Praise for *Blackhear...*

'King Arthur as you've never seen h...
just capture lightning, but command...
of blood and desire. A masterwork of urban fantasy – and
the coolest thing you'll read this year'
Samantha Shannon, author of *The Bone Season*
and *The Priory of the Orange Tree*

'The screaming neon of *Blade Runner* meets the medieval
steel of Arthurian legend in a world that's dizzying in scope
and imagination. The boldest, smartest, most adventurous fantasy
I've read in ages – and it's really f***ing fun'
Krystal Sutherland, author of *House of Hollow*

'Arthurian legend meets urban fantasy in a
brilliant, bloody wild ride'
Jay Kristoff, author of *Nevernight*

'Outstandingly well-crafted and absorbing
urban/epic/alt-reality/mythic fantasy read'
Juliet E. McKenna, author of *The Green Man's Heir*

'This rocks!'
Fantasy Book Critic

'Prepare for a politically charged, addictive read'
The Fantasy Hive

'*Blackheart Knights* takes these familiar stories and makes them
into something that is new and inventive – a gritty, grimdark
take on a futuristic London. Well-written, compelling and
packaged in a way that keeps the reader guessing. Think of
this as an old-school thrash metal gig like Slayer or Metallica
at their heyday – loud, fast, fun and satisfying as f***'
Grimdark Magazine

'Fun, gritty and imaginative twist on an Arthurian legend.
It's an urban fantasy retelling where knights ride bikes rather
than horses and compete in gruesome fights in an attempt to win
money and fame. I haven't read anything like *Blackheart Knights*
previously and I don't think I ever will again, it's a very unique
contemporary take on a well-loved tale'
Library Looter

Laure Eve is the author of critically acclaimed fantasy duologies *The Graces* and *The Curses,* and *Fearsome Dreamer* and *The Illusionists*. A British-French hybrid, she was born in Paris and grew up in Cornwall, a land suffused with myth and legend. She speaks English and French, and can hold a vague conversation, usually about food, in Greek. She is very English about comedy and very French about cheese. Selling comic books in foreign languages, loosing a variety of blood-curdling screams into a recording booth and striking odd poses as an artist's model are just some of the things she has done for a living.

Also by Laure Eve

Blackheart Knights

The Graces
The Curses

Fearsome Dreamer
The Illusionists

BLACKHEART GHOSTS

LAURE EVE

Jo Fletcher
BOOKS

First published in Great Britain in 2023
This edition published in 2024 by

Jo Fletcher Books
an imprint of
Quercus Editions Ltd
Carmelite House
50 Victoria Embankment
London EC4Y 0DZ

An Hachette UK company

A CIP catalogue record for this book is available
from the British Library

PB ISBN 978 1 52941 181 2
EBOOK ISBN 978 1 52941 180 5

10 9 8 7 6 5 4 3 2 1

Typeset by Jouve (UK), Milton Keynes

Printed and bound in Great Britain by Clays Ltd, Elcograf S.p.A.

Papers used by Jo Fletcher Books are from well-managed forests and
other responsible sources.

This one is for D –

Baker, detective, lover of noir,
and all-round extraordinary human being.

(You contain too many impressive multitudes for anyone
to believe you as a fictional character, so you're not in the book.)

PART I

Come close, lover, listen in.
I know just where to begin.
Dip my hands in your past sin.

—Flowers for Kane

CHAPTER I

Riverlands, Evrontown
Two Weeks Ago

Silent buildings watch the river give birth.

A watery figure emerges from its black-mirror depths, heaving and crawling up the scud bank of gritty mud some enterprising salesperson had, one time in the recent past, named a 'beach'. There is a sign to this effect, unnoticed by the figure as it stumbles past, except as a convenient lever for one hand to grip in its desperate haul away.

The figure reaches the top, mud giving way to hard, packed dirt and a maze of rearing warehouses beyond. It takes trembling steps, dripping and leaking as it moves, its boots damp thumps. Weak moonlight picks out the drops clinging to the stubby hairs on its bowed head. Cross-strings of riotous city light on the river's far bank bisect the horizon behind its stumbling form.

It trips, topples to a knee, and the defeated crumpling in its shoulders suggests it might not get up again. There it stays, one moment, two, and the riverland's warehouses seem to nod to each other and themselves – just another victim.

Then the figure jerks, heaving upwards as if electrified by the sudden terror in giving up. Stumbling on, leaving dark footprints in its wake, it disappears down an opening as wide as a boulevard between unnamed storage facilities that rear far upwards.

The warehouses mark its departure in silence.

'Your desire?' asks the gargoyle in a flat, featureless voice.

The projection hovers a foot out from the building's front wall, thrusting into the space of anyone who dares approach. The figure examines the gargoyle's fixed, open mouth and wide stare. The projection flickers once and then holds steady, its light matrix sophisticated enough to vaguely mimic the appearance of stone.

Whimsy. Who'd have thought the Silver Angel capable?

'I need to see Garad,' the figure tells the gargoyle, and then gives a violent cough.

'No one by that name lives here,' the gargoyle states.

'Garad, I know it's you,' the figure insists. 'Let me in.'

'I don't know you.'

The gargoyle projection must conceal a capturer, pointed directly at the face of anyone on the approach.

'Please,' the figure whispers. 'Please, I can't—'

She gives a great shiver and then collapses. It goes too slowly to seem real, knees folding and toppling the body forwards, which rebounds off the panel and swings the opposite way, stumbling back down the steps and pitching down on to the hard concrete street below.

When the figure knows more again, she finds herself lying on her side wrapped in blankets, her back pressed against a long spread of delicious warmth. A heated wall. More blankets soften the hard ground underneath. The rest of the room is sparse, bare and clean and well lit. A weapons rack is pushed into the far corner. Contortionist poles cut the room's right third, fixed into ceiling and ground.

The figure levers herself upright by increments, elbows to hands to sitting. She is in the training room of Garad 'the Silver Angel' Gaheris, which is just big enough for one. She remembers being hauled up in arms and carried, but theoretically, knowing it was happening, rather than feeling the press of it, as if it were all done an inch away from her skin. It has taken perhaps hours, perhaps a lifetime, to get to Garad's from riverside, and her whole body had grown numb, leaving her trotting unsteadily on stump legs with feet she couldn't feel.

Someone in the room speaks.

'How do you feel?'

It's Garad, sat on a chair a little way away with a short sword laid across their knees, held there with one casual, gentle grip. The chair has been placed outside of the figure's immediate range of motion. The Silver Angel has a reputation for caution.

The figure checks herself. Her nerves tingle and burn, revitalised from their slow freezing. She rubs her close-shaved head, relishing the feel of stubble and hard skull underneath.

'More alive,' she says. And then, as if it just occurred to her, 'My thanks.'

'How do they callian you?'

'Ghost,' she says.

'Ghost,' Garad echoes.

Ghost simply waits.

'I don't know anyone by the name of Ghost,' Garad says.

Their expression is composed, even at ease, considering they have a half-drowned stranger in their secret apartment, the one no one is supposed to know about, because secret apartments are the sort of thing you make provision for when you're as famous as Garad.

'I'd be surprised,' agrees Ghost.

'We've never met.'

Ghost says, 'No.'

This is not quite true, but there's nothing to be done about it. Some things are necessary in the moment.

'Why are you here and how did you find me?' Garad asks, then pauses. 'And why are you so wet?'

Ghost's gaze settles briefly on the hand curled around the sword grip. Those long fingers held deceptively loose, fingers that had dealt crushing damage to their opponents over one of the most illustrious careers in the history of the Caballaria.

'Someone just tried to kill me,' Ghost says. 'I'll save you the bother of deductive reasoning – it involved a lot of water.'

'How unfortunate. Had you made them angry?'

'I think he mostly just enjoys it.'

That was to shock, and judging by the look on Garad's face, it did its work.

'As to why I'm here,' continues Ghost, 'I'll get to that in a second. As to how I found you, well. How many people besides me know the location of this secret foxhole of yours?'

There is a heavy silence.

'One,' Garad says.

'Neh.' Ghost nods.

'*She* told you.' Garad leans forwards, and their fingers don't look so loose any more. 'Finnavair.'

Ghost swallows a sudden lick of fear. Nods again.

Garad sits back. 'She's dead,' they say tonelessly.

'I know.'

Silence.

'You look a little like her.'

Ghost shrugs. 'Neh, you're not the first person to tell me that.'

'How did you know her?'

'I'm her sister.'

This hits.

'I thought she didn't have family,' Garad says.

'Not officially,' Ghost agrees. 'Anyway, not much of a family. There's just me.'

'What do you want from me?'

'Fin sent me here.'

'Why?'

Ghost holds up a hand. 'First,' she says, 'I want to tell you my story. It explains everything, I promise you that. And at the end of it, you get to do whatever you want with me. 'Cord?'

'I don't like stories.' There is definitely a grippy look about their hand. Their sword point nudges its way towards Ghost.

'Funny, I thought you were a Caballaria knight,' Ghost retorts. She is trembling – whether from fear, exhaustion, cold, or all three is hard to say – but her tone is resolute. 'It's past midnight, and you don't strike me as the late-night bacchanal type, so I'm guessing you've nowhere else to be. You already know I've no surprises on me; you'd have searched me when you scraped me off your doorstep. Si Finnavair, though now she be through Marvol's door, is the reason I'm here. And I have a story to tell you. A blow-this-city-wide-apart kind of story. And considering how London's going these days, you might want to give it all a fair listen. 'Cord?'

Garad is a statue.

'Do we have an accord?' Ghost demands.

''Cord,' Garad says. 'Talk.'

7

At that, some of Ghost's tension melts, enough to pull the blanket close and huddle into it.

'Got any alcohol?' she ventures.

The silence grows ominous.

Ghost sighs. The warm wall at her back steadies her enough to start it. Her eyes half close.

'Showing up like a bad surprise at people's doors is turning out to be a habit of mine,' she admits. 'Because it all began a lot like this.'

CHAPTER 2

Shuttershill, Alaunitown
Two Months Ago

When Leon Manus Dei Pendegast o'Launitown opens his door to her, it takes him a moment to understand what he's seeing, which he can hardly be blamed for.

'Who are you?' he says suspiciously.

'Good eventide, Si,' Ghost courteously begins.

'Ehn? Si? I en't a knight, and I don't want any of whatever yer selling.'

'You *were* a knight, a Rhyfentown guard captain, and I'm not selling anything.'

That gets his attention, as she'd hoped it would.

He peers at her. 'How the fuck would you know about that?'

'We've a friend in common,' says Ghost.

'Who?'

'Finnavair Caballarias o'Rhyfentown.'

'You think I'm friends with famous people? Besides, she's upped and disappeared on everyone.'

'She's not disappeared,' says Ghost. 'She's dead.'

Leon goes still. Then he gives a short sigh. 'Thought so.'

Ghost holds tight. She's already given him two shocks, and if she pushes him, he may well shut the door in her face just because. The light spilling around his frame has the weak, low-set quality of poor accommodation, and the man himself is hard to read. He has a craggy, rocklike face amid the outline of a hopefully benevolent troll.

Finally he remembers that she's there. 'Well?' he asks. 'What do *you* want, then?'

Ghost is careful. 'She gave me your name, said you help people in trouble.'

Leon doesn't move. 'Come to call in the debt, have we?' he says.

'If that's what gets me through the door.'

He suppresses a snort, turns it into a sniff. 'I see.'

His eyes roam over her, taking in the white and grey allegiance charms that hang from her collar chain, and the tattoo on her hand of a small, ornate key, marking her as Marvoltown-born. There's little fashion about her – she's dressed to move – but maybe he notices that her clothes are well cut, good quality, marking her out from these surroundings with subtle notes.

Then he moves ponderously backwards, inviting her in.

Ghost suppresses the urge to collapse on him in relief as she follows him through the narrow hallway and into his apartment beyond. It's as shabby as she suspected, a one-room clutter, void of any prettying features that might at least denote a home, rather than just shelter.

It took her a while to track Leon down. He left Rhyfentown and came here to Alaunitown years ago, and Fin hadn't known exactly where he lived now. Even these days, moving districts isn't quite as easy as a song. Leon's fall, if Ghost is any judge, was a high one. Guard knights might not get paid as much as Caballaria knights, but it's still a trickly career if you can get it, and he was a captain, no less. Now he's in a one-room in a shit-streaked part of a totally different dis'.

'Go and sit over there, warm up,' he orders Ghost, pointing to the far wall. A large square of it has been painted a different colour of drab than its surroundings to denote the heated section, and underneath the square sits a sagging, open-backed divan.

'I'm fine,' Ghost says.

'You're shivering.'

Ghost reconnoitres herself. 'So I am. It's cold out.'

She settles on the divan, but Leon continues to stand.

She appraises his physical appearance. One of his eye sockets is devoid of an eyeball, sporting instead a stretch of puckered skin over jutting rims of skull bone. He lost it in his youth, in one of London's many inter-district clashes, and has apparently always refused to wear a face overlay, eyepatch or anything that would conceal it, sporting his wound like a badge of pride.

She can't help it. She probes the more recent wound. 'How's life after knighthood?'

'I barely remember the before,' he says, the short words speaking loud of long-nurtured hurt. 'That's all over, long time now.'

Nothing much harder than being an ex-knight. Ghost should know.

Now she's one, too.

'So what happened to Fin, then?' Leon asks. 'Whole of Rhyfentown dis' has been in an uproar looking for her, so the glows say.'

'I don't know,' Ghost says. 'I just know that she didn't come home.'

'Maybe she's hiding out at the palace with the King.

11

They are lovers, after all,' says Leon, his gruff voice curdled with disdain.

'No, she's not there.' This doesn't feel like enough, so she adds, 'I'd know.'

'Some people think he's done something to her,' Leon muses, 'and Cair Lleon's covering it up.'

'Why would he, after risking so much by publicly announcing their relationship? No, something else happened.'

Leon folds his arms. 'So you live with her.'

'Lived.'

'Lover?'

'Sister.'

'Fin was a war orphan; she never grew up with no sister.'

Ghost shrugs. 'I came along later.'

'I thought she never knew who her family was.'

'She didn't. I found *her*.'

'Hm,' Leon says with satisfaction, 'after she got rich and famous, I war'nt. Why'd she keep you secret?'

'Fifty questions and a throat smile if I get any of them wrong?' Ghost replies pleasantly.

'You showed up at *my* door,' Leon points out. 'And I still don't know who you are.'

'I'm Ghost,' says Ghost, 'and that's all I can give you. Will you help me or not? You told Fin she could send anyone your way.'

'That was a long time ago,' says Leon.

'Debts still need to get paid.'

He tips his head in acknowledgement. Evidently it was a deep one, the debt between them.

Leon rubs his face. 'So what do you want? Trick? En't got any.' He gestures wryly to their surroundings.

'No.' Ghost pauses. 'I need work.'

12

'Work?' Leon echoes, astonished. Then he breaks into a stuttering laugh. 'Saints. You keep them surprises coming. That why you're asking about my old life, is it? Well, I can't get you into the guard. Those bridges were burned.' He turns momentarily reflective. 'Incinerated, really.' Then he looks her up and down. 'Anyway, they'd never let someone as tiny as you in. You look like you can barely hold a sword up.'

'I'm not talking about the guard,' says Ghost. 'I'm talking about what you do now.'

'And what do I do now, Lady Stranger?'

Moment of truth.

'You hunt godchildren,' she says, smooth as cream, though her heart, stuttering through a few sudden bumps, disagrees with her voice.

Leon cocks his head.

It seems to be the least favourite of all the surprises she's thrown him so far.

'Very knowledgeable, our Fin, for someone I hadn't seen in ten years,' he says, after a dangerous pause.

Ghost nods. 'She kept track of you.' Softer: 'She cared about you. She said you were a bit of a pere to her, when she didn't have one.'

Leon grunts. 'Very talky, wasn't she.' But Ghost can see her carefully chosen words have landed a hit – the crags of his face seem softer in turn. 'What do you want to be a God's Gun for?' He eyes her. 'It en't a good choice.'

'I don't have another.'

''Course you do. Pretty thing like you.'

Ghost laughs. 'If I didn't need you so much right now, I'd give your face a kiss of my fist for that.'

'Just a joke. Saints. Fin had a sense of humour, at least.'

'I'm not Fin,' says Ghost.

'No,' says Leon sourly. 'But whoever you are and whatever you've done that you're running from, you still got choices, and I'm not the best of them. I don't work well with others.'

'Couldn't you just introduce me to whoever hires you, so I can at least—'

'Don't work like that. It's shadier than a well's end, this business. You got one lot of people thinking we're little better than bounty hunters, the other lot thinking we're worse than that, and if anything goes wrong, no one's coming to rescue you. The ones hired you deny all knowledge, and then you're fucked. Add to that, it's badly paid, hard on the body, worse on the mind and you spend all yer time on yer own.' He folds his arms. 'Which suits me fine, I don't like people. So you can already see how this en't going to work out.'

This last part rings untrue – from what she's seen so far, Leon strikes Ghost as someone profoundly lonely – but the rest sounds about right.

Still. No choice. Not for Ghost. This is the only avenue she's got left.

'Well, you're not a pere to *me*,' she says, 'so how about a cock rub as a token of my gratitude?'

Leon's one good eye narrows. He strides across the room and takes her roughly by the arm. For a minute she wonders if he's marching her into a back room for a rough game – and frankly, she's in admiration at the sudden, bold show of energy – until she sees that he's hauling her to the front door.

Bad play.

He unlocks it, shoves her through.

Bad, bad play.

'Wait,' she protests, 'I'm sorry, I just thought—'

14

'You thought wrong. Get out.'

Saints, he's furious.

Ghost turns quickly, searching for another in.

'There's no need to take things so damn serious, it was just a suggestion,' she tries. 'Wait, you can't do this, you're in debt to Fin!'

'Can't be in debt to the dead,' he says.

'Yes, you can, it's called moldra lagha!'

Leon shuts the door in her face.

Fuck. Fuck. Fuck.

'I'll just keep coming back!' Ghost yells desperately into the door.

Leon's muffled voice gruffs its way through the metal. 'And I'll just keep ignoring you!'

'Neh? Forever? I don't have any work, remember? *I've got nothing better to do!*'

Silence.

He's gone. Gone into his cave and left her all alone.

Then she hears it. A short, annoyed sigh on the other side of the door.

Ghost grins in relief.

CHAPTER 3

Cair Lleon, Blackheart
Five Months Ago

This is the communications hall of Cair Lleon, in the palace of London's King.

It is a cavernous space, bereft of furniture, brightly lit with nowhere to hide. The sizeable herd of glows interviewers and their capturers are corralled by belly-level gates of iron that bisect the room, keeping them back from the King's dais by a good few metres. They'd have to take a mighty leap to get over them, Wyll reassures himself, with an impossible run-up among the tangle of glows machinery and the knots of people manning it all. He is far enough away to be safe.

Wyll sits on the King's chair, flanked by the King's Saith, that inner circle of most trusted advisors who are, by now, almost as famous as he. His appearance this morning was greeted by a rising tide of applause, whistles and calls from the knot of glows people. Some are eager to approve recent events, some notably less so, Lucan tells him – but it's hard to tell which is which in the noise, because when it's loud enough, it all sounds the same.

Some commentators see the King's recent public declaration of his lover, the fighter knight Finnavair 'the Fair Fae'

Caballarias o'Rhyfentown, as a step towards stability and solid-ification, and a hint towards new progeny to strengthen the weakened line of Rhyfen. Some see it as a pointed unification between societal tribes. Opinion is loudly divided on whether this is a positive or a negative, but there is one thing everyone agrees on — the story is a decently sensational one. The once scandal-touched bastard-turned-King has chosen a once dirt-poor street rat-turned-celebrated knight to be his official mate. You don't get much better than that on the glow shows.

The first thing commentators will later pick up on is that the King appeared a little preoccupied, perhaps even subdued, for such a happy occasion. Then again, Artorias Dracones has always been unusually shy about this area of his life. The second thing is that the lover herself was notably absent.

'Our timing was poor,' Wyll says to the interviewer who asks where she is. 'The Lady Finnavair has had to go into imme-diate sequestering for her next fight. She takes her duties to the Caballaria as seriously as I take mine.'

'Did you get time to, ah, say goodbye before she went?' asks the interviewer, amid a roll of laughter.

'Next question,' Wyll answers, and the laughter swells.

The next question duly comes — 'How did you first meet the Fair Fae?' — and is easily answered, as are the next few. Lucan has prepared him well for them, and particularly the one they've been waiting for, which comes from a well-presented inter-viewer with a sour frown.

'Sire, our watchers dearly want to know this most of all — why choose a Rhyfentown street rat as the King's official lover? Just what message are you intending to send with this choice?'

'It wasn't a choice,' Wyll says. 'No one consciously chooses who they fall in love with. I think her background gives her strength of character, as mine did me. Those who get easy beginnings are in more danger of complacency, which can so often lead, in my personal opinion, to weakness.'

The well-presented interviewer says no more, but many around him whistle at the blow.

'What do your family think of the match, Sire?' another interviewer calls.

'Such as they are?' Wyll drily replies, which earns him fresh laughter. 'Anyone who isn't in favour of my happiness would surely have only shameful reasons for not being so.'

An adroit play – tamer questions now follow, citing a general lack of desire to be counted among the shameful, and just a few minutes later, the session is well concluded by the King's charismatic communications advisor, Lucan Vastos Fenestris o'Senzatown.

'You can take it off now,' Lucan says. 'It's just us.'

He stands in front of Wyll, all business. They are in Art's private palace apartments, together with the rest of Art's Saith. Scattered behind Lucan are the others – Brune, her bladed legs sheathed in appropriately sharp-cut black trousers. Fortigo, the King's personal vastos since the day he took the Sword nineteen years ago. Garad, the Silver Angel themself, and now retired King's champion. Finally Lillath, the King's Spider, leans against the nearest wall with her face set to neutral.

With an effort, Wyll lets go of his illusion. He sees his transformation reflected in the faces around him. Between blinks, their warm and beloved Art disappears, replaced by the Sorcerer Knight's cold, hard lines.

'Saints,' murmurs Fortigo. 'I—' He checks himself, and says no more.

'Terrifying, isn't it?' Lillath cheerfully replies.

Wyll ignores them both. The usual post-illusion fatigue is beginning to set in, not to mention the dip from the adrenalin rush that carried him through those interviews, and he needs to sit down. He fumbles his way to an armchair, a comfortable high-backed affair that is rapidly becoming his favourite spot, and sinks into it.

'I think congratulations are in order,' Brune says. 'That was quite convincing.'

'There were some errors in deportment,' ponders Lucan. 'We need to practise more.'

Lucan's approach to practice can best be described as painfully anal. Another round of that and Wyll might break.

'This subterfuge won't hold for long,' Fortigo says quietly. 'There's already talk around the palace about why the King missed all his appointments for a week. Granted, the assumption is that the Lady Fin was the cause, but if he keeps missing them—'

'We need more time,' Lucan argues, 'until we have a better plan in place. Just a few more days.'

'What do you want to do then?' mutters Wyll. 'Go on and announce that the best ruler in a century has been assassinated by his own secret godchild daughter?'

The ache that chases a complex illusion is starting up in his bones and it's making him peevish. He can hear it, but he doesn't care.

'It wasn't an assassination,' says Lillath. 'It was *moldra lagha*.'

'Oh, good,' Lucan retorts. 'You and the rest of the commentators can spend days quibbling semantics while London descends into chaos.'

'She was working alone, Lux.'

'There's no way to know that for sure.'

'There's no way to know anything for sure,' Lillath evenly replies. 'But the interrogations have been pretty thorough.'

Wyll resists the urge to scoff. He'd lay a ton of trick down that he's the only one who knows what 'thorough' really means in the hands of someone like Lillath.

'That's no guarantee,' Lucan says. 'Red has been knight-trained in mental-strength tactics as well as the physical, thanks to *his* beneficence.' He nods to Wyll.

'Lux, come on—'

Wyll stirs. 'He's right. She's been trained by the best. We can't guarantee that she didn't have help,' Lillath's mouth opens to argue but Wyll rides on, 'even if she was unaware of it herself.'

'Well, obviously whoever is behind it wants the Sword,' Brune observes. 'And obviously they're absolutely fine with killing whoever stands in their way.'

A heavy silence follows this. Wyll can practically feel the fear rising off them all and beginning to stink up the room.

'She was yours, Wyll,' comes a low voice. 'You found her. You nursed her, you made her into a knight. And then you brought her into the palace.'

Garad is a darkened, towering presence at the back of them all. An angel indeed, wings protectively spread. Saints know they've never been on the best of terms. It was at Art's request that Garad took on a younger Wyll and trained him up as the next King's champion, with all the diligence their imperious piety required. Always done in service to their first master, the Caballaria, and their second, the King, and all against their own personal judgement.

It must be hard, Wyll can admit, to like your usurper. It must be even harder when your usurper is a godchild. But that doesn't mean he has to take bigoted shit from them.

'I know what it looks like, Garad,' he retorts. 'But I loved him. I served him. Same as the rest of you. Do I need to prove it with my fists?'

'I'm not too old for it, *Sorcerer Knight.*'

'Stop it,' Brune cuts in. 'Fighting like this solves none of our problems. I think we can all agree that saving Art's life at Mafelon may just negate the probability that Wyll would want to conspire assassination now, don't you?'

Garad's silence says a lot. It says, for example, that Mafelon was three years ago. It says that things change, as all things must.

'What about Fin? Excuse me, the Lady Finnavair?' Garad asks instead.

Lillath stirs. 'She's still missing. Her trainers haven't seen her since that last bout. You know, the one where Art—'

'—made a fool of himself?' Garad says frostily. 'How could we forget?'

Garad the Monk, they are known, their romantic life so opaque it's been speculated not to exist. It might just be that famed disdain for public love, or it might be something more. From its inception, Garad had struggled to hide an animosity towards the relationship between Fin and Art. Wyll has occasionally wondered if their steadfast adoration of their oldest friend ever had the tinge of romantic love. Has Garad hated every girl Art ever turned his head for because of it?

Lucan shrugs. 'Maybe she's in hiding? It must have been rather overwhelming, having the King of London invade the end of your fight and declare his love for you in front of the entire world.'

'What about her friends?' Garad asks. 'Don't they know where she is?' Silence greets this. 'For the love of the saints, she must have some.'

'She does,' Lillath says, nodding. 'She's friends with Red. They've become quite close since Red moved to Blackheart.'

The news drops like a trick bomb.

The group exchange glances.

'Are we saying,' Lucan puzzles it out slowly, 'that Art's illegitimate daughter and his recently acknowledged lover conspired to murder him, or . . .?'

Garad abruptly pushes off from their slouch against the wall. 'This is ridiculous. Why are we wasting time playing idle speculation games? What does it *solve*? Art is dead, and we're sitting around play-acting, *lying* to everyone, and using a godchild to do it. It's disgusting. It's immoral.'

By all means, thinks Wyll, *say what you really feel about me.*

'Garad,' Lucan's light voice holds a warning tone, 'we need to stick together on this. If any of us give even a hint of wrong, to anyone, everything comes tumbling down. You see that, don't you?'

Garad steams.

'Garad? Are you with us?'

Even with the eyes of the room on them, the eyes of their oldest friends, there is no crumbling. It deserves a begrudging amount of respect. It's hard not to respect Garad, even as it is easy to mock them.

'I won't lie like this for much longer,' they say.

And suddenly Wyll can almost see it – the effort it has been costing them to do it, like a heavy, mottled grey demon that squats on their shoulders, weighing them down, claws sunk into their back.

22

Lucan poorly conceals the look of bafflement engendered by someone to whom lying comes as second nature.

'A few more weeks,' he repeats.

Garad gives a stiff nod, pushes off from the wall, and leaves the room.

The door closes with a quiet click.

Lucan twitches.

'Let it go,' Brune says to him. 'They're in pain. Let it go.'

'Well, who here isn't in pain, Brune?' Lucan's smile is furiously brittle. 'Who here isn't having to go on and pretend that their heart hasn't just been ripped right out of their chest? But you lick your wounds on your own time. Here and now, we stay and we fix this, together. If anyone else disagrees, by all means, head for the door.'

No one moves.

Lucan nods. 'Good. Now let's make some plans.'

And then he looks at Wyll.

'What?' Wyll says warily.

'The Fair Fae's disappearance is worrying. If she was a part of this, that gives us a lead. We need more from the . . . daughter' – Lucan hesitates over the word, as if to admit that Red is Art's daughter is to admit that his sainted Art once made a mistake – 'and if direct application hasn't produced anything, maybe subterfuge will do it.'

'Subterfuge?' echoes Wyll. 'What exactly do you expect me to do, pretend I don't want to rip her apart with my bare hands?'

'That would be a start,' Lucan says. 'I have an idea.'

CHAPTER 4

Garad's Apartment, Evrontown
Two Weeks Ago

'Leon was true to his word,' Ghost says to Garad. 'A couple of nights later he took me along on a job.' She reflects. 'That night was the start of it.'

'Of what?' Garad asks.

'My downwards saunter into the seven hells,' Ghost replies, and gives them a humourless smile.

Machine Sounds, Alaunitown
Two Months Ago

Leon is easy to spot, even when he's trying to hide.

He sits at a table near the front, tucked to one side: the darkest spot in the room, specifically chosen. Nothing more than a thin sketch in the dank bar light, but his outline is distinct – a shabby, slabby hill. He may be past his prime, but you'd think twice about testing a mountain troll, even an old one. The stage tricks behind him give him a mean glow, leaving his front in shadow. Music licks around his shoulders as he pauses, eyeing Ghost.

The bar he has asked her to meet him at is deep into the inner dregs of Alaunitown. It was once a workmanlike industrial area, filled with nothing but old factories and cramped, indifferent housing. Now there are lofty, scrappy eateries housed in old flecter-glass production plants. An artistic collective squats in the top two floors of an abandoned chemical storage facility. Street diners that only serve blue food, or only open every other night, dot the streets in between the plant workers' housing blocks, worming their way through the cracks.

The bar is called Machine Sounds, named for the slick, clinging kind of music currently seeping through the underground scene like bike oil. The band on the stage right now is so-so. The singer's pretty good – their lyrics are more suggestion than word, evoking a sensory feel of ecstatic misery – but it's a shame about the beat-keeper undercutting all the singer's hard work, pissing over the vocal atmosphere with arrhythmic, damp rattles.

Leon raises a boot and gives a gentle kick to the chair opposite him, which skids out from under the table and connects with Ghost's shin. She lowers herself on to it and sits, waiting out the noise. The band comes to the end of their last number and a buzzing silence descends on the apathetic bar.

'Thank you,' the singer says sullenly.

Ghost leans forwards into the lamplight of the table. 'Got your message to meet here,' she says.

'So I see,' Leon replies with a grunt of amusement.

'Only I'm not too sure how.'

Leon shrugs. 'Neh?'

'Well, I said I'd contact *you*, remember?' Ghost gives him a friendly smile. 'Because you've no idea where I live.'

'Ah, I have my ways.' Leon gives her a clumsy wink, and she laughs in return, which keeps his guard down while she leans in and grabs his collar, a loose construction of rubber just large enough to slip a hand in and tug 'til the choking begins.

Leon's eyes go wide and he struggles for the next breath. Ghost hopes he doesn't get it; he blew the last foetid one right into her face.

'Listen,' Ghost says in a friendly tone, 'I don't like people knowing where I live. When people know where I live, I don't feel very safe. You can probably tell. So how did you find out, and who else knows?'

Leon's skull-crusher hands appear and grip the table edge instead of her. Either he's gone soft in his old age, or he doesn't want to escalate this.

'Relax,' he wheezes, 'relax, saints! After you came to me that first night, I followed you back home, all right?'

'Oh,' Ghost says, 'well, I feel better. Why?'

'You know where I live, now I know . . . where *you* live—'

Damn, he has a point. Also his cheeks are definitely looking a lot more purple than before.

Ghost lets go.

Leon pulls hurriedly out of her loosened grip, and then gives her a hurt glare.

He'd asked Ghost why she wanted to become a God's Gun, and she'd made a joke about needing something to do, because she wasn't the sort who could just sit around. No one could, in her opinion, but some people managed to persuade themselves of it, and then more often than not ended up finding more destructive ways to get through their time.

Truth was – well, the truth wasn't for him. Fin might have trusted the old git, but Ghost did not, because Ghost could not afford to trust anyone. Except now the shame has begun for her flash of temper – not for the anger, but for the fear it represents.

'Sorry,' she says. 'You're right. I'm a stranger, and . . . fair's fair.'

Feeling safe enough for some righteous anger, Leon opens his mouth, but he gets no further than that because just then all the lights cut out and the bar is plunged into darkness.

A sound comes from the stage: a voice sing-talking in the blackout.

The bar holds its breath, trying to work out the threat.

No threat, as the stage lights stutter back in, or at least not an obvious one. The light picks out a figure in a lurid pink and yellow wig, the colours of the fat sugar snakes you can buy fistfuls of for pennies in the Neon Markets that sprawl their way across the Kingdom tip of Senzatown. The singer wears transparent boots up to the knee and thin clothes that are more strap than garment. They undulate very gently from side to side, gripping the microphone tight between both hands, eyes closed soft as if they don't know where they are, hadn't really thought about it, just wanted to sing to themself.

Ghost hears Leon's grating laugh, feels his warm breath on the side of her face.

'See something you like?' he says.

His face is now an unnatural pink from the stage-light spill. Ghost leans back, tries her best to ignore the singer in her peripheral with the insistently haunting voice.

She must be failing though, because Leon says, after a swallow of his drink, 'Don't worry, you'll get an up-close view. She's the reason we're here.'

His head tips to the stage.

27

Nettled by his insinuation, Ghost tries to regroup.

'You asked me to travel halfway across the dis' to watch some dregs-bar warbler?'

'You're here to be my second; watch and learn. Maybe use that terrible temper of yours, in case things get sticky.' His tone turns acidic. 'Course, now the whole place has seen you try to strangle *me*, so we're not exactly presenting a united front to our quarry. Thanks for that, by the way.'

Ghost sorts through the clues. 'Is that what I'm supposed to be? Your protection?' she asks.

'What's so bad about that?'

'I gave violence up with my old life.'

'Really?' Leon meaningfully adjusts his collar.

'Sorry,' she offers again.

He'll use it as ammunition every chance he gets to cover up his embarrassment. Least she can do is act contrite for him.

Leon sniffs. 'If so, you can get me another throat greaser. My neck hurts from all that choking you did.'

Ghost presses a button and moments later a server appears, responding to the wink of the projected light above their table. While she orders, Leon rises from the table and goes to speak to the bored-looking guard standing in front of a rusty chain wall fencing off the back of the bar, and presumably, private rooms beyond.

Ghost finds her attention drifting back to the stage. The singer has opened her eyes, though she stares beyond the crowd, beyond the bar and into another world. So convincing is she that Ghost finds herself drifting along with her, somewhere airier than here and full of longing. When the singer finishes, she disappears, walking off into the back lights as if nothing else exists beyond them, and Ghost feels faintly cheated, as if she'd woken in the middle of a particularly pillowy dream without the chance to have its satisfying conclusion play out.

When Leon returns to the table, he throws back his new drink and Ghost wordlessly presses for another.

'So,' she says. 'Who are we trying to find tonight?'

'Cassren Grenwald.' Leon fishes in his jacket pouch and comes up with a data coin. He presses the tiny catch on the coin's side and a fuzzy white light throws out from the coin's flat surface on to the bar table's dark surface. Words and images flicker through the light in a slow scroll. It will play all the data it has and then start again in an endless loop, over and over, until its charge runs out.

Leon flicks the catch again, freezing the data run. The bar table shows a face made of light – a capture of a woman with dark, unblemished skin. Small, round build. An elfin-like face, rendering her younger than she might actually be.

'She doesn't look like the type who might need to disappear.'

'Neither do you,' Leon says. 'And she's a schoolteacher.'

A puzzled Ghost opens her mouth to keep probing, but they are interrupted by the arrival of someone at their table.

'Heard you wanted to talk to me?' they say.

It's the singer, but it takes a moment. She has abandoned her lurid wig and transparent trappings and is dressed now all dark and demure, with long hair slicked close to her skull and coiled up like boat rope at the back of her neck. Even her gaze is different. On stage she was dreamy-smooth, but off it and she's gained a sharp, jagged focus.

'You're a good friend of Cassren Grenwald,' Leon says to her.

The singer does not reply, but if she were a cat, she'd be bristling.

'How do they callian you?' Leon asks.

'Flowers For Kane.'

'How do they callian you when you're not singing as Flowers For Kane?' Leon amends.

'I don't switch it on and off,' says the singer. 'Anyway, you must know, since you already know so much.'

'Pretend I don't, and we're doing the thing that polite people do,' Leon says.

'Delilah,' says the singer venomously, and no more.

It's the height of rudeness to give someone only a quarter of your name, even in this part of town. The singer's being a bitch, and it's raising the temperature all round.

'Well, Delilah,' Leon says, 'they callian me Leon Pendegast o'Launitown, and I've been asked to find your friend Cassren—'

'By who?' Delilah says with obvious contempt. 'Not her family. Not anyone who cares about her. They'd never send a dog like you to chase her down.'

Leon endures this without comment, and Ghost finds her hackles rising for him.

'All right, friend,' she says quietly, 'I'm the only one who gets to insult him, and I don't really feel like sharing the fun. Want to back down a step?'

Delilah turns her attention to Ghost. 'And who are you?'

'I'm his protection,' Ghost says, and it sounds only mildly embarrassing to her ears.

Delilah is ice. 'Oh, Guns need protection from their prey now, do they? Shouldn't it be the other way around?'

Leon clears his throat. 'I'm just trying to find Cassren,' he says, 'and not to hurt her.'

'No, you'll just brand her like you own her, won't you?'

'It's a tattoo,' Leon interrupts, 'like the ones you got on your arms, lady, only probably a lot less painf—'

'You'll put her on that fucken *list*,' Delilah continues, her voice rising over his, 'and then she'll become a target, plain and simple. She'll be prey.'

Leon looks stony. 'Prey for who?'

Delilah shakes her head.

'Can I just—?' Ghost raises an interjecting hand, and then shoots Leon a shocked look. 'You're a God's Gun?'

Leon returns her glance. His eyes narrow. His mouth opens.

Luckily, Delilah rides right in. 'So ashamed of it you don't even tell your own protection. Can't say I'm surprised.'

Leon downs his drink and slams the cup on to the table hard enough to make her jump.

'You tell her running only makes it worse,' he says to Delilah, and then nods to Ghost. 'Let's go.'

'I can't tell her anything,' Delilah says, 'I haven't seen her in weeks. You can't find her through me; you're looking in the wrong place. Shouldn't you be questioning the ungrateful cur who shopped her?'

'You mean the good citizen who reported a crime?' Leon says as he rises from the table.

Ghost visibly winces.

'I mean the prick who punished her for trying to save a life,' Delilah snarls.

'She was unregistered,' says Leon, 'so it was his legal duty,' and walks out.

Ghost risks a glance at the furious singer before she follows.

★

Outside, Leon leans against a wall and lights up a sicalo, inhaling deeply. Fat jasmine-scented clouds plump their way through the air.

Ghost sidles up.

'What the fuck are you playing at, Lady Stranger?' he says, every word bitten off.

'I'm sorry,' says Ghost, and this time she means it. 'The whole bar already saw me at your throat. Figured I'd ride it out.'

Leon snorts. 'Saw a chance to kick me again and took it?'

'Delilah needed to like one of us, and it got obvious pretty fast that it wasn't going to be you,' Ghost says quickly. 'So I figured I'd play dumb about the God's Gun thing. But now, see, maybe she'll talk to me.'

'And what,' says Leon through furious smoke plumes, 'makes you think you'll get the chance to do that?'

'Come on, Leon,' wheedles Ghost, and then tries a bit of distraction. 'What betrayal was she talking about? What happened, exactly?'

Leon looks out across the street. 'Cassren Grenwald is a soothsayer,' he says, 'and a good one, so it appears. She was found out when she had an episode a couple weeks ago, shouting to someone she worked with that he'd better stay home the next day or he'd die. Of course he didn't heed her. He was killed in a street crash – some idiots hopped up higher than the stars stole some rich man's quad, took it for a ride, lost control. Ploughed right into the man as he crossed the street. Cassren was outed as a genuine soothsayer by someone who'd overheard her prophecy to the poor man. She took off soon after that.'

Ghost whistles through her teeth. *That's what you get for caring – shopped to the Guns.*

'And Delilah's her friend, is she?' Ghost muses. 'I'd bet a bit more than that, judging by the barking she did back there.'

Leon shrugs. 'En't close to the worst I've had. She was all yap.'

And she only got yappier with your antagonising.

'And not much for the laws against magic either,' muses Ghost. 'Definitely a sympathiser. Maybe more.'

Leon perks up. 'Activist.'

'Maybe. Why, do you chase those down too?'

'Not officially, but if we can find them, the local guard'll give us a nice bonus.'

Now there's potentially more trick to be made, his pride has righted itself quick enough.

'Let me see what I can find out,' Ghost suggests. 'A test, see if I'm good enough. I'll get her a drink, be sympathetic, tell her I don't like Guns either. She's angry, I can work with angry.'

'She's a self-righteous little sot,' mutters Leon. 'Where'd we be if we all just ignored the law and did whatever we wanted? Law's law. No exceptions.'

Even ex-guards don't necessarily believe that – or not ones with any intelligence to them. Laws shouldn't be steel but bamboo, made to take a bending, depending. Whatever life's been throwing at Leon lately, it's made him rigid.

He is looking at her speculatively. She tries to look sweet. Likely fails.

'You've got a temper, underneath all that cuteness,' he comments, 'and it's served you well so far, no doubt. I'd lay trick down you've seen some things, but it gets murky as the seventh hell from here on in. Don't get much below the line than a Gun. You need to get used to the world under the world.'

Ghost is diplomatically silent. Let him think whatever he

needs to think. As long as he's trotting along the wrong path about her past, all's well.

Leon holds out Cassren Grenwald's data coin.

'Go on, then,' he says. 'Impress me.'

There are, as Leon describes it, three types of people who join the God's Guns.

There are the ones who think godchildren are a danger, think they're doing society a favour. A few even call them blasphemies, refuse to name them godchildren at all. They say they're doing the saints' work, finding the blasphemies and getting them tagged for all to see. Ghost has seen them on street corners before, preaching to the passing apathetic.

This kind usually have a story that might explain their hatred. They have a bet go really bad, or someone they love take ill and die. They go to a soothsayer to try and fix the problem, only the soothsayer can't give them what they need, because who can fix the fall from peak to trough in the choppy sea of life? It just happens, the nature of existence. Only, people need someone to blame, so then it becomes the godchildren's fault for turning out to be just as subject to the whims of an indifferent universe.

The second type, according to Leon, is the one you most often come across, and the best at the job. They do it to earn their trick, pay their bills, and that's it. They don't think about it. They've trained themselves not to. Ex-knights, often times, like Leon.

And like Ghost.

Then there's the third type. This is the rarest one, but they turn up every so often. They'll gun fine for a while, but each time they close a job, it seems to chip at them. Soon enough they're asking why it is they have to chase godchildren down like animals. Then it can often be a short hop from sideline empathy to a full-blown cause.

Leon had a recruit, once. So young, so eager. Too eager. Of course, it turned out he had connections to one of the most violent and notorious godchild activist groups, in it to play a double game and try to scupper Guns work any way he could. Leon spotted him a mile off. Turned him in himself. He got a big bonus that day. Hit the betting bars that night. Good night.

Which one am I? Ghost asks herself. *A punisher, a compartmentaliser or a sympathiser?*

She arrives at her apartment just as the sky starts shyly flaunting the promise of dawn. It's an attic space in a once grand old building that, from the outside, looks and smells of history, and on the inside smells only of damp and ancient cooking fat. It's pretty clear at the moment, with only a few temporary guests drifting in and out of its hallways. They leave her alone, and she leaves them alone. No one here has much worth stealing.

She boots open her front door – it sticks in wet weather – and does a careful, weaving dance that takes her through the labyrinth of candles layering the floor of the main room. Slender taper candles stuck into the tops of dark green absinthe bottles, black candles stoppering up the tops of Tanker whisky bottles, wide stumpy candles basking in metal saucers and glass basins, red candles in spindly waist-high holders, the kind made from cheap gold but painted copper to look more expensive, and black iron trident holders holding three wax stumps apiece.

The place has a generator that runs fine, with a stutter and cough now and then, but light is not what the candles are for. The sheer number of them is a little unnecessary, but they serve a double purpose – no one but her can get through them without knocking one over, so if anyone breaks in, she'll get a warning. And frankly, they look pretty.

They remind her of another life.

It's always been funny to Ghost how candles exist in two states – a cheap necessity for the poor, and a glorious luxury for the rich. Cair Lleon, the famed palace of the King of London, has a ballroom ceiling filled with black iron chandeliers that hold hundreds of candles apiece. A thick and sturdy pulley system lowers each chandelier carefully to the ground when the candles need to be replaced. The ballroom isn't used very often. When it is, and the candles are all lit, and a thousand sparkling flames float above the crowd, the sight remakes the world into a fairy tale.

Ghost peels off her clothes and wraps herself in sleeping blankets, sinking on to her simple pallet bed and curling up. In one hand is the data coin Leon gave her. She presses the tiny catch on its side, and a fuzzy white light crawls up from the coin's flat surface into the darkness of her lofty one-room home. Words and images flicker through the light in a slow scroll, highlights from the life of the missing Cassren Grenwald.

Silly girl should have kept her mouth shut. No doubt her family knew, had always known. If she made a prediction that accurate, chances are it wouldn't have been the first time, and normally it starts to show young, especially in someone with that much power.

This girl is a rare one.

Despite the big integration promises made by the current regime and the deregulation of the district borders just a few years ago, inter-dis' cooperation is largely a joke. The best way to disappear is still to jump districts. Leon had told her to start with Cassren's home and look for anything that could lead

Ghost on to friends or family members who could be hiding her, getting her false identification markers for another district, going by another name, building another life. Doing everything, in fact, just like Ghost.

It feels like setting herself to hunt down a version of herself.

She wonders what Cassren feels, and where she is, and if she's lonely.

She wonders what she'll do if she finds her.

CHAPTER 5

The Royal Stable of Cair Lleon, Blackheart
Five Months Ago

'You couldn't have known,' says Art gently.

The room beyond the King's familiar shape is sheathed in darkness, but he is sitting close enough to the firelight to accent his expression, which is one of deepest sympathy.

Wyll stares into the fire. 'Well, then, that just makes me unforgivably stupid, doesn't it?'

'No, Wyll, it doesn't.'

'I'm your champion. I'm supposed to defend you.'

'My champion, yes,' Art replies, 'not my personal guard. You can't protect the people you love from every harm under the sun, no matter how much you want to. Everyone dies.'

'Not everyone is murdered.'

'I'm the King,' Art points out. 'People often want me dead. You said that to me, once.'

'I remember.'

'It rather stuck with me.'

Wyll snorts. 'How could it not?'

'You were a troublesome cub.'

'But when I grew up I got boring?'

'On the contrary,' Art retorts, 'the trouble only multiplied.'

Wyll feels himself begin to smile, the familiar banter melting him, comforting him, and in that comfort he finds renewed horror. He pulls sharply away from it.

He is not allowed comfort.

Art notices the shifting change, of course.

'You couldn't have known,' he tells Wyll again, a touch of rebuke in his tone. 'You can't read minds.'

That, thinks Wyll, *is the gift I should have been born with. Not this useless talent for making moving, talking lies*.

'Stop doing this, Wyll,' comes a new voice: a brittle, flat voice, with none of its usual undulating playfulness.

Wyll looks up to see Lillath lurking at the doorway to his private rooms.

'Ah, your Spider has arrived,' he tells Art. 'Maybe we can ask her how *she* failed, too.'

Lillath's eyes are fixed on the illusory Art with an expression of unmistakable disgust.

Art shakes his head. 'Lil never met Red. No one did – until me, right at the end there. You kept her a secret from all of us.'

'What if I hadn't?' muses Wyll. 'Would you still be alive?'

'Stop this,' Lillath snaps. 'Get rid of it.'

Wyll leans back in his chair, forces his humming muscles to relax. His brain clambers down a notch. Moments later Art disappears, as if he never was.

Wyll actually hears Lillath breathe out.

'Why do you keep doing that?' she asks, her composure regained.

'What a stupid question,' Wyll says mechanically. 'He's gone. I don't want him to be. So I bring him back.'

Silence.

Another piece of evidence that they really do live in this new, awful reality. Back in the old one, Lillath de Havilland, Spymaster to the King of London, would have skewered Wyll for being so rude. Now she just moves a little closer, watching him.

'Oh, stop looking at me like I've lost my mind,' Wyll says, feeling the sudden, deep resentment that comes from shame. 'I know it's not him. I know I'm just talking to myself. I'm aware. Okay?'

'Everyone talks to themselves,' Lillath replies. 'You just externalise the conversation a little more than the rest of us.'

Wyll says nothing. He lets her settle into the chair opposite, the chair where a moment ago his faked, conjured version of Art had been sitting, making him feel less alone, and ashamed of the need.

Lets her. Ha. Lillath can go wherever she likes.

'It's only been a few days,' she says. 'I can't let him go yet either. It's hard. He's dead, so that means he shouldn't be here. And yet I keep seeing him everywhere. I sit down to send him a message, and I have to remember all over again that there's no longer a him to send a message to. So when I walk into your rooms and see him sitting there, you'll have to forgive me if I don't handle it well.' She pauses. 'It's your fault for being so damn talented. Your illusions are so real.'

'Try touching them,' Wyll says.

'Right. Next time I suspect someone is a fake, I'll just punch them in the face.'

Weak jocularity. Another facet of human behaviour in the face of an event too horrorful to withstand.

'How are the torture sessions going?' he asks.

Lillath gives him the kind of look that suggests this sort of insinuation might be a little too obvious to sting.

'You mean the interviews we've been conducting with the prisoner?' she asks.

'While she's chained up, drugged and kept perpetually awake,' agrees Wyll.

'Well, saints,' Lillath comments, 'it's almost as if you feel sorry for our young King-killer.'

'It's regret at the waste of an exceptional fighting talent, that's all.'

'I'll have to take your word for it.'

'You never saw her fight?' Wyll asks, surprised.

'When would I have the time to get merry and go and roar at a bout?'

'It must be tough, being the royal Spymaster.'

'It is,' Lillath mourns. 'I haven't done anything fun for ages.'

She is watching him in that way she does, her face set to mild apathy and her mind set to cut.

'I may not have an idea of Red as a fighter, but she's a good communicator,' she muses.

'Neh?' Wyll says. 'I confess I never found her a scintillating conversationalist.'

Lillath laughs. 'She's not much of a talker, I'll grant you. It's more the impressions she gives between the grunts.'

He knows he is supposed to ask. He knows disinterest is as telling as eagerness. He has to look like he cares about Lillath's interrogation of his former lover – but how much is too much? What's the right amount to indicate his innocence?

'So,' he fumbles, 'what are your impressions so far?'

'She's used to being alone,' Lillath ruminates. 'Until recently. But she keeps pushing that new feeling away. Camaraderie, intimacy. Love. It's all new to her, and it scares her.'

'Love?' Wyll repeats, while his heartbeat climbs. 'With who?'

Calm. She doesn't know just how far things got between you and Red. She only knows that you were her mentor for a short time.

Don't give her any reason to suspect more.

'I don't know,' Lillath says. 'But whoever they are, I'm not yet sure whether they helped her do this. She has definitely decided to shoulder the burden alone. Her guilt is all over her. It colours every feeling she has.'

'Good,' says Wyll. 'I hope she suffers.'

Lillath just looks at him.

'Why not,' she says quietly, 'think instead about what kind of life she had that led her to see the death of her father as her only path?'

'No,' Wyll retorts. 'Everyone suffers. Not everyone chooses to react the way she did to their suffering. She deserves everything that's coming to her.'

Lillath continues to study him. He hates the feeling of wondering what she sees.

'So what do you think about Lucan's idea?' she asks.

Wyll gives a short laugh. 'I think it's stupid.'

'Why?'

Here it is – the real reason for her visit. Lillath never moves without purpose.

'Red won't confide in me,' says Wyll. 'Saints only know why you all think she would.'

'Come,' Lillath coos, 'you must have spent *some* time alone together.'

'Barely any,' he responds, while his head fills with Red sat above him swaying like a tree in high wind, speared on his rigid, straining cock, her thighs clamped around his ribs.

With an effort, he banishes the memory.

'Well, it's worth a try,' he hears Lillath say.

'I disagree. It's pointless.'

'Wyll,' Lillath says with a pained smile, 'what makes you think this is a request?'

His heart throws out a few arrhythmic beats, threatening to make a mess of things.

'I see,' he says.

'Unbelievably, I'm not sure you do.' Lillath gives a short sigh. 'Finnavair isn't the only one under suspicion. You got an assassin the audience with the King that ended his life. A neat way to prove that you weren't in on it with her is to help us find out who was, don't you think? No one wishes you a lifetime of having to live with the guilt of being used, but at least it's easier to swallow than the alternative.'

'Maybe for you,' murmurs Wyll.

Lillath is not often one for pity, but he can see it on her face now. It makes him want to kick. Illusions push at his insides, begging to be set free. Ghosts demanding to live again.

'I'll call for you tomorrow,' Lillath tells him.

When he next looks up, she is gone.

In the corner of the room, Wyll spies a familiar figure lurking. She hangs in the air like a rainbow, her long dark hair a twist of rope over one shoulder. She is an invitation, a tease, a painful reminder of something he can never have again.

She hovers there a moment more before she too fades, and Wyll is left alone.

CHAPTER 6

Garad's Apartment, Evrontown
Two Weeks Ago

'So Leon begrudgingly let me take on the Cassren Grenwald job,' Ghost says. 'And off I went, an eager dog sniffing down the trail, so bloody desperate to please.' She shakes her head. 'You know, I hate soothsaying. That's the one godchild talent that can never be a gift. It's only a curse.'

Garad is staring at her intently. 'Why?' asks the knight.

'Because,' Ghost replies, 'it's not a good thing to know what's in your future, itso, or you'd just sit in a cave and hide forever. If someone had told me then what would happen to me over the next few weeks, I might have thrown myself into the river at the start, save the enemies I was about to make the bother of doing it themselves. I can understand that man not wanting to believe Cassren's death prophecy about him and just getting on with it.' She shrugs. 'It's just how we all have to live, every day.'

Sunnyside, Alaunitown
Two Months Ago

Cassren Grenwald's apartment is in a quiet, unassuming area.

Scraggly trees gamely line the narrow boulevards, the air suffused with a sense of chatty, bubbly peace as dusk descends and the last of the day-timers make their way home for dinner and bed.

Ghost moves up to the entrance of Grenwald's apartment block. Security is lacking around here – someone has wedged the front door open with a brick. Ghost slips into the building as easy as a dance, following the stairs up to Cass' place on the angel level, within kissing distance of the sky.

Ghost had told Leon not to bother paying anyone off to get a copy of the apartment key – she had the kind of childhood that taught her to be good with locks, and luckily this one's the kind of vintage that makes it easy prey as the world moves on. Thirty seconds under the trick pick she procured at a local market and the cheap electronic yields with a soft bleep, the door swings open and the room beyond materialises, shrouded in curtained dimness. She closes the door behind her as silently as she can, the better to take a decent look around without alerting any neighbours.

It is a cosy, crowded L-shaped place, unexpected alcoves stuffed with trinkets and flecter-glass space-makers dangling from ceiling hooks. You might have room to breathe, even in a little place like this, if every available surface was not covered in books. Books in piles surrounding a warm armchair with a sagging dip in its cushion. Books on the window shelves, on the kitchen table, scattered across the rug in the middle of the floor. When Ghost pokes her head into the bathroom, she sees three books piled on top of the plumbing box and one more on the floor beside the bathtub.

Ghost likes books fine. They look good on a shelf. They're like lamps or paintings, a decorative statement for the wealthy – but nothing about this is decorative. Cassren's books are in a shocking state of disarray, as if she doesn't care a trick penny for their outsides. 'Well worn' is a generous description. If Ghost didn't know better, she'd assume the girl had a pet bear who used them as chew toys.

Other than that, the apartment is neat, but not excessively so. There are dirty dishes still stacked up by the sink. A heavy cup perched on a low table, doing its best to grow a mould-based civilisation in its depths. If Cassren has made a run for it, she's done it fast, as if she were startled into it rather than working to any kind of plan.

The far wall catches Ghost's eye. It was part hidden on entry by the apartment's unusual shape, but as she edges around the corner, the wall comes into view in all its strange splendour.

Coiling wreaths of lusciously painted vines stretch across the brick, in green hues that range from fern to emerald to sunlight, before edging all the way down into midnight blue. Among the foliage are heavy-lidded eyes, hidden until you stare and they begin to stare back.

Intertwined with it all, in a handwritten script that flows like a river, are the words:

Ware the banished children's return
     they have been wandering in the wilderness and their
        hunger
  is
    death

Ghost traces the words with her eyes, trying to shake the strangely heavy feeling they give her. The whole thing must have taken days, weeks. If Cassren doesn't own this place, her landlord is going to be *livid*—

'Art critic or thief?'

Ghost's shoulders twitch, registering a noise behind her.

The voice comes from the direction of the doorway, clear as a bell in the quiet.

Sloppy. She should have heard someone coming.

She turns. Standing in Cassren's now open doorway is Delilah. The most immediate thing Ghost is struck by is her hair. At their first meeting it had been obscured by her stage wig and then the bar's dim lighting. Bathed in the light of the golden hour streaming through the apartment's tall windows, it is a warm ginger, streaks of copper and burnished brass showing through, sparkling like trick wiring.

'Oh,' says Ghost nonchalantly, keeping the fast beat of her heart under wraps. 'I didn't realise anyone else had access.'

'So . . . thief,' Delilah replies, but a half-smile hovers over her mouth, and the belligerence of their first encounter is notably absent.

'This is about finding Cassren,' Ghost protests. 'I'm allowed to be here.'

Rhyfen be fucked if she has any idea what legal powers Guns have, but hopefully the savage songstress is equally ignorant.

Delilah's arms are folded. 'So you're a Gun now? That was quick. Forced down your disdain for the career, did you?'

'I need the trick,' Ghost mutters, dialling up her embarrassment for her audience. 'We can't all be singers with a voice like a sultry angel.'

The compliment lands. She can tell because Delilah flashes a little belligerence, as if to compensate.

'Then I'll stay and watch you work,' she says. 'I'm allowed to be here too.'

A game of who blinks first. Fine.

Ghost gestures to the wall. 'Her work?'

Delilah nods.

'Interesting way to spend your lone time.'

'Right. What do *you* do to relax, shoot kittens?'

'I've never touched a gun in my life,' says Ghost.

'Strange approach to your new profession.'

'The name is historic.' Ghost quotes Leon. 'It doesn't mean I'm literally working for some god, does it? And it doesn't mean I carry a gun around.'

'But you can, if you want. Legally.'

Ghost shrugs.

'And use it,' Delilah says. 'If you want.'

Ghost widens her eyes. 'You're *fun*.'

She picks up her jacket and walks towards Delilah and the door. The former looks surprised.

'You're leaving?'

'Nothing to find here except an obtuse wall poem,' Ghost says. 'Plus, you're annoying.'

Delilah's mouth hangs open. 'I'm what?'

'You're worse than a tricked jude who's throwing the bout.'

'You're comparing me to corrupt Caballaria adjudicators?'

'You sound insulted,' Ghost replies in her mildest voice.

'I'm not into the fight,' Delilah protests.

'That's a little like saying you're not into life.'

'Oh, let me guess, you go to *all* your local bouts.'

'My,' Ghost comments, 'looks like we're at opposites in every way that counts. Good day to you.'

A silent Delilah lets her move out into the hallway.

'Wait,' she hears Delilah say.

Ah, I knew she wanted something.

Ghost keeps going towards the ascender, but she makes sure she's slow enough to be caught up to.

'You've got it all wrong,' Delilah calls behind her. 'Cass didn't disappear because she was afraid of being arrested—'

Ghost swipes her hand though the laser call-rod and hears the whirr of machinery as the ascender clatters into life.

Delilah is approaching, her boots clicking and her voice rising. 'She disappeared because she was killed. One of them killed her.'

Ghost tuts. 'One of who?'

'Her *clients*.' That last word is said with bone-melting acidity.

All right. Time to bite. She turns. 'Clients,' she says.

'You don't know about them?' Delilah looks triumphant. 'They're all commons, every one of them. The sorts of people who'd use her illegal services for their own gains, and then get murderous when they don't get the answers they want. Or maybe she saw too much.'

'How do you know she's dead?' Ghost asks. 'Seen her body, have you?'

'No,' Delilah says, 'but she's not the first. She'll turn up in a few weeks, somewhere in the docklands. It'll look like she drowned. They'll call it self-end, and they won't even look for more evidence that it could possibly be anything else.'

The ascender chirrups as it reaches the angel floor.

'You're a soothsayer too, I take it,' says Ghost.

'No, no,' Delilah snaps impatiently back, 'everyone knows about this. It's been happening around here for months, maybe years, but no one cares. There's a pattern, and something's going on, and no one cares about it!'

Ghost opens the ascender's gate and steps inside. 'So open up a dispute with your local about it.'

'Don't you think we've tried that? None of you do anything. They just keep killing godchildren and getting away with it.'

The fury is fear. Whatever the truth, Delilah believes what she says.

'Sorry.' Ghost shakes her head and closes the gate. 'I just find the alive ones.'

'Your little fire-spitter,' Leon says, 'might have something.'

'When,' Ghost retorts, 'did she become *my* little fire-spitter?'

'When you got her to talk to you.'

'I didn't get her to do anything she didn't want to.'

They are sat together at another bar, this one close to Leon's place, his dank and dark home away from home. No floor should suck at your shoes. The lighting is so bad the servers are little more than shadows.

'More than I got,' Leon says.

Ghost shrugs. 'Well, I am prettier.'

'You got assets I don't, that's all.'

'She wasn't looking at my chest, Leon.'

'I was talking,' Leon says, 'about your eyes. You got twice as much as me, anyone looks better sat next to a cyclops.'

'Please, war veterans clean up at the right places.' Ghost gives him a winning smile. 'So did you reach that friend of yours at the district records place?'

'Neh,' says Leon, and produces a data coin. Ghost reaches out for it but he snatches it back. 'Wait, you don't get your paws on this one. I got to get it back to him. These things get traced if they go for a walk.'

Ghost pouts. 'So what's on it?'

'Death records for the area. Asked him to compare the last year with previous tallies, like you said.' Leon's brows rise. 'Drownings are up, and not just by a tickle. It en't exactly a common death note around here – or rather, it's real common if you're a particular type.'

Ghost is eager. 'A godchild?'

Leon shakes his head. 'Syndicate. Favourite way to get rid of rivals.'

Syndicates. The street families who run business in illegal trading and Wardogs tourneys. If there were any godchildren among them, they'd hardly likely be registered.

'Some of those drownings could be godchild,' she muses.

Leon shrugs. 'No way of knowing.'

'What about deaths of registered godchildren?'

'The local registry list is on the coin, but it's short.' Leon's voice dries out around the edges. 'This ain't one of the more law-abiding areas in the dis', don't know if you've noticed.'

Ghost leans back, disappointed. 'So there's no way to prove that someone's drowning godchildren specifically.'

'What does it matter?' rumbles Leon. 'If Cassren turns up drowned, then the angry singer might have a point. Either way, your job is to find her. Talk to her family yet?'

'No.'

'Why not?'

'Hard to talk to someone when they won't talk back,' Ghost says. 'It's a real conversation stopper. They wouldn't let me in the door.'

Leon sucks his teeth. 'Ah.'

'Ah,' agrees Ghost. 'Listen, man. What do I do next?'

'Dig into her life. Think where she'd be most likely to go. Can't track her without finding her trails.'

'She's a damn schoolteacher,' Ghost says, massaging her forehead.

'She's also a soothsayer,' Leon remarks. 'What about the man who shopped her?'

'He's a common.'

'For all you know. Maybe he's hiding her now.' Leon shrugs. 'Last place you'd think to look, no?'

CHAPTER 7

Cair Lleon Clusterloc, Blackheart
Five Months Ago

The grip on Wyll's arms threatens to separate balls from sockets.

He is dragged between two members of the royal guard, drooping and stumbling along a narrow hallway. The walls he passes are transparent, the small rooms beyond them harshly lit, devoid of comfort and impossible to escape.

The procession ends at a door. He hears an electronic beep. He is hauled through, noisily dumped on to the hard floor and locked in. The two guard knights don't even spare him a glance, their gazes reserved for the door's locking mechanism. Satisfied that everything is as it should be, they move off in silence, their boot taps receding.

Finally, he is left alone.

Or not quite alone – there is one other person down here in Cair Lleon's own special prison, in the room opposite his. So far, they have not made a sound.

Wyll stirs weakly, pulling himself upright with trembling arms. When he does so, he sees her. She is staring at him. Across the corridor's modest width, they lock eyes.

It is the first time he has seen Red since the day – just over a week ago, or a lifetime ago in a different universe – that she came to him, battered, bloodied and half-dead, begging him to get her a private audience with the King.

Trust. The mistake he keeps making. He has sworn to himself that he will never make it again.

Red is staring at him with naked wonder.

'You can't be here.'

Her words float through the space between them.

'Trust me, I wish I wasn't,' Wyll croaks.

He stifles a cough – a little too performative – and settles for curling up against the transparent wall.

'What are you doing here?' Red says. It is less a question and more an accusation.

Wyll replies, 'I'm in trouble.'

Red just watches him owlishly.

He leans his head back against the wall, wondering how best to prise her open. This whole idiot plan has been rushed. Lillath has sent him in here with only minimal strategy. She'd thought it would be enough that Red's suspected partner-in-crime turn up in the same situation, that just the sight of Finnavair would lower guards enough for tell-tale gleaming nuggets of truth and secrets and shared confidence to shine through.

By all accounts they had very recently and rapidly become friendly, Red and Finnavair, and for no particularly obvious gain on either side – suspicious in itself. Additionally, when one is the official lover/soon-to-be-spouse and the other the unacknowledged child of the same now dead man, well, only fools pass over such coincidences.

They have to be in this together somehow. A pair of scheming snakes.

Wyll glances down at his hand, resting on the cell floor. He sees slender fingers cast in tones of hazelnut, smaller and more delicate than his own battered, knotted digits. Still, Finnavair Caballarias o'Rhyfentown is a fighter of no small renown, and she works hard for it — the palms are rough with calluses, and the third finger on the right hand is mildly crooked from a badly healed break some months prior to now. He is particularly proud of this small detail. He has studied her. Red, of course, is probably too far away to pick it up, or wouldn't notice it even if she wasn't, but it's the detail that fuels authenticity. Wyll pays attention to details. It is one reason, he believes, that he is so good at what he does.

Didn't pay attention to the details of Red, though, did you?

His father's voice, filled with bitter satisfaction. His long-dead father talks often to him, usually to criticise.

'How long have they had you in here?' he asks Red in Finnavair's musical, streets-tinged voice.

'I don't know,' Red says. 'A few days. It's hard to tell without windows or clocks.'

Every line of her is wary and tense. She doesn't trust Finnavair's appearance. Maybe Lillath is wrong and they weren't such good friends after all.

'Do they know?' Wyll asks.

Red is silent.

'Know what?' she replies at length.

'Come on,' coaxes Wyll. 'They aren't capturing any of this. They don't, not down here. They watch the hallways, but they can't hear in our cells. It's so there's no record of anything that happens.'

'How do you know that?' Red dubiously asks.

'Art told me.'

His name is supposed to electrocute them both. Evoke some shared response. Instead, Red curls even deeper into herself. He cannot read her. He needs to be closer to her, but he and Lillath agreed that up close was too risky. What if she tried to touch him? She'd know immediately that something was off, that he wasn't Finnavair. He'd still feel like him underneath the illusion – wrong body shape, wrong musculature.

'Red,' he calls softly. 'Come on. Do they know?'

Do they know what? Something. Anything. Whatever you like.

Just give me something.

'What do you want from me?' asks Red.

She sounds weary. Lillath told Wyll that she spends most of her time asleep. Her muscles stand too stark, pushing too hard against her fatless skin. They shouldn't have drugged her so much, but it was hard to argue against. They all saw the storm she created without even touching anything, just standing there and raging at her father sitting feet away, until the receiving room was torn apart and his throat was crushed.

They are afraid of her. And they are right to be.

'You know what they said to me?' Wyll tells her. 'They think we're in this together.'

Her head rears. 'Why would they think that? You loved him.'

Wyll just waits.

'I've told them I did it all on my own,' says Red. 'I've said it over and over. Why aren't they listening?'

Success. He has roused her.

'They say they have evidence otherwise,' he says, kindling the spark. 'They want to execute us both.'

She shakes her head. 'No. No. That won't happen.'

His laugh is bitter. 'I don't know how to persuade them otherwise.'

56

'You tell them it was all me,' she demands. 'Tell them that you hate me.'

The expression on her face is one of perfect acceptance, as if hate would be a foregone conclusion.

'They know we were friends,' Wyll tries. 'People have seen us together.'

'No, they haven't.' Red delivers this with considerable irritation. 'Hardly anyone knew about us. I mean,' she amends, 'about our official relationship.'

Her eyes stray momentarily, as if looking for capturers. Wyll feels a little lost. There are inflections here that he doesn't understand.

'Friends is an official relationship in your head?' he asks.

She doesn't like the question. 'I wouldn't have called us friends. I never got the impression you had me as anything so equal.' A flash of something. Hurt? It seems her relationship with Finnavair is a little more complicated than Lillath's sources had suggested.

'I'm sorry,' Wyll says. 'I didn't mean to make you feel like that.'

'Yes, you did. You kept me at arm's length every step of the way.' Red glances at him sidelong. 'And I did you. And here we are.'

'Here we are,' Wyll echoes, stalling.

'Don't you want to know why?' Red is staring at him. Intently focused.

'Why what?' he responds.

'Why I did it. Why I killed him.'

Wyll notices his breathing has sped up. He tries to slow it down.

'After all, you had no idea what was really going on, did you?' Her voice rises.

He supposes she performs for the capturers she seems convinced are there. Smart.

'No,' he agrees. 'I didn't.'

'So ask me.'

'I know why you did it. I know you're his daughter.'

'It must hurt.' She is trying to goad Finnavair. 'You must
want me dead. Why are you sitting here playing silly games
with me?'

'They arrested me! I'm not here by choice.'

'Moldra lagha,' Red says, 'gives you a claim to my life.'

'Moldra lagha is a stupid, antiquated law that ensures all we
ever do is kill each other,' Wyll hotly replies. 'Besides, I wasn't
his acknowledged lover, or not until recently. I'm low down on
the list; I'd have to wait a while before I got my turn.'

Red barks a laugh.

'Well,' she says in acknowledgement. 'True enough. But you
told me you weren't lovers. You said he was like your brother.
Was that a lie?'

Like a brother? Why would Finnavair have said that? She and
Art had been seeing each other in secret for two years, and the
way Art talked of her, on the rare occasions that he was goaded
into mentioning her at all, was very much not with a brotherly
kind of affection.

'I was about to marry him,' Wyll says. 'We gave up doing
that with brothers a while ago, and I think civilisation is the
better for it.'

'*Marry* him? I . . .' Then something passes across Red's face,
some clear, cold wash of shock.

She sits back.

'Who do you think you look like right now, Wyll?' she asks.

His mask drops. He feels it go, a sharp exhale after holding breath to pain.

Red watches him curiously.

'Saints, for a moment there I really thought they'd arrested the Sorcerer Knight himself,' she says, 'but you . . . you're pretending to be Fin, aren't you?' Her head tips. 'At least, you *think* you are. I wondered why you were talking so strange.'

A mirror. He needs a mirror. He was Finnavair when they dragged him into the clusterloc, he knows he was. Fuck. *Fuck.* When had the illusion dropped? Why hadn't he felt it go?

'Wyll,' Red says, and his name in her mouth again claws his heart to ravaged raw meat. 'Why are you here?'

They stare at each other. He feels the shame of the sham; he feels disgust, horror, exposure, like being caught pulling his own chain out in the open. Why isn't he in control of this?

why isn't he in control of this

'They wanted to try tricking you into revealing who helped you,' Wyll finally admits. 'And because they can't find Finnavair, they think it's her. They asked me to pretend to be her to get it out of you.'

He pictures Lillath cursing at him from behind a capturer screen.

Red is stiff. 'Fin didn't help me. She tried to stop me. She failed.' Her hands make a gesture of 'as you can see'.

'Where is she now?'

'Wherever people go when they die.'

What little light there is seems to drain away.

'You can't be serious,' says Wyll.

Red is blank and hollow. 'Why would I joke about that?'

He remembers the way she turned up at his door that

night – the night she came to him, the night she got him, unknowingly, to help her get the audience with Art that would end his life. She had been cut, doused in blood, her throat half crushed. Her throat is, even now, dappled with blooms of sickly yellow-purple bruising. He had almost forgotten about the state of her in the shock of what followed. She never did tell him who had done that to her.

She is telling him now.

'If that's true, where is Finnavair's body?' he asks.

'Marvoltown. You heard of the lost station? Terminal? It's underneath street level. There are a set of steps in the grounds of an abandoned bone house in Daeccenham that'll take you down there.'

Lies don't usually get so specific. Such details can so easily be disproved.

'No one helped me get here,' Red says. 'Every step I took, I took alone. Why is it so hard to believe that I came here by myself? That I got myself sponsored? I trained, I fought, I found my way in, I did it all on my own—'

'On your own?' Wyll spins back. 'What, not a word of thanks for the Sorcerer Knight, the King's own champion? Without me, you wouldn't even have got close.'

She just shakes her head. 'Is that what you torture yourself with? I used you. You didn't know. There's no guilt here for you.'

There it is, in plain speech.

I used you.

No plan to get herself out of this? Not one lie, not a blame laid at another door?

'You're sentencing yourself to death,' says Wyll.

Red gives him a look of cutting disdain. 'Did that years ago, the moment I decided to avenge my mother.'

'So,' he drawls thoughtfully, 'you get to be a spirit of vengeance. How wonderful for you. How pure, how easy. But you're still a human being, no matter what you tell yourself. Being a monster is a convenience.' He spits on the ground. 'It's weak. It's pathetic. It means you don't have to take responsibility for the things you do. It means you don't have to face the fact that when you ended his life, you ruined mine.'

He gets what he wants. She is startled out of her chilly torpor. Her mouth opens, but he doesn't want to hear it. He does not want her excuses.

'Not to mention the fact that you'll push this city to the brink of war,' he says. 'Do you even comprehend the knife-edge we're bleeding our feet on, right now? Do you understand what happens when everyone finds out he's dead? Do you care?'

And he loses her again.

'They'll find another King,' she says, turning her face away as if he has disappointed her. 'They always do. No end of people wanting to tell everyone how to live.'

'Well, of course you'd have that view of it, when you have no idea how hard it is, how each decision weighs on you like, like,' he casts around, 'iron chains. You think it's fun, being King? You think he had a *merry good time*?'

'Are you sure you didn't love him?' Red says darkly.

Peevish brat. Idiot child. Weak, disgusting traitor.

'Of course I did,' Wyll hisses. 'More than anyone I've ever known.'

She looks away. Did he imagine a flicker of hurt across her face, or was it really there? Was it, *was it*, and why did he need it to be?

'Someone else was in charge of this assassination,' he insists, trying to insult her. 'You shouldn't even have been able to pass basic knights' training by yourself.'

Red is silent, turned to the wall.

'If I did have help, I didn't know about it at the time. So what good is it telling you now?' she mutters.

Shit, now we're getting somewhere.

'What good is it protecting them?' Wyll asks.

'I'm not protecting them. If you want to know who they are, ask the palace guard.'

'What do you mean?'

Red leans heavily on her shoulder as she curls on her side against the wall, as if she doesn't have the strength to hold herself up. He wants to take her into his arms. He wants to tell her that everything will be all right, even though it won't, even though it feels like it may never be again.

'You think you're the first to come to me like this?' Red mutters. 'I've had others. Offers. Those walking meat-slabs you call guard knights are, presumably, suitably bribed, and then in come the visitors.'

'Who?' Wyll urges. *Saintsfuck, does Lillath know about this?*

But Red does not answer. Her eyes are closed.

'I don't want any of it,' she says. 'I just want to be left alone. If you're going to kill me, just get on with it.'

It dawns on him then: she never expected to make it past the first rocky terrain of adulthood. Everything she has done over the past year has been with the heady freedom of expected death. Any consequences soon to be inconsequential, at least to her.

But there are worse things than death.

'You won't get an arena execution, Red,' says Wyll. 'You won't even get a secret execution. You'll live out a long life – for the want of a better word – just like this. Drugged. Chained. This grey, listless twilight. They'll never let you go. Death would be a release, you see, a freedom, and they don't want you free.'

He might as well have flayed her open. She looks wounded, horror-struck.

He should be rejoicing. He is rejoicing, he tells himself. He is winning, and winning must always feel good, or what use is it?

'I really thought you'd come here to kill me,' says Red.

It almost sounds like a plea.

He considers telling her that he thought of it, on his way over here.

He considers being that kind, and that cruel.

'If I were lucky enough to have a choice,' Red continues in a dream-rippled tone, 'that's the death I'd ask for. To meet you in the arena. A fight to the end.'

It is as though she has plucked his recent nightmares from his head. In one, he is dragged protesting to the pit floor, where Red stands ready and waiting, weaponless. Art watches them both from the royal box. He points down to his champion in front of the baying arena, and then holds his arm out straight and slowly squeezes his hand into a fist. *Kill her.* Wyll has no choice. He looks into Red's eyes as he draws his knife. Her huge eyes leak tears as she wails, wriggles like a wounded rabbit, pleads and begs . . .

But there is another version that haunts him. A version much like their very first meeting, where this colt-like masked unknown danced constantly out of his reach, dazzling him with her grace, slippery as a fish, until he finally had her pinned to a wall, felt the thick give of her heaving flesh against his, felt the thick give of her arm flesh underneath the point of his blade, and when he felt the vibration of her guttural scream through his arm, he fell joyously, dangerously in love . . .

'I miss the fight,' says the diminished creature before him, and suddenly he hates everyone who has dared suck the life and passion from her like this. *What is this impulse in us to subdue danger until it becomes pitiable in its safety?*

Her head rolls in his direction.

'If I met you in the arena at my full strength,' she continues, 'I'd kill you, Wyll. I'd rip you apart with every muscle and bone I have. I'd claw at you until you were nothing but ribbons. Until every sinew string, every scrap of your flesh, was mine. I'd make a nest of what was left and I'd curl up in it and I'd feel peaceful, and complete.'

For the first time since he came in, Red smiles, and as she does so, her face is lit with a luminous, fragile beauty.

It is, without a doubt, the most romantic thing anyone has ever said to him.

He paces under Lillath's watchful gaze.

'Wyll, what happened?' she asks.

'How dare you send me into that!' His incandescence feels good. It masks.

'Your illusion was perfect, at least to me,' persists Lillath. 'Why didn't you look like Fin to her? Why could she see through it?'

'Well, let's review. Perhaps due to me skipping in there looking blithely like someone she's already killed?'

'A boast,' Lillath suggests.

'Have you found Finnavair alive and well?' demands Wyll.

She hesitates. 'Not yet.'

'That's because she's dead.' Wyll points out. 'Go see for yourself.'

'Good idea,' Lillath says in the kind of patient tone reserved for people who are several steps behind her. Of course she already has people on their way to the location.

'Heed me, Lillath. That girl in there ended one of the best knights in the Caballaria, and then went on to kill a King. You have to execute her, and do it now.'

Wyll's voice has a noticeable wobble to it. Irritating.

Lillath just watches him. No one ever comes out from under the Spider's thoughtful gaze without a scratch.

'She's too valuable,' she says at last.

'And what about all these people that have been coming to see her? Aren't you the least bit curious to know who *they* are?'

'Of course. It's in hand. Wyll, you need to calm down, I have this under control.'

Wyll laughs. It sounds deranged, even to him.

'Under control,' he repeats. 'Well, good for you. But if you want to keep Red alive, you leave me out of it. Because if you let me near her again, I'll kill her, you understand? I'll fucken *kill* the murderous bitch.'

Lil is wary, small before his rage.

'Which one first?' she asks quietly.

'What?'

'Fuck or kill?'

Wyll points a finger at her, dismayed to see it tremble. 'Get out of my way.'

She makes a minute nod towards the door.

He sweeps past, barely aware of the guards fumbling and scattering in their haste to unlock the outer gate and press away from his path. Perhaps they are a little disturbed by the horse-sized dogs stalking in the wake of the Sorcerer Knight, growling and drooling swinging strings of saliva to the floor, their teeth too big for their jaws. He lets them exist until he is outside, at which point he dismisses them with an irritated flip of a hand.

But he doesn't even notice the small boy, a boy that looks just like a child-aged Wyll might. The illusory boy follows in the wake of the illusory dogs, tears tracking silently down his apple-shaped cheeks, his feet bare, completely alone.

CHAPTER 8

Garad's Apartment, Evrontown
Two Weeks Ago

'Now I must admit that in the next part of the story,' says Ghost, 'I don't come off too well. But we're only human, itso? Gwanhara forgives the growl of our groins, as they say.'

Her attempt at light humour falls into the black hole of Garad's silence and disappears, never to be heard from again.

Well. There's oft been a joke or two about the Silver Angel's own claims to humanity, considering their at times robotic approach to the gilded role that life has gifted them, so perhaps it wasn't the best thing to say.

Ghost clears her throat. 'So,' she continues, 'I went back to the bar.'

Machine Sounds, Alaunitown
Two Months Ago

Ghost sits at the high-top in Machine Sounds, playing with a drink.

Liquid the colour of black mountain honey sits in a squat round spirits flask, served chipped but otherwise naked. It's full night, but still too early for this bar's main crowd, it seems. Funny how a place like this can feel like it's hooked up to a trick power relay when it's stuffed out with people, but when there's not enough to jump-start the air, the worst of it shows. The old, juddery wall projections. The brassy, cheap table lamps. A pervasive down energy, so strong it's almost a smell. The smell of boredom, the smell of too much time to spend tearing yourself apart for every mistake you've made, every wrong you've dealt and been dealt.

The next time the lone server wanders past the high-top, Ghost stops them.

'Is Delilah on tonight?' she asks.

The server gives a half-hearted frown. 'Who?'

Ghost recalls her singer name. 'Flowers for Kane.'

'No, she's here Tuesdays.'

The server ambles off, their walk a yawn.

What are we doing here? Ghost asks herself.

Working the job, says the other her. *Delilah is the only path we have, since the last one we took was such a disaster.*

The other her – the voice in her head that she argues with, that reminds her of things she'd rather not remember, that picks at her scabs and sits in her head observing her life and running a commentary on her choices, the one that she sees staring back at her from any reflective surface, another Ghost with a mind of her own – has a point.

She has come straight here from a visit to the man who shopped Cassren, a fellow schoolteacher by the name of Jessen Magisteras Arshawl o'Launitown. Jessen had a face as bland and round as a bowl of milk cake. Smile as wide as a yawning cat. Features arranged all suspicious when she beeped his door horn, but on learning that she was a Gun, his whole demeanour changed and he became welcoming, beckoning a 'come in, come in'.

Which, on reflection, was a bad sign.

'It just baffles me how this culture has become about coddling lawbreakers these days,' Jessen confided to her as they perched together on a pair of pale featureless chairs in his pale featureless house. 'After all, if they've done nothing wrong, there's nothing to worry about. But they all choose to be illegal, don't they?'

'Do they?' Ghost replied, managing to spin it into an agreeable tone. Not that it mattered. The man was the type who didn't need a listener, just a silent wall to bounce his opinions against.

'It's really a question of those who want to fit in, and those who don't. Those who want to be part of the *community*.' He waved a hand, his eyes wide with the righteous innocence of those just making sense. 'They need to integrate more, that's what I'm saying. I don't go visiting Senzatown without knowing about the customs there, do I? Learning some of the local slang? Eating the food? It's about *fitting in*. If you don't want to fit in, well . . . that's on you, isn't it? You'll have to deal with the consequences of that.'

'I do love their dukka eggs,' commented Ghost.

Jessen paused, caught off-guard. 'What?'

'Dukka eggs. The Senzatown dish. The one where they make it three ways with different spice mixes, and you take a bite in turn from each one—'

'Oh saints, I can't stand that muck,' he said dismissively. 'It's not proper food, is it? Let's be honest.'

'Right,' agreed Ghost. She was not altogether sure what proper food was, but she'd scoop shit off the street and have it on toast if it were the opposite of whatever this one liked to chew. 'Listen, I'll be out of your ears soon as I can, I just came to get a couple of details straight. For my report. When you overheard Cassren telling your colleague that he was going to die the next day, did you believe her?'

Jessen exploded a laugh. 'Of course not. She was acting like she'd sniffed a bucket of boost.'

Boost, Ghost surmised, was some Alaunitown fashion drug of the now.

'So you've never believed in soothsayers,' she said.

'Saints, no. They prey on the soft-minded to make their trick.'

'So sorry.' Ghost smiled and shook her head. 'I must have got bad information. I thought you shopped Cassren for being a godchild.'

'Shopped? What does *that* mean?' Jessen said with some disdain.

Jessen was the type who liked people to know which level of society he sat in.

'Reported,' Ghost amended.

Jessen's brow was furrowed in an effort to follow her. 'Well, yes, of course. I'd never make a false declaration, if that's what you're suggesting.'

'Not at all,' said Ghost, 'just that if you don't believe in sooth-sayers, why did you report her for being one?'

'Well, it wasn't necessarily that I—Um, I was just being care-ful, that's all; it doesn't mean she has,' Jessen blustered, 'magical powers, does it?'

'So which is it?' interrupted Ghost. 'Either you don't believe she's a soothsayer and so you made a false declaration, or you do believe and you shopped her for trying to save a man's life?'

The conversation had gone a little downhill after that. In any case, the pudding-faced fool was not hiding Cassren. No one is that good at playing idiot.

Ghost lets out a sigh and knocks back the last lick of her drink. She'll just have to come back another night and see if—

Damn. That's a bit of luck at last, for here comes the lady herself, and it's not even Tuesday.

It looks like Delilah is Delilah tonight and not the singer Flowers For Kane, as there's no sign of the sugar-coloured wig or the strap clothes. Still, people stare as she goes past. She has a 'notice me' quality. And Ghost is noticing.

She pushes away from the high-top, gets close to Delilah's path. The latter lands eyes on her, and the reaction is good enough.

'What are you doing here?' she asks with astonishment aplenty, and – perhaps wishfully thinking – a kind of surprised pleasure.

'I came to find you,' Ghost replies.

'Why?'

Show your belly and get her defences down. It's the only way with someone who runs on anger.

'To tell you that you were right.'

'About what?'

'I looked into drownings,' says Ghost. 'They're unusually high around here. They've been presumed syndicate deaths, so it's hard to tell how many might have been godchildren.'

'I can tell you how many were,' Delilah replies. 'It's fifteen in the last year.'

Ghost stares at her as her brain dredges up the numbers Leon gave her.

'That's almost all the drownings,' she says.

71

Delilah makes a 'told you' shrug with her slender shoulders.

'How would you know how many of them are godchildren?'

'Just because your officials don't,' Delilah mocks, 'you don't think a tally is being kept elsewhere?'

Ghost holds up her hands. 'Fine. Your sources are better than mine. Now, as much fun as it is to continually tear my head off, wouldn't you rather be hydrated while doing it? Got time for a drink?'

Delilah goes watchful as a cat.

'What,' Ghost goads her, 'scared to be seen with a Gun? Thought you said you're not a godchild.'

'I'm just trying to decide how attractive you are,' Delilah says. 'Far more damning for me to be seen with a plain.'

'You wouldn't even be talking to me if you thought me plain, lady,' says Ghost, and kicks the chair opposite her out with her foot, shunting it into Delilah's thigh. 'Anything you want for the first round.'

Delilah's jaw twitches. 'Anything? Even the long-aged whisky they keep locked up in the back?'

'I'm not cheap when it comes to drinks.'

'No, just where it counts.'

Ghost laughs despite herself. It's been a while since she's crossed someone who can parry and thrust so easy, even if it's with words as weapons instead of swords.

They order up and Delilah settles, looking at her.

'How do they callian you?' she asks.

'Ghost.'

'That's about as real as *my* stage name.'

'Well, you appear to know about Guns, so you'd know that they don't love to use real names.'

'Yes, of course. Without a name, it's harder to find you when there's blame to be laid.' Delilah's small mouth twists. 'Ghost is apt. Ghost in, ghost out. No foot in the real world. You know that executioners used to do the same, back in the days before they could hide behind glow screens, when they had to be out on the stage where everyone could see them? They'd wear hoods so none of the watching crowd would ever know who they were.'

'I'm surprised you don't think it's a Gun doing the killings,' says Ghost. 'Say one of them has slipped off their leash and started giving the hunting a bit more of a literal ending.'

'Maybe it is. It makes sense, doesn't it?'

'Only if you're too prejudiced to apply logic. Maybe you don't know enough of the lifestyle, so let me tell you. Guns don't get paid much – they're murky official at best, so help is hard to come by, and they're shunned by damn near everyone on both sides. Only people without much of a choice choose to be a Gun.'

'My tears are at the ready,' Delilah says.

'Resources, you tart-tongued beauty. You can't just drown fifteen people and nothing happens – not unless you have trick and you have connections. Despite what you may think, a killed godchild is still a problem to solve for the local guard – besides which, none of those fifteen were even registered. As far as everyone knew, they were commons. So why haven't there been any disputes opened up for their deaths?'

Delilah takes a pull of her drink, baring her throat a little. Tiny glimpse of throat, soft skin.

'I don't think it's a Gun,' she says after her swallow.

'No, you think it's a client. You want to tell me more about that?'

Delilah shrugs. 'Cass was a powerful soothsayer. People pay

a lot for that. Privately – it's illegal on both sides, so both sides keep it quiet.'

'How did she find these clients?'

'Word of mouth,' Delilah says vaguely.

'Do you know any of them?'

'She was very careful.'

Which is not a no.

'How would I find these clients to talk to?' asks Ghost. 'She doesn't strike me as someone stupid enough to keep a book of all their names and addresses written out all neat and legible.'

'She wasn't.'

Helpful. But something about Delilah's manner says *she* might know a way to get to these clients. A couple more drinks might do the trick, and if it doesn't, well, nothing lost.

As if she's read Ghost's mind, Delilah reaches out for a server, a friendly grab for the arm, and murmurs something to her, too quiet for Ghost to hear. The server nods assent, and then ambles off.

'Neck needs more greasing?' enquires Ghost.

'Message service. I just cancelled my evening plans.' Delilah gives her an appraising look. 'You're more interesting.'

'I'm flattered. Sad for your plans.'

'My plans'll understand when they catch sight of you.'

Ghost cranes her neck around the bar. 'They're here?'

'Wouldn't it be funny if they were?' Delilah leans back. 'Also I ordered the long-aged whisky on your trick.'

'Well, it'd better be a knockout.'

'The cost'll make you think so.'

Ghost smiles. 'You're not going to like this next question.'

Delilah nervously pats her hair. 'None of them have been a treat so far.'

'If Cassren was so powerful, how did she not foresee her own death?'

'Everyone knows it doesn't work like that. Soothsayers only see the likeliest possible future, if all the players involved keep on the course they're on. The trouble with human nature is it's fickle.' Delilah turns sour. 'Change your behaviour, change the game.'

There is a popular glow show about a fictional team of vastos investigators working out of some sleaze-fest in the downs of Senzatown. One of the team is a soothsayer with special dispensation to use his ability – a dispensation that doesn't exist back in the real world – whose catchphrase 'change your behaviour, change the game' has infiltrated the latest trends of dis' slang. Other than that – and a rippling torso – there's not much else to him.

Trouble is, the majority of soothsayers are mostly useless. Their predictions are too inconstant and too vague to apply to anything or anyone specific. You need someone powerful who can turn those visions and nigglings and twinges and dreams into accurate sketches of the future – and the powerful ones are very rare.

Cassren was very rare.

More drinks arrive. Delilah takes a big gulp of hers.

'People think if you've that much power, you'd want to show it off,' she says, swirling the rich amber contents of her glass. 'But the more power you have, the more likely it is people will try to ride it for their own ends. Know what it's like to be used for what you can do?'

Ghost is silent.

'It's compassion that fucked Cass,' Delilah says with a bitter tinge, designed, it appears, to mask a more profound sadness.

'Powerful godchildren are only rare as hen's teeth because they learn, practically from birth, to keep quiet about it.'

'Not all of them.'

'No,' Delilah agrees, 'but the Sorcerer Knight is one in a million.'

'You admire him?'

She snorts. 'Are you playing? Hard to admire someone who hates themself as much as he does.'

'You think he hates himself?'

'Why else would he have chosen to be a target?'

'Some people think it's brave. He's an example of what could be for godchildren.'

'He's never allowed to use his magic,' Delilah says. 'He's not a godchild. He hasn't changed anything for his own. He conformed, and he knows it.'

'For a common, you know an awful lot about all this.'

'I knew one, growing up. The mild, registered kind. The kind who can make a toy hover to amuse a baby, or tell your mood before you walk in the room. Nothing heavier than that.'

That explains a little, but not Delilah's anger, nor her defences.

'What's your story?' she asks, more softly. 'Why become a Gun?'

'Not much else open to me right now,' Ghost replies.

'Why not?' And then, impishly, 'Did you do something bad?'

Ghost says nothing.

Delilah pauses. 'Sorry. I'm prying.'

Ghost shrugs. 'It's all right. Needed a quick exit from a former life. I got caught between two people and I chose badly.'

Delilah brightens. 'A love gone wrong! You should write a song about it. Knew you were a heartbreaker soon as I saw you.'

'I'm the one got my heart broken. The one I wanted gave me the heave, and the other one was about to.' Ghost gives a wry smile. 'So I shed my old skin and made my escape from London.'

'More snake than ghost.' Delilah appraises her. 'But you're back, now.'

'It'd be easier if I'd just stayed away,' Ghost muses.

'Some people don't like easy lives.'

Ghost laughs. 'That they don't.'

'So you don't have anyone waiting for you at home?'

'No,' Ghost responds, and Delilah looks pleased.

'Do you want to come to mine?' she says. 'I have a better whisky than this, and it's not far.'

No way to suppress the surprised laugh this provokes.

'Well,' says Ghost, 'you're very direct.' Truth be told, she finds honesty as seduction pretty hard to resist.

'I'm also good at reading a room, for a common. And I think I'm right in saying we've both been thinking about each other's beds.'

'Only because you're curious about where the enemy sleeps.'

Delilah smiles. She's drunk, realises Ghost.

I'm drunk too, realises Ghost.

'You're not my enemy,' she says. 'Cass' killer is. And you're trying to find them too. Anyway, this isn't about that. Despite my best efforts, I like you. You're . . . intriguing.'

You're supposed to be in hiding, Ghost's other self reminds her.

She gives the warning her usual due consideration.

Two breaths later and she's making her way towards the back of the bar, following the twisting back of the copper-haired will-o'-the-wisp ahead.

They reach the outside, broaching the swirl of cold, foetid air.

Delilah takes her hand, but the angelic singer's attention is else-where, gaze hopping around the concrete stretch.

'I just want to make one stop before we get to my place,' she says vaguely.

'I could eat,' Ghost agreeably replies. 'Big appetite.'

'Not for food.'

'Not quite what I meant either.'

Delilah gives her a look, and then a laugh. 'You're something.'

Suddenly her attention is all on Ghost, twin beams of a gaze, both hands holding Ghost's.

Something, says Ghost's other self to her, *might not mean what you want it to mean.*

'Can we get those dough balls studded with frogs' legs they do round here?' Ghost suggests. 'There's a vendor down the way.'

She feels Delilah squeezing her hands almost too hard for seduction.

'Cass belonged to a group,' she says. 'Did I tell you? They were investigating the drownings around here.'

'You didn't.'

Delilah is looking intently into her eyes. 'Well, you should talk to them.'

Back to business? This girl has an odd bedding technique.

Ghost nods. 'I will. Tell me about them tomorrow.'

'Mmm,' Delilah demurs, 'I think they want to meet you now.'

She cocks her head to the side.

Ghost looks around.

Figures come up from nowhere, several of them, looming large, forming a tight circle it would be hard to break through even if she wasn't feeling very unsteady on her feet.

The fucken whisky, her other self says. *No wonder you're acting so slow-dope, she* dosed *it—*

'Fabulous,' Ghost manages, and then – with time for one last irritated thought about how smug her other self is going to be about being proven right – everything goes dark.

CHAPTER 9

The Royal Stable of Cair Lleon, Blackheart
Four Months Ago

Wyll returns to his own rooms so preoccupied that at first he doesn't even notice the girl asleep in his bed.

The Royal Stable of Cair Lleon is, in his view, a luxurious prison. It is for this reason that, despite it being his official place of residence, he has never really lived there. A rebellion against both security and tradition – the latter normally upheld even for the King's own champion – but Art had just laughed when complaints were made about how often Wyll found ways to sneak out of the stable to go roaming, and suggested they stop trying to cage a fully functioning adult human who also happened to be a master thwimoren. Against the tricks an illusionist can play on your mind, the only defence is not to play.

So Wyll got his freedom, quietly taking over an old power station going to ruin in an unkempt corner of Marvoltown – its history as the site of a galdor wall adding to its allure – and made it his private, secret residence. His one concession was that it was at least in the neighbourhood of Stredforthe, close to the Blackheart border and only a twenty-minute bike ride away from the palace at good speed. Only Art knew where the old power station was located, and only Art allowed him to have it.

But Art is dead, and with him the privilege he had bestowed – privilege Wyll is only just becoming aware of, now that he feels its absence. His talent has made a prisoner of him. Art's old Saith needs him close at hand, ready to assume their dead leader's form at a moment's notice.

Impersonating the King of London: a crime so enormous as to be unthinkable before now – but then again, things are only unthinkable before they happen. Order and rule are illusions more persuasive than any he could ever make.

It is late in the afternoon when Wyll stumbles back to his rooms, having worked himself too hard at training. Despite a lengthy cool-down, his muscles retain a tremble, and he feels more drained than he'd like. But it's the best way, the only way, to get through each day. When he punishes his body, he shuts down his mind to cope with repairing it, numbing any thinking it might have been planning on. Right now, he doesn't want to think. Right now it scares him, the places his mind wants to go.

Like the paranoia, for example. He could really do without that. He is already half convinced that his rooms are full of hidden capturers, the work of Lillath, or perhaps even Lucan, to keep him under watchful eye. Or . . . no, saints. He is seeing shadows where there are none. His mind is on its habitual punishment parade, having him jump at nothings or succumb to delusions. When it gets really bad, which isn't often, his magic leaks out even when he doesn't mean it to, conjuring meaningless terrors that strain his nerves. His bed, for example. In the sliding dark of this winter's afternoon, he'd swear that there is a lump in it, the suggestion of a body under the covers . . .

The lump shifts, and Wyll's heart stops. A second later and

panic kicks out an attack dog, going on horse-sized, its sheared haunches gleaming with rippled muscle as it approaches the bed.

The lump rustles. Bedclothes crumple and shift and a head materialises above them.

'Get out of my bed,' says Wyll. He opens up the dog's jaws and rolls out a growl like an ancient, stuttering engine.

A stranger stares back at the dog. Mussed hair. Sleepy, dazed look. Not scared enough for someone who just got woken up with high menace.

'Didn't you hear me?' he demands.

After a bleary, protracted moment, the girl focuses on Wyll. 'I fell asleep waiting for you,' she says.

Wyll examines her. She looks younger than him, but maybe it's the bed look, the dazed expression on her face. Her hair is chopped short below the ears, her cheeks are round, her mouth wide and open soft.

'I don't know you,' he says. 'Get out of my bed, now.'

'I have to show you something,' the girl says, her voice higher. An urgency has crept into her mien. 'Please.'

Wyll's nerves kick. The dog growls. The girl looks at it, her eyes wide, but she doesn't move. He really doesn't know her.

'Who are you?' he snaps.

'Gennivy,' she whispers. 'I'm Gennivy. I'm a serving vastos here.'

'I've never seen you before.'

'I have to show you something,' she repeats, staring at him.

Is that what feels off about her, that she's high as a cloud right now? Her behaviour is dazed but single-minded, and apparently she's unafraid of giant, aggressive dogs. Wyll banishes the illusion. The Gennivy girl is still focused on him and doesn't even appear to notice its departure.

'How did you get in here?' he asks. 'What do you want?'

'I have to show you something,' she repeats, growing more fractious. 'Please.'

And with that, she rips down the bedcovers, rising to her knees. She is completely naked, her flanks tight as she moves.

'Oh no,' Wyll says, and a different kind of fear takes hold. 'No, listen. I'm not interested.'

This is not the first time someone has found a way to offer themselves to him like this, but no one has ever made it all the way to his private bed before.

'Don't do that,' he says, 'just—'

More frightened commands, ready to babble their way out of his mouth, sputter out as his gaze latches on to her body. At first he dismisses them as sloppily drawn tattoos, simple words daubed across her chest and stomach:

PINECONE
VESPERS
V

It takes him a moment to understand what it means.

Saints alive.

It's Viviane. Viviane is in London.

And just like that, Wyll's buried past surfaces like a corpse in a river.

It was more than four years ago now, and Wyll was a still-tender nineteen years old, eager to prove himself, precocious and anxious, hurt and trying to hide it. Artorias Dracones, the King of London and the only man who had ever been kind to Wyll, had sent him away. Out of London, the First Kingdom, and to Barochi, some dull agricultural city in the Third Kingdom, where it would hopefully be much harder for him to cause a scandal simply by existing.

Si Carrivuthen, the minor Third Kingdom diplomat Wyll had just been placed with, headed a relatively modest retinue, though his influence was well documented. A small, fastidious man with expensive taste, his function, as far as Wyll could tell, seemed to be to hold as many formal dinners as possible, serving as a kind of oiling mechanism in the machine of Third Kingdom politics.

Wyll had spent the last two years in households like this one, learning the ways of the elite, but he felt particularly lucky to be placed here. Here was someone willing to take him in and protect him and teach him how to move through successful society, where the transgressions made less sense and any fall from grace seemed so much higher than before. Up until now, he had spent his life being tolerated, hidden away or ignored, but this house was different.

In Si Carrivuthen's house, he was prized.

'Do you know what that thing does?'

Wyll looked up to see who dared interrupt his reading time. His gaze discovered a knowing smile framed by light, fluffy hair and topped with deep, soft eyes crinkled into half-moons.

He hadn't yet met this one. They definitely weren't at his formal introduction ceremony yesterday. He'd have remembered.

The newcomer nodded to the collar around Wyll's neck, and only then did he realise he had been fingering it without realising as he read his book, tugging it gently from his skin.

'It's a collar,' he told the knowing smile. 'A mark of allegiance.'

The newcomer leaned their head to one side, as if his pretty innocence was the world's most wonderful joke.

'It's also a castration device,' they said.

The collar Wyll wore was a thin, flat band of smoked flecter glass encasing a delicate spiderweb-thin latticework of pale blue-tinted aluminium in the colour and pattern of Si Carrivuthen's house. The Si had fastened the collar around Wyll's neck himself on his arrival, in full ceremonial view of his existing retinue.

'There,' Carrivuthen had said, after adjusting the fit to his satisfaction. 'Now you're of mine, and under my protection.'

His fingers had cupped Wyll's chin and the pad of his thumb had run along Wyll's jawbone, before tenderly letting go.

The newcomer plopped into Si Carrivuthen's expensive reading chair opposite Wyll's, their own version of Si Carrivuthen's pretty collar winking at their neck. On the newcomer, it looked like an accessory as deliberate as any well-chosen ink. On Wyll, it looked more like a punishment.

'What do you mean, it's a castration device?' he asked.

'I call it the Choke,' said the newcomer. 'You'll find out why.'

He stared at them. They wanted him to ask more, so he wouldn't. He knew this game.

'Fascinating,' he muttered, and overtly returned to his book.

'So what's your trick, new toy?' he heard the newcomer ask.

Keeping his eyes on his book, he frostily replied, 'I'm no toy.'

'Right. You're here because of your long history in diplomatic work. What is it? Not another soothsayer, I've had enough of their vagaries. Come on, be interesting.'

He didn't want to tell them, but somehow it found its way out of his mouth anyway.

'Thwimoren.'

The newcomer whistled. 'The wicked white horse of godchildren. Carr must be pleased with himself; he's been looking for one of you for years.'

'I'm no white horse either,' Wyll snapped back.

'Don't take offence,' said the newcomer with some amusement. 'Thwimoren have a bad dog reputation, that's all. You can blame Edler Feverfew for that. He's dead, he won't care.'

At the mention of that notorious name, Wyll's heart crushed itself into a tiny ball, while the rest of him wanted desperately to follow suit.

No one knows, he told himself. *I've a different name, different official parentage, the King made sure of that, no one knows . . .*

'Who's Edler Feverfew?' he asked with studied curiosity.

The newcomer sounded surprised. 'The old King of London's personal illusionist. The reason the new King exists. You're telling me you don't know that story?'

'Oh, him,' Wyll quickly amended. 'I forgot his name.'

In his head, the newcomer said, *You forgot the name of your own father?*

Out loud, they sounded unsuspicious. 'Hard to get away from it. Taint by association. Never make mistakes, Wyll. They don't get forgiven for people like you and me.'

He studied the newcomer. Large brown eyes, glossy warm as chestnuts, reduced all their other features to unremarkable. The kind of eyes that made you think of messy beds and tangled sheets and rainy afternoons, watching the world outside drip and run, as your thighs were parted by soft hands and your hard—

Wyll blinked.

The newcomer smirked.

'What's *your* designation?' he asked brusquely, trying to cover up the previous thought apparently blaring out from his face.

'Designation?'

'What kind are you?'

'The come-and-get-it kind.'

'I mean,' Wyll commanded his blush to depart and hoped to the saints it obeyed, 'what kind of godchild?'

'I prefer to remain mysterious.' The newcomer leaned back into the reading chair. 'Show me something of yours.'

'Here? Now?' He looked quickly around the empty room.

'This is the Third Kingdom, Wyll. Magic's legal here.' The newcomer considered. 'Somewhat. In any case, you've landed yourself in the house of a godchild fetisher. Magic will be demanded of you on a nightly basis. He'll want to show you off, so my advice is to get some practice in.'

'I can't just . . . do it.'

'Of course you can.' The newcomer grinned. 'You're just being shy.'

They were right. He wanted to show off.

He concentrated.

The newcomer turned, movement catching their eye. Through the open door of the reading room trotted a neat little dog with clipped, marbled grey fur and trimmed chops. It moved noiselessly across the rugs to reach them both, and then settled back on its haunches.

The newcomer examined it. 'Is it just visual?'

The dog opened its mouth and gave a petite bark.

'Huh,' they said.

Wyll blinked and the dog disappeared.

'I won't do it again, then,' he grumped.

The absent-minded newcomer, still gazing at the area of floor where the dog had just been, finally noted his tone. 'What?'

'You didn't look impressed.'

'Oh no, it was very real. But it's just . . . a dog. It's hard to be impressed by a dog. It could have just trotted in off the street.'

'No, it couldn't,' Wyll said, but privately he took their point. What kind of boring idiot conjured a common rat-catcher?

'I'm just saying, maybe you want to think more . . . unusual,' the newcomer continued, waving a hand.

They wanted a surprise. He could do surprise.

'What's your favourite animal?' he asked them, and then closed his eyes.

'I like snakes. Make me a huge snake.' They grew enthusiastic. 'One of those really giant ones as thick as a forearm. And lime green. No, wait! What's that one with the crazy black and red pattern that looks like . . .' Silence. 'What the *fuck* is happening?'

The last was said as a sudden, breathless squawk.

Wyll opened his eyes.

A vast golden hall surrounded them.

The walls were millennia away, the ceiling higher than the sky. From it dripped enormous ironwork chandeliers, holding a thousand candles apiece, tethered from dropping on their heads by thick, taut chains. At one end of the hall was the royal dais, a raised platform with a frantically filigreed throne as its centrepiece.

The King once confided in Wyll that he hated that throne. He had often tried to swap it with a plainer chair, producing pained expressions on the faces of the palace vastos whose entire meaning revolved around making him look as magnificently royal as could be without overstepping the wide boundaries of good taste.

The newcomer's mouth was stretched wide open, eyes bigger than a frog's. Their hands gripped the arms of the reading chair from Carrivuthen's house. Wyll didn't remember what the chairs in the palace ballroom looked like – besides, he'd learned that the illusion was generally more impactful if something remained of the real world to disorient the viewer even more.

'Where the fuck are we?' they said, gawking nakedly.

Wyll didn't know it yet, but the sight of the newcomer undone was a sufficiently rare moment to warrant imprinting it in memory.

'In the ballroom of Cair Lleon,' Wyll replied.

They gave out a hysterical laugh. 'A snake, I said. Make me a snake. Not the ballroom of a damn palace.'

'I thought this would impress you more.'

Their eyes latched on to his, shining with delight. 'You were right. Saints dead and alive, this is unbelievable.'

Wyll's heart swelled.

'What happens if I try to reach that chair over there?' the newcomer asked, pointing at the tiny royal dais a lifetime's walk away. Even their voice sounded like it echoed through an enormous space, instead of a small reading room. He was particularly proud of that detail.

'Well, you'll bump into the reading room wall long before you reach it, no doubt,' Wyll said with a laugh.

He watched them examine their surroundings, lost in wonder. It had been so long since he had conjured for someone else. He'd forgotten the shameful thrill it gave him, that addictive pleasure flush, but now he felt it again and wondered how he could have gone so long without it—

His throat gave a sudden squeeze. He coughed, choked, felt the slow bloom of panic as his body began to struggle, the tight band across his chest as his lungs tried to inflate with nothing inside.

As all Wyll's concentration focused on trying to breathe, Cair Lleon's vast ballroom vanished, unveiling the rather more ordinary dimensions of the reading room. The newcomer's gaze rested on Wyll's gasping face with a calm and watchful air. They didn't realise what was happening. He wanted to scream at them *something's wrong, get help, please help* but there was no air with which to scream.

Then, as quickly as it had appeared, the squeezing sensation at his throat stopped. Air rushed in through his gaping mouth and he coughed, his hands spasmically gripping the arms of his chair.

'I'm sorry, Wyll,' said a new voice. 'I hope that didn't hurt too much.'

In the doorway stood Si Carrivuthen, a frown painting his face.

'Are you all right?' he asked.

Wyll sucked in more air, unable to speak. He simply nodded. He could breathe. That must mean he was all right.

Carrivuthen moved into the room, coming swiftly to Wyll's side, his hands reaching out to cup Wyll's face, his eyes full of concern.

'Oh good,' he said. 'I really am sorry. I asked you to stop, but you must not have heard me. Wyll, you have to be very careful with your magic. You are precious here, and celebrated, but unfortunately I am still subject to the constrictive laws of our otherwise wonderful Kingdom. Listen to me carefully. You must only ever perform magic with my expressed permission. Never without, and never *ever* outside these halls. You understand? The last thing I want is to get you into trouble. You are precious here, and celebrated,' he repeated, 'but that makes you vulnerable to . . . people who don't see the world the way I do.' His hands dropped to squeeze Wyll's shoulders. His gaze was earnest, even a little guilty. 'You see?'

Wyll nodded. He saw.

Carrivuthen's concerned eyes crinkled. 'Thank you! Thank you, Wyll. Well. Now that unpleasantness is out of the way, may I tell you how extraordinary that was? Just incredible. You are more luminous than I ever dared hope. Don't you think, Vivi?'

The newcomer, who had been still and silent in the chair opposite, gave a pretty smile. 'Oh yes. I don't think I've ever seen anything like it. He'll make a glorious centrepiece for your next gathering.'

Carrivuthen rocked back on his heels. 'I think you're right.' His eyes were milky and kind. 'What do you think? Can you do something like that again, in front of more people, when I ask you to?'

Wyll's heart sped up in anticipation. 'Yes, Si.'

'Call me Carr.' He stood up and moved to the newcomer's side, his hand stretching out to grip their shoulder. 'And I see you've met my lovely Viviane.'

Wyll and Viviane locked gazes. They smiled. Wyll quickly looked away before they could see the murderous fury in his eyes.

I call it the Choke.

You'll find out why.

The trickster had goaded him into showing off just to land him in trouble. Jealousy, he assumed. Still, at least he now knew how it was going to be here. He had spent his whole life in hostile company and he knew very well what to do. He had to show them who the meaner dog was, as soon as he could.

First chance he got, Viviane was going down.

CHAPTER 10

Garad's Apartment, Evrontown
Two Weeks Ago

'Were they godchild activists?' asks Garad. 'The people who jumped you?'

Ghost gives them an annoyed glance. 'I'm getting to it. Can I have some alcohol yet?'

'No.'

Ghost sighs.

Hidden Treasures, Alaunitown
Two Months Ago

When she gets the light back, she finds herself being stared down by cold black eyes.

Their owner glares at her from its perch atop a large cabinet directly opposite, a pear-drop creature forever frozen in a low belly prowl. Its face fur alternates in thick black and white striping, arrowing down to its snout.

'What in seven hells is that?' she hears someone say in a slow, stupefied voice.

Her mysterious surroundings grow noticeably quiet, the

murmurs she hadn't realised were there thrown into existence by their sudden absence.

'*That*, my interesting proposition,' a voice replies, 'is a badger. A preserved corpse can be worth a fortune, to the right buyer.'

Ghost raises her heavy head, feeling as though her brains are sloshing up the sides of her skull. Nestled into a soft, sagging armchair a few feet away from her is an outlandish figure covered in a fretwork of metallic threads, like a spider draped in its own web, with a glass pipe dangling from their fingers to catch the light. Wrist rings and arm cuffs cover their bare fore-arms from hand to elbow. The slightest movement elicits a tumble of clashes and jangles and janks as they knock together.

'Badgers are a myth,' ventures Ghost, at which point she real-ises that the slow, stupefied voice is in fact her own.

'They were real once. Extinct now. Victims of fashion.' The outlandish figure tuts sorrowfully.

Ghost tries to catch up, but all this glue in her head is making it more of an ordeal than she'd like.

'Don't worry, it'll wear off very soon,' says the outlandish figure, with what Ghost decides to think of as inappropriate amusement.

'You kidnapped me,' she slurs indignantly.

'Don't be silly, I don't have the upper body strength,' the out-landish figure replies. 'Sugar and Joln Chimes kidnapped you.'

They nod past Ghost towards the back wall. Ghost tells her body to turn around, but it takes a disconcerting amount of time for it to obey. Eventually she twists in her seat and takes in the two silent figures stood behind her. One is in stiff leathers and a wide-brimmed hat that hides their eyes. The other is tall and rather solid-looking, with prettily rolled rows of hair that hang around their shoulders like snakes.

They are both slouched against the wall six feet away, a decent distance, and they haven't tied Ghost down. If she can ascertain where the nearest exit is, she might be able to make a break for it. It feels oddly hard to be afraid right now, even though she knows she should be. Everyone else in the room does seem vastly more awake than her, which is, admittedly, a slight disadvantage.

'*Sugar?*' she says.

'Ghost?' Snake hair stonily replies.

'Fair,' concedes Ghost.

'They callian me Moth,' the outlandish figure supplies.

Ghost turns back to Moth. 'Where's the treacherous witch sometimes known as Delilah?'

Moth shrugs. 'Don't take offence, Delilah doesn't usually pay anyone so much attention. I think she likes you.'

'She *drugged* me.'

Moth considers this. 'It's flattering, if you think about it.'

It was the damned whisky, ever her downfall. Being sober'd be so much less dangerous, if vastly duller. Dullness has always been Ghost's real fear, the thing that would kill her quicker than anything else. Boredom ensures that the few reasons to get up in the morning disappear as fast as a promise made to a lover you've grown tired of.

'So I suppose you're going to explain why I'm here, then,' says Ghost.

'You think so?' Moth mildly replies.

'Look, even the treacherous witch doesn't think it's a Gun doing the drownings. And this won't get you anything in return. No one's going to care that you plucked me. Guns don't work together. Guns don't even know who each other are.'

Moth takes a drag from her pipe. 'Funny,' she says through

curls of smoke the colour of rotting plants. 'I thought you were working with Leon. Cos *he's* a Gun.'

Nothing worse than a stranger who knows your business.

'As his protection,' Ghost says. 'On the Grenwald job.'

'You don't act like protection.'

When the play is unclear, go silent. It makes other people talk more. Code names, stuffed badgers, shops full of mysterious junk – Moth is a theatrical type, no doubt, and theatrical types need to perform.

Moth gives a little nod. Ghost hears a rustling of movement, quick footsteps behind her, and then feels a sudden pressure on her upper arms, holding them in place, while something cold and thin and gelatinous is pressed across her face. Her vision goes utterly black as the thin gelatinous thing covers her eyes, pressing stickily to the sockets. Her body, galvanised by adrenalin, jerks and struggles, to no avail. The scuffle is brief.

Ghost stops moving.

'What in merry fuck?' she pants.

'It's just a blinder.' She hears Moth's distinctive, now disconnected cadence. 'A darkening overlay.'

'I know what a blinder is,' Ghost snaps.

'My apologies. Now Sugar has your arm to help you balance. Please stand.'

'Fuck you.'

A hard, cold sensation pings the back of her neck.

'You feel that?' murmurs a voice by her ear. The erstwhile Sugar. 'It's the mouth of a shooter pressed up against your spine. Neh, I've one and you don't, Gun. That's ironic, itso? Now stand up.'

It's remarkable how steadying are the varying degrees of hard threat pressing against her soft, vulnerable body.

Between the vice grip around her upper arm and the rigid metal at her neck, Ghost manages a pleasingly fluid standing motion.

Calm suffuses her guts – the remnants of whatever drug had put her to sleep, or that quiet you get in the eye of a danger storm, the one that comes when it appears impossible to escape. She's been in this eye before. She knows this eye of old.

'Listen,' she says, as she is shuffled slowly across the floor, 'you don't have to torture me, cos truthfully I don't know shit about any of this. I'd hate to be the cause of your wasted time. Don't make me feel bad, now.'

'Oh, stop babbling, this isn't torture,' says the voice beside her. 'It's just a test.'

'A test? What kind of test?'

No one answers. This Sugar person is bent on pulling her arm out of her socket to get her to move, and frankly it's working, pain being a superb motivator.

'It seems like a nice secret club you've got here,' Ghost says, 'but regretfully, my social calendar is tamped fuller than a pipe bowl at a philosopher's social. So maybe we could skip the testing part and get to the part where I walk out of here and go back to my life and you go back to yours and we never speak again?'

'Senza be fucked, she talks a lot,' rumbles a third voice from behind. Presumably the behatted Joln Chimes.

'Just get her into the cellar,' says Moth from a distance.

'The cellar?' Ghost says. 'Why is the test in the cellar? Why not all out in the open like normal tests?'

'What's the matter?' the voice beside her murmurs. 'Scared of the dark?'

'The test is in the *dark*?'

'Stop flirting and get her down there,' Moth says.

The clunk and *breep* of a door lock. A brush of new and different air flow. The awful sensation of yawning space where there was none before – or at least, none the senses could pick up, though it was of course always there, whether sensed or not.

How many hidden and secret things behind doors and beyond the feeble scope of sight? How many times has she passed something that looked like nothing? What lurks beyond, what lies beneath, crawling, squelching, reaching towards her with spindly, inhuman arms . . .

This is supremely unhelpful, Ghost tells her other self. *Could you desist?*

Well, what kind of thing do you *think would be locked up in the fucken cellar?* the other her snaps.

'Stairs,' Sugar barks. 'Go easy, there we go—'

Chafing at the bit, heart pounding, Ghost descends.

When they reach the bottom, she is shuffled forwards, and then comes a horribly long pause.

Whatever monster waiting for her breathes long and slow: *inhale*, *exhale*, with unnatural uniformity. A feeling of hulk and bulk, a thing too big for the space that tries to contain it.

Machinery.

Of course. Torture can be hands-off. No need to ruin your clothes with blood spurts.

Nevertheless, Ghost begins to relax. Somehow a machinery's blank indifference is easier to stomach than the focused sadism of a living creature. She'd take function over intent, every time. The hands on her grip harder, holding her in place, and then there is a gentle, feather-light sensation on her cheeks like spider feet, momentary, gone again and then back, growing in size and weight.

Something is touching her face.

Ghost stares blindly out from the overlay's prison of darkness, feeling panic kick underneath her like a spooked horse. There is no escaping this. All that remains is endurance.

The alive thing presses against her skin, tickling the downy hairs on the planes of her face and making each one of them shudder in horror. She hears a sound, a gasp. Then a very human kind of 'ah', surprised or pleased, hard to say which. She cannot tell which of her would-be torturers utters it.

The touch on her face disappears.

Shuffling footsteps. Heavy, glutinous breaths, leading away from her. Creaking, sounds of movement.

Only then does the grip around her arm relax. Only then does the cold metal pressure on her neck ease off.

'Walk,' says a voice.

Ghost takes an unsteady, directed totter. She nearly falls up the stairs, but at least she's allowed the use of her hands this time. Back up top, she is pushed through the room, then a hand on her arm brings her to a stop. With a sucking noise, the overlay is slowly peeled off her face.

Ghost blinks in the light of the junk shop. Moth and Joln Chimes are in front of her. Sugar must be lurking behind. Whatever happened in that room, whatever they saw, looks to have impressed the shit out of them all. Their faces are cocktails of admiration and eagerness.

'Well,' Moth comments, pleased as pie, 'Delilah's instincts are good, I'll give her that. Sadly, life has taught me the art of suspicion. I had to make sure for myself.'

'Make sure of what?' asks Ghost. It feels required, and sometimes she likes to play the part assigned for her.

Moth grins, rolling the glass pipe stem back and forth between her fingers.

'I know who you are,' she says.

'Lady, *I* don't even know who I am,' drawls Ghost, while foreboding trickles its acid through her stomach. Was that what the face-touching in the cellar was all about? They can't have seen through the surgery, it was top trick. The scars don't even show.

Moth is smiling indulgently.

'You're a godchild, my dear,' she says.

A lifetime's worth of permutations flip through Ghost's brain, a thousand reactions that could push them to do this or that; a million alternative scenes stretch away across the universe inside her, most of them violent.

For once in her life, she resists the urge.

'Oh,' she says. 'That.'

Moth has the deliriously pleased expression of a dog with a marrowbone in its jaws.

'Don't worry,' she assures Ghost. 'Your secret's safe with us.'

Ghost keeps her racing pulse under wraps with an affected yawn.

'Are we boring you?' rumbles Joln Chimes.

'Your pardon,' Ghost says. 'I'm getting sleepy. Usually when I ply a girl with drinks it's at least with the chance of a bed game at the end of it. But there's been a lot of drugs tonight and no release. I think my body's given up.'

'You're not going anywhere 'til we say,' Joln Chimes threatens.

'Hush,' Moth admonishes. 'She's on our team now.'

Ghost snorts. 'No, I'm not. I'm a Gun.'

Moth turns on her a gaze of happy threat. 'Neh, you are.'

The implication lingers, grows fat.

'You want a Gun working for you,' Ghost says slowly.

'She's a fast one,' quips Joln Chimes.

'Doing what, exactly? What exactly is it you do?'

'This and that,' Moth says.

'Activists.'

Moth flaps a hand. 'Think of us as a support network.'

'For illegal godchildren.'

'Like you.'

'I don't need a support network, but my thanks for the offer. I'm touched,' says Ghost, while her mind churns, the other her swearing a lot and coming up with nothing useful.

'Not really an offer,' rumbles Joln Chimes.

'You'll do us a favour from time to time, that's all,' Moth says.

'And if I say no?'

'Leon gets to know who you really are, turns you in himself, and you wave goodbye to freedom.' Moth leans forwards. 'But nobody here wants that. We can help you. We can protect you.'

We can blackmail you.

Fuckity fuck.

A lifetime of keeping it from everyone she's ever met, ordering every little thing about her existence so it doesn't show, so no one can possibly tell, never letting anyone get too close, running when they do, shedding lives over and over, dying and being reborn again and again . . .

Well, it loses its charm, over time. Truth be told, Ghost is tired.

She's had enough of running.

'This test machine you've got in your cellar,' she says. 'It can prove I'm a godchild?'

Moth nods.

'How?'

Moth just shrugs.

'Nothing's ever been able to do that,' Ghost tries.

'Until now,' Moth says. She sounds absolutely sure of herself. She wears confidence like a musk. She at least believes in it.

'Who made it?' Ghost asks.

'I did,' Moth replies.

'Didn't peg you as an engineer.'

'I'm a woman of many talents. Now, how's about the deal?'

'The deal where I do whatever shady shit you want and in return you don't ruin my life?'

'That's the one.' Joln Chimes is grinning.

Ghost promises that smug mouth a future punch. 'Well,' she speculates, 'you could get Leon down here and show him your test machine, but I've got the feeling you don't want anyone to know that thing exists, or you'd have it on the market by now. So I'm at a loss as to how you'll be proving it to him.'

'It'll be on the market soon enough,' Moth says. 'But you'll never be outed, that I can promise. Long as you're with us, you're safe.'

'I'm not *with* you, Lady Moth,' Ghost snaps. 'I'm not with *anyone*.'

'Lone wolf gets old fast.'

'Well, I still like it just fine. I've no knight in your fight. Leave me be and I'll do the same. I'll drop the Grenwald job. Tell Leon I couldn't find her. Walk out of your life. Forget you exist as you'll do for me. Counter-offer.'

'You don't give a shit about what's being done to your own people?' Joln Chimes rumbles.

Sectarianism. In Ghost's experience, it's nothing but a fucken nuisance.

'No, I don't,' she tells him. 'World's a terrible place for most everyone in different ways, not just me.'

Joln Chimes surges forwards. His sweet comrade in arms, or whatever they are, grabs his wrist, trying to steady him. Ghost backs off fast, keeping him at arm's length.

The idiot's got her closer to the door, at least.

'That's it?' Joln Chimes shouts at her. 'Oh well, nothing to be done about the state of the world, never mind, I'll just go on hiding like a mouse, taking care of my own selfish hide and fuck everyone else?'

Ghost keeps them all in her sights.

Make him angry. Make him swing again.

'Playing righteous victim doesn't absolve you, friend,' she says.

'What's that supposed to mean?'

'How many people have you hurt along the way on your cruise for justice?' Ghost quirks a brow. 'Got any deaths on your soul?'

A hit, and faster than she had anticipated – Chimes goes for her, bearing down like, well, a big old bear. She turns and bolts, expecting to feel his hands on her back.

'Let her go,' she hears Moth say.

'Saintsfuck that,' Sugar declares, 'she knows too much.'

'She knows about an antiques shop,' Moth says, with the disparaging surety of someone who has protection. Could be local guard, could be syndicate, could be some secret godchild overlord. Who cares, as long as it gets Ghost out of here and away from these idiots?

Still, as she opens the door, she expects to feel a shot from Sugar's shooter – her back is a mess of knots waiting for the pain it thinks is about to explode all over it. But nothing comes.

The door bangs closed, and Ghost runs.

Outside, the night has the coolness of near morning, a

moment's relief from the promise of another day in this cold storage box masquerading as a city. Looming sky-kissers and squat storage spaces. Tight rows of those old fisherfolk dwellings. She could be anywhere along the entire river.

It'll be a long way back home.

And it won't be the last she'll hear from *them*, either.

We're not running, the other her says. *Not this time.*

So I should become a Gun rat, work both sides? she argues back. *That sounds like a nice and safe new life, doesn't it? That'll end well for me, that it will.*

Don't be such a coward, says the other her. *You're used to dying.*

CHAPTER II

The Royal Stable of Cair Lleon, Blackheart
Four Months Ago

The vastos girl Gennivy comes to slowly, blinking mutely at the steam in the air.

'You're awake,' says Wyll, standing above her. 'Good. Please take a bath.'

Several more frustrating seconds pass. He can practically see various situational signals sluggishly penetrating her brain. Bath. Steam. Lying on the floor. Wrapped in a blanket. She catches sight of her bare feet. Then she looks up at him with – ah yes, there it is: naked fear. A look with which he is all too familiar. He feels his temper rising to match and tries to leash it.

'You're in my bathroom,' he prompts. 'Do you remember how you got here?'

Gennivy looks around. 'No,' she croaks.

'Do you remember getting into my bed?'

Total shock. A confirmation glance. Then, at the end there, a repulsion she is too dazed to hide.

Calm. Art's voice appears in his head. *It's not her fault.*

Then his father pipes up, *She thinks you're disgusting.*

With an effort, Wyll controls his tone. 'I need you to get in the bath and wash yourself.'

The girl looks up at him. 'What?' she says.

'You have some kind of paint all over your chest and stomach. You need to wash it off.' Wyll pauses, pushes it out. 'Please.'

She opens up the blanket and examines herself. The words are stark and clear on her skin, daubed in no doubt Caballaria-grade performance paint, designed not to budge from friction, or from sweat. She's going to have to scrub.

'It's warm,' Wyll says. 'The bath. There's soap just there. Take your time. I'll wait outside.'

He turns, leaving the girl a bewildered puddle on the tiles.

'I don't know how I got here,' she blurts at his retreating back.

I know, he wants to tell her. *I'm sorry.*

But out loud he says nothing, afraid of giving too much away. He simply leaves the bathroom and closes the door behind him, tight with humiliation.

It's Viviane all over. No one else could control people like they could.

Pinecone. There's only one place in all of London with that name, and vespers is only two hours away. He doesn't have much time to get there.

As Wyll dresses for the ride ahead, the past crowds his brain, muscling in on the present, filling him up with the memory perfume of someone he prayed to the saints he'd never meet again.

The guests were long gone.

Wyll felt pleasantly woozy, floating in a fug of alcohol and post-conjuring fatigue. He was tricked out. It had been small stuff – giving a corpulent blonde a head of raven-black hair, or

105

materialising a cat on the lap of a minor Lord – but with thirty guests to entertain, individually and en masse, the night had taken its toll.

His centrepiece, conjured via Carrivuthen's careful preshow directions, had been making the roast duck look like a pink cake covered in sugar-cream star flowers, giving the gift of delighted confusion to the mouths of their guests.

Viviane had been there too, but in what capacity Wyll had been unable to ascertain. Every time he'd caught sight of them throughout the evening, they had been glued to Carrivuthen's side, whispering in his ear, as subdued and watchful as he was garrulous and open-armed.

Whenever Wyll began to flag, Carrivuthen somehow knew and was instantly there, offering him a drink or a small bowl of whatever course out of the eighteen dishes they were currently on, murmuring encouragement and bravos, tirelessly flitting between attending him and keeping every guest charmed. He was good at it – the kind of person adept at making everyone he met think well of him.

Now he sat in his private study with his two beneficiaries, bafflingly alert as he sipped a digestif while the dining room and kitchen bustled with the clean-up behind closed doors. Viviane was sprawled out on their back on a nearby divan, glass held loose in one dangling hand.

'You were magnificent,' Carr said to Wyll, who, despite his fatigue, managed a pleased blush. 'What you can do is truly extraordinary. It should be celebrated, not hidden away by the fearful. Alas for our current leaders. But here, at least, in these four walls, you can indulge in your true self. And I can reward you for it. Come here to me?'

He never commanded. He always asked, curling the ends of

his sentences upwards like a hesitant beg. Viviane's eyes tracked Wyll as he rose from his slump in a chair and took the empty spot next to Carr, who reached out as he sat and ran a hand through his hair.

Wyll had become used to such touching, though it had taken a while. His experience of intimacy up until now had not, he realised, included anything like the casual physical closeness that most people seemed instinctively attuned to. He felt deficient in this regard. He felt his own lack, and consequently his own eagerness to make up for it.

'How do you feel?' Carr asked Wyll.

'Tired.'

'Not too tired, I hope.'

Wyll just smiled in response. He had the urge to lean into Carr's hand so that he could feel the press of it better against his head, and tried to resist.

'*I* know how you feel.' Viviane piped up from their repose, sounding a little alluringly in their cups.

'Oh?' Wyll raised a challenging eyebrow. He had got used to Viviane too, as much as anyone could.

'You feel wanted, for the first time in your life,' Viviane told him. 'You feel loved.'

Wyll just laughed. What else to do when your secret feelings had been plucked straight from your chest?

'Is that true?' Carr asked him.

Wyll shrugged, giving up and pushing against the hand in his hair.

'How awful,' he heard Carr say with a sigh. 'You are the best of us, but you get treated like the worst. It should be a crime.'

'Maybe one day it will be,' said Wyll, his mocking tone suggesting shameful hope.

A hand came under his chin, turning his head to face Carr, whose milky eyes looked pretty – right then, the prettiest thing he'd ever seen. Carr's neatness felt like assuredness. Like a comforting kind of power.

'You are safe here, Wyll.' Carr's voice dropped lower. 'And very much wanted. Do you understand?'

Wyll tried to nod, but the hand on his face restricted his movement and he laughed again. This was all so silly and seductive and strange. His embarrassment, his defences, had all melted away like spring snow. He felt an overwhelming desire to be kissed, undressed and played with.

You're drunk, he told himself.

He knew that, but he didn't care. Being drunk gave him permission. Being drunk felt like being free.

'How long have you been in my household now, Wyll?' asked Carr, as his fingers pushed agreeably against Wyll's scalp.

'About six months.'

'Vivi,' he heard Carr murmur, 'have we given our lovely companion a proper welcome yet?'

He heard a low, loose laugh from the other side of the room. 'Not yet.'

'Wyll?' Carr said. 'Say no if you don't want this.'

Stop this? Stop being held, being wanted? Saints, what a bleak prospect. Who would ever say no to love?

He was manoeuvred so that he sat facing out from the couch and Carr nestled behind him, one hand still on his skull.

'Say no any time, do you understand?' Carr sounded a little stern, and Wyll knew he was supposed to respond.

'Yes,' he managed. 'I mean . . . I understand.'

Viviane arrived, trickling up from the floor to nestle in between his thighs. They'd stripped off their top, laying bare

108

the flat planes of their chest and sinuous torso; wrapped trousers were slung low around their hips. Their hands found his waist, his chest, and began to undo the soft, expensive shirt he had been given to wear to dinner.

His head was held by Carr's strong grip, his warm hands, as Viviane leaned in to kiss him, pressing their whole length against his. Heat bloomed and suffused everywhere they touched. They pressed themself against him like a cat's back arching into a hand, then reared back, limber fingers twisting at his trousers, undoing and freeing and pulling a grateful sigh from him as the pressure eased and the straining parts of himself could spring free.

With his normal shame somehow in retreat, he looked down, fascinated by his own willing exposure. Viviane flicked eyes up at his and they caught, and then curved into anticipatory half-moons, and then their mouth opened wide, wide as a snake's swallowing prey, and engulfed him. He watched them do it, felt himself seemingly grow four times his size in every way possible, his whole being tightly focused on each overwhelming sensation – eagerly trapped in a wet, hot cavern, the thrill of its suck and pull, how dangerous it felt, how helpless he was, the grip of fingers on his thighs holding them parted and steady, the hands that held his neck, the back of his skull, the press of both front and back, one body in front and one behind, the soft mouth at his front and the hardness he could feel bulging insistently against his spine, the incredible comfort of it, how could a human being live without that press? How had he lived without that press?

As he gasped on his climb towards the finish, the wall lights in the study, set to long-night dim, seem to grow in brightness until they screamed. He heard Carr laughing in utter delight.

The illusion leaked away with his fluid, the light flickering and fading out as he disappeared into Viviane's throat, all thoughts of vengeance against the trickster utterly forgotten.

Because he was wanted, and he was loved.

The bike is sleek, and he's managed to dirty it up over the years with heavy rides in the outer dis' limits of London, where roads are more like tracks strewn with rubble and the hilltops keep the snow that melts on the grounds below.

Its engine is built silent, but with the additional mod of an artificial whine when it kicks into higher speeds, a mandated requirement so the street-trotters can hear it coming. It slips him along rain-greased roads, skating across ribbons of dark ground streaked in tinny shifting lights from the flashing street signs above.

No one ever thinks about rooftops, wouldn't even recognise their own neighbourhood from bird level, but Wyll likes to look up at the world beyond his head. Up there are species rarely seen on the ground, unfamiliar ecosystems and a strange terrain of spires and turrets, microforests made of spindly transmitters and power nodes. The birds rule as kings and queens of the airy rooftop world, full of cool wind rush and muffling, scudding clouds. Dare to dip lower and enter hell, filled with hot light and cacophony, and populated with too many tall beings ever to count, crisscrossing their dimension in a ceaseless, Sisyphean rush.

Wyll flies along the ground, trying to mimic the birds, his bike clearing a path. He wears his usual outdoor incognito gear of smoked helmet and patchless Blackheart leathers. Passers-by would assume him to be a guard knight, and he goes too fast for them to note the lack of detail, or tut at the illegality of an unaffiliated, incognito rider. A tut is all he'll get thrown his way, though – illegality is often a technicality for people like him. Like the birds of London, he lives in a different world, but unlike the birds, it is not a world he can fly free from any time he likes. Just as with everything else in life, privilege has its consequences. The bike gives the illusion of freedom, but no one knows better than Wyll how ultimately empty illusions are.

A hard ride takes him to the right spot on the bank of the Thames, sunset chasing his back. Across from his gaze, floating serenely in the middle of the river, is the sprouting isle known as the Pinecone. An ancient place steeped in history and myth, most famously said to be the hideout of Saint Alaunis, the very place where he made Calevel in secret, that mysterious weapon that could somehow render a powerful godchild as helpless as any kitten-weak common. Calevel was ultimately destroyed in the Lysander War, and the pieces long lost. There are entire sects of historians who have dedicated their lives to tracking them down, to no apparent avail.

These days, the Pinecone is an icon of the modern age, bristling with communications tech, a creature of silver, grey, copper and black. Forbidding and forbidden, its few sanctioned visitors are those tasked with its upkeep.

The only way to get to it is by boat, but at one point in its thousand-year backstory, an enormous tunnel was dug, though never to completion, with the aim of creating a huge, incredible thoroughfare underneath the river itself. The project was finally abandoned as too dangerous when, determined to show how safe it was, the probably mad construction magnate who had headed its creation insisted on hosting a lavish all-night dinner party with the cream of society within the tunnel's semi-complete walls, setting the whole thing up at two hundred metres across and twenty-three metres below the river's surface. This brave gamble was unfortunately lost when, three hours and several courses into the meal, the tunnel suddenly flooded and everyone died, including the construction magnate.

Tech has moved on since then and the half-complete tunnel no longer floods, but there has not yet been another magnate with the inclination to finish it. So it remains, shored up and echoing and strange and dark – but not forgotten.

There are always people who can find a use for such a place.

Wyll secures his bike, hoping to the saints no one is idiot enough to try attacking it for parts (anyone wandering around this empty, desolate place would hardly constitute a casual passer-by), and leans an arm into the spindly river grass that grows untamed along the banks. His hand comes back up attached to a handle attached to a door in the ground, which opens with barely a whisper. Someone's keeping that door oiled.

Beyond the door are steps leading down into a murky gloom.

The way is lit with strings of self-powered trick lights stapled into the walls, a makeshift but serviceable solution. He wonders who concerns themselves with the upkeep, and then decides that he doesn't want to know.

The steps end abruptly at an open doorway, and Wyll looks through it into a vast, circular cathedral, strobed by bigger lights flooding the curving walls, highlighting their painted treasures. A girl with a face like a wolf shimmers on the ceiling, her lips bigger than Wyll, a vast goddess stretching over his head. Rhyming couplets from the book of Saint Alaunis carpet the ground. The names of the dead adorn the smooth brick, a tunnel of remembrance. Fish leap across walls and flash their scales.

'You came,' a voice calls.

An indistinct figure emerges from the shifting light. Doe eyes and lips are parted in an almost smile, as if they know a secret about you that you haven't yet worked out for yourself.

'It's been a while,' says Viviane.

Wyll eyes them. Saintsdamn it, his pulse is skipping.

'Not long enough.'

Viviane cocks their head, looks around at the dark brickwork. 'This takes me back.'

'To what, exactly?'

Their smile is wicked sharp. 'To the last time we were underground together.'

One wonderful thing about Si Carrivuthen's house was the impressive training rooms, housed underground in its labyrinthine cellars. The diplomat frequently entertained Caballaria coteries, and fighter knights had been known to guest there for weeks.

Life with Carr was like sinking into a warm bath. Wyll's daily struggles with his sharper emotions, with remembered pain or anger or loneliness, became muffled, as if now behind a wall. He could hear them thumping from time to time, but only to register, not to react. He would feel relief if he stopped to think about it at all, but he never did.

He was too preoccupied with the painful business of being in love.

It was true that Wyll had never been in love before, and it was true that he was in love with Viviane. It was undeniable to his secret self, though to anyone else he would rather die than admit it. He tried to deem it pathetic, inconsequential, momentary – anxious to be anything but the naïve, inexperienced young lover he suspected himself to be. But whatever he called it, the feeling itself remained – stubborn, huge, filling him up wall to wall and pushing out everything that didn't feed its obsessive sincerity.

Useless to Carr until the next social function, Wyll spent much of his daytimes alternating between the training rooms and the library. Boredom was death, and an existence as an ornament quickly wore thin, so he had turned his attention to expanding his training regime, slicing his time into designated blocks, shifting from one activity to the next, pushing his limits of strength and dexterity, breaking his body carefully, in multiple, tiny ways, to rebuild it in new directions. It was frequently dull, always hard, and often made him grind out tears of frustration and effort – but it was absorbing, the satisfaction spreading within him over time better than any party drug.

Except recently. Recently his focus had been off. There were days when all he wanted to do was lie around, dozing and spinning long scenarios in which the lithe trickster who had his heart and his cock in their hands took centre stage. It was often almost too much to propel his body into the training room and get to work.

During a long, empty afternoon and a particularly exhaustive attempt to master the scythe, Wyll got that itch between his sweating shoulder blades, the warning system alerting him to another presence. When he looked around, Viviane, crossed of arms and faint of smile, was standing in the doorway to the cellar training room he had been dancing around for the last hour.

Carr often travelled, taking either Wyll, Viviane or both along with him. Between that and the guests as a near constant presence in the house, Wyll almost never got a moment alone with Viviane. He wanted them to be trapped the way he was, compelled and fighting the constant need to beg for any scrap of special attention. Their infrequent bedroom encounters were always orchestrated by Carr, and always as a three. It was not that encounters with Viviane alone had been forbidden, exactly – or not officially. It was just that the opportunity never seemed to be there.

Until now.

'You do look your best when you're sweating, I've noticed,' said Viviane.

Wyll dropped the scythe and nearly cut off his own toes. After swearing profusely and mumbling about needing practice gloves with better grip, all under the amused gaze of the trickster before him, he straightened.

'How long were you standing there?'

'There's no need to be embarrassed,' purred Viviane. 'You move beautifully. I had an idea of your grace from our brief encounters, but I have to admit seeing you in training is quite something else.'

His face, he was sure, had reached a truly luminous shade of red.

'My thanks,' he mumbled.

'Where did you learn all that?'

'Past benefactors had very good trainers. It kept me occupied and out of the way.'

Viviane's face softened. 'I'm sure.'

Wyll gave an awkward shrug. 'I didn't mind. It's all I wanted, anyway. I was grateful.'

'All you wanted?' Viviane echoed.

'I'm going to be a knight.'

The arms uncrossed. The gaze looked him curiously up and down. 'Godchildren can't be knights.'

'He's going to fix that.'

'Who?' Viviane's quick mind made the leap. 'The King of London? You think he cares?'

'He cares,' Wyll said stubbornly. 'He'll send for me when it's time.'

It sounded naïve even to him – but he had nothing else to hold on to for his future.

Viviane, perhaps wisely, did not press it.

'But you only train your common talent,' they said. 'What about the illusions? Why don't you practise them?'

'I do, with Carr. He has me doing them practically every week.'

'Cake tricks. Harmless fluff.' Viviane was brimming over with a contempt they'd never shown before – or at least, he now supposed, never in front of their benefactor. 'You can't possibly be stretched by disappearing the fat bald Lord's gut and reappearing his hair, or making the Lady look as young as she did on her no doubt disappointing wedding night. Saintsfuck, Wyll. You make wine cups look like bread rolls, all the fools laughing uproariously when someone tries to eat one, and you think *that's* using your talent?'

'Carr is kind and generous to me. The least I can do are those small things.'

'Carr is using you, silly boy.' Viviane shook their head. 'Wyll, why do you think a small-time diplomat like Carr is so keen on having godchildren around?'

'Why are you so keen that I hate Carr?'

'Hate? Who said anything about hate?' Viviane gave him an appraising look. 'I just think you should understand the situation.'

'And you're the one to give it to me straight?'

'Who else? It's us and it's them. Always has been. Always will be.'

Wyll had often wondered what kind of life Viviane had had before this. He knew so little about them. However it had been, it had certainly taught them not to trust.

Viviane leaned against the doorway, taut and intense of eye. 'They have a deal. Carr and Cair Lleon. They give Carr a useful asset like you, and he gives them . . . information.'

'You mean he's a spy for London.' Wyll snorted. 'That's ridiculous.'

'No,' Viviane coolly replied. 'Just good sense. He has a similar deal with some low-paid frog in the Kembrian government. How do you think he got me?'

'You're from Kembri?'

Viviane gave an assenting shrug. 'Fourth Kingdom, birthed and grown.'

Kembrian. It was something. A piece of the puzzle of Viviane.

Their energy changed, pulling back as if they could sense his hunger for more of them and didn't enjoy the feeling.

'But,' Wyll was desperate to keep them talking to him, 'all I do for Carr is cake tricks, as you call them. How is that so useful for him?'

'He'll step you up. Once he thinks you're ready. People still take a risk with a magical fuck, even in the loose and idle land of Barochi. You'll take the hapless groin-led guest to a room with capturers, all the better for future coercion. However elastic *their* morals, their families, spouses and business colleagues might, alas, be less forgiving.' Viviane gave him a small, knowing smile, waiting for him to work it all out.

'Carr wouldn't have me do that,' Wyll said.

But he already knew that Carr would. Because that was how the world worked, wasn't it?

'It doesn't matter,' he insisted in the face of Viviane's smile. 'I don't care. We all have to pay our way for a comfortable life.'

But he did care, and no doubt it showed. He *hated* that, anything showing.

Viviane was studying him.

'What?' he snapped.

'You must have come from a very bad place,' they said softly, 'if you think this is the best it gets.'

'So that's what *you* do for him? Fuck his guests so he can blackmail them? Tell him how best to manipulate all the fools who get drunk at his table? What an amazing use of *your* talent. Neh, I know you're a mind reader. It doesn't take a genius to work it out, the way you're glued to his side and whispering in his ear the whole time.'

Far from angry, Viviane was cool. 'Actually, that's not quite it. I'm a persuader.'

Wyll frowned. 'A persuader?'

'I don't make you do anything you don't already want to do,' Viviane said quickly.

Wyll's frown deepened as implications trickled cold down his spine.

That first night, with Carr and Viviane in Carr's study. How unusually relaxed Wyll had felt with the two of them. How eager for their combined touch. It had been a relief to feel, for the first time in his life, a simple, joyful want, unfettered by the shame of inexperience or judgement.

'But how would I *know*?' he said. 'How do I know anything I do around you is what *I* want to do?'

'People don't work like that. Things happened in your childhood that make you react certain ways. Not to mention the food you saw someone else eating last week, the books you read, the people you talk to, the people you *listen* to – saints, we're all a mess of influences at the purest of times. You've never made a single decision alone, not in your entire life. No one has.' Viviane had the knowing exasperation an adult wore when talking to a child. 'You know mind readers can't actually read minds, don't you, as if they're turning the pages of *The Book of You*? How anyone thinks they could pick out just one thought from the maelstrom of anyone's brain is . . .' They shake their head. 'It's more animal than that. Impulses, emotions. I can feel *those*. And so can you. People give signals in their reactions to you, don't they? And you interpret those signals to determine how they feel. They're angry. Sad. Confused. Jealous. I'm just very good at picking up signals. I . . . tune into someone. And it goes both ways, like opening a door between two rooms. I can feel you, but you can also feel me. And if I feel relaxed, let's say, or frightened . . . well, when we're in tune, when the door is open . . . so do you. That's all. That's it.'

He felt examined. Rummaged through. He wondered if they knew how he felt about them.

Idiot. Of course they knew. Why else would they be playing with him like this?

He wondered if how he felt about them was his doing, or theirs.

'How did you end up here?' he asked.

'Same way as you.' Viviane caught his gaze and held it. 'I'm dangerous, and I need to be contained.'

'I wasn't sure if you'd get my message.'

'She was hard to ignore,' Wyll curtly rejoins, willing himself to keep his feelings, his mind, under lock and key as the figure approaches, their boots giving clipped echoes against the tunnel floor. His heart disregards him, fluttering with nerves.

Viviane laughs. 'Cute, isn't she? I thought she might be to your taste. She looks a bit like me, don't you think? That was why I chose her.'

They stop close enough. Half their face is lit ghost-white with projection lights. The other half rests in darkness, rendering their smile enigmatic.

'No,' Wyll says shortly.

'No, she wasn't cute, or no, she doesn't look like me?'

'Viviane, stop.'

Viviane stops. Their head tips to one side.

They look just the same, like they walked out freshly made from his memory. But they are no illusion. The poor girl in his bath is testament to that. Besides, he'd never conjure Viviane to keep him company, not when he has spent the better part of the last three years attempting to forget they exist at all.

'You're embarrassed,' they say. 'Are you a prude these days? How wonderfully antique of you. Is that part of the deal when you join the royal house?'

'You didn't have to scrawl your summons on her body. You could have just sent me a message.'

'How?' Viviane mocks. 'It would have just ended up in the giant pile of other message coins marked "Sorcerer Knight adoration mail" – which eventually gets melted down to make a new helmet or something for you, I suppose.' They laugh at Wyll's expression. 'It's never even crossed your mind that it's someone's job to do something about all the junk that gets sent to the palace by your adoring hordes?'

'You used her,' says Wyll.

Viviane shrugs. 'And she'll use someone else. What's your point? It's like complaining that the world turns.'

He remembers the horrified way the vastos girl had looked at him, like the mere thought of him touching her made her want to vomit.

'She didn't remember what you'd made her do,' he says. 'You never used to make people forget.'

'Let's say I've grown as a person since our paths last crossed. I'm sure you have too.'

'It wasn't persuasion, it was force. Is that how you do things now?'

Their eyes crinkle. 'You sound angry with me. Your Caballaria persona is quite the grump, you know. How funny that people don't know what a lovely shy boy you really are.'

'Were.'

Viviane just looks at him, that infuriating faint smile playing on their mouth that he remembers so well, that smile that says *I know exactly what you're feeling, because I put it there.*

'You must get this a lot,' they say, 'but I see you so much on the screens that I feel like we've been friends still this whole while.'

'We were friends?'

'We were something.' They are too close, suddenly, and he can't stop the flood when it comes, pieces of memory of a naked Viviane, hair stuck to their forehead with sweat, that same smile on their face as they bucked on him like a sure horse rider urging a stallion to jump.

He must not let them in. Last time he did that, people died.

'What do you want from me?' he says, and his frost at last makes them falter.

'Maybe I just wanted to see you again,' they say.

121

'No one ever "just wants to see me again". I'm usually a means to an end.'

Viviane raises a brow. 'How cynical. Where are the stars in your eyes these days? Beaten out of you by the privileged life you lead?'

'You know nothing of my life now. As far as I know, you're a leech like all the rest, come to suck.'

'Like all the rest?' Their smile sours. 'I was the one who *helped* you. I got you out from sucking minor diplomat cock and back to sucking major royal cock. And now look where you are. Because of me.'

Wyll doesn't bother to try and explain to them, yet again, that Art was never his lover. Viviane believes in fucking people over in a rather more literal way than most.

'Mafelon,' they say.

It is the word he has been waiting for. The weapon he knew they would deploy, the detonated bomb. Mafelon is a knot of scar tissue on his soul, a taint, a constant reminder of his own ugliness.

'Oh,' says Viviane knowingly, 'you don't care? You know I can blow up your life any time I like. I just tell everyone what *really* happened that day and it's over for you.' Their vicious tone turns in a blink, goes soft and persuasive. 'All this time I've kept the secret of how you won back your saintly King's trust.' And now the smile is back. 'I assume you've never told him how you almost let him die?'

And saints, he nearly says it. It almost vomits out of him as thick, phlegmy guilt: *I did let him die. He's dead, and it's my fault.*

He can feel Viviane watching him, savouring the struggling they can see. They think they're in control. They always did.

'No, I haven't told him; I haven't told anyone,' Wyll says.

'I'm protecting you as much as you're protecting me. We can do this, Vivi, we can take each other down – but why? We agreed that day to bury it. Just before you decided to completely disappear on me. Remember?'

They retreat, defences rising. 'I had to. You know that. To protect us both.'

'And now, after all this time, you show up just to threaten me? What do you want?'

They are still, no doubt weighing up their next play.

But what if it's not that? What if they came back just to see him again, because they miss him? It's stupid, he knows, the thought of a needy little child, but—

'I need your help,' they say. 'I'm close to something big.'

The hopeful wave building inside Wyll crests and begins to fall.

'What kind of help?' he asks.

'I need something retrieved.'

The wave crashes, soaking him in disappointed fury.

'What?'

'A map,' says Viviane, with all the careful blankness of someone trying to disguise how much more of a thing it might be than just a map.

'What exactly is it you do these days, Vivi?' Wyll asks.

Vivi shrugs. 'I get things for people. I'm an intermediary.'

'I'm not stealing anything for you,' Wyll flatly replies.

A tut. 'It's not theft. It's being sold.'

'Why can't you buy this map yourself?'

'I have a rather recognisable face these days. And sadly, without your power to disguise it.'

'There must be a dozen people you could persuade to get it for you,' Wyll retorts. 'Why me?'

'Because I need you to look like someone the owner of the map would sell it to. Just occasionally, your arrogance is justified. I've never met another thwimoren like you, Wyll. No one can do what you do.'

Wyll searches for the trap he fears is there.

'Come on, Wyll. It'll be an adventure. I know how much you love wearing other people's faces.'

Viviane's voice is a horse bit, tugging and guiding. Wyll feels its pull and gallops hard the other way.

'No. That's my answer. I won't be part of whatever coney-crazed plan to change the world you have today.'

Viviane looks put out. 'So you'd rather carry on being rich and adored until you get too decrepit to look good in the paint, and then retire somewhere remote and count your glory days on your fingers 'til you die? That's a worthy life, to you?'

Grasping. That's the word for the look on their face.

'I think you need to work on your sales pitch,' Wyll says.

'Still a coward, I see. You're so disappointing up close, aren't you? No wonder you keep everyone away from you.'

All the old wounds are still there, welling up with blood.

'This was a mistake,' says Wyll, 'and I'm leaving.'

'Wait,' they reply. 'Wyll, I'm sorry. I'm sorry, okay? Please.'

The 'sorry' strikes him as sure as a bullet. Viviane does not say sorry.

They move restlessly, as if searching for something. 'I know what this looks like. I've no right to judge how you live. We all do what we can to survive, don't we?'

Their anxiety lowers his hackles. Smooth, confident Viviane, the only Viviane he ever knew, is all gone. This one appears vulnerable and unsure.

'What do you do to survive?' asks Wyll.

They just shrug. 'What everyone does, I suppose.'

'What does that mean?'

Instead of answering, they say, 'I've always been impressed at how you manage to fight without using your magic. I can't imagine how frustrating that is.'

It is. He feels it, suddenly, as strongly as if he is standing in the arena pit. 'I'm a castrated circus horse,' he says. The joke is too bitter to be funny.

'Like trying to dam a tide, neh?' Their tone turns gentle. 'It must be hard, never able to be who you really are, not even for a moment.'

'Under the eyes of the world, no less, just waiting for you to mess up,' he agrees.

'Trick is no compensation.' Viviane shakes their head.

He feels tired. Whatever else there is to think about Viviane, at least he could always be honest with them, godchild to god-child. They were the first one who showed him how to let go.

They were the first one in other ways too, and that kind of thing leaves a mark.

'It's a shame you didn't use my gift,' Viviane says. 'Feels like you could do with the release.' Their smile blooms once more, reading his emotions as effortlessly as ever. 'She'd have enjoyed it, too.'

Wyll snorts. 'Would she? Or would it have been you riding her mind, enjoying it for her?'

'Not the first time we had a proxy fuck, itso?' they purr. 'Or have you forgotten?'

His groin tightens and he does not need to look down to know that it shows. 'No,' he says. 'I haven't.'

Viviane moves close enough to kiss. Panic thrills up and down. He tries to stall them.

'This was different,' he murmurs. 'The girl you sent me was scared of me.'

'Maybe, but she was also aroused.'

'How could you know that?'

'I could feel it. It's an open door, what I do, remember? It goes both ways. You get a little . . . emotional bleeding.'

He feels the simple warmth of another body against his, a craving that he never realises he has until it happens. Viviane's pillowy lips stop just short of his, their hot breath caressing the surface of his skin.

'Remember how it feels to have a lover who isn't scared of you?' they whisper into his ear.

He feels their teeth tug gently on his lip.

Red.

Red wasn't scared of him.

The thought of her fills him with a swelling tide of still-fresh pain. The shock pulls him out from under Viviane's kiss. They hesitate against him and then push in again, but he puts his hands on their shoulders and presses them away.

'What's wrong?' they say.

'This isn't going to work, Vivi,' he says. 'I'm not the way to what you want.'

They pant an annoyed laugh. 'Saints, what's the problem? You won't even just fetch something for me? After all we've been through together?'

Viviane the seductor. Viviane the persuader. It used to beguile him. Now all he sees is desperation. This is not about him. This is about what they can get him to do for them.

'I asked you to come with me, after Mafelon,' says Wyll. 'I could have protected you.'

'I don't need your protection,' they snap.

'Just this *map*, then.'

They try to soften. 'Wyll—'

He shakes his head. 'Enough. I'm not your pet any more.'

'No, now you're someone else's,' they hiss.

Again, Red flashes through his mind.

He lets go of their shoulders and turns, walking away.

'Wyll, stop!'

And this time he can hear the *push* Viviane puts into their voice, but it doesn't work. He is no suggestive serving girl, and the hold they once had over him is gone.

More than anything, it is relief he feels.

He can hear them calling that they'll tell everyone about Mafelon, that they'll ruin him.

Go ahead, he thinks. *The one person I didn't want to know about it is dead.*

CHAPTER 12

Garad's Apartment, Evrontown
Two Weeks Ago

They lean forwards. The sword across their lap catches the light.
  'You're a godchild,' they say tonelessly.
Ghost looks up into their blank mask of a face.
  'Neh,' she says, steadily enough. 'Why? Gonna throw me out?'
Garad narrows their eyes. 'Why would I do that?'
Because you've done it before.
But Ghost swallows that thought — not time for that, not yet — and continues her story.

The Dugs, Alaunitown
Two Months Ago

Ghost sits huddled in her bedroom, surrounded by her candles, her warning and her protection. Strange how sticks of light can make a body feel safe.
  She feels violated, as if Moth, Joln and Sugar — and Delilah, oh, especially that manipulative little tartlet — took something from her she wasn't prepared to give. But what? All that happened was that she was led blindfolded into a room where

something touched her creepily on the face and made a decent guess about her godchild status. For all she knows, the whole thing was some bizarrely staged nothing designed to frighten her. But to what end?

An urgent warbling starts up from the stairs, interrupting her assessment of last night's fuckery. Someone in the stairwell, incoherently crying or talking, hard to tell, but either way, doing it to themselves.

Ghost sighs, relaxes, her shoulders coming down. There's something strangely safe about that noise. The building might house some crazy people, but at least the crazy here is a known quantity. They're all too lost in their fractured worlds to intrude into hers.

There comes a frantic knocking at the door.

Usually. *Usually* too lost.

Ghost eyes the door. It's pretty unbreakable, but that Chimes was a meaty bear. Then again, did he really seem like the knocking type?

'Ghost!' calls a muffled voice. 'Ghost, are you there? It's Delilah!'

Ha.

Ghost gives it a wait.

The knocking continues. The wailing from the stairwell climbs in intensity.

'Ghost, if you're in there, please—'

Ghost heaves out a sigh. If the double-dealing songstress keeps banging like that, it'll leave a mark, not to mention she's upsetting the wailing neighbour.

She takes her gun from underneath the bed. It feels strange in her hand, still. Too heavy, a dense pendulum pulling on her arm. She supposes Leon won't have cause to get her one until she proves herself on this Grenwald thing, but it felt more prudent not to wait around for his grudging approval. She's never been in any guard, so she's not had cause to touch a gun before, and they're hard to come by otherwise. Took a lot of trick to get it.

Now to see if it actually works.

She sidles up to the door. 'Fuck yourself,' she says through it.

The banging pauses. The wailing continues.

'You *are* there,' comes Delilah's voice. Relief, it sounds like. 'Please, I just want to talk. I'm alone. They don't know I came here.'

Ghost shifts the gun in her hand, a reassuring tic. 'So?'

'Please, can I just come in? Your hallway is . . . it's very noisy.'

'That's just Shouty Shera. No need for nerves, she's not the kind of crazy that hides a knife.'

'That's her real name?' Delilah sounds amusingly shocked.

'Of course not,' Ghost says through the door. 'It's just the name I gave her.'

'You haven't bothered to learn the right one?'

'She doesn't even know what world she's in. You try asking her for her real name. Go on, I need a laugh.'

'I can see why you'd be angry with me,' says Delilah.

'I'm not angry. Where I'm from, kidnapping is a sign of affection.'

'West Rhyfentown, right? Where you're from, originally? I know you've got a Marvoltown tattoo and all that, but you've also got a faint accent.' Delilah sounds apologetic for her sharp ear.

The Marvoltown tattoo is not exactly a feint. In a sense, Ghost was born there. Marvoltown, the Death Saint's dis' – the saint of death, but also rebirth, change and the unknown. He has become, in recent times, as much Ghost's patron saint as violent old Rhyfen.

'What do you want?' she snaps at Delilah.

'I came to help you find out what happened to Cass.'

'Seems to be code in your world for something else involving idiots with stuffed badgers and blindfold tests.'

'I'm sorry about that. They heard you were sniffing around. They wanted to know if they could trust you.'

'There's no test in the world can determine that,' Ghost says. 'About anyone.'

Silence.

Shera continues to wail, but the urgency has gone, and with it the sense of danger. Maybe she's a sensitive; maybe she can hear the energy in their exchange softening, feel the hackles going down. Who knows these days who is capable of what.

'I trust you,' she hears Delilah say.

What in seven hells is this lady about? asks her other self.

'I'd love it if you went away,' Ghost says sweetly.

'I can't.'

'Why not?'

'I just can't.'

'Why me?' Ghost asks the world.

'Because you showed up. At the bar. You looked into drownings. You came to find me to tell me. You cared.' Delilah's voice rises desperately. 'No one's ever cared before.'

Ghost opens the door.

The face before her is a charming mix of defiance and vulnerability, its pretty features sharp with some heightened emotion – whether from her earnest words or the warbling behind her is hard to tell. She catches sight of the gun in Ghost's hand, stiffens, wisely decides not to raise an objection.

'Why aren't your testy friends helping you find Cass' killer?' asks Ghost.

Delilah tightly shakes her head. 'They're not my friends. They're Cass' friends. Anyone who sniffs around gets a look-at.'

'Why would a group of godchild-lovers be so paranoid?'

'They're not activists,' Delilah says, 'if that's what you're thinking.'

'I never said what I was thinking,' Ghost replies, 'and that's a nice intellectual word for fools playing at righteous heroes. Now, you must have some bait to hook me with, or you wouldn't have trekked all the way here to get nothing but a shut door.'

Delilah looks cunning. 'I got you an invite.'

'To what?'

'The kind of party you'll never even hear about 'til you get an invite.'

'I don't feel like dancing right now.'

'Not that kind of party. It's where Cass meets her clients. They'll be there – one of them in particular, he's high up on the predator list. If anyone knows what happened to her, it's him.'

'And why haven't you questioned this rich prize yourself?'

Delilah gives a short laugh. 'There are two kinds of people who get invited to this party: farmers and cows. Glapissant is a farmer. You're a cow. I'm just the help. He won't talk to me, that'd be like talking to a waiter.'

'Did you just call me a cow?'

'A very special kind of cow,' Delilah amends.

'Special how?' Ghost asks, but she already knows.

Delilah just widens her eyes.

'No,' says Ghost, and makes to close the door.

'Wait!' There is panic in Delilah's voice.

'I've spent my whole life keeping this from everyone I've ever known. Only one person has ever found out who I really am, and it cost me *everything*. You hear me? It's why I had to burn my old life and run.' Anger makes her honest. Honesty is a luxury she cannot often afford.

'The lover who rejected you,' Delilah says. 'You told them, didn't you? You thought you could finally trust someone enough to show them who you really were, but they didn't react the way you'd hoped.'

Ghost struggles with a sudden, sharp dig of claws in her heart. She'd thought, with time . . . ah, well. Pain is pain. It doesn't slough off, it calcifies.

'Happens to us all,' she says eventually.

'Not everyone is like that,' Delilah urges. 'At this party, you'd be desired like you've never been before—'

'What makes you think I want that? I just want to be left alone! But I can't, can I? Your friends made sure of it.'

'I'm really sorry.'

She actually looks it. Can't really blame her for all of it, either – Ghost had been the one to chase her down for answers on Cassren, eager to prove herself, eager to show off. Trouble of it all is she isn't the hiding sort, even when she needs to be. Never was.

Ghost sighs, rubs her neck. 'Not only are they holding my secret over my head like a sword on a string they can cut any time, but you want me to announce it to a whole den of 'launitowners?'

'Go as a Gun, then,' Delilah quickly amends. 'I'm there to sing, so I can get us in the door, but her client's too hard to reach otherwise. You'll never be able to find him any other way.' She's as insistent as an itch. 'These people don't exist, the way you don't exist – unofficial, outside the normal rules. This is the only way you'll get to them.'

'At a party,' Ghost scoffs.

'I told you: not like any party you've been to before.'

The pretty thing is standing her ground, staring Ghost down, face stripped back in a tempting new way, a way that could even mean honesty.

Ghost feels her resolve soften and run like butter in a hot pot.

My darling, says the other her, *isn't your libido part of the reason why you had to dump your old life?*

Shut up, Ghost tells the other her.

And didn't you thereafter swear that you wouldn't let it get you in trouble ever again?

Shut up.

And yet here we are, trills the other her.

Shut up.

CHAPTER 13

Si Carrivuthen's Household,
Barochi, Third Kingdom
Three Years Ago

Mafelon.

Scar on the soul of London.

One of many corpses Wyll has buried under the floorboards of a room somewhere in the back of his mind. A room he has mostly managed to keep locked, to prevent anyone from ever discovering those corpses, the embodiments of each terrible thing he has done, each secret he must keep. He was doing a decent job of it until the sudden reappearance of Viviane.

Young Wyll's arrival into Carr's retinue had heralded a surge in the diplomat's popularity. He delightedly told Wyll that he had been inundated with requests for meetings, all to see the dazzling thwimoren up close.

At dinners and lunches and soirées, Wyll performed small feats of illusion for them – nothing much really, not a huge stretch for him, but enough to elicit gasps and claps. He made huge cakes disappear from the table, or turned them into roasted haunches of meat, while the diners made a fuss of sampling the food and delighting in the confusion it sent into their brains, with tongues expecting shredded sticky salted flesh but tasting fluffy spun sugar, chewy candied fruit. He made kits and pups appear on tables, sending them stalking between the candelabra with their adorably chubby paws, all the while feeling the claws of Viviane's words sinking into his heart.

They were right, this was a waste of his talent, and his time. How long was he supposed to stay here, getting fatter in mind and body, until one day he went to conjure something more than a cake trick and found he no longer could?

Among his few personal belongings was a thick bundle of letters from the King, careful to give no identifiable detail and always signed from his nameless 'uncle', but full of warmth and wit and affection. After two years of correspondence, the missives had, in the last few months, stopped coming. Not one letter. Not even a brief, regretful note explaining how busy things had been, how he'd write soon. *Nothing.*

Late at night, when he was alone in the dark with his fears and no distractions, he had started to wonder if Art had forgotten all about him, pondering if it was a deliberate kind of forgetting. Despite all his bold talk to Viviane, he was afraid – afraid of being considered too much of a liability to make space for, of being suppressed, forgotten. Abandoned.

After that night in the training cellar, he had begun to feel as though Viviane, too, was avoiding him. They disappeared a lot. Carr was too preoccupied with the business of his life to care, but for Wyll, a Viviane appearance was just about the best part of his day, and he noticed, painfully, how few of those he was now getting. Between that and Art's continuing silence, he was lonely, which made him desperate, a potent hunger that not even his punishing daily training regime could sate.

One night, when Carr was out at some elaborate function

with people who didn't necessarily enjoy the presence of god-children as much as Carr did, when Wyll was trying to keep his miserable ardour at bay with a late-night session on the ropes and heard the door at the far end of the corridor bang shut – the door no one really used that led from the back of Carr's villa to nowhere much – he prowled out of the training room to investigate. He opened up the door a sliver, saw the unmistakable figure of Viviane walking away and seized his unexpected chance. He ran back to the training room, pulled on the thin housecoat he'd left there, feeling it stick unpleasantly to his sweat-soaked skin, and followed Viviane.

The sky was tumbling fast as he left, and it gladdened him. Twilight was a velveteen time for lovers, for spilling sins and secrets. Carr's villa was on the outskirts of a rich town, an uneasy limbo between city and countryside, neither one nor the other. Here things were prettier, cleaner and less chaotic than the twisty organic intestines of London he had grown up with. The villas here were filled with people who preferred both more space and more rules. Verdant, rolling countryside surrounded the town, the trees and fields neat and tamed, a showcase for the death of change. The light out here stayed brighter for longer, too, and so it was easy for Wyll to pick out the familiar figure receding along the road.

The distinct shape of Viviane moved at a clip, and Wyll followed at the awkward spider dance done when you wanted to catch up but did not want to be noticed until you did. He wanted to tap them on the shoulder, make them shriek, hit him, the giddy camaraderie created in the wake of sudden threat extinguished.

Then, perhaps, they could talk alone, finally, for the first time in weeks.

He wasn't completely stupid. He knew it likely that Viviane had another lover. Carr was possessive, which was why Viviane would wait until he was out of the house to visit this mysterious person. Wyll just wanted to know who he was up against, to make his case, prove to Viviane, with all the fervour of a first-time lover, that everything they wanted they could get from *him*.

So enraptured was he with these near-future imaginings that he almost lost them when they turned off the road and plunged into a vast field of hulking geothermal chimneys. The ghostly white fluted tubes reared into the sky, sending never-ending cloud plumes trickling from their mouths. The ground vibrated softly with their hum, as though a sprawling beehive was buried in the ground beneath.

Like a dog which'd lost the trail, Wyll circled uncertainly once or twice, then plunged into the strange hum, moving hurriedly between the tall pale stacks. There was no question of going back now, and no question of pretence. When he did catch up with them, it would be clear that he had deliberately followed them. But what would they want to traverse a giant generator field for?

The answer lay on the other side. When Wyll broke out from the field, he found himself next to a wide stretch of river, and on it a floating carnival. A small flotilla of boats in a jumble of shapes and sizes had been lashed together, connected by makeshift ladders and swing ropes. There were people out on deck, moving shapes lit by a roving rainbow of trick lights, some hanging on to rigging arching dangerously out over the water below, a black ribbon sprinkled with dazzling, dancing lights. A smell of cooked meats with the tangy notes of seafood perfumed the air, riding on the strains of music and laughter.

Wyll moved closer, wooed and lured, his goal temporarily forgotten. It was a scrappy kind of party. The lights were a mismatched range of large iron floor lamps, dangling bunches of flecter-glass globes, utilitarian rhomboid search lights and sticky chrome trick strips tacked to surfaces, as if each guest had brought their own light source.

The boats themselves were made of welded spare parts, rubber treads, wheel spokes, repurposed shipping containers, even – from what he could see – bike parts. It was not the kind of place he'd ever expect to meet a knight, so it was reasonable to assume those bike parts were illegitimately obtained—

'Lost, are we?'

Wyll startled. The figure who had spoken was crouched bankside on an overturned storage crate, wreathed in smoke. A mass of hair lay like a rag-rug on their curved back and their feet were in utilitarian-looking thigh-high boots.

No one would come upon this flotilla hidden behind a power farm by accident. Best to act with purpose.

'I'm here for my friend,' Wyll said to the booted smoker. 'Viviane.'

'Well, of course,' said the smoker. 'We were joking, weren't we. Go on in.'

Wyll blinked. That was easy. He nodded his thanks and walked to the first boat's edge, floating steady an inch from the bank – never hesitate; hesitation meant you didn't belong – and stepped across, leaving the safety of steady ground.

The boats were peppered with knots of people, talking – arguing mostly, it sounded like – while they ate and drank, standing or sitting around on upturned crates, blanket piles, repurposed barrels. The blind adrenalin of Wyll's single-minded pursuit of Viviane was wearing off and he began to feel uneasy.

This was not his party, his world. He didn't belong here. But he hadn't come all this way just to turn tail. He needed to find Viviane, even if it was only to apologise and leave – but maybe there was a chance they would relent and let him stay . . .

As he wandered around, his ears caught conversational strings –

'Of course it's not utopian, but it *could* be, if the totems of greed were pulled down—'

– and he got a few nods from the boat strangers, nodding back, surprised and comforted by their friendliness, though making it clear that he couldn't stop to chat, not right now. This wasn't much like Carr's parties, where the social hierarchy was so rigid it dictated who could speak to whom, even what kind of conversation they could have.

Viviane was still nowhere to be found, and he was now several boats from shore. Losing heart in the entire endeavour, Wyll savagely and silently cursed his lovesick idiocy and began to pick his way back to the bank, unhappily contemplating a long journey home in the dark. Saints, he wasn't even sure of the direction, having followed Viviane like a mindless rabbit.

'Hey,' he heard someone call in his direction, 'where've you been?'

Wyll turned, eager, confused, somehow thinking it could be Viviane, but the one speaking was a tall shape in a ridiculously bulbous hat.

'Oh,' he said. 'I'm sorry, I—'

'Don't be sorry,' said Bulbous Hat, a trifle impatiently, 'just get in here and thrash this out with us, would ya? Peke is spouting total trout guts again.'

Bulbous Hat and their companion, presumably the trout gut-spouting Peke, were sitting together on upturned crab pots.

'No one's suggesting *actual* assassination, are they,' said Peke in a heavy, sombrous voice. 'You're being dramatic.' He was a surprisingly small figure, at odds with his voice – lithe and wiry like a little hunt dog.

'It's *delas*,' Bulbous Hat insisted. 'Working with that kind. Makes me want to spit my dinner in the *riviere*.'

'We're not working *with* them, are we,' Peke said patiently. 'We're using them, aren't we.'

'That's how it starts,' Bulbous Hat morosely replied.

'There's this radical crazy who grew up in one of those monotheist cults,' Peke continued, ignoring his companion's negative attitude. 'She's the one who wants to do it. She's the one who *suggested* it.'

'How in seven hells do we even have a connection with this *she*?' Bulbous Hat rolled their eyes despairingly in Wyll's direction. The word 'she' was said with the tone of 'sludge rat'.

Wyll stood frozen, trying desperately to work out how to get away. This did not sound like a conversation of which he should be a part. Assassination? Radical crazies? Hopefully they were all riding high, or just having fun with him, even if they did appear to be entirely sober.

Peke nodded in Wyll's direction. 'Viviane knows her. Says they grew up together. Itso, Vivi?'

His eyes connected with Wyll's. A relieved Wyll looked around – but there was no sign of Viviane. Meanwhile the pair sitting on the crab pots were waiting and looking right at him.

The moment grew too fat. The three of them began to struggle with the weight.

'You're talking to me?' asked Wyll at last.

Peke nudges Bulbous Hat. '*They're* on a journey.'

Bulbous Hat snorted. 'You only got here a few minutes

ago, I saw you arrive. Brought some of your own, did you? Share it out.'

'What are you on, Viv?' Peke said. 'Titon'll be fury-dancing if he thinks you've turned up flying to the meeting. Don't antagonise him, neh? You know how seriously he takes all this.'

'Well, someone better be if we're planning on killing the King of London,' Bulbous Hat airily replied.

Wyll's utter confusion took on an alarming new flavour.

Peke spat. 'Stop yelling it, you cockworm.'

'Why? Everyone on this tug's in the group, it's the safest place *to* yell it.'

'And I just said – did I not just say? – that no one's killing anyone,' Peke drove on. 'You're not listening. You never listen. It's a *fake* assassination. The crazy's the only one who's going to think it's real, and then she and the rest of those terrorists she's in the mix with get ripped apart by the palace, and they're out the game. They won't even get to fight it out in an arena. It'll be a mass execution for them that dare touch the Blackheart King.' He dusts his hands. 'One less group of bilious godchild-killers in the world.'

'Peke, stop fucken talking *right now.*'

A sharp new voice cut Peke's throbbing bell tones in two – and then there was Wyll's quarry, standing feet away, a look of total furious shock on their face.

Wyll raised his hands, his heart gladdening at the sight of them at last, and began to explain himself, but before he could get anything out, Viviane stepped up and punched him in the stomach.

'Can you at least lower the gun?' asked Wyll in the meekest voice he had.

The cold, blank muzzle of the weapon in question currently occupied the majority of his attention, as if lit by torchlights with arrows pointing to it from all directions. Viviane's hand and arm behind the gun, and their face beyond that, occupied a fuzzy, unimportant second place.

'I didn't realise I was doing it,' he pleaded. 'On Iochi's own face, I swear it.'

'It wasn't the face of a saint you were making, Wyll,' Viviane said in a terrible new voice of ice. 'It was *mine*.'

The way they'd just let him walk on to the boats. The nods from strangers. Peke and Bulbous Hat's familiarity with him.

A lot of things had suddenly begun to make sense in the last few minutes.

'It's happened before,' Wyll protested. 'I don't realise what I'm doing. I can't control it.'

'You took my *face*.'

Saints, they sounded disgusted.

They hated him.

'It's just bent light and sound,' mumbled Wyll. 'It's not *real*. I didn't mean to. I just followed you here because I wanted to talk to you. I don't know what this is. All this.' He looked helplessly round at the boat walls, intimately cramped around them. They were having this out belowdecks, just the three of them. Wyll, Viviane, and a great big hole-maker. 'I just . . . it was *you* I wanted to see. So I suppose my brain tried to give me what I wanted. In a manner of speaking.'

A long pause. The gun muzzle seemed to yawn bigger.

'Does Carr know you can do this?' Viviane asked.

'You've both seen me conjure other people—'

'But I've never seen you *wear* them. And there's only one other thwimoren that's ever been able to do that.'

Wyll's heart dropped and dropped and dropped.

No one had ever been able to prove that godchild talent was genetic. It missed the next generation almost as often as it hit, and it was rare that exact talent was duplicated. But Wyll's father was the one who taught him how to paint his illusions over himself to look like another. Who else could he have learned it from?

He looked past the gun to Viviane, and Viviane looked past the gun to him, and they knew, and he knew. There was only one way to go from here.

'I heard you want to assassinate the King of London,' he said. His life hung in the balance.

The gun lowered a fraction. Viviane laughed and shook their head, their expression one of amused resignation. 'Double dead, is it?' they said. 'I expose you, you expose me?'

Wyll sensibly kept quiet.

Viviane let out a sigh. 'Fake bullets. She'll have a gun, but it'll be loaded with fake bullets. They pack a sting, but they don't break flesh.'

'What's the point of pretending to kill him?' asked Wyll tentatively.

'Best way to get rid of them,' Viviane replied.

'Who?'

'The enemy.'

'Who's your enemy?'

'Those who want humanity to stay small and mean.'

'Don't treat me like a child,' Wyll said. 'I'm not. Explain it.'

But Viviane kept silent.

'You're a revolutionary, is that it?'

'Such disdain! But underneath, I think I detect a faint tang of fear.' Viviane smirked. 'Don't worry, I've always been too pragmatic for idealism. Anyway, this isn't my show.' They caught his surprise. 'I'm flattered, but I'm only a member of the organisation, and low down at that.'

Wyll remembered the affinity and respect in those casual nods, the ease with which he could walk through strangers. Viviane was lying, but he was not sure why.

'You can trust me,' he said.

They gave him a look of patronising amusement. 'I don't know you, Wyll. You think sucking someone's cock means you ingest their personality too?'

'I think for you it might,' dared Wyll.

Viviane laughed. 'That's not exactly how my talent works, but as analogies go it's pretty good, so there's a win for you. What else have you got?'

A test, see if he had the brains of a child or a man. Right then.

'You've got knights in the mix. They're helping you. Maybe financing you, or getting you access to the King.'

It was hardly a big leap – boats made out of bike parts, a gun in his face – these were knights' things, untouchable to all other mere mortals – but their surprised look still gave him an undeniable rush of pleasure, a little tightening just below the groin. Viviane had really screwed up his wiring. Somehow pleasing them made him happy, and in more than one sense of the word.

'Well,' they acknowledged, 'who's the trickiest of them all? Such an endeavour needs appropriate financing.'

Yes indeed. There was barely anyone richer and more powerful in the world than a knight. Their lives must race as easy and free as a bike ride. Wyll wanted – oh, he *wanted* – such a life for himself. But which knights would align themselves with assassination, even a fake assassination? Who stood to gain from it?

Wyll shook his head. 'Why would anyone do something like this?'

Viviane's doe eyes grew sharp. 'We all have good reasons. You think it a game?'

Hard to think of it as a game with a gun pointed in his general direction.

'I meant your would-be assassin,' he said. 'Why would she do this?'

Viviane shrugs. 'Haven't you ever felt the bright fire of righteous fury? She thinks she's on the right side, and she'll die because of it. There's no changing that kind of mind, so why not use it to your best advantage instead? Point that zeal in a more constructive direction.'

Wyll was suddenly struck with the absurdity of this conversation. This couldn't be real. It just couldn't. He came here to confess boyish, heart-pounding love, a feeling so wonderfully innocent, a feeling he longed to return to, before a time when he knew that the object of his adoration could be so frightening, so out of reach. A wiser part of him understood that he could not hope to catch up to where Viviane lived, and that he wouldn't want to, anyway, but that wiser part was not in control.

Right now he was only visiting Viviane's world – but maybe he could find a way to stay.

'What happens if the assassin succeeds?' he said. 'What if she . . . throws the gun away when it's not working and pulls a knife?'

'She won't get that close,' Viviane replied.

'How can you prevent that? Will you have someone else there, someone on your side?'

A pause, enough of one to know that the answer was no.

Wyll's mind began to whir, eagerly looking for a way in. 'Where's it happening?' he asked.

'My darling, the more questions you ask, the less likely it is that you get to leave this room.'

But Wyll wasn't listening. 'It's got to be some kind of diplomat function,' he muttered, thinking furiously, 'otherwise why involve you? You're getting her in there somehow, aren't you? Through Carr. He's involved too.'

Viviane's laugh was abrupt. 'Carr doesn't know anything about this. For a politician, the clot is curiously averse to anything political. All he knows is that he gets to attend an important function with the King of London and his coterie.'

Wyll looked up at them. 'So *you're* going to be there, if you're arranging it.'

'No, Carr will be going alone. Security doesn't allow any attendees a retinue. Wyll, I think it's about time you—'

'I can be there,' Wyll interrupted.

Viviane abruptly stood and paced forwards, the gun held loosely at their side. 'You're an innocent. You know nothing about any of this. Do not involve yourself.'

'Stop insulting me,' he snapped, with the reckless vigour of someone who did not care to understand how dangerous the situation was. His was a mission of love, and love always won. 'An hour ago you didn't even know that Edler Feverfew was my father. What else don't you know about me?'

Viviane stared at him. He held their gaze, while inside he trembled like a rabbit.

'Yes,' they murmured, 'what else don't I know about you? Why don't you tell me?'

It felt like an invitation and not a challenge, warm and safe as a bath.

'I know the King of London,' Wyll said.

The little misshapen boat door behind Viviane opened, and in walked a small man with long, corn-coloured hair and a pair of the fiercest eyes Wyll had ever seen on anyone who wasn't a bird of prey.

Behind his shoulder crowded a small knot of people, angling in to take a good look at the interloper. People, Wyll now knew, who had been listening in the whole time.

'Hoy, thwimoren,' said the hawk-eyed man. His smile was lopsided, as if he didn't quite know how to wear one. 'My name is Titon and I'd just love to hear more about your relationship with the King.'

Viviane's gaze had transferred to Titon and was locked there as if by magnetic force. The others on the boat had said his name, but even in that brief mention there had been deference and just a little fear, warning Wyll-as-Viviane not to get in trouble with him – but Viviane wasn't looking at Titon with any kind of fear.

Suddenly, it was all so clear. Titon was the man that he had come here to discover, to size up, to see if he could beat for Viviane's love. Titon was his rival.

Viviane liked strength. Carr was weak, using other people's power to get his own. But this Titon, he was strong. His personality filled the room so much you could choke on it. How could Wyll prove that he was stronger than a man who would plot to fake-kill a King?

He'd have to be the man who actually carried it out.

'Why are you getting involved in this, Wyll?'

Dawn's pink was edging the sky by the time they reached Carr's house. It had been a long night of discussion surrounded by hard, mistrustful faces: a long night of pleading his case with strangers who looked as though they'd rather throw him in the river. As soon as Viviane started to advocate for his idea, though, hackles went down, and acceptance came curiously fast after that.

People tended to feel whatever Viviane wanted them to feel.

Even so, they had been tasked to watch Wyll closely, to stick to his side and survey all his doings until the operation was over. He would not be able to speak, move or toilet without Viviane's knowledge. It was exactly the kind of attention from them that he had long been fantasising about, but there was no need to tell them that.

And now, he supposed, he was no longer a child but a man. It was not the thrill he was expecting to feel when he finally stepped over that line, more a kind of vague, sickly dread at the dangerous unknown that life had suddenly, over the course of one night, become.

'If you're doing this for me . . .' Viviane ventured.

'I'm not,' Wyll snapped.

This was not just about winning Viviane.

When a younger, more naïve Wyll had signalled for help, Art had come. Art had rescued him. In return, Wyll had promised he would save Art's life, reasoning that someone always wanted the King dead, so the opportunity was bound to come along sooner or later.

He just hadn't expected it to be by his own hand.

But maybe if he did this, he would prove to Art that he was useful, worth having around, maybe even worthy of being a knight. Art would invite him back to his side instead of sending him away to more spineless users like Carr for another two years.

The King of London would never make him do bed and cake tricks for low-level ratshit politicians. The King of London would never make him do *any* tricks.

He wanted them both to love him. Viviane and Art. To love him and to want him.

He said none of this out loud, of course, but as always with Viviane, he had the embarrassing notion that they could somehow see it on him anyway.

When they finally reached the back door to Carr's silent villa, Viviane stood on tiptoe and kissed Wyll on the cheek, as though all was easy and well.

'You can still get out of all this,' they whispered. 'I promise, if you say no, they won't hurt you, they'll just let you go. I'll make sure of it. Think it over.'

But there was no need to think it over. He already knew what it was to gamble his life for what he wanted. He'd done it before, and he'd do it again.

Mafelon was his chance, and he took it.

It went perfectly.

Wyll's previously secret connections with Cair Lleon were made plain when Carr was persuaded to make the request to bring Wyll and it was surprisingly granted. Carr, only too happy to have a way to get closer to the King, gladly took Wyll with him to London to attend the soon-to-be-infamous diplomatic dinner at historic Mafelon. The extremist would-be assassin – no doubt manipulated by Viviane, under Titon's supervision – took her chance. Then Wyll took his, stopping her with a masterful, dramatic display of illusory prowess in front of a cowed crowd made up of many of the most powerful diplomats in the Seven Kingdoms. A shocked and grateful King

Artorias had no choice but to give Wyll the public recognition he so badly craved, and keep him closer ever after.

Art – his mentor, his father figure, his saviour – died without ever knowing the part Wyll played at Mafelon, for which he feels nothing but relief. But if Viviane should choose to expose him now, especially when he is already under suspicion for Art's death . . . everything could come crashing down. So much of it already has, and he cannot afford to lose any more. He will disappear into a black hole and never climb back out.

He'll have to get Viviane their damned map.

And then he'll have to come up with a way to ensure that they cannot ever threaten his life again.

CHAPTER 14

Garad's Apartment, Evrontown
Two Weeks Ago

'So you went to this . . . godchild party,' says Garad, with a mix of eagerness and subtle disdain.

Ghost draws on a sicalo, enjoying the feel of their rapt attention.

'Strap in,' she comments, 'because it was the longest and weirdest damn night of my life.'

Loisnes, Alaunitown
Two Months Ago

'I feel ridiculous,' Ghost grumbles, tugging on her flimsy jacket.

'You look incredible,' Delilah says by her side.

'Generic flattery doesn't work on me.' She pauses. 'Incredible? Really?'

'Neh,' says her preoccupied companion as they stride along the street, hopping a data coin from one rounded knuckle to the next, casually dextrous. An anxiety tic.

'How does anyone walk in these things?' Ghost asks the sky.

Delilah glances at Ghost's feet. 'Claws are tricky. You get the right of it after a bit of practice.'

Ghost struggles on in the seventh-damned bird shoes. Apparently they wouldn't even get a claw in the door if they weren't appropriately dressed to theme, and tonight's theme is 'animalia'. Fucken make-believe. Why did all secret things have to have such silly rules to them?

'Who invented this lunacy?' Ghost grumps. 'Who woke up one day and said, "You know what would be a fun thing to do? Walk around on claws. And let's not mess about – saints, no, if you do a thing, do it all the way – so let's make sure they completely hobble people's range of motion so they can barely take a step without wobbling over. And let's make them out of materials that sound like bone dice rattling in a cup when they walk the street, announcing their presence for a mile in every direction—" '

'Joln Chimes was right,' Delilah says. 'You talk a lot when you're nervous.'

Ghost side-eyes her.

She's all done up in the soft pale pinks of cats' snouts and she's got legs that go on forever. Shimmering on her neck in pellucid pearl is a registration tattoo. A temporary fake, of course – and therefore illegal – but where they are going, the daring little flaunt will be admired for it. They love godchildren so much at this party that it's admirable to pretend to be one.

'Been talking about me, have we?' she asks Delilah.

Delilah snorts. 'You think a lot of yourself.'

'I'm used to adoration.'

'Well, don't get used to it with me.'

Ghost smiles to herself. They wobble-click along rain-damp

roads, striped in bright-bleach shop signs and 'buy me' flash strobes. They pass a Caballaria bet shop, its window fronts taken up with moving projections of the latest public bouts, in order of importance. Ghost finds her eyes straying to the fighter names, flashing in proud streaks across the flecter glass – and then she wrenches them away with an effort.

'So you're expected to entertain tonight?' she asks Delilah.

'I'll sing for my supper. Just a short display; they've a few people booked. It's only just started up, and it'll go on late 'n' long.'

Ghost checks the time on display at the shop they pass. 'It's past midnight now.'

'Okay, Grandma,' scoffs Delilah. 'It's a sun-up thing. You go 'til the light hits you.'

'Huh. How will you know? Can't see shit underground.'

'What makes you think it's underground?'

'Aren't all secret things?' says Ghost.

'No. Sometimes they're in plain sight.' Delilah gestures at the building coming into view ahead.

It's a tall, featureless obsidian cube, plunked in the middle of a street and crowded on all sides by far more ornate buildings from London's long, varied past. Subtle it is not.

Ghost halts. 'That's a building?'

Delilah nods.

'I hate to be obvious, but there's no door.'

Delilah wiggles the coin in her fingers. She presses its catch, springing its projection into life. A thick, double-pointed symbol in summer-sky blue shimmers into the air above the coin. It looks like a W.

Delilah holds up the coin and trains the W symbol on to the blank black wall in front of them.

There is an immediate answering glow from the wall's depths. A panel slides away, revealing a small slot. Delilah deposits the coin in the slot. They watch it eaten up by the building with a satisfied chirrup. Smooth mechanical sounds come from beyond, but the wall does not change. It is still wall. Very much wall.

'Well, that was a disappointing result,' Ghost remarks. 'What do we do now?'

Delilah gives Ghost a triumphant look and walks straight through the wall. Disrupted light bends around her with a silent fizz.

Saints alive. The wall is a *projection*.

Ghost's body, despite all evidence, expects resistance, clenching tight as she walks into the wall – but there is only air, a clean and sharp passage to the beyond.

And beyond is *vast*.

The first several floors of this megalith have been sacrificed for a hall with a ceiling that disappears into the stars. A plainly tiled floor stretches away into other lands. Dotted around the space, in various attitudes of squatting or hugging or perching precariously, are objects. None are smaller than human size, and several loom larger than Ghost's own apartment. One is so big it takes up an entire corner from ceiling to floor. Made of intricately patterned twists of metal, it stands brash and alien, man-made but only just. It looks like the real-world approximation of a mathematician's nightmare, and staring at it too long gives Ghost a strange vertigo.

'What is all this?' she manages. Her voice skips across the tiles to where Delilah stands with a look of cool amusement on her face.

'Art,' says Delilah. 'Come on. Ascender's at the back.'

'What, the ground floor isn't big enough for a party?' Ghost grumbles. The claws on her feet click across the tile, each answered with rebounding wall clicks until it feels like being surrounded by a swarm of skeletal locusts.

'The rich live high,' answers Delilah.

The ascender is easier to spot than the front door, but only just. It glides noiselessly into place, a plain glass box like a display case. They click on to its transparent plate of a floor.

'You look nervous,' observes Delilah. 'Not used to the elite world, I take it.'

'Not really,' lies Ghost.

'It's easy. Just pretend you're there solely for their amusement.'

'I know that game.'

They share a look.

'You're sure Cass' client will be there?' asks Ghost.

'Sure as I can be.'

'Glapissant,' muses Ghost. 'I feel like I've heard the name before.'

'He runs a few different things. Mostly tech, so I hear.'

'What does he look like?'

'Like a frog,' says Delilah.

'Is that what he's dressed up as tonight?'

'You'll see what I mean. Stick close to me. Be cautious about anything you're offered. Blue food and drink are usually the safest bet.'

'Why blue?' a baffled Ghost asks.

Delilah shoots her an entertained look, clearly enjoying the innocent company of a provincial good girl.

'Blue's the designated safe colour in Alaunitown,' she says. 'The stuff you give to first-timers. I think the practice originated with the bordels and their nervous virgin clients. They'd

156

wear a blue ribbon so the meretrix would know to go easy on them.'

Before Ghost can reply, the ascender – so quiet the only thing that has told her they are moving at all has been the sight of the walls of the ascender's shaft flashing past through the glass walls – sleeks to a stop.

The door opens on to a riot of life.

Knots of sprouting, feathered, scaled and furred augmentation dot the space. Ears and tails, claws and paws, tentacles, wings and skin grafts – some temporary, some not – headdresses, elaborate jewellery, clothing drapes and shoes, all designed for a queasy invocation of the historic – outdated, some might say – casual casting of godchildren as something exotically bestial, something organically monstrous.

These people, by all accounts, being the cream of Alaunitown society, cannot be outdated. They would say they dictate fashion, and where they lead, everyone follows – but in Ghost's opinion, they're usually the most outdated of the lot. People at the top don't tend to like change all that much, in case it leads to them losing their privileged spot.

Glossy, thick music, assured but not intrusive, can just be heard oozing underneath the chattering buzz. Ghost feels a hand slipped into hers, which was dangling previously slack and unfettered by her side. It's a pleasant shock – but one look at Delilah's face shows the performance of it. She is not Delilah, not here – here she is Flowers for Kane, transformed through will and attitude alone.

'Follow my lead,' she says, with the quiet assurance of the coveted, and they set off into the crowd. As they go, Delilah relieves circling platters of their sparkling drinks and grabbable parcels of food, and points out faces in soft undertones.

'That one's a Welyen,' she says, as they move past a skinny man covered in a dense, thickly clustered array of giant ostrich feathers and already looking sweatily regretful at his costume choice. 'A cousin underling or some such, but apparently he has the ear of the Lady Orcade herself.'

'What are all the projections about?' asks Ghost. Many people in the crowd are clutching large black data coins sprouting an array of different faces.

'They're menus,' Delilah says.

'What do you mean?'

'I mean, people come here to buy and godchildren come here to sell. I told you this was how Cass met her clients.' Delilah glances at her. 'You know, if you just told people what godchild class you are, things would go fast as a bike. Even if it isn't a rare one, every person here would be punching each other out just to be near you—'

'Ask me again,' Ghost cuts in, 'and *I* might start punching out.'

'I've no idea why you're so secretive about it,' grumbles Delilah.

'Your happy kidnapper friends have enough weapons pointed at me already. Here, I'm a Gun and nothing else. That was the deal. If you don't stick to the deal, I might be forced to make trouble. This place means nothing to me. I'll get us kicked out quicker than a stray cat in a kitchen and you'll never get to sing for this shamble of kambion-loving richies again, itso?'

Delilah looks away, across the crowd. Her mouth opens, closes. 'Listen,' she begins, 'I didn't want—'

But Ghost never finds out what Delilah didn't want for a large paw clamps around her upper arm.

'Flowers for Kane,' says the bear who owns the paw – literally a bear, the woman underneath dressed to fit the animal and big enough to own it.

Delilah nods.

'You're due in the Chrysalis Room,' the bear says. 'Let's go.'

'My invite is coming too.' Delilah indicates Ghost. 'To watch me.'

The bear examines Ghost. 'Do you have a pass for the Chrysalis Room.'

Ghost observes how the question is delivered as a statement, as if the bear already has the answer and is merely playing out the required dialogue without enthusiasm.

'Yes,' says Ghost.

'Show me the pass.'

'All right, no,' says Ghost.

The bear grips Delilah's arm. 'Then you'll see her afterwards.'

Delilah's protests are weak, as if things are immovably set. She turns her face back to Ghost as she is led away, mouthing sorries and indications to wait for her here.

Which Ghost is not going to do.

She watches their path, then follows at a cautious distance, notes the door they slide through at the far end. When she gets there, however, it doesn't open. There is no handle; there isn't even a panel.

She considers, looks around, and then tries to poke a hand through it – which promptly comes up against extreme solidity. Not another projection, then. Saintsdamn it.

Mercifully, her brief door attack seems to have gone unnoticed by the crowd at large, as though – much like the larger party – if they don't know about the Chrysalis Room, it doesn't exist to them. Secrets within secrets. She wonders how many layers there are.

Well. No good standing here like an idiot. Time to make friends, see if she can't snag herself a client for a little question time.

Three fruitful cocktails and five fruitless conversations later, Ghost finds herself in an open side room, contemplating a ceiling covered in snowy-white wings and wishing she'd had less to drink.

'They're real,' comes a voice, 'if you were wondering.'

Ghost turns to find the owner of the voice standing close by. He is handsome, in a predetermined sort of way, as if he'd been made in a factory where they have a set number of models to template from, though they made the mouth of this model a little too wide. His skin is waxy and damp, like he has just walked out of a steam room. Presumably he has partaken of the circulating platters and is currently riding high. How irritating will this interaction be?

'What do you mean?' she asks, dealing in.

'They used to belong to actual birds,' the handsome man replies.

'Huh.' Ghost looks back up at the drooping wings, now cast with a grimly sad tint. 'Why do that? Fake ones can be made just as well.'

'Oh yes. Pay enough and you wouldn't be able to tell the difference.' The almost handsome man nods upwards. 'They're a little tatty and pathetic up close, truth be told. The fake ones often look a lot better, and they don't degrade over time the same way. But that's not the point. The value of a thing, or at least, its perceived value, comes from arbitrary determinations. If it wasn't once part of an organic body that could actually fly, then it's just play-acting, isn't it? And play-acting isn't worth as much on the markets.'

Ghost gives a pointed eye-sweep of the room. 'I feel like the current crowd might disagree.'

The man laughs. 'Ah, that's posturing for you. People with real power don't normally need to display themselves.'

He is notably dressed rather plainly in comparison to the rest of the crowd.

Ghost nods. 'Didn't you just do that by inference?'

The man glances at her and laughs again. 'You're quick.'

Impressed rather than insulted. *Good.*

Ghost indicates a woman standing nearby who sports a pair of thick horns spiralling up from her sculpted hair, the ridges smeared in pearlescent paint. 'I bet those cost a night's worth.'

'Well, naturally,' the man agrees. 'It doesn't matter what they *look* like. It's what she's been told they should cost.'

His eyes rove down the length of Ghost, and quite baldly at that. It goes on a moment too long, too impersonally; the sensation is not unlike being scanned and weighed by a machine.

'Trying to determine *my* worth?' she asks.

'Naturally,' he repeats, his voice vague. 'So what can you do?'

'What are you looking for?' she serves back with what she hopes is a game smile.

The man smiles, and with a definite loss of friendly this time.

'I'm very specific in my tastes, so why don't you tell me about your talents and we'll see if you're a match.'

Ah. He thinks she's a godchild.

She quickly heads him off that road, 'Actually, I'm trying to find someone else, someone I'm supposed to meet. Funny story, I don't know what he looks like. But you seem like the kind of man on handshake terms with everyone who's anyone. Help a helpless out?'

161

She's never been good at doing naïve, but plucking his social-standing string might play.

It works – barely. The man raises an impatient brow.

'His name is Glapissant,' says Ghost. 'He's in tech. I know that doesn't close it in much in this kind of a room, but I don't have a lot to go on. However, I can tell by the expression on your face that you know exactly who I'm talking about; is he famous or something?'

'What do you want with him?' the man asks.

His entire demeanour has changed. She just scored a hit, though it's hard to say what kind.

'I just want to ask him a few questions.' She makes a fast choice – she has to catch his interest somehow. 'I'm not a godchild. I'm a God's Gun.'

It works beautifully – the man's jaw drops. After a moment, he stutters a laugh. 'Alauni-damned, you're a brave little cat.'

'I just want to talk to this man about a godchild he knows,' Ghost says.

The man studies her. Ghost gives back a whole lot of earnest innocence.

'Unregistered, I take it,' he tests.

'So the rumour goes.'

'There aren't any unregistered godchildren here, Si,' says the man. 'Promise.'

The Si is a mocking deference. God's Guns don't get the privilege of a knight's designation.

'Of course not,' Ghost says smoothly, 'but he knows one.'

'What makes you think that?'

'So the rumour goes,' Ghost says again, 'but he could refute it all, of course. Just rumour, after all.'

'After all,' the man agrees, 'though rumours are often worth a lot in a room like this. One well-placed suggestion and suddenly one can find one's value taking a rather bruising tumble.'

'Well, it's just a conversation. A private one, if he prefers.'

'Mm,' the man says. 'But you'll have to do better than that to get to someone like him. See – if you're not a godchild, Glapissant won't meet with you. And even if you were, you'd have to be one of the rare ones. That's the only kind of meeting he'd take.'

'Well,' says Ghost, 'I've got some information that'll interest him. Information that has more value than a magical cocksuck.'

The man's face turns nasty. The effect is so sudden and immediate that Ghost finds herself ready to duck from a swing he might take at her. And then it's gone again in an instant.

'Some might go in for that sort of thing,' the man says primly, calmly enough. If she hadn't just seen the utter disgust on his face, she'd take it for no more than a touch of prudishness. 'And considering how many kambion-fuckers there are at this otherwise illustrious gathering, I can see why you'd think that was the deal. But as we've already established, people do talk, and none of the talk about him has ever run to that taste.'

It's strange, muses Ghost, *how much split thinking goes on in the human head. You can hate and love the same thing at the same time, and take no extra trouble to keep the two juggling away. Is it because he cannot see godchildren as human, so the thought of fucking one of them fills him with as much repulsion as the suggestion that he fuck a dog?*

'My mistake,' says Ghost. 'But he's here, I take it?'

The man shrugs. 'If he was, he'd be in the other building.'

'The other building?'

'You didn't think this was the whole party, did you?' the man says. 'Let me show you.'

163

He leads the way, Ghost eyeing the back of his head as she follows. His hair is slicked down, but too thin to carry the grease, so the effect is limp and wet.

They come out to a balcony, a tiny thing no one would look at twice unless they like riding a vertigo high – but like the rest of this place, there's another layer to it. In this case, a contraption that looks like a crude interpretation of a bird's exoskeleton, complete with stringy feathered wings that look about as able to hold a body aloft as a paper bag. It rests on the balcony edge, just about big enough to fit a human. The youthful figure holding it in place is clutching its tail feathers with the careless air of a toddler gripping the foot of a toy baby.

The man moves confidently forwards. The youngling in charge of the contraption starts strapping him into it. Not one word is exchanged. Another invisible pass to the next hidden layer of this secretive world.

'What is that thing?' asks Ghost.

'A glider,' the man replies.

'To glide where?'

'The other building,' the man says, and points across the vast, empty chasm that yawns between this solid mass and the next.

The glider mech is busy cinching and adjusting. The man waits patiently, his gaze on Ghost.

Ghost peeks over the edge of the balcony. The ground is so far away that it feels like another world, a queasy window into an alien time and space. A parallel set of cords run from the lip of their balcony and arrow across the emptiness to the other building, disappearing into the thickness of a hair strand each. The cords tremble and wobble in the wind. They look about as thick as a thumb. Two thumbs' width of cord and a fistful of feathers and glue holding you from a soaring splatter death.

Ghost gives a short laugh. 'You're a lunatic.'

The man shrugs. 'The building across from us is sealed from the inside. There's no other way in.'

With the help of the glider mech, the man clambers on to the ledge. His trouser leg catches against the stone, riding up enough to flash a small tattoo on the inside of his ankle, the kind of placement that conceals rather than shows off. Ghost manages to catch the rim of a small wheel etched into his skin, its spokes ending in tiny flower bursts, before he adjusts himself.

'You're really going to do this?' asks Ghost incredulously.

'So are you, if you want to meet Glapissant.'

'You don't even know if he's there.'

'I said that *if* he was here, he'd be *there*.' The man nods over to the building behind him, looming an eternity away. 'But to be more accurate, he's not there *yet*. I'd estimate his arrival in about, oh, let's say thirty seconds' time.'

With a scuffle of his polished shoes, he pushes off from the ledge.

Ghost feels her gorge rise. She rushes to the balcony edge.

The man soars into the distance, the feathers on his wings fluttering. The parallel cords whip and sag with his weight. Nothing snaps. He makes it to the other side without fanfare.

That quiet surety. The way no one approached him the whole time they were talking. Not so much with the glazed reserve saved for the inconsequential as a kind of affected blankness – the kind people do when they recognise someone important and are trying to pretend they haven't.

Someone is coming back. The cords give a series of frenzied bounces. A tiny figure launches from the other balcony and grows in size. Ghost and the glider mech watch their approach together in silence. Either the arriving attendee is less practised, or the arrival is less graceful than the take-off, accompanied as it is by jouncing and swearing and creaking and a very ungainly clamber-scramble over the balcony edge by the stranger. Evidently they've been sufficiently filled with whatever secretive tricks they have going on at the next level to return to this one.

Ghost turns to the glider mech as he disentangles the last of the contraption from the sweaty, sweary arrival, who stumbles off into the dark behind them.

'You know how they callian the man who just left?' she asks.

She already knows the answer, but she's hoping that she's wrong, because surely no one can be that much of a bastard.

The glider mech looks at her with the stupefied boredom of the sober at a raging bacchanal. 'Of course I do,' he says.

'How?' When the mech hesitates, she loses patience. 'Speed it up, brainfried, he's escaping me.'

The glider mech tosses her a look of disdain. 'That's Glapissant o'Launitown,' he says, 'and I'll thank you not to surprise-test my faculties, okay, because I haven't touched any party candy all nigh—Hoi!'

Ghost has one leg in the contraption and is hopping clumsily on the other clawed foot in an effort to stay upright.

'Hoi,' the glider mech says again, 'you don't have a pass for the other building!'

How the fuck can all these idiots tell that just by looking at me? What is it, a hairstyle code?

'Help me get over there, or by the saints I'll be a bitch about it,' Ghost snarls at him.

The glider mech shrugs. 'It's your funeral.'

No room to reverse now, the mech is cinching her in and all too soon he's done – 'That's it?' she asks, hating the nerves in her voice, hating that he can hear them as he grins and says,

'That's it,' and she's on the ledge herself, wind whipping at her tiny, pulpable bag of flesh.

She does, in a moment of private shame, contemplate not stepping off.

Then she feels a sudden pressure in the small of her back — a *shove*, is one way to put it — and then

FUCK

FUCK

FUCK

screams the other her inside, and Ghost has to agree.

Death calls from the ground. It feels like her entire body rolls inside out, wet guts in the air and skin all crinkled and folded up next to her bones. Air currents push at her with astonishing force, but the cords hold her on course—

The building in front of her is a blank mountain and there is no time to build any new fear on just how fast it's coming up on her, its impossible growth in less than the heartbeat it takes to keep her alive one moment more, and then it zooms to every corner of her vision and her whole body clenches, preparing for the moment she smears into it like a squashed fly, but then she flits through the opening she barely perceives and something tightens, jolts her hard like a rag doll, stopping her motion enough for the glider mech at the other end to grab hold of her and ease her down.

Buckles and straps are fiddled with, barely felt on her skin, her whole body numb from shock.

'Ah, definitely a glider virgin,' the new mech pronounces with a satisfied smile. Older than their counterpart, and — impressively — even more irritating. 'First time is the fun time, neh?'

She'd quip something sweet right back if she could be sure

that her insides would stay inside when she opened her mouth. Ghost stumbles away from the mech through a dark narrow space, only one thing on her mind now.

Glapissant, you smug rat turd, I've got questions and you've got answers.

This is not the airy halls of the apartment-palace she just flew away from. This is more like a network of hot, dark caves, one leading into another, which lead to two more, and so on, all occupied by owlish creatures in various attitudes.

Some sit at tables, having their fortunes read in the dark blush, lights pitched as low as an erotic nightmare. Some are having other things read, judging by the moans. There are no doors, no delineations of privacy. A medley, a free-for-all, a show. An anxious glut mistaking subjugation for desire, pulled together by that unspoken feeling they seem to sense in each other. Or maybe they're just so bored that anything excessive seems like a good time. An odd smell surrounds one such coupling, so forcible it makes Ghost step back in surprise – a metallic stink that hangs heavy and razor-sharp on the air.

She can feel its pull, that longing to live in the velvet dark like this, that floating comfort of a dream. The work comes in making your wake life as good to be in as your dream life, because if you neglect it, you'll soon find yourself chasing worse and worse ways to spend more time dreaming than being awake. And a whole life spent asleep is a quicker way to death.

Sooner or later you have to wake up.

Ghost makes a hasty exit and selects another opening at random from which echo shouts, and hopefully not of the coupling kind. The lights in here are an eerie shadow-blue and in those dark bleach casts, everyone looks dead. Blue is the safe colour, Delilah said, but right now Ghost doesn't feel it.

She heads towards a small group of people standing in front of a squat man in a face hood who shout-mutters phrases across their heads. Ghost hovers near the back, trying to make out the game, but it's not a big crowd, and the squat nuntias raises his voice, his face hood's beak pointed directly towards her.

'Buying or selling? Buying or selling?' he croaks.

Ghost hesitates, floundering.

'Come, come,' the squat nuntias coaxes impatiently, 'you can only be here if you're one or t'other, buying or selling?'

'Buying,' Ghost says.

'Very good, very good – now this next one, Ladies, Laerds and Lords,' quick as a blink he's back to addressing the crowd at large, '*this* one is from our very own pelleren in the next room!' His fingers hold up a small vial for all to see. 'Our pelleren's talents are known far and wide – his deft hand at floating and pitching has awed every 'launitowner who's ever seen it – *very* desirable, very desirable *indeed*, one of the strongest talents in the dis', Ladies, Laerds and Lords, which is why we start *this* bidding at a thousand trick, come on, a thousand a vial, who'll give me a thousand?'

It's blood in the vial.

Got to be.

But – a thousand trick? Over a *year* of electrical power, just for a spoonful of some pusher's body juice? It's an obscene joke. Ghost feels a scoff at her teeth – but already hands in the crowd are going up, three at least, and the nuntias goes to it, rapidly pitting them against each other, holding the vial up all the while, its sloped edges giving off a mean glint, the liquid inside coloured black in the room's shadows.

They're buying godchild blood, and judging by the moans, it isn't the only bodily fluid for sale. But why? What could anyone

169

possibly do with the blood? There's never been a successful synthesis of whatever it is that makes a godchild a godchild. The best the biology meddlers have been able to come up with so far is a weak ability to tell when someone has used their magic – fluctuations in energy fields or some such; she doesn't pretend to understand how – and there's the ever-thriving market in trinkets and salves and potions and wearable items to ward off magic or bring it forth, not that any of that junk actually works.

Saints, if everyone knew there was a thousand-trick market for godchild blood, they'd be selling off their own kids for the fortune . . .

Ghost feels a shove at her side and stiffens, reaching out automatically and clutching at the body there, pitching forwards and reeling the attacker into the nearest wall.

Her attacker gives an outraged squeal and sags. It's Delilah. Her bare legs fold up, knees grazing her chin.

'Saints, I'm sorry,' Ghost says, 'I tend to react badly to being touched without prior warn—'

Delilah's giggling cuts her off. Her skin has a sheen and her eyes won't focus, sliding aimlessly around the room. When Ghost tries to help her up, she can barely stand unaided and almost falls down again.

'I take it blue isn't your favourite colour,' Ghost says.

Delilah giggles some more and mumbles under her breath. It sounds like 'no virgins here'.

She's high as a cloud – too high. And in this den of eager hyenas? Someone's going to mistake that fake registration tattoo on her neck for a real one and start advancing, and she's in no state to stop anything she might not want.

Ghost looks around and curses. Delilah's of no further use, not like this. Either Ghost wastes her time standing guard over her for the next however many hours until she comes down, or they get out of here and she can come down in safer environs.

Besides, she's never going to find that shit-weasel Glapissant in all this. He's greased his way to ground by now, and even if he hasn't and she does find him, he'll just play with her some more. She doesn't have the power to do a damn thing in this murky place.

'Where we going?' Delilah mumbles, a solid ten minutes into Ghost dragging her around in her efforts to find a way out.

'Home,' Ghost says shortly.

'Your bed or mine?' Delilah leers, which is only alluring when her head isn't lolling all over the place and she doesn't look like she's two steps from a vomitarium.

Trouble.

Nothing but trouble with this girl.

CHAPTER 15

The Consilium, Blackheart
Three Months Ago

The collar of this saintsdamned fashionable jacket is too tight.

The lights in this saintsdamned marble room are too bright.

The drone of this Consilium meet is simultaneously soporific and intermittently jarring, as if his body is demanding sleep but his mind, sensing a threat, keeps jerking him awake.

Wyll looks out across the sea of faces, a faceless sea, elevated like an island on the King's throne. This used to be Art's vantage point, above, away: a single node from which all radiates, London's powerful spread out from the Consilium's round table like spokes on a wheel, behatted and outfitted in the colours of their district. Each district ruler is sat at the table's rim, with representatives spreading out behind them like a pie wedge-shaped cloak.

This is what power sees. Strange, lonely, dislocating, intoxicating – as though you could disappear underneath the power itself.

One face is turned towards Wyll with a contemplative air – Julias Consilias Dracones o'Rhyfentown, the silver-haired head of what remains of Art's extended family. For decades now he has trodden a careful, successful line, growing from severe diminishment to quiet, fat power, siphoned off from the distant relative on the throne like a tic on a dog.

Wyll dredges up a quick montage, formed from hasty lessons with Brune. Julias has reached the autumn of his life without one official lover ever announced. He keeps to himself, rattling around the Dracones seat in northern Rhyfentown alone, save a retinue of serving vastos. He stays in the background of the political arena, rarely imposing his opinion on the Consilium. One of the more unpopular district heads in Rhyfentown's recent history, by all accounts. Not loud enough and not quick enough to violence for the tastes of his district's rowdy populace.

Wyll strains to recall what he was told about Art's relationship with Julias. Cordial in public. In private? But why is he still staring at Wyll? Did they have an argument recently, or—

Saints, is his illusion slipping?

Wyll glances at Brune, but she is busy mediating a debate. Lillath hovers at the back of the room. A pre-arranged signal – the flash of her tiny handheld light directed into his face – would alert Wyll that something looks wrong, but there is no flash. Lillath stands still and calm.

Relax. Between the stupid high collar they have him in today that lines up to his cheekbones and shields half his face, and the sheer distance from the throne to the rest of the crowd, they can barely see who might even be behind it, never mind any nuance of expression he is failing to convey, or some minor facial scar he forgot to include.

He watches a vastos place a tablet in front of Julias, and then wait respectfully as he reads the message written on the tablet, erases it and writes a brief reply.

Wyll tracks the vastos as he weaves his way through the

chairs, crossing the district divides and heading into the pearl- and copper-coloured wedge of Alaunitown. He hands the message tablet to Horath, the notoriously grim-faced personal vastos of the Lady Orcade, renowned head of Alaunitown, today dressed in sprays of white feather. Horath passes it to his Lady, who begins to read the message—

'—Sire?'

It is said quietly in his ear by his own attending vastos. There is a mildly anxious cut to the Sire, as if somewhere, something has gone wrong.

Wyll raises his head. *Sire.* Today, Sire is him.

He gives the room the clear nod required for his attention.

The Lord of Evrontown, a fatuous idiot of mean capabilities ('a hearty, straightforward thinker', Brune had recently sternly corrected him), nods back.

'Forgive me for interrupting our King's internal struggles,' he says, fleshy lips curled into an unconvincing smile. 'Perhaps he is meditating on his recent news. I think I can speak for all when I attest to my own preoccupation with it and all its implications. It was quite the shock.'

Wyll stares at him with blank incomprehension.

Evrontown mistakes it for silent aggression.

'I mean to say,' he continues more sharply, 'it is strange to me that after announcing the Lady Finnavair as your official lover, you now hide her away from plain sight like a guilty secret. Has there been a recant? Has the Lady changed her mind?'

Some laughter greets this, soon stifled when the Lady Orcade, Lady of Alaunitown, speaks up.

'Evrontown,' she chides, 'who has time for gossip when they've a district to run?'

Evrontown shuts his mouth. Orcade smooths back an errant

strand of hair and looks around the Consilium. She has the kind of manner that seems quiet and retiring until she chooses to draw attention to herself, at which point she could sit in silence for a minute and still hold the room.

'Our King,' she continues into the tense hush, 'has been London's ruler now for nineteen glorious years. He has spent most of his life in service to it, the youngest monarch ever to take the Sword. His dedication to his people cannot be faulted, even if, perhaps, we haven't always agreed on his ideas.' Orcade gives Wyll a reassuring smile. 'He does come from a historically rambunctious family.'

General uneasy mirth greets this succinct assessment of decades of intermittent civil war under Art's notorious father, his predecessor.

'The demands upon him cannot be overstated,' Orcade continues. 'I think he has earned a little privacy – some time with the lovely Lady Finnavair in peace.'

'Some time away from the pressures of the Sword,' suggests Gwanharatown. 'Saints know I could do with a break myself. Ha.'

'Ha,' Iochitown joins in. 'I know just how you feel. It's quite exhausting, isn't it.'

More hearty gobbling as the group competes over the strains of leadership. They don't know Art is dead, but to them he might as well be – they've already decided that his time is over. Vultures. Nothing but fat vultures picking over a carcase.

High up in the rafters comes a rustle of heavy wings, and the faintest sounds of hissing.

It takes Wyll a moment to realise that he has inadvertently conjured vultures. With a sudden prickle of sweat he dismisses them. No one else appears to have noticed.

Evrontown clears his dogged throat. 'Still, we are wondering whether Si Finnavair will be making an official appearance at some point, as is the usual protocol.'

Do not look at me every time a question is asked that you don't know how to answer; it makes you appear weak, admonishes a past Brune in his head. *Give yourself more time by repeating the question as a puzzled phrase.*

'An official appearance,' Wyll echoes.

When nothing more appears to be forthcoming, Evrontown takes the reins once more.

'After all, as the acknowledged lover of London's only King, congratulations are in order.'

'She is a knight in one of the most high-profile Caballaria circuits,' Wyll rejoins. 'Sometimes she has a bout almost every week, or so it feels.'

It's enough for protocol.

Usually.

'Sire,' Evrontown maddeningly persists, 'please forgive me for correcting you, but Si Finnavair has not been at Caballaria for weeks. All her scheduled bouts have been cancelled. She has gone underground like a fox to its hole.'

A smattering of laughter greets this sly allusion to her roots. Art had always insisted the crowd who loved her as a street orphan-made-knight would love her as a street orphan-made-knight-made-royal paramour – but while the general crowd might adore a romantic story, the rich and powerful are far more pragmatic. All they see is a public stunt and a poor-quality choice.

'Understandably, she might want a little space post-announcement,' Wyll barely hears the Lord chuntering on, 'but hiding at the palace suggests a lack of training in the proper protocols. Your public gesture at her last bout a few weeks ago, while romantic, was hardly appropriate.'

With an effort, Wyll reaches for the rehearsed lie. 'Cair Lleon is working very hard on an official event of declaration, to which you will of course be honoured guests. I'm told it'll be the gathering of the season.'

'What about the rumours?'

'What rumours?' Wyll's tone is more than a little sharp.

Evrontown looks flustered. He glances around for support, but the hall is awash in avid silence.

'If we could just see her—' he begins.

Brune is cutting him the look that means *shut this down immediately*.

'Si Finnavair is not a dancing horse,' Wyll says. 'She will undoubtedly make herself known again when she feels able.'

'Is she currently staying at the palace?'

That was Gwanharatown, a shrewd woman with manner-isms reminiscent of a hunting bird. When she dives in, she does it fast.

'Why do you need to know where she is?' Wyll counters.

'My Lords and Ladies,' Brune cuts in, 'is the whereabouts of the King's bed-player really a topic for today's political debate? We have much to achieve in this session, so let's stay on course.'

'Are you keeping her against her will?' asks Iochitown, his brush moustache a-bristle.

Wyll can't help it – he glances at Lillath. She is mute at the back, too far away for him to see the expression on her face, but her arms are crossed and she is still. So no help there.

'What a ridiculous and frankly dangerous suggestion,' he shoots at Iochitown.

'Then why all the dodging, Sire? A simple question needs a simple answer. Where is Si Finnavair?'

Wyll's temper clamours for his attention like an anxious dog.

His gaze swings around the room. Each pie wedge of district representatives is mute in their eagerness to hear their leaders speak for them. The leaders themselves are *agreeing*, for saints' sake, backing each other up, when normally by now, according to Art's lifelong complaints, they'd be at each other's throats.

This feels like a coordinated effort.

Julias Dracones, Lord of Rhyfentown, rises to his feet with his hands raised and says, 'Please, please.'

The rarity of this event does what the King's authority could not – it quiets the room.

'We are alarming and confusing our King,' says Julias. 'That should not be our intent. Let us speak plain for once.'

A ripple of wry chuckles.

'Sire,' continues Julias, 'the problem, as ever, is of rumouring. For an explanation, I turn to our esteemed Lady of Marvoltown.'

Marvoltown, a rotund jollity of a woman who can normally be counted on to inject levity into the proceedings, has a solemn look on her face.

'A concerning report has recently reach me,' she quietly begins, 'from the guard knights who cover the area of Daeccenham. Several weeks ago, they found a body in an underground tunnel. With no family coming forwards to claim it, it's been a difficult time with identification. But it does quite dramatically resemble the Lady Finnavair.'

A thunderous silence reigns in the hall.

'This sounds like a joke,' Brune begins.

'Perhaps,' Marvoltown cuts in, 'an identification from the King himself—?'

'You want our ruler to take time out from holding London together to personally eyeball a rotting corpse?'

'Of his own deceased lover? Yes! The implications alone—'

The spot that Lillath currently occupies flashes with sudden, alarming intensity.

The signal. He's losing the illusion, fuck, *fuck*.

Around Wyll rises the sound of arguing voices like angry birds taking flight, while he sits amid the cacophony and desperately tries to control himself—

A sudden, bone-jarring crash cuts through the noise. There, near the back of the room.

It is Garad, standing, having dashed their chair against the marble floor. Tall, terrible, silent.

For one moment, Wyll is deathly afraid of them. For one moment, it feels as though the entire room is, too.

'I know Fin personally,' says Garad into the quiet. 'I will identify the body.'

The Consilium watches their long-legged figure stalk towards the doors. Guard knights eye them as they pass, hands tightening. The Master of the Key frantically scrambles at the massive locks and finally, breathing a sigh of relief, opens the doors to let them out.

Lucan closes the door and rounds on Wyll. 'What the fuck happened in there?'

'What happened? What happened? I'm sick of pretending to be someone I'm not,' Wyll says, 'that's what happened.'

He is crowded on all sides by Art's Saith in a private antechamber, away from prying ears.

'You were doing fine until they started asking about Fin,' Lucan says.

'Listen, lying may come easily to you all,' Wyll bites back, 'but I have a problem with lounging around and talking about people as if they're still alive.'

'We don't know that Finnavair is dead,' Lucan says. 'That's just something Red boasted about.'

'It wasn't a boast,' Wyll says. 'It was a confession.'

'Oh, for saints' sake, they're just trying to score wounds—'

'They are,' Lillath cuts in, 'but they're not shooting blanks. It's Finnavair they found.'

A thunderous silence greets her statement.

'Why didn't you tell us?' Lucan asks.

'I didn't know right away. The local guard had already found and removed the body before we got to it. Discreet investigations took time to verify the particulars.' She looks unusually grim about the mouth. 'The discovery was supposed to be contained, but obviously one of the guards was unable to resist temptation. I'll find out which one.'

'Who cares who it was? It's out, and now we have to do something about it.' Lucan closes his eyes and sinks on to a chair. 'Saints, what a mess.'

Brune looks old. 'Well, at least Garad stepped in. We can control the narrative through them.'

Lucan utters a muffled scoff. 'You thought that was rehearsed? That was Garad gone rogue. Lucky they didn't have their sword on them, or they might have started swinging it.'

'So . . . what are they going to do?'

'What do you think? Go and eyeball a corpse in Daeccenham, drawing every eye in London with them as they stride. And saints help anyone who stands in their way.'

Brune hesitates. 'If it really is Si Fin, can we not ask Garad to lie, buy us more time—?'

Lucan brays a laugh.

Lillath shakes her head. 'I think we've lost this one,' she says softly.

'That attack in there was too coordinated,' Brune muses. 'Si Finnavair is dead. Red had a visitor recently, but none of the capturers caught it and none of the guards saw anything. Something is going on. Someone has a plan. I just can't see it. We're running out of time.'

'Do you think they know about Art?' Lucan is anxious, frizzing. 'Saints, what do we do if they know?'

He's like a panicked child who wet the bed and can't face his mother finding out.

That's his father Edler's voice in Wyll's head, sounding cold and distantly amused.

'We keep Art alive a while longer so we can find out what's going on,' says Lillath.

'Right,' Lucan says. 'Because up until now we've been sitting down and waiting for the answers to shit themselves out of us.'

Lillath makes a haughtily scrunched face. 'Crude, Lux.'

'Wyll can buy us a little more time, at best,' Brune says. 'You can't illusion up a personality. People are starting to notice that the King is – how do I put it? – out of sorts.'

'Come on, he just needs more coaching. He's been doing well up to now, hasn't he?' Lucan says to the others.

'No,' Wyll snaps. 'I'm not doing it any more.'

Lucan spreads his hands. 'It's just a few more days.'

'Did you not hear me say no?'

The room's energy shifts, growing taut.

'I heard you,' Lucan says.

'It's as if you want to pretend he's not dead,' Wyll says, 'when he very much is. This is stupid.'

'Stupid? I'm stupid for mourning him?'

'You're not mourning him. That's my point. You're behaving

like a child screwing its eyes shut so what it can't see doesn't
exist.'

It is embarrassingly easy to move away from Lucan's wild
swing.

He is not a fighter, Wyll reminds himself. He probably never
had to move fast in all his life.

The rest move equally slow. They catch hold of Lucan, wres-
tle him 'til he's clamped down. Lucan doesn't break free. He
doesn't want to. He just wants to show his anger, not use it. He
subsides.

'You know,' he pants, 'acting like you've stoically accepted
his death is the same as my pretence that he's still alive. You're
avoiding the pain you know is there waiting for you.'

Wyll scoffs. 'You don't know my pain. I lost a brother.'

'And I lost my oldest friend, you cold fucken prick. I've spent
my life with him. At his side, loving him, supporting him,
arguing with him. Most of my entire *life*.' Lucan stares him
down.

Wyll looks away, oddly affected by his admission.

'Could I ever replace Art for you?' he asks. 'In all
seriousness?'

Lucan looks surprised, then a little uncomfortable. 'No. Of
course not.'

'Then why do you have me pretending I can?'

Lucan sighs, a gusty, defeated sigh.

'I have to go.' Wyll stands up. 'I have a bout coming up to
train for. You know, in my other life as the Sorcerer Knight.'

'It isn't fair,' Brune says quietly to Lucan, 'what we've been
asking him to do. It's time to let Art go. Plan for what comes
next.'

Wyll doesn't wait for the formality of goodbyes. They know

where he is going and where to find him. He cannot escape them. He cannot escape this. He knows his constant rudeness makes them dislike him. They see it as a lack of respect. What they don't understand is that he uses it as a wall between him and the rest of the world. It shuts him out, but it also keeps him safe.

And it keeps them all safe from him.

When he reaches his rooms in the Royal Stable and closes the door on the world beyond, there is someone waiting for him. He is about to bawl out the intruder – how many people are getting access to his supposedly private rooms nowadays? – until he realises who it is.

His hackles lower.

The visitor is seated in the sunken receiving room with his legs crossed, tight and compact as ever, fingertips pressed together in that irritatingly performative intellectual manner he always adopted.

'You're losing control,' says Edler, watching his son sweep in and collapse on to the bed with his head in his hands.

'Go away,' Wyll tells the floor. 'I want to be alone.'

'Well, *I'm* not the one conjuring me.'

Wyll rubs the heels of his hands against his face. Why does his father always turn up when least wanted? Is that what he uses him for? To face the things he doesn't want to face?

'They're weak,' the Edler illusion says. 'They're letting London fall into the wrong hands. Wyll. Listen to me.'

'I can't help but listen to you,' Wyll snaps back.

'I understand your fear, but you *know* what needs to happen.' Edler is insistent. 'Don't you remember all the conversations we had about London's future?'

'How could I forget?' snarls Wyll. 'While the other kids I

183

knew were playing with their toys, I was trapped in your study with you talking politics.'

'Don't be pathetic,' Edler says. 'Childhood is preparation for manhood. And I prepared you, did I not? I prepared you for a world that would have chewed you up. You know what it takes to survive. It takes power. It takes being on top. And right now you're someone else's pet, just like you always are, just like you always have been.'

Leave me alone, Wyll tries to think, but Edler takes up his whole head and there is no space for anyone else.

'You know what it will take,' that awful wheedling voice urges. 'What will it take?'

And just like it was when Edler was alive, Wyll has no power not to answer. 'A godchild in control of London again,' he mutters.

Edler sits back, satisfied.

'That was your dream, not mine,' Wyll insists.

Edler leans forwards. 'My dream is yours now. There are only two choices, Wyll, remember? Predator or prey. Which are you?'

The words are painfully familiar, every phrase said a thousand times before, dredged up from the hazy child memories of his father. With a desperate gesture, he winks Edler out of existence.

Then he curls up on the bed, unable to stop imagining Lillath watching him, suspicion darkening her features like storm clouds.

CHAPTER 16

Garad's Apartment, Evrontown
Two Weeks Ago

'After the disaster party,' Ghost says, 'I went to Leon. I will admit, I didn't tell him everything. Didn't really think the whole "me being an unregistered godchild" thing was information he necessarily required at that exact point in time.' She pauses. 'But it was enough to get him all riled up.'

Wardogs Bar, Alaunitown
Two Months Ago

When Ghost arrives, Leon barely turns to acknowledge her. His attention is dragged elsewhere, eyes on the action, forearms leaning on the sides of the fight ring, within blood-spray distance of an imminent Wardogs fight.

Wardogs, the shadow twin to the Caballaria, grown out of street businessfolks' ability to provide for a need when the more sanctioned version fails. It used to be huge, too big and too established to take down, as swollen as London's population of poor, all those who could never afford to settle any dispute in the proper way.

Even the advent of the public Caballaria circuit several years ago, designed to be a free version to serve every citizen from every background, didn't kill Wardogs. Some fights need to get settled in private, with fewer eyes on them. Wardogs is not lawless. It has its own strict codes and the punishments for transgressions are generally harsher. It is run by people who know very well the exact cost of a life.

Insisting they meet at a Wardogs fight to talk instead of a bar or his apartment, like a normal person, is another test, one of the small tests Leon is giving her, probing her ability to move comfortably in the world he inhabits. She'd find it offensive if she wasn't smart enough to realise that it's his way of recovering his pride after the kicking she gave it when she made him look weak at that first meet with Delilah.

She brings Leon up to speed. Moth and her band of snarly strays. The strange party Delilah took her to, and the encounter with the slippery Glapissant.

When his name comes up, Leon gives a big sniff.

'That rat-fucker,' he says.

'You know him?'

'Reputationally. He's some big grease in tech. Rich as rich is rich. From Senzatown, originally.'

Ghost thinks of the allegiance tattoo tucked away on the man's ankle. She knows she's seen it before, but she can't dredge up where. A wheel with flowers on the spoke ends. The wheel symbol is classic Senzatown.

So he has old allegiance to some Senzatown notable. So what? Everyone collects allegiances as they move through life. And now he's a big tech man in Alaunitown, the big tech dis'. What does it mean? Does it mean anything?

She does wish she could remember where she's seen that damn tattoo before.

'What would such a man want with a soothsayer?' she muses.

Leon grunts. 'One that actually works? They'd be a trick machine for anyone, never mind some big rich business just dying to know how to get even bigger and richer. Trouble is, I've never heard of a soothsayer could actually predict anything useful. The good ones are mad and the rest are cons.'

'Cass wasn't mad. She was a schoolteacher.'

'Then maybe she was a con. That'd certainly be enough to get her dead, if someone like him found out she wasn't on the up.'

'She was real,' says Ghost. 'She predicted her colleague's unfortunate ending, didn't she? Anyway, whatever Delilah says, I'm not convinced Cass is dead, and she didn't run off because of Glapissant.'

'Neh, she is,' Leon says, 'and who's to say?'

'Oh Leon, where's your positivity?' Ghost reproaches. 'I can find her, just give me some more time.'

'I wasn't funning. Cass Grenwald is dead. Her body got found this morning, after you went out dancing with the local kambion-fuckers at their sky orgy.'

Ghost feels her skin furred by some internal breeze. She searches Leon's face for confirmation, but there's no need. Leon wouldn't lie about that. There's no trick to be had for a dead body, and neither of them will get paid.

'Where?' she asks.

'They dredged her up from the river.'

Fuck. She wonders if Delilah knows. 'Murder?' Ghost asks, while her heart thumps and a handsome-faced man with a too wide mouth and a clammy sheen to his skin dances through her head.

'All I know, it's a drowning. It'll be stamped as self-end for the least amount of fuss.' Leon sounds satisfied, like he has it all worked out. 'Sweet lady schoolteacher with a dangerous side-play, for trick or for kicks, maybe both. Who's to say. Either way, it don't matter. Our job ain't investigatory vastos, now, is it?'

'You just said they're going to stamp it self-end. That isn't much of an investigation, Leon.' A thought strikes Ghost. 'I could talk to the guard, tell them what I've found out about Glapissant.'

Leon grunts, the closest he gets to a laugh. 'Why?'

'Why? To find her killer.'

'What for?'

Ghost stares at him. 'What for?' she repeats.

'If they don't like the verdict, her family can open up a dispute,' he says with dismissive finality.

'That doesn't stop me telling my side to the guard, help them out.'

'You want to stay unnoticed, don't you? Have yourself a nice new shady life? Making a fuss with the local guard about a dead unregistered godchild with shady connections is the opposite of that, I'd say. You're a Gun now. Act like one.'

He's got a point, says the other Ghost.

Around them, the ring fills with spectators – a mix of roughs who work from the bottom rungs of the local syndicates, and family types, their kids scrabbling in the dirt floor to pick up empty trick coin casings and trade them between each other in gleefully nonsensical deals. When the fight starts, they'll be hoisted onto their parents' backs to get a good view of the violence.

Leon grunts as the woman next to him turns to speak to her neighbour and the brim of her enormous hat grazes his ear. It's an overdone creation, heavy with animals fashioned from varied metals and tinkling with district charms. It's probably her best hat too, Ghost thinks, as if the woman is out to a Saints' Day celebration instead of some grunt fight.

'What else did they do?' Leon asks. 'That activist group.'

'You mean apart from drugging me and dragging me to an antiques shop in the anus end of the dis' for a little chat-me-up?' Ghost shrugs out the smooth lie. 'Nothing.'

'They just let you go?' he asks her.

'All they got was a Gun tracking Cass down. I don't know what they wanted to hear, but it wasn't that.'

She side-eyes him, watching the rumination. Leon is one of those whose efforts at thought show up like his skull is transparent and his brain a whir of turning cogs.

'What'd you say the ringmaster gave her name as?' he asks.

'Moth,' Ghost supplies. 'But it's made up.'

'I've heard that name before, recently. She's a seller. She's got—' He falters into silence.

'Got what?'

Leon turns to her with renewed energy. 'You need to go back there.'

Ghost scoffs. 'What? No. I told you, they're all shady as shit. I don't want anything more to do with them.'

'Well, you'd best pop a change-of-heart pill, because I want you to.'

She studies Leon's face for clues. 'Why?'

'There's rumours about that one, and there's trick to be got if we can prove those rumours true,' Leon says.

'What rumours?'

He won't tell you, and then you can stop trusting him.

But he does.

'She's got a weapon,' he says, with the certain authority of the gossip fiend. 'It's some new shit to catch godchildren with. How about that? No more guesswork. You just point this thing at anyone you like and you can see if they're a godchild, registered or no. It'll make our lives as easy as breathing.'

Machine sounds in the darkness. Mechanical breathing. Clicks and such. It felt like something really big in the room. Or maybe it *was* the room. And then that feather touch on her face.

'There's nothing that can do that,' Ghost tries.

Did it with you, though, didn't it?

'This is Alaunitown,' says Leon. 'They might be a sneaky load of bastards, but they got the resources and the brains here.' His tone is the begrudging respect afforded to a dis' that can do something better than his own place of origin.

'What, a new Calevel?' Ghost says. 'A holy sword for the modern age?'

'You can mock all you like, but I've heard about this thing from higher-ups.' He gives an authoritative sniff. 'People like that en't got no reason to lie.'

In Ghost's experience, social status in no way guarantees reliable intelligence. The elite are as prone as anyone else to get all excitable about made-up stories, and are more often a target for them in a bid to siphon off some of their carefully hoarded power.

'I'd never lay down a bet without proof, though, so let's get some.' Leon eyes her. 'How's about it?'

He has the starry-eyed gaze of a cockfight regular who thinks he's on to a jackpot chanticleer.

'How do you think I get proof?' says Ghost. 'Moth and I didn't exactly become firm friends.'

'You're in with them now. Find a way.'

'I'm not *in* with them.'

'You just got taken to an orgy by one of 'em. I'd say you're at least on speaking terms.'

'It wasn't an orgy,' Ghost says, but without much conviction.

'What's the problem?' demands Leon.

'I don't want anything more to do with those jacksters, that's the problem.'

He gives her a patient look. 'Sometimes in life we have to cosy up to people we don't much like to get what we want.'

'Don't patronise me, Leon,' Ghost says.

Any reply he might be mustering is drowned in the sudden swell of noise that greets the two fighters striding out into the pit before them. One is a bare-chested bear dressed in cheap drags, a real street thug – but the other has some good armour and a couple of throwing knives that flash as a nice set. He has the posture, too, a residual pushback of the shoulders that speaks of his past. Ex-Caballaria, for sure.

The nuntias confirms it with a guttural precis of each fighter's back story. Disgraced ex-knights enjoy a dubious double-edge on the Wardogs circuits, admiration and envy turned to hate. There are few things a crowd like this enjoys more than the high brought low.

The noise dies down. They circle each other, strung tense.

Leon keeps his eyes on the fighters as he murmurs to Ghost, 'You like this?'

'Not really my scene.'

'I could enter you. We could make some tidy trick. You're so tiny the odds against you'd be laughably low, and they'd love you being an ex-knight.'

'What are you talking about?'

'You. Ex-knight. It's obvious.'

'Is it?' Ghost says, while her heart hammers.

Leon smirks. The ex-knight in the ring goes for the first hit, a vicious left swipe with his short sword.

'Nice life,' Leon says above the roar around them. 'Makes me wonder why you left it.'

'Neh? Why'd you leave yours?' retorts Ghost.

'I asked first.'

'Ask again,' she replies through a forced smile, 'and I'll get sad.'

Leon holds up his hands. 'Curiosity saves.'

'In my opinion,' Ghost says acidly, 'people only invoke that idiotic "curiosity saves" proverb to justify their own fucken nosiness. Curiosity won't save you this time, Leon.'

'It got me an awful lot on you,' he remarks. Instead of his usual defensive aggression, Leon's all poise. Alarm bells begin to ring just as he confirms the reason for his new-found confidence. 'I know who you've been haunting in yer spare time, Ghost.'

Ghost grinds out a laugh. 'You can't be so stupid as to have followed me again.'

'Why d'you come to Alaunitown?' he asks.

'Same reasons you did.'

'Rhyfen-accented with Marvol tats on yer skin, as if you deliberately want to confuse people so they can't decide what you are.'

'People move around, these times. It's not so strange.' Ghost eyes him. 'You did.'

'Know what it cost me to come here and start again?

Everything. People only move when they're desperate or they're up to something. And you, secret sister to a dead street-rat knight, I know why you came here, *here* of all places, to this part of the dis'. They don't live that far away, do they? Walking distance, in fact. Close enough for you to go visiting often, standing for hours opposite, waiting for them to come out for a little look. And then come out they did, one time, and I couldn't believe my very own peepers.' The naked, punchable triumph in his voice. 'The Silver Angel themself, eh? That's who you came here for. Not me.'

The best thing, according to Ghost, about being trained as a knight — it taught her how to control the violence ever present at her fingertips, the muscles that scream for immediate release when confronted with any kind of threat. All right, occasion- ally it spills out before she can leash it — nobody's perfect. But imagine how much worse she'd be if she'd never had that train- ing. Imagine what kind of animal.

So when she does not immediately punch Leon, she feels rather proud of herself.

She'd never had him down as a tiptoeing follow-artist, not even after that first time he claimed to have trailed her to her apartment. She'd presumed he'd just got lucky, that was all. She'd had a whisky or two, wasn't paying attention. Who'd have thought a shambling mountain could be so good at keep- ing hidden? People surprise you. Think you have them down, and then — something like this.

'So I'm a crazy fan,' Ghost says. 'You got me.'

Leon guffaws. 'Neh, you're a violent ex-knight who bolted from her old life, wants to become a Gun, friends up with god- child activists and hangs around the door of one of the most powerful people in the First Kingdom, who also just *happens* to

be a known godchild-hater. I'm no brain, but I'm no fool neither. And you've been taking me for a ride ever since you talked
yer way through my door.'

Saints-be-fucked.

He thinks she's an activist.

He thinks she and Moth's group are working together.

Leon interprets her silence as victory. 'I told you when we
first met, there are three kinds of people want to be a Gun. Do-
the-jobs, vengeance-seekers, and sympathisers. I had you
pegged as a vengeance-seeker, if I'm honest. But I reckon I have
the right of it now. You been playing a real dangerous game
with me, and I think it's time I deal in.'

'Are you . . .?' Ghost stops, concentrates on the fight, trying
hard to swallow the laugh she can feel bubbling up. 'Are you
trying to *turn* me, Leon?'

He can sense her mirth. Unsurprisingly, it does not go down
well. But, come *on* – couldn't be helped. Both sides thinking she
works for the other? Both trying to recruit her for double games
at the same time? Life is sometimes just too much. You have to
laugh, or you'd scream 'til you coughed up blood.

'You listen to me, you sneak.' Leon's tone now has an admira-
bly vicious tint. 'I don't know what you and yer kambion-loving
friends are planning to do to the Silver Angel and I don't want to
know. I leave what's not my business well alone, you hear? But
I'd lay down a ton of trick you don't want them finding out about
it ahead of time. Because, girl, that's not just one of the most
powerful Caballaria knights there ever was that you keep visiting to stare at, but the palace too, and then you're *royally* fucked.'

He sounds almost joyful.

'You've got it all wrong,' Ghost grinds out, but she can see it's
too late. His head has already galloped off where it will.

Ah, let him think it's political, the other her says. *What matters is that he's utterly correct about one thing — you do not want Garad Gaheris knowing about you.*

Not yet.

'I don't want to know anything about it,' Leon warns. 'The less I know, the better.'

'Just enough to get what you want,' Ghost mutters.

'Neh, a better life,' he sharply retorts. 'Guilt's a luxury when you spend all your time trying to keep your head out the water.'

Inevitable, really, though she'd hoped he wouldn't turn out so damn predictable. It hurts when people behave the way she expects, because she always expects people to behave like the selfish shits they are, underneath it all — her included, to be fair — but there's always the tiny hope that they won't. Cynics are the most hopeful people around, desperate to be proven wrong, taking it harder than most when they're not.

'Now, you could kill me for what I know about you,' reasons Leon, 'but I got some insurance against that. I know it doesn't look it, but I got people primed to miss me. I played my first hand in that game soon after you showed up, you understand me?'

'What, Leon, going to such trouble?' Ghost simpers. 'If I didn't know better, I'd think you're keeping a heartbeat back for me.'

'That's just me playing it safe,' Leon evenly replies, looking out over the sanded pit. 'Old habits. Truth is, I don't think you got it in you to end me. I reckon you're sweeter than you like people to think.'

The ex-knight takes a thick punch to the forearm — he spits a shock as his hand opens without his consent, dropping one of his two knives to the ground, where it's kicked away from reach.

His arm hangs at his side, numbed into uselessness – but he has one more.

'Well, shit, now you're just being nasty,' says Ghost.

Leon doesn't laugh. 'I need this. Ain't had a break in a long time. My life's mostly been near-misses. You wouldn't understand how much harder that is than just five decades of drudge. Low expectations is a much easier way to live. Sadly, I've one of those self-torturing dispositions, cos I can never help wanting to be back on top. But I never am. And you . . .' He gives a helpless shrug. 'You were, and yet you took a jump to the bottom. Reckon we're two of a kind there. But I can put you back on top. I can. I can get you noticed again. All it'll take is a word, here and there. Just a little trickle to get a flood of interest in you going.'

The air smells hot with violence. Ghost snorts, the sound lost in the grunts of the fighters, the thump and rattle of desperate feet on sanded grit. This is the problem with hanging around the same person for too long. Through pure osmosis, they come to know how to hurt you best. Is this how it always is, a part of every human stratum, no matter the upbringing or the current means?

Are we just an untrustworthy breed?

She turns to Leon, reluctance grinding out of every word. 'And just how am I supposed to get back into Moth's place to lay eyes on this blessed weapon? I can't imagine she'll answer to a polite knock.'

Leon raises brows. 'Did Fin ever tell you how she first met me?'

Ghost sighs. Back in another lifetime, a Rhyfentown guard knight had picked up a fourteen-year-old street rat stealing from a bike store, intent on selling on any parts she could make off with. Leon had taken pity on her, spared her the stain of a stint in a clusterloc. She must have impressed him somehow, because after that, he had taken her under his wing.

Ghost gets the inference. At least the lockpick she procured to get into Cass' apartment will get another use. As she watches the fight, the ex-knight goes down heavy, blood spraying from his open mouth.

She knows just how he feels.

CHAPTER 17

Ravensbrink Kill Ring, Iochitown
Two Months Ago

Within the velveteen depths of Iochitown, the district named after London's patron saint of spies, thieves and performers, moves an unassuming man with an air of neat bureaucracy.

Ravensbrink, Iochitown's biggest weekly meats market, has an odiferous reputation. This is due to the kill ring at its centre, which is used all day to end the lives of batch animals – primed for their next manifestation as succulent dishes at nearby eateries – continuing the market's longstanding tradition of selling its wares as fresh as it gets.

The crowds are thronged with private buyers, kitchen vastos hailing from larger, wealthier households who have the resources to take on a whole segmented cow and sell on the parts they don't use. The fashion-conscious claim their intricately carved ear cuffs are made from far rarer and infinitely more expensive deer bone, but if you haven't bled trick for it, chances are it's cow, and if it was bought from a Iochitown jeweller, chances are it was a Ravensbrink cow.

The neat man currently making his way through the market is dressed in a wrap outfit of black and burgundy, the dominant colours of Iochitown born and bred, and as such, he could not be less conspicuous as he weaves through the crowd, many of whom sport filtration masks in the latest styles to combat the smells of offal and layers of blood old and new.

Bright, racing trick lights beam briefly on his balding head and skitter over the soaked ground he walks on. News projections slide across his face and hang in the air above. He passes a hologram on a plinth – a beautiful, scantily clad man beckoning him inside the open-roofed warehouse behind with a crooked finger and a suggestive smile. One kind of meat selling another.

The person he came here to see is standing with their back to him at the kill ring's circular viewing side, facing the action. Their thigh boots are cinched tight and their short jacket is adorned with allegiance charms sewn on to the thick fabric. Their hair is bundled under a cap and the backs of their ears glint with the tell-tale loops of a face overlay.

The neat, bald man makes straight for them, but a tall woman steps into his way, and another shorter man follows up on his other side. Gun holsters bulge at their hips. Private guard.

'Where are you going?' asks the taller guard.

The neat, bald man nods to the woman standing ringside.

'I have an appointment,' he says, raising his reedy voice over the noise of the surrounding crowd and the animal grunts beyond the barriers.

'Who's that with, then?'

The man hesitates. 'Should I not say their real name? Are we being spies?'

The taller guard does not smile.

'Why don't you,' she says in a pleasantly unpleasant tone, 'tell me the name of the person you think you've an appointment with.'

The neat man has been prepped for this.

'Ladymere,' he says.

'And your name?'

He resists a smile. 'Barochi.'

The taller guard raises a brow. 'You're named after that country up north that's nothing but wind farms?'

He shrugs. 'It's nice. Breezy.'

The taller guard leaves. The shorter guard briefly hovers his hand at his hip. The so-called Barochi resists the urge to roll his eyes – he is supposed to be intimidated and he should try to act the part.

He watches the taller guard approach the short figure standing ringside. He catches a glimpse of the figure's overlay-plastered profile as they turn their head a little to listen to the guard talking into their ear. The overlay gleams with intricately painted scales, perhaps a nod to Iochitown's district symbol of leaping fish – or perhaps they just like glitter.

Barochi watches their lips move. Beyond their mouth lies the kill ring's sanded floor, stained brown with old blood.

The taller guard returns.

'Ladymere would like to know what the first trick you ever showed them was,' she asks.

'A grey dog. Remind her that I've come a long way since then, would you?'

This is relayed. The neat, bald man calling himself Barochi cranes his neck to try and see how this goes down, which moves his body forwards just a little. The shorter guard tuts, then taps his gun with a finger.

Ladymere listens to the answer and then, finally, looks back at him.

They nod.

The taller guard knight beckons. Barochi moves forwards, feeling a weight shift behind him as the shorter guard takes up the rear. The crowd around them, unaware of the game in their midst, press out of the way only at the jostling insistence of the guard knights in their move to clear a path.

Ladymere turns their head as Barochi appears at their side, peering at him in amusement.

'Wyll?' they say into his ear.

'Viviane?' he responds in a reedy murmur.

Viviane's gaze roams his face. The scales hide their contours but there's no mistaking their eyes, those inviting depths of melted chocolate.

'The detail is amazing up close,' they say. 'Even better than I remember.'

'Practice.'

'Tut. How illegal of you. Who is this dull little thing you've chosen as a cloak?'

Wyll shrugs. 'A man I once met. Before Carr, in another Kingdom. He'd been imprisoned five times for mass fraud.'

'You met him in prison?'

'Oh no. When I met him, he'd become a politician.'

Viviane gives an appreciative laugh.

'So, Ladymere?' Wyll asks drily.

'It's my name nowadays. Did I not mention that last we met?'

'You did not. Code names and passwords?'

They shrug. 'You don't spend a lot of time in Iochitown, do you? This is the trickster dis', Wyll. Theatrics are much akin to breathing.'

'A little over the top?'

'Says the man currently pretending to be someone else?'

'Well, yes, but I don't have to try so hard,' he says, affecting a modest air.

'You're in a good mood,' Viviane observes. 'Can you change your personality along with your face?'

Wyll's grin is as wide as a frog's. There is no denying the giddiness he feels when he is not himself and has the power to pass anonymously through the throng without a glance tossed his way. No eyes on him. Invisibility – despair for some, freedom for others.

'If we'd met in Pinecone again,' he says, 'I might not have had to disguise myself.'

'Couldn't be helped,' Viviane replies. 'Things are heating up. Crowds are less conspicuous.'

Things are heating up. Never a good line when said by someone like Viviane.

Beyond them, a pig gives a great squeal as it is led scuffling into the sanded pit. It knows what comes next. Intelligence is often a curse.

With some reluctance, Wyll asks, 'What are you involved in now?'

'Have you ever noticed,' muses Viviane, 'how meat market kill rings and Caballaria arenas are essentially the same thing?' They side-eye him. 'That makes you a cow.'

Dodging his question by trying to rile him.

'What's heating up, Viviane?' he asks.

Viviane waves a hand. 'Just you keep your head in the mud, Wyll, it's safer. Now, your message said you'd changed your mind. What have you changed your mind about?'

Wyll looks out over the pit. The pig's burly owners hold her hefty bulk still between them and then draw a quick, precise knife across her throat, accompanied by a smattering of fist-on-palm approval from the crowd at their neatly professional handling. Their salesman quickly begins to take bids before the blood can cool too much.

'I'll get your map for you,' says Wyll.

A pause of silence – perhaps surprise.

'And in return?' asks Viviane.

'You hide someone for me. Get them out of London.'

Viviane is quiet so long that it draws his gaze back to them.

'For a moment there, I thought it was my amazing charm that had changed your mind,' they say eventually. 'What is it, some scandalously unacceptable lover of yours?'

'Something like that,' says Wyll.

'Saints, is it a common?' Viviane grimaces.

Titon was a common. Apparently it is only acceptable when Vivi does it.

'No. She's a godchild.'

'Oh dear.' Viviane perks up. 'One too many magic tricks, 'ware the clanging of the clusterloc. What did she do, tell a rich man's fortune wrong?'

Wyll lets their mind go where it goes. They'll be far more inclined to help out a fellow godchild, and curiosity about meeting a lover of his will hopefully be too hard to resist.

'She's a little more dangerous than that,' he warns.

Viviane raises their eyebrows. 'Well, she'd have to be to attract you, now, wouldn't she?'

He does not know what to make of that, and lets it slide.

'Vivi, she's, uh, volatile. Bad temper.'

'Again, pet, just your type.' Viviane turns to the ring with a flash of scales. 'I like her already.'

It may be the world's worst idea to put Red and Viviane in a room together, but it's too late now. Besides, it might not even come to pass.

First he has to help Red escape.

'Just . . . don't try to recruit her to whatever you're running,' he says to Viviane. 'Just help her disappear. Wherever she wants to go, whatever she wants to do. I'll pay for it. That's my price for getting the map for you.'

The full press of Viviane's scrutiny bears down. He feels its weight.

'You always let us get too close, don't you, Wyll,' they say.

'Vivi, stop.'

Their brows rise. 'You never did enjoy any reminders of your truest nature. But fighting yourself, well, only you get hurt. Life gets a lot easier once you embrace it.'

'I never did enjoy the clumsiness of your insight,' Wyll mutters.

'Fine.' Amused Viviane, the one he hates the most, the one who persuades him that nothing he says or does will ever be a surprise. 'Why aren't you going with her, wherever it may be?'

'I'm not interested in becoming an outlaw.'

'And the real reason?'

'She doesn't want me.'

He says it before he realises that he has. Viviane's gift at work, perhaps.

'Are you sure it's not because she senses that you already have a love in your life?' They give a delighted laugh at his look. 'Oh, not *me*. I'm talking about your King and saviour. Even I couldn't compete with him.'

'You never tried,' says Wyll. 'After Mafelon, you chose to go off with Titon.' The short sentence hides a wound never fully healed: first heartbreak, the sharpest kind.

They must be able to sense it, but instead of softening, they harden. 'I went off with Titon because it was the only good choice I had.'

'Stop. You're free to be with whoever you want, Vivi, but don't pretend you leaving was *me* rejecting *you.*'

'I go where I'm needed,' Viviane coolly replies. 'As well as where I'm wanted. And after Mafelon, it was very clear that you no longer needed — and you barely wanted — me.' Before he can object to every way in which that is the most shamefully inaccurate reading of a situation since the dawn of time, they sweep right on, 'Anyway, there's hardly any point in being jealous of the dead.'

Wyll's heart stops.

They cannot know. They cannot *possibly* know. They don't read minds, and he has been so careful around them, so careful never to betray any feelings about Art—

'You hadn't heard?' Viviane can feel his shock. 'Titon got himself killed in a round-up a while back. He had a guard spy in the ranks, apparently.'

Wyll's heart starts again.

'I hadn't,' he says, and then, awkwardly, 'I'm sorry.'

Viviane gives a careless shrug. 'Now he's a minor footnote in the annals of history.'

Wyll searches their face, but it is too hard to say whether they even care about Titon's death. They always were an excellent performer.

That means it's not Titon who wants the map.

'Who do you work for now?' he asks.

'I never *worked for* Titon, like some common foot soldier. I was something infinitely more valuable, thank you.'

The first flash of irritation he's seen. He lets it drop. No good provoking someone with whom you're trying to cut a deal. Presumably the map is for some new activist group, some new version of Titon, some new master Viviane deems powerful enough to stand at the side of to whisper in their ear. It's not his business, and he doesn't want to make it his business.

'Passage out of London for this map,' he says. 'Do we have a deal?'

'We do if you tell me what's going on in the palace,' Viviane wheedles. 'The rumour mill is grinding.'

'What do you mean?'

'Please. It's one reason things are heating up in the kitchen, or haven't you noticed? The most popular theory is that your dearest love Artorias is about to be ousted. Some sort of coup in the wings. My trick's on Evrontown, they've been suspiciously outspoken in recent times.'

Wyll summons every ounce of control he has. 'I know as much as you do.'

One advantage of donning an illusory face: it's much harder to read him. After all, Barochi is a stranger to Viviane.

After a long moment, they turn back to the kill ring. 'I seriously doubt that, King's champion.'

'They don't tell me anything. I just get sent into the ring to fight.'

Viviane sighs. 'You know, I don't put up with this obstinacy from anyone else. If other people I work with held back like you do – well, let's just say they wouldn't do it for long.'

'Is that a threat?'

'Would I threaten my business partner? We've a deal, *Barochi*.'

'Do we?'

'Get me the map,' Viviane says, 'and I'll get your girl out, no questions asked.'

'She'll have more than one shadow,' Wyll admits. 'And they'll be good.'

'Lady Popularity.' Viviane is dismissive. 'It's not a problem.'

It might be, but he's rolled the dice on this one now. Risk for reward.

'I feel bad,' Viviane muses. 'I think I get the easier end of this deal.'

Wyll looks at her. 'Why? You have to make someone with major attention on them disappear. All I have to do is buy a map.'

'You haven't met its owner.' Viviane's laugh is of the sinister kind. 'And their asking price will be high.'

'You've the resources, I warrant.'

'Right enough,' Viviane agrees. They link their arm through his and squeeze. 'Oh, Barochi, my love. We've come a long way from petting for Carr, you and I.'

Wyll is less sure of that.

Sometimes it feels like he still wears a damn collar around his neck.

CHAPTER 18

Garad's Apartment, Evrontown
Two Weeks Ago

'What with everyone just lining up to blackmail me,' muses Ghost, 'I'd never felt so damn popular in my life. Leon could make the kind of trouble I really, really didn't want, if I didn't do what he said. So I did.'

'Did you come here to try to kill me?' Garad asks mildly.

Ghost shakes her head. 'No. Leon guessed wrong about that.'

'Then what do you want from me?'

'I'm getting to it. Let me get to it, or throw me out. Now which is it to be?'

Silence.

Ghost nods, and carries on.

Hidden Treasures, Alaunitown
Two Months Ago

It's the little differences that catch you most, Ghost reflects as she draws on her sicalo.

It's tickled her to discover that the sicaloes they sell here come in district colours, the tobacco neatly wrapped in thin skein

208

papers of pale yellows or copper. It's a common enough thing; it simply hadn't consciously occurred to her before she'd bought some that Alaunitown sellers would prioritise their own district brands before any others. Her favoured Rhyfentown sicaloes, dark red with the faintest earthy tang of licoresse, can be found here, but only in specialist stores, and at a premium.

Curls of smoke float serenely across her view of the ramshackle building across the street. It's been dark for more than an hour now, which, judging by the past few days' careful assessment, tracks with its usual habits. It's well into the night and the trick-light sign outside its front door has been switched off, dormant until the dawning of a new day's chance to sell weird junk to the good people of the area.

Well, the other Ghost tells her, *nothing is going to change with another few days of watching, is it? What are you waiting for?*

Courage, she supposes, but most people get it wrong – no one has courage innate. Courage is made in the moment, a sudden, arbitrary choice. So galvanised, she pushes off the shadowed wall she's been hiding against and crosses the street, keeping to the unlit parts, one arm cupped protectively around the bag that weighs down her shoulder – and her future heart – with its contents. In there, she has water, the means to make fire and a polymer gel normally used in construction that will take care of anything still ticking after the first two elements have done their best.

She'll carry the stain of what she's about to do, but it's the only way to throw off the double chokehold currently around her neck. Leon can't blackmail her to steal a test machine that doesn't work, and Moth can't prove what she is with nothing but melted parts.

She could, if she needed to, convince herself that she's doing it for all godchildren everywhere. Give a nice righteous hue to her doings, self-forgiveness through the moral high ground – but fuck if she doesn't hate people like that, who don't have the guts to understand, never mind accept, themselves. Those people are all twisted up. Those people are the most dangerous kind. They're capable of the worst horrors you've ever dreamed, and some you haven't yet, simply because soul-sick acts can be forgiven if you've made yourself believe you're in the right. That shouty idiot Joln Chimes might be headed down such a road, if she's a decent judge.

No. She knows that she doesn't much care for most of the human beings she reluctantly shares this planet with, be they godchild or common. There's only been two people who managed to make her worry for their survival more than her own, and they were both more powerful – and more protected – than she'll ever be.

She removes a trick lockpick from an inside pocket of her jacket, crouches at the back door and sets to work. It takes several tries and longer than she'd have liked, but eventually she's through, the door sliding open without a sound. Moth's place didn't exactly have the air of technological advancement required for a silent alarm, but you never know – in which case, she might have to move quick.

Then, as she slides along in the dark, Ghost hears the last thing any would-be thief wants to hear – the sound of voices.

Fuck. Fuck. With all the lights off and no one in or out the last hour? What kind of conversation goes on in the dark?

One you are probably not supposed to overhear, whispers the other her.

Ghost stands stiff in the gloom. Two voices, from her straining ear – Moth's unmistakable rangy scrape, like a virtuoso

210

violinist gone rogue, and another, much lower tone, clipped and neat.

She inches glacially closer. She has to see where they are. If they're tucked around the corner, away from the cellar door, there's a chance she can still sneak in while they're deep in their talks, wait for them to leave, and then go to work on that damned machine.

Right, says the other her. *And there's a chance that fish could hoist themselves up on their tails and start walking.*

Ghost ignores this, still coasting on the courage and the adrenalin that got her here. Then she hesitates, curiosity pricking at her. Just who is Moth talking to in such secret, late-night fashion?

Might be good to take a little look, at the very least to get a read on the situation. If she can get up to the gallery . . .

The voices lower to background murmurations as Ghost creeps away, slipping up a little stone staircase at the very back of the shop to the top floor. The gallery door is wedged open – never been closed, it looks like, forever anticipating the moving feet of commerce. Up here, the voices carry loud and clear. They must be right below.

Ghost drops into a squat and begins, cautiously, to monkey forwards.

'—sell it to?' the clipped, neat voice drifts up to her.

'Why, what's your stake in the game?' Moth replies. 'Trying to find more recruits for your secret little training schools?'

Silence.

'Neh,' Moth says. 'You might say I've heard of you.'

'They're not training schools,' the man replies. 'We fund housing for the trickless. Support for the under-represented. Charities.'

'Oh, I know what you call 'em officially. Unofficially, they're training schools for godchildren who wouldn't be able to learn how to use their magic any other way. And now you're on the hunt for a bigger intake.'

'You have it wrong,' the man says with eminent politeness. 'I'm just a numbers man. I sort funding, that kind of thing. In any case, those charities represent the interests of Blackheart itself.'

'Oh my, well, saints alive.' Moth sounds amused over impressed. 'Never thought I'd be attracting that kind of attention. Closest someone like me will ever get to Cair Lleon, neh?'

'I don't represent the palace in this matter.'

'So who do you represent?'

'The people your machine will most affect.'

'What, all of them?' Moth laughs. 'Is there anyone with that much say so in all of London, apart from the King himself?'

Ghost crouch-sidles on to the small gallery that houses the rarest items in Moth's eclectic collection and overhangs the ground floor. There is a light, in fact, crawling weakly up the walls from below, not bright enough to penetrate the shuttered windows from the outside. She painstakingly inches her face closer and closer to the edge of the gallery floor.

The tops of two heads come into view, square in the midst of armchairs. One head is piled with an assortment of silver combs and dangling charms – Moth's apparently usual tinkling-trash finery – and the spartan-mopped head of her visitor. Too hard to see his face from here, though. He's dressed in dark, unassuming clothes, barely noticeable next to Moth's multi-fabric blare.

'Listen,' Moth continues, 'you're not the first to come knocking. I've had more than one syndicate, as well as one or two . . . let's call them "businessfolk", armed with enough trick to buy half the dis'. You're going to have to move fast if you want it.'

'How will I know if it works?'

'If you're a godchild, it'll see. And if you're not, it won't.'

'Hardly more impressive than a back-alley "flip a coin" fraudster,' says the visitor evenly.

'It does more than that,' says Moth, 'as I'm sure you've heard, since you've taken the trouble to come all the way here.'

A pause. 'A living map of every godchild in London,' says the visitor, and even Ghost, from her lofty vantage point, can hear the eagerness in his voice.

Moth's silence is acquiescence.

'That's impossible,' muses the visitor.

'Everything's impossible until it's done.' Moth is smug with the utter assurance of someone who believes in their own words.

'How did you create it?'

'It's been fourteen years in the making,' comes the deliberately vague reply.

'And here you are, selling it to the highest bidder.'

'Am I a saint?' Moth says, evidently stung by his accusatory tone. 'I've some arrogance to me, but not enough for that. Who should have the right to determine who's worthy and who's not?' She looks the visitor up and down. 'Why, you think you can choose? Go ahead.'

'It should be the King,' says the visitor.

'I thought you said you don't represent the palace.'

'I don't.' The merest hesitation. 'But the King is in charge. That's really the point of having one.'

'Please, everyone knows each throne-taker gets it through corruption and whim, not merit. Anyway, fine – say he's a good King. How about his Saith, though? His most trusted advisors? You'd better hope they're good people too – and not only that, but with the same stake in the game as his. And then there's the

Consilium: seven districts, each with their own agendas, pulling things every which way. Are they all good people? Do they want what's best for everyone, or only for their own? Is that going to work out for the rest of London?' Moth steeples her fingers. 'Turn the sooth ball every which way you like, you won't get the answer you're looking for. Hells, flip the runes for it. It'll make about as much sense as any other way.'

'Cowards leave it to others to make the choices,' says the visitor quietly.

'Cowards? You don't know what I have the stomach for, my Lord. You don't know what I've done. You don't know the first thing about me.' Moth is all steel, the visitor all silence. 'Now. Are you serious about an offer or not?'

'Show me,' says the visitor simply, and as Ghost tracks them making their way over to the cellar – the 'test' room with that clicking, clanking machine – she realises what a narrow escape she just had by dawdling to listen to their talk. If she'd have gone straight down there to put the torch to it as she'd originally planned, she'd have been caught inside the cellar with no way out.

Curiosity does sometimes save, it appears.

Moth and her visitor disappear down the cellar steps, and the door closes fast behind them.

Ghost gives a noiseless sigh and settles in to wait it out. Hopefully neat-little-numbers man won't be making an offer so good he walks out with the machine tonight – and only then does it occur to her that she has no real sense of how big it is. She remembers the mechanical breathing, the clicking and pumping, and the touch on her face – so at least as tall as her, then, but what does it weigh? She reassures herself with the thought that the prospective not-from-the-palace-or-at-least-not-officially buyer looks like he could hold up a hand for nothing much heavier than a drink. That machine won't be going anywhere.

For a minute there, she'd let herself hope the man would have an obvious connection to the Cass Grenwald case, but first guess is no – a 'launitown businessman like Glapissant has no obvious connection to Blackheart, and the neat-little-numbers man doesn't seem the type to attend a black-market godchild orgy. Appearances can be deceptive, of course, but if he's got bigger stains on his heart than inflating some numbers on his monthly reports, she'll hand in her brain for a tune-up. Men like that don't know true violence. Men like that—

—shout a lot.

She can hear him. It has to be him; there's only one person with that voice pitch in the cellar. A muffled bass fury.

And then a high-pitched squealing, like a cat being squashed in an industrial press.

Silence. Silence after a scream is not often, in her experience, the gentle kind.

Ghost trains her gloom-adjusted eyes down on to the cellar door.

Nothing – maybe it was a cat, after all – but then the door bursts open and Moth comes stumbling through it. Even in the half-dark, it's pretty obvious she's not walking right, dazed and lumpen, and the man comes chasing after her – and somehow he's not as small as before, somehow he looms.

'*That's* your test machine?' he shouts. '*That's* your machine? You evil *crow*. You—'

He takes hold of her. He looks too big, now, too strong, like his sizing suddenly got all messed up. He shakes her like a rag doll. A lot of what happens next is unclear, because Ghost sees smoke – fire smoke, and now it's rolling through the room thick and fast, billowing upwards from the cellar like a living thing, and it's time to leave.

There's only one way out from the gallery, and they're going to see her, but better seen than dead, so she takes the stone stairs, and when she gets to the bottom, creeping out, Moth is alone, a crumpled mound on the floor of her junk-stuffed shop, and the man is nowhere to be seen.

Ghost creeps past her still form, and then hesitates with an annoying sense of guilt at leaving her here – *for what and why? The woman kidnapped and threatened you* – but then she hears a shuffling at the cellar door.

'Hoi!' the man shouts.

Ghost risks a look. He has reappeared at the top of the cellar steps, like an enormous demon among the smoke curdling around his form. He has something in his arms, a big bundle – of blankets? Clothes? It doesn't look like it's big enough to be that machine she heard – and his face is painted with a look of shocked fury.

Ghost's legs scream at her to run.

Ghost orders them to stand still.

'Who are you?' she says.

'Who are *you*?' he counters.

Stalemate. Smoke's getting bad. They haven't got long before this gets too hard to escape.

'Moth!' she shouts, but Moth doesn't move. Her eyes are shut, her jaw slack.

The man steps forwards at her shout – somehow a threat even when he's laden down with whatever he's carrying – and Ghost gives it up.

Not your fight, says the inside her. *Get out.*

She bolts for the back door. Evidently the buyer had the same idea as her – to destroy the test machine – and that's good enough right now; someone else is taking care of her problem with a good old rip-roaring fire, and it'll consume everything in there, there'll be nothing left, nothing—

Ghost makes it across the street and turns, risking a quick lurk.

Nothing.

No billowing smoke. No orange glow lighting up the insides with its dull, angry tint. The shop is as dark and silent as the moment she first arrived.

But she *saw* that smoke. It was immense, billowing the promise of imminent destruction.

Though, now she thinks back, there was no *smell* . . .

The shop's back door bangs open. The numbers man struggles outside, that big bundle still wrapped up in his arms. She watches him heave across the road to a waiting quad car, open the door and deposit the bundle in his arms inside. It's clearly heavy enough to be awkward, but curiously pliable and floppy for a machine – though who in seven hells could say what tech that can tell godchild from common should look like?

The man shuts the quad door and straightens, looking around the street.

Ghost shrinks into the shadows, heart hammering fast.

He seems to stare right at her.

Then he moves on, turning and disappearing back into the shop.

She contemplates creeping back to find out what's going on—

And then hears the unmistakable flat crack of a gunshot.

No need to see anything to know what just happened.

Ghost turns and escapes on the quietest feet she can muster, keen not to join Moth beyond Marvol's door via another bullet from the buyer's gun.

As she flees, she thinks on how it looks like Leon just lost his jackpot, and how, at least in this case, he is right about his life's recent run of misfortune. Someone got to the world-changing machine first, and was ruthless enough to avoid having to pay.

Now all she has to do is convince Leon that she had nothing to do with it.

CHAPTER 19

Stredforthe, Marvoltown
Two Months Ago

When Red wakes, she must feel as though she has travelled into the past.

She comes to in Wyll's bed, in Wyll's hideaway, the secret place he began bringing her to not so long ago, though it feels like a lifetime since. The bed sits in one corner of an abandoned power station's ground floor, a lofty monument to largely defunct technology. The bed, the floor, the marked-out training square, every inch of the wet room, every available wall – Red's body has been imprinted on them all, leaving invisible psychic smears. Her smell has been rubbed into his sheets and seeped into the brickwork. She was the invader, but he unlocked the city gates.

He sees her stirring from his vantage point a good distance from the bed. He doesn't want her to think he's been watching her in her sleep, though that is exactly what he has been doing. He approaches slowly, a serving plate in one hand and a large cup of water in the other.

'You're awake,' he says. 'You must be hungry.'

He sets the plate and cup on the small table beside the bed and then backs off. Red is mussed, confused, and deeply lovely with it. Saints, the thrill of seeing her in his bed again, as if time really has been rewound and all is as it was mere weeks ago, when he lived in the blinkered bliss of ignorance.

Red stares down at the plate, its hard lacquered surface covered in delicately steamed parcels of spiced, sap-drenched goose, or fish and fennel. A street vendor who goes door to door in the area to sell them always stops here nowadays – Wyll has become a regular customer. The vendor is a cheery older man originally from outside the Seven Kingdoms and appears to have absolutely no idea who Wyll is, which just adds to his value.

'They're delicious,' Wyll says. 'I promise.'

Red scents the air.

'They taste even better than they smell,' he offers.

Her eyes roam her surroundings.

'Is this real?' she asks, her voice still burred from sleep.

Wyll nods. 'I couldn't conjure this place. It's too complex an illusion.' At her sceptical look, he adds, 'Besides, it doesn't benefit me to lie to you about where you are. I brought you here for a reason.'

'What reason?'

'We'll get to it. You can relax, no one knows you're here. Eat.'

Red stays still. 'You haven't poisoned them, then?'

Wyll impatiently clicks his tongue. 'That's a coward's death. Whatever I could say about you, I'd never treat you as a coward.'

She feels heartened by the anger in his compliment – and, too hungry to keep resisting, reaches out towards the enticing plate. It's all he can do to stop himself from doing the same.

He doesn't know why, but he expects her to eat with a little self-consciousness. People tend to, with an audience. Instead she scoops up a dripping parcel and stuffs it into her mouth, making a chute of her jaw as if to throw the chunks into it as fast as she can. She eats three like this in a breath.

'Clusterloc food must be bad,' Wyll comments.

Red's cold eyes shift to his. He immediately regrets the joke.

'So why'd you bring me here?' she asks as she chews, gaze fastened to the plate and only occasionally flickering upwards, as if food is the point of this and Wyll comes in a distant second.

'To offer you a way out,' he says.

Red smirks with bulging cheeks. 'I thought you said these aren't poisoned.'

'You're so sure that's your only future at this point?'

She shrugs.

'Why do you act like your fate is set?' Wyll asks.

'I don't know how else to act.' She watches him for his reaction. 'That annoys you.'

'That pleases you,' he shoots back.

She acquiesces to this with a lopsided smile. 'Gotta get my kicks where I can, these days.'

She is sitting up straighter, her demeanour livelier. The food is working.

Good. Time to dial it up a notch.

'How did you know I was the way to him?' Wyll asks.

Him needs no further signifier.

'I didn't, not for certain,' Red says. 'It was just my best chance. I knew I had something you liked.'

He is sure she knows the double meaning of her words.

'Magic,' he comments, dismissing the other unspoken suggestion. 'You played the game very well, for a novice. High risk, high reward.'

They might as well be dissecting a bout, the way a trainer and fighter would do together post-fight. He supposes this is all she's been made to talk about in the past few months. Even horror becomes banal with repetition.

'Have you been practising your talent?' Wyll asks.

Red snorts. 'Yes, the clusterloc guards love it when you break the law in front of them.'

'I don't see the problem. The worst has already happened. What are they going to do, arrest you?'

She studies him for signs of seriousness. 'They drug me. They chain me. What d'you think I can do when I'm like that?'

'You're not chained right now.'

He can practically see her harden at his come-on. He knows that sudden spike of hunger. The permission to let go, just once. The tantalising promise of release, the promise to feel again so hard that you lose yourself in the process—

'You always asked to see me exposed, didn't you,' says Red. 'Whatever I gave you, it was never enough.'

She is definitely feeling stronger, strong enough to flirt, tap back.

'Because you were lying,' Wyll replies.

'I never lied.' She looks him up and down. 'I just hid.'

'Not very well.' Wyll finds himself getting hotter as pain stirs under his skin. 'I knew you were hiding something, I just didn't know what it was. But I would have found out. A few more days . . .'

'Yes,' Red says baldly. 'That was why I had to move so fast at the end. It was . . . a mess.' She shakes her head, apparently in disbelief that she managed to pull it off.

'See, you did lie to me,' Wyll says. 'You pretended to want me to get where you needed to be.'

It was supposed to come out a strong and irrefutable state-ment, but tears threaten – sudden, strange, humiliating. He swallows them down.

'That wasn't a lie,' Red says, skirting vehemence. 'I was going to . . . get you out of the way. But I couldn't. You understand? I almost ruined everything because I—'

He burns to know the rest of that thought, but she wrenches herself away from it.

'I already told you not to feel guilty,' she snaps. 'Why are we talking about this? It doesn't matter. I'll be executed in a few days anyway, and then it'll be over, and you can forget about all of it. You can pretend I never existed, if you want. Why am I here?'

She is restless. Her blood must be fizzing by now; it'll be harder and harder for her to keep control.

'I told you,' Wyll says. 'A way out.'

'No.' She is flat. 'No political wrangling. I won't be used like that. Just kill me.'

'This is not a political game, it's an escape,' he says. 'Through me.'

He watches her absorb this.

'You're just going to let me go?' she says slowly.

'That's far too risky, they'll hunt you down,' Wyll replies. 'But you can stay here. Under my protection. I can guarantee your safety here. No one knows about this place.'

Red looks around. What does she see? Does his sanctuary look more like punishment than comfort? Does it feel empty? Does he?

'No one except your driver,' she says, expecting him to backtrack.

'That would be taken care of.'

There. A flash of shock. Not as cold in the bones as she tries to be.

'You'd kill him?' she tests.

Wyll shrugs. 'He's in the way.'

The echo of her words is not lost on her.

'What am I supposed to do here?' she asks.

'Train,' he says. 'Eat. Sleep. Read. Live. I'll bring you anything you need. I'll bring you anything you ask for. Anything in my power to give you – it's yours.'

This sinks in. He is one of the most powerful men in London. She really could ask for anything she liked.

Wyll gathers his courage. 'I'd do whatever it takes to make you happy,' he says.

Did it sound like he'd rehearsed it? Did it sound true?

Red licks her fingers clean of pastry flakes and sticky threads of sauce, collects herself and turns, assessing her surroundings. The bed isn't beautiful, but it is large and comfortable, and there is no shortage of space. She sweeps over the training square, the weapons rack, the heavy chest full of equipment, the shelves on the side stocked with medicines, salves, bandages.

'I haven't even shown you the second floor,' says Wyll. 'I have acrobatics equipment that will blow your mind. You can practically fly. And on sunny days, the rooftop has an exquisite view. You can sun-soak like a cat. And there's a garden. Miniature fruit trees. Herbs. I've grown most of it myself.'

He is rewarded with her full attention. She is looking at him as if he is new to her. Perhaps he is, now.

'You'd be here too?' she asks.

He cannot tell which way the question points.

'When I could be,' he responds. 'But you'd often have the place to yourself.'

'They're just going to let me go? They'll let you do this?'

They, not *you*. Good.

'Of course not,' Wyll says.

She understands the implication.

'Why?' she demands. 'Why risk yourself for me?'

Courage, Wyll.

'Because I want you,' he says.

He watches the weather of her face. She is right: she doesn't lie – or at least, she's extraordinarily bad at it. Despite her efforts, emotions radiate from her like fanfares. It's one reason her talent can be so powerful, though she never quite grasped that side of it.

'I don't understand this game,' says Red.

Her movements are calm but tight, like a coiled spring.

'It's simple,' Wyll responds. 'The game is one of keeps. As in, how I get to keep you.'

'Keep me.'

He just waits.

'Why should I trust you?' she asks.

'Why shouldn't you? The alternative is death.'

'Not necessarily.'

'You just said you'd rather be executed than be used for political ends.'

Does she even realise that the bed pillows are levitating behind her, that it's her doing it, like a manifestation of her state, the anxious hovering she is doing, caught between mistrust and longing? Longing to get out of her predicament, likely. Not longing for him.

Time to see how far she'll go.

'Or,' Wyll says, 'you could try to kill me now and escape.'

It's practically a sound, the key of her rising, frantic energy, like the electronic whine of his bike when it kicks into higher gear.

Wyll gestures across the room. 'You're closer to the weapons rack than me.'

He sees the decision made. Which decision, he waits to discover in an agony of suspense. He watches her lever herself slowly off the bed, come to standing, start to move. She looks like she could punch through the distance between them to eat him. He begs his body to stay still. He must not threaten or spook her. He must wait and see what choice she has made.

She approaches him. Up close, her eyes are haunted, sleepless bruises smeared underneath in purple shadows. When he does nothing, she reaches out, and he lets her. He lets her press into him. He lets her mouth brush his. He lets her choose. He lets her win, because with Red he wants to lose. He wants to submit to her, the power in her that so easily seduced him and had him begging at her feet for any way to make her happy; he is drawn to her like the sea, drawn to it as a reminder of how small he is; he loves to be reminded of how small he is, he wants to be someone's pet, the focus of all their attention and love as pain, he *wants* it—

Arms wrench his backwards, torn away from her, and for a second, he thinks they're being attacked – and then he feels a crushing force on his chest. His feet leave the ground, his whole body hovering impossibly, pinioned in nothing by nothing, and then *rushed* backwards. Red rapidly recedes in his vision and his back connects hard with a wall, the crushing force on his chest holding him there, feet dangling inches from the ground. It is like being encased in stone.

Red holds him bodily away from her, far out of reach, cocooned in awful pressure. It is, Wyll realises, the most helpless he has ever felt. Movement is laughable. His lungs cannot inflate enough to breathe. His life and his death are hers.

This is how Art felt as he died.

Red stares at him, breathing hard, hands spasmodically clenching at her sides.

'Don't come after me,' she says.

She disappears from his rapidly darkening field of vision. He concentrates on trying to sip in enough air to survive.

He hears the front door bang.

Seconds or years later and the awful crushing pressure that has become his world disappears. Wyll drops painfully to the floor, falling forwards on to his hands and knees. His gorge presses in a feeble desire to release the contents of his stomach, from relief more than anything else.

Footsteps echo across the floor.

'Are you okay?' asks a concerned voice.

Wyll waves a hand.

A few moments of deep breathing – and a false start or two – sees him slumped on a divan, Lillath standing across from him, alert and watchful. Two of her personal guard knights have materialised from their hiding places to prowl the room, presumably on the lookout for threat even though the threat just escaped.

'Fuck,' he says finally, eloquence currently out of reach.

'Yes,' Lillath agrees. 'Well done. I thought you'd misjudged her, but your play was a good one.'

'Yes. Isn't it strange she'd react badly to going from one prison to another,' Wyll mutters.

'There are worse things,' Lillath comments.

Wyll just shakes his head. His body aches, but a quick assessment reveals no warning signs of lasting damage. Still . . . that power, that strength. Saintsfuck.

As if Lillath can read his mind, he hears her ask, 'Can she do that without Tidal?'

'I only dosed her a small amount,' he replies. 'Just enough to get her barriers to drop. She'd have tasted it in the food otherwise.'

Lillath cocks a brow. 'So – yes, she can.'

Wyll says nothing.

'Well. How reassuring that we've let her out on to the streets.'

Wyll says nothing, more obstinately. They've been over this ground.

'At least we have eyes on her this time,' Lillath says. 'They're very good. She won't notice, and they'll only intervene when they need to.'

If Lillath picked them, they won't just be very good, but the best. He just has to hope that Viviane wasn't lying about their own resources.

Hope, risk, try, fail, try again, in ever more dizzying circles.

'I suppose they were told they didn't need to this time,' he says pointedly, a deflection to hide any possible leak of his thoughts on his face.

'Sorry about that. Obviously we wanted to let her think she escaped on her own.'

'Well, you watched everything else,' Wyll mutters, 'why not my death too?'

Though what could have happened before that . . . If Red had tried to seduce him, he would have let her, and Lillath and her accompanying knights would have watched it all. Out of everything he has done that led to this, it is the complicit invasion of his privacy that most appals him. He feels humiliated and disgusted, and mostly by himself.

'She wouldn't have gone through with it,' Lillath says reassuringly.

'Once you've killed your own father,' Wyll retorts, 'there aren't many more restraints left to break.'

Lillath sounds intrigued. 'Speaking from personal experience?'

His laugh feels like it strips his throat on the way out. 'Not one of my favourite rumours.'

'No, but useful. A person who is capable of murdering their own kin is capable of anything.'

It feels like she means this in more ways than one. It always feels like this with Lillath. She gives off the perpetual impression that she knows more about you than you do.

'I did what you asked,' says Wyll. 'Now leave me be.'

'For now.' Lillath rises. 'Rest up. We might need you again soon.'

He stiffens. 'What for?'

'You're a natural liar, Wyll. I'd use you more if I could be sure you'd ever do anything that didn't serve your own wants.' Her smile is slight.

'Am I supposed to feel shamed by that? Pure altruism is a myth. There is not a selfless animal on this earth. I'd think a Spymaster might know that better than anyone.'

She inclines her head. 'I've seen people do some strange things in my time. Now just relax. You've done your part. Let us do ours.'

She stands there as if waiting for an ending bow or a hand touch, some pointless gesture of civility. When Wyll does not move, she takes her leave without a word, her knights circling her impassively, minnows around a shark.

He hears the boom of the power station's huge door, and its locking mechanism click into place.

Shadows grow long across the floor while Wyll sits and hates himself. That he felt there was no choice just makes it worse.

He could only shake off Lillath's suspicions by betraying his murderous former lover. It was that or face the clusterloc himself. His life so far has often seemed little more than a series of prisons, but he isn't too stupid to understand that at least the one he currently occupies is a comfortable one.

There are, as Lillath said, worse things.

Planted in Red's pocket is a small data coin, a recording of Wyll warning her that she is being followed in the hopes that she will lead the Spider to her co-conspirators. Telling her to lay low for two days, and then on the third, to meet a mutual friend at a specific time and place, a friend who will help her leave London. After that, she is on her own. Just the way, apparently, that she wants it. And Wyll wants to give her what she wants.

He just has to pray that Viviane can get Red out before the Spider makes her move.

And in the meantime, he has a map to buy.

CHAPTER 20

Garad's Apartment, Evrontown
Two Weeks Ago

'After Moth's death,' says Ghost to Garad, 'it all went downhill pretty quick.'

Leon's Apartment, Alaunitown
Two Months Ago

'Leon, you big bear,' hisses Ghost.

She taps on his door again, shifting uneasily from foot to foot. He's there – the smoked windows of his poky place glow dully with internal light. She knows the buyer-turned-murdering-thief didn't follow her – he couldn't have with his hands so full – but every quad she's seen on the way over here looked like the one he bundled his stolen test machine into – a dark box on wheels, just like every quad out there. She knows this is all just the paranoia of residual adrenalin, and if Leon would open up his damned door and let her get in out of the open, she could finally climb down enough to make sense out of this eventful evening.

The door disappears from underneath her hand as it opens,

and her pulse slows with relief – only to climb back up again as she is confronted with a stranger's face. His blank, shark eyes latch on to hers. She takes a step back. Not normally one to give ground, but when it's three against one . . . Behind him she can see two more, crowding through Leon's narrow doorway and out on to the street.

All three strangers have differing builds but one thing in common – strength. The two big ones merely exude general menace, but the smallest, a wiry man with boat knots for arms, looks like he could dig your grave before he put you in it.

Alarms ring. Ghost gives the wiry one her best version of a pleasant smile.

The wiry one looks her up and down.

'Bad night?' he asks.

Evidently recent happenings have her too shook for the best version, then. She drops the smile and settles for closed shop.

'Could get worse,' she says, taking the strangers in. They are casually dressed, but with a vague air of uniformity, as though they don't spend a whole lot of time in regular clothes.

The wiry man jerks a finger towards Leon's doorway. 'Your friend is in.'

'Oh, not my friend,' Ghost says. 'I don't live round here, I'm going door to door for the campaign.'

'Campaign?'

'Neh, the campaign for,' Ghost nearly misses a beat – saints, she really is off her game tonight – 'the degunning campaign. You must have heard of us. We advocate for the abolition of guns. Bring unregistereds in by more harmless, peaceable means, we say. Trank darts, or, or, sleepers in their food. You know.'

'Mmm,' wiry man says, with the air of an agreeable sceptic. 'Neh, I think I *have* heard of you.'

Ghost keeps her expression to an air of blank naïveté.

'Late time to be knocking on people's doors about politics,' he continues.

Ghost shrugs. 'People are more often in at night. Daytime I just get a lot of empty homes.'

The wiry man nods. 'Tricky move.'

'I have my moments.' She is relaxing into the role, just a little bit, enough to feel like she has this in hand, when she sees the tattoo. It is on the wiry man's neck — and he has so many she almost misses it, jumbled in among the rest and half obscured by the rise of his collar.

It is a tiny, seven-spoked wheel, with a rose flourishing on each spoke.

'Well, I won't keep you from your proselytising,' the wiry man says. 'A word of warning — man inside's a Gun by profession. Might be a hard nut to crack.'

'My favourite kind,' Ghost says.

He walks past and out into the night, the two large silent hills moving ponderously after him. They don't bother to close the door behind them.

Ghost waits, agonisingly, until they have disappeared round a corner, then waits longer, as long as she can stand it.

Then she goes inside and closes the door very firmly behind her.

She finds Leon steeped in his favourite armchair, staring at nothing.

'Just met your three friends,' she says.

He looks up. 'What?'

'The menacing fellows coming out your place just now.'

Leon goes back to staring at nothing.

'Weekly card game, was it?' prompts Ghost.

'What's it to do with you?'

Ghost watches him a while.

'I take it the visit wasn't friendly.'

Silence.

She lets loose a big sigh. 'Well, at least you're already in a bad mood. I always think it's best to get unpalatable news when the shit cart's already upturned, itso? Much better than tainting a good mood, when there are precious few of those to come by as it is—'

Leon thumps the arm of his chair with a meaty paw. 'Spit it up, whatever it is.'

So she does. The black-market sale of the test machine. The neat, bald buyer who looked like he'd cry if you shouted at him, turned furious killer thief.

She keeps the whole appearing/disappearing fire thing to herself. Either she hallucinated that smoke, or the buyer is a thwimoren of truly fantastic talent. There's only one in the world with that kind of ability, and it's safe to say the Sorcerer Knight is not skulking around back-alley junk shops doing deals with crazy activists. At the least, someone as important as that wouldn't be dirtying his hands himself, he'd send a troop of well-trained knights to do it for him – not some crazy numbers man.

No. There's another thwimoren on the loose, at least as good as the Sorcerer Knight. Whoever he works for has a powerful weapon in their hands.

She turns her attention back to Leon, waiting for the blow-up sure to come over the knowledge that he's lost his ticket to success.

He rubs his face. 'All right. That's over with, then. Best to leave it alone and get to the next job.'

Ghost swallows her pout. It made for quite the dramatic

story, her night so far, and she did, she admits, get some enjoyment out of telling it – but the pay-off only comes with an eager audience, and so far the audience has all the eagerness of a poisoned rat in its death throes.

'Leon, listen,' she says, probing carefully, 'I tried, I really did. But you never said anything about other players in the game. That man was a surprise I couldn't plan for – he got there first, and now I'm the only witness to Moth's death. And I was only there in the first place because you blackmailed me into it. All in all, it's been a hell of a week.'

'Well, what do you want, a back rub?' Leon snaps. 'You were never there and you don't know shit, and who can prove otherwise?'

'Well, *he* can,' Ghost points out reasonably.

'How's he going to find you? Just drop it, Ghost. It's all over. We made a play and we lost.'

The *we* grinds her gears, but now doesn't feel like the best moment to follow up on that one.

'I'll have another job for you soon, neh?' Leon flaps a hand in a gesture of dismissal.

Alas for them both how well this goes down with Ghost, especially when she cannot shake the feeling that she's being fucked with from all angles.

'I'll finish up the Grenwald job, then,' she says, testing.

'You'll not. What did I just say? I'll have another job for you soon. In the meantime, keep your head low; spend some of that trick you have tucked away in yer spare boots on women and wine.'

Ghost stands zapped and wobbling, adrenalin doing its drum dance along her insides and pushing her all off-balance.

'Let me see,' she says thoughtfully, 'if I've got everything straight. I chase a soothsayer who turns up dead. Someone's drowning godchildren. I get collared by a woman who's got a machine to find out any godchild, even those who don't want to be found out. I go to a party where the people who run this town trade up bits of godchild for trick. I watch the machine thieved and the woman killed. And now I come here to tell my blackmailer boss about this exceedingly conspiratorial string of events and I find a bunch of private guard knights who work for Cass' client – and possibly her killer – coming out of my boss' den. And now my boss tells me, "You know all this crazy shit's been happening recently? Forget it. Forget all of it and go and get fucked." And to that I say that I've had my taste of being fucked recently, Leon, I've quite had my fill. I'm feeling very much like I'm being bent over in a non-consensual way, so you best start telling me what's really going on, because I'm having a pretty bad time and I'm just itching for someone to blame.'

His gaze is narrowed on Ghost. 'How do you know they're working for Glapissant?'

'The tattoo on his neck, Leon. A wheel with flowers? Glapissant has the same one. I don't know whose it is, but I know it's Senzatown. But why would a Senzatown elite have a 'launitown businessman on their loyalty list? And why would they be collecting up godchildren for drownings?'

'Stop,' says Garad.

Ghost stops.

'A seven-spoked wheel, with roses at the end of each spoke. That was the allegiance tattoo you saw on both Glapissant and these private knights visiting Leon?'

Ghost nods, demonstrating a look of quizzical innocence on

top of the careful appraisal of Garad's tight expression, scanning for any emotions they've been too slow to quash.

'Recognise the tattoo?' she asks.

Garad cuts her a look. 'It isn't mine, if that's what you're thinking.'

'I know very well it's not yours,' Ghost patiently responds. 'But you're Senzatown elite too – or you were once upon a time, before you moved to Blackheart to become a Caballaria knight, itso? Maybe you've seen that symbol before. Maybe you know whose it is.'

Garad shakes their head. 'You have it all wrong.' But it is said in the wavering tone of someone who doesn't quite believe their own convictions.

Ghost waits until Garad becomes too aware of the silence.

'Continue,' they say, and so Ghost does. There'll be time enough for pressing when the story's done.

Besides, Ghost already has a good idea who that tattoo belongs to.

'I don't give one rat's sac about whatever some elite is or is not doing with unregistereds,' Leon says with the fake patience of someone past their patience limit, 'because that is not my saints-damned job. That is an investigator vastos job, and I don't do that job, do I? I chase down unregistereds, and the last one I got given to chase down is dead. Job done, Leon doesn't get paid. Meanwhile the bills mount up and the trouble piles on and now I've got some fucken private prick knights breathing down my neck because *you* went to a party and pissed off their employer. What the fuck is *wrong* with you? How can you not see what the only course of action is at this point? We've been warned off. They came, they menaced, they muscled, and we're done, okay?

No more chasing down Cass Grenwald, no more foot-working at tricky rich parties, no more chasing after whatever that crazy activist bitch got herself shot over. It's finished. Done. Ended. All the words that mean stop, all right?'

'I can rip these blinders off,' seethes Ghost. 'I can find out what's really going on, just give me *time*—'

'You'll never see shit from where you are, and neither will I,' Leon raps back. 'That's just how it is for people like us. Look, I'm sorry I sent you into it. That's what you want? All right, have an apology. Best savour it, it only comes round once in a lifetime. I've been *told*: either we let go of this, or we let go of our fondness for breathing.'

That's enough for Ghost to pause.

'It en't just about you,' Leon continues, every syllable edged sharp. 'I'm the one in range. I'm the one they'll fire at. If you don't leave it alone, we're both dead. You'll do what you damn well please, I'm sure. But by all the saints, I'll take you down with me. You understand? I'll take you down.'

For the first time, Ghost can see that his obtuseness isn't about fear, it's about fury. He's trying very, very hard not to lose whatever tenuous hold on it he has. She's been so wrapped up in her own wrath that she hasn't seen his own.

This whole situation twitches her fist. It's been a hard night, and a bit of near-death can make a girl reckless. Leon is unmovable as a stone tor and there's nothing more to be done here.

After swearing blind she'll let the whole thing drop, Ghost leaves the coward brooding in his chair and heads out into the night.

There's only one place she wants to go right now. Somewhere she can hurt.

CHAPTER 21

Private Bone House, Blackheart
Two Months Ago

The sounds hit him first.

Hissing and clicking and beeping, seeping through the door. A strange mechanical alien, a giant locust filling the room, chittering and spindling across the tiles—

Wyll pulls his imagination up short, composes himself and codes into the lock. The door opens with a quiet swish.

In the room beyond, the light is kept dark, as per the patient's needs. Her body is little more than a bundle of sticks, though the private medic attending her is doing her best to change this. She has assured Wyll that the nutritional deficiencies of the first fourteen years of the patient's life will be corrected, as much as they can.

The medic, Nyma Parnere, is bent over a glow screen. She looks up as Wyll enters, her pleasant face calibrated to concern.

'How is everything?' asks Wyll quietly.

Nyma glances at the bed in the corner, surrounded by its hissing and clicking machinery, its occupant asleep among the sheets and pillows like a mouse burrowed in its nest.

'Better,' she says. 'At least, her metrics have improved.

But she's very weak. I'd guess she's been like this her whole life.' Nyma gives a helpless shrug. 'I don't really know what's wrong with her.'

Nyma is both an extremely talented medic and refreshingly direct, two reasons why Wyll thinks well of her. She has nursed him through many fight injuries, both the official and rather more unofficial kind, and she is both loyal and discreet, another reason Wyll thinks well of her.

'Her illness might be linked to her talents,' he says. 'If what I've heard is true, the kind of thing she can do is so draining that it takes too much of a physical toll for her to function normally.'

Nyma's eyebrows rise, and her expression turns thoughtful.

'Like she has an imbalance of power in the body,' she says. 'The energy required is too great, so she can never replenish or repair enough to get herself back to the healthy middle.' Her gaze catches Wyll. 'Where did you get her from? Is she family of yours?'

Of course, sometimes Nyma's directness is a hazard rather than a benefit.

'No, she doesn't belong to me,' Wyll says. 'I'm just looking after her for the moment.'

'Then who does she belong to?' asks Nyma, but Wyll does not really have an answer for that.

The hastily scribbled message he received via a nervy Gennivy this morning read simply:

Your package never turned up.
Do you have mine?

Saintsdamn Red for not acting on his offer to get her out of London. The idiot is probably wandering around Blackheart streets telling anyone who'll listen that she should be executed for treason.

Red or no Red, no doubt Viviane will be coming soon to collect their coveted map. Did they know that the map is a living godchild? Did they keep that from him? It's possible. When he saw the poor girl hooked up to that machine in the cellar of Moth's junk shop, when he'd looked around and realised that she *lived* down there, and that Moth, her own mother, was selling her off for what she could do . . .

Something very old and very brittle inside him snapped.

Wyll knows about living in cellars, and he knows about parents like Moth, parents who see their children as something to use over something to love.

Viviane will be angry with him, because Moth was not supposed to die. But he can be angry in turn that their end of the deal has not been met. They will protest that they cannot be blamed for Red's refusal to pick up on his offer, which is hard to argue against – but what Red doesn't know is that now he has another way to find her. She will, as Lillath has suggested, have run to the only friends she'd have left – her co-conspirators.

He has to move quickly, but he can get to them before Lillath does. He can see for himself who plotted to kill Art. *He* can decide what their fates should be – not the Spider, not the Saith, not anyone who might hesitate when they should kill because they're too afraid of how it would make them look.

He will make the kill. For Art.

If this map actually works, that is. Because if Moth was right about what she can do, she is nothing short of a miracle.

Wyll hears a rustle of movement from the bed. Fine, sweat-soaked strands of hair sprawl weakly over the pillow's desert mounds. Two eyes, glistening and wobbling, are uncooked eggs on the pale plate of a face. The mouth, a thin, puckered gash, opens.

'Where's Mama,' says a barely voice.

Nyma raises her eyes to Wyll's. 'It's all she's been saying, over and over. I haven't even got her name out of her.'

'Where's Mama,' the girl in the bed says again.

'What's your name?' asks Wyll gently.

'Where's Mama.'

'Your mother told me you can do something special. I'd like you to show me, if you can.'

'Where's Mama,' the girl's voice rises to a scream, her gaze wild and unseeing. 'Where's Mama! Where's Mama! Where's Mama! Where's Mama! WHERE'S MAMA! WHERE'S MAMA!'

The words lose all meaning, now an animal chant, a howling dog.

Nyma takes Wyll's arm and manoeuvres him out of the room, hunching under the sonic storm like a woman caught out in the rain without a shield.

The door shuts. The girl's mindless shouts are dulled to a manageable background.

They look at each other.

'I come when called, never any questions asked,' Nyma begins.

'Yes,' Wyll replies. 'I like that about you.'

'But that's a very sick girl you have in there. Where are her family?'

'Not around.'

'We can't get her mother?'

'It's interesting to me that you assume that would be a good thing,' Wyll says. 'As if the ability to procreate automatically makes you the best at looking after the thing you made.'

'Legally, it does, until proven otherwise,' Nyma says stubbornly.

'Her mother proved it otherwise.'

Nyma looks at him as if she is trying very hard to believe him.

Wyll sighs. 'It isn't only trick that buys your quiet, is it?'

Nyma just nods, as if this is an entirely expected move. 'I know what I owe you. I know without you I'd be in prison, or worse. But how long does that last? One day I might come up to a line I cannot cross, no matter what it costs me.'

'Is today that day?' asks Wyll.

Nyma stands as if in thought while the milliseconds tick by and alternate future timelines flash through Wyll's mind – but he forces himself to wait for her decision. Nyma's loyalty is no doubt due in large part to the trick paid and the debt owed, but also due to something more indefinable. Respect, perhaps. Wyll suspects that if he ever treated her as less than an equal, all the trick and debt in the world couldn't prevent the dust trail she'd leave in her wake as she accelerated firmly out the door.

'No,' she says at last. 'It's not. Look, I know you have a thing for helping our kind. I know you've made it your cause. But that girl in there can't survive without constant care. She will never be able to make her way in the world alone, you understand me? Are you really willing to take that on?'

'No, of course not,' says Wyll, 'she's only a means to an end. I need you to help me assess what care she needs and secure it for her. The best and most discreet you can find. Whatever it costs.'

He waits for Nyma to decide their fates.

She rubs her forehead, tired from the moral battle she just fought. 'Si,' she says shortly. 'Under the usual name, I assume.'

Wyll nods.

Once she has departed, to return in a few hours with what equipment she has decided is necessary in the meantime, Wyll turns his attention back to the living map he has stolen.

She wants Mama? She'll get Mama.

It takes a moment. He studied the woman as much as he could on his meeting with her, but an hour or two in someone's company isn't enough to get the full range of their expressions, so there's none of the finesse of his usual work. He assesses himself in the mirror. Good enough, especially in dim lighting under the eyes of a half-mad child.

Wyll stands still, allowing himself to sink away just a little more. It's not enough to slide someone else on like a costume. Costumes affect the insides too. It's the point of them, in fact. Otherwise, why wear something that doesn't change you? Whether it be to make yourself feel thewy, foppish, fuckable, haughty, sweet or lithe.

When he is ready, he enters the makeshift sickroom, crossing the room to the chorus of machine birds chirruping, machine animals breathing.

The pillows rustle. 'Mama,' says the map.

Then she falls silent, as if this much expression has already exhausted her.

Wyll approaches the bed, running through his mind how Moth had spoken to her bed-bound daughter in front of him. The things she had said to make her map show off her skills.

'My girl,' he says fondly. 'My dear girl. Now, my girl, can we do a little work today, hm?'

The map watches him owlishly as he takes the seat next to the bed.

'Can you find someone for Mama?' he coaxes, leaning forwards and taking a limp, damp little hand in his. 'Your favourite game to play, isn't it? Finding people? Showing me what you can do?'

The map stares at him, drinking him in. He forces himself still, forces himself to believe that she believes what she sees.

Finally the map gives a faint nod. He feels the press of her fingers on his, a weak tightening.

He has wondered if he would feel it, the map's rummaging through his mind. He has also wondered what else she might pick up on when she's in there. Could she see things about him he never wants anyone to see? Will it ever be possible to know how she works? Does it matter? Should he try?

'Who?' the map demands, and Wyll shakes off his fears. Too late to back out now.

What had Moth said about this part? All you needed to do was focus on the person you wanted to find and think of everything you know about them, everything you feel about them, for as long as it takes. Someone you know is much easier for the map to find – there are more reference points. A stranger takes longer.

Wyll concentrates. He conjures Red's face in his mind. He forms her expressions – the guarded one, the loose one, the one she had when she was on top of him, the one she had when he had his hands around her throat, the slip and twist of her body in the footage of her first day at knight's training, the fall when she gives herself over to the fight.

No one remembers a person exactly. Memory is a feeling, an ever-changing approximation, and all he has is the impact of the person on him, not the person itself. His Red envelops him, suffuses him, and he bathes in her memory smell.

He feels a faint scratching inside himself, as if an insect is walking over the delicate spongy ridges of his brain. It is a deeply strange feeling, too unknown to decide, yet, whether unpleasant or not.

Thank the saints it doesn't take long.

The Red in his mind shifts, taking on her own life, moving independently, away from his imaginings. Now the map has control of his fantasy Red. He watches, fascinated, as the Red in his mind walks about in a room, in a house.

Then the map shows him who else is in the room.

When Wyll realises where she is, he feels a cold dread creep its wet fingers around his heart and squeeze. Saints alive. *This* is who was behind the assassination? *This* is who has been helping Red?

When Lillath finds out, things are going to start exploding.

'Good girl,' Wyll tells the map, and strokes her limp hair.

PART II

Struggle like a rabbit
Dangling on the snare
But you're the one that put you there.

— Flowers for Kane

CHAPTER 22

Garad's Apartment, Evrontown
Two Weeks Ago

Ghost's throat hurts.

She's looking at Garad, but Garad stares hard into the wall past her head, lost in some ferocious thought of their own, reviewing her story so far, maybe, looking for the clues, that insistent tickling at the back of their mind that suggests there are connections to make.

Ghost's throat hurts, and Garad will get there soon enough, so this part of the story she does not relate.

This part of the story is just hers.

Wardogs Bar, Alaunitown
One Month Ago

Ghost is looking at a fight board.

The names are unfamiliar, but then again they would be because this is Wardogs, and she doesn't move in the kind of circles that know those names, or not quite yet. Give her enough time to sink all the way into the silt.

A half-drunk tank of headpuncher dangles from one hand as

249

Ghost contemplates the board, her recent talk with Leon a sourer taste in her mouth than the drink. His words chase a tail in her head, round and round. *Either we let go of this, or we let go of our fondness for breathing.*

The old her was the thinker. The new her, *this* her, prefers to take a swing at things first. That's what she's for – violence. She looks up at the board again.

'Thinking of putting your name down?' says an older man hanging next to the board. He has a keen gleam in his eye as he looks her up, down and sideways.

Wardogs fighters, unlike in the regular Caballaria, aren't pre-determined. There's no chance to meditate, train, hole up in a monastery and get massaged and fed all day. You put your name down on the day's chalkboard, and you get randomly picked. In that way, it's a lot more brutally fair than most Caballaria bouts, being left to chance, but there are a million other ways it's not. Corruption is as rife here as anywhere else, and with a heftier price to pay for the losing side.

Ghost shrugs. 'I might.'

The man gives a derogatory chuckle. 'Pretty thing like you, someone's got to miss you.'

She picks up the chalk. 'You'd think so, wouldn't you?'

'Careful,' the man says. 'I was only joking with you. Don't get that lovely face mashed up.'

'I'll duck.' She's lucky – or unlucky, depending on your point of view – that it's a quiet sign-up day and they need the fighters, or she wouldn't get a look in. There are several empty spaces on the board, just waiting for a new name to fill them up.

'Come on, you're too small!' the man scoffs. 'It's a question of sheer strength. Most of the mecs you'd be up against would mince you.'

'The big ones are slow,' Ghost says.

'Well, I'm sure you're speedier, and you could give them the run around, but what you gonna do when they catch you?'

'Get hammered into the ground, I expect,' says Ghost. 'Only I have a trick they don't.'

The man grins. 'And what's that, then?'

'Most people can't get back up from a hammering.' She bends to the board and prints her name. 'But I can.'

Once upon a time, two knights met in a monastery when they really shouldn't have.

Really, as Ghost remembers it now, it was the fault of the young monk in charge of her stay there. He was newly initiated, that much was obvious, and nervous. Hadn't locked the monastery's layout well enough into his mind yet to navigate with the unconscious ease of training. He went wrong.

Really, as Ghost remembers it now, it was also the fault of her opponent. Despite being one of the most recognisable faces in London, they had that day decided not to wear the standard chainmail hood mask required of knights while on the move around the buildings. It's a failsafe, really – the rituals of a pre-Caballaria fight are elaborately designed to prevent two opponents ever meeting while sequestered in the same monastery. They are never allowed to move outside of their designated room without being accompanied by a monk, they use separate training areas, and there is no communal dining area, not for guest knights – all meals are brought to their room. Even were there a mistake and their paths managed to cross, at least the hood mask would provide some anonymity.

But Garad wasn't wearing theirs. They later claimed it was the first time they'd ever done that, and had honestly no good reason for it, decrying either laziness or hubris. Later they'd come to see it as a deliberate influence, as though the saints had wanted them to meet.

Two small mistakes by themselves wouldn't have mattered much, but together changed both their lives.

The monk could be forgiven. The layout of that particular monastery was admittedly confusing. The halls were set as occasionally interlocking spirals, illustrating the idea of two people following a similar path but on different sides, moving side by side yet separate, blind to each other, as humans tend to move through life. Except these spirals occasionally interlock with a gap between walls, allowing the monks to move more freely than their knight charges, and it's through one of these gaps that the two knights caught sight of each other. Another coincidence – a moment later and they would each have passed an empty gap. But they crossed the gap at the same time, and it was only for one second they could see each other clear as day, but one second was enough.

They both stopped short, drawn to sudden movement. They both looked at each other – Ghost with her features and hair covered in heavy folds of tight chain that pooled on her shoulders, Garad with a naked face, sharp and lean and opaque under the pale hallway lights.

The Silver Angel themself. The King's own champion. Hair that famed shock of white. Figure loaded with rangy, muscular power. Legendary, beautiful, iconic.

'Ah, fuck it,' they said, and gave a short, cross sigh.

The next clear capture from Ghost's memory collection was set several hours later. She was sat alone on a bench nestled among the luscious greenery of the monastery's rooftop garden. It was high summer at that time, and despite it being late evening, the sun was still fat and gorgeous in the sky, pendulously low and golden warm.

The rooftop garden served both as a gracefully designed oasis from its heat and a traditional tribute to the Saith. They had altar spaces aplenty inside, but the garden was, to Ghost, its loveliest offering. Seven artworks dotted the green. One was a small stone fountain carved to look like Evron's face, with cupped hands below, water pooling in his palms and spilling downwards as an offering to the thirsty. There was a seven-spoked stone wheel, long Senza's own symbol. The sundial on a tall plinth in the centre, where it would catch the light best, was for Rhyfen, ever associated with the fire of the sun. Iochi had a small pond, dotted with the mottled spy fish that were his trademark, slippery and tough to spot. There was Alaunis, made as a fox out of copper wire mesh, with clusters of black pearls for his eyes. Gwanhara's carved hand rose out of the undergrowth, covered in crawling ivy like intricate jewellery, with a key resting in her palm. Next to the hand stood a stone-carved door to nowhere – or at least, nowhere you could see – as Marvol's doorway to death and the unknown.

In her memory, Ghost was sat clutching a short, folded letter in one hand, looking at the doorway, or rather through it, when Garad appeared in the garden. Ghost watched their languid approach from the safety of her bench.

'Well,' they said when they were close enough, as if the two of them knew each other so well that polite introductions had been put in a box marked "wastes of time", 'I'm being replaced. You?'

In reply, Ghost held her own letter aloft.

'A paper recall?' Garad raises a brow. 'Vintage.'

'Public stables can't afford to use the glows networks,' Ghost replied. 'Officially. Unofficially, we're an under-resourced herd of dinosaurs whose approach to the latest in communications tech I'd describe as "apathetically baffled".'

Garad picked their way to the bench and sat next to Ghost, who found her heart beginning an uneasy thrum. They'd met before this, but only ever at grand Caballaria functions, surrounded by others and constrained by etiquette. This casually intimate nearness was new and strange and, according to her heartbeat, thrilling.

'It's my fault,' said Garad. 'Us both being replaced. After we saw each other, I insisted. Sent a message about it right away.'

'So did I,' Ghost replied.

She was still concentrating on the stone doorway, or at least pretending to, but there was no denying the surprise in Garad's voice.

'You did?'

'I did.'

'May I ask why?'

Ghost glanced at Garad. 'What d'you mean, why? It's in the Code, that's why. Fighters aren't meant to know what they're fighting for or who they're fighting against, to preserve the purity and integrity of the bout. I'm aware most people don't take it seriously, but I do. Besides, it's a waste of time to go through the bother of these elaborate set-ups to make sure we don't meet beforehand, if at the quick we're just going to throw up our hands and say, "Oh well, never mind." Why bother with *any* of the rituals, then? You render the whole thing meaningless.'

Garad gave a great laugh. 'Well said.'

'I get riled too easy,' Ghost confessed, now feeling the hot flush comedown on the other side of sudden anger.

'It's a sin to hide passion.'

It was Ghost's turn to be surprised. The great unreadable Silver Angel, whose private life was locked tighter than a miser's purse, enthusiastic on showing passion?

They looked away from her and across the garden, clearing their throat.

'This is one of my favourite Saith shrines in the dis',' they said, gesturing at the artworks around them.

Ghost nodded. 'Mine too. Mostly cos it's quiet. Half the fighters I know who've stayed here pre-bout don't even know about it. Can you imagine being so incurious?'

'You'd have to have an inclination to think upwards. Most people just look ahead.'

'Ah well,' says Ghost agreeably, 'I think it's because I'm a bit of an escape artist. There's a bit of Iochi in me, despite being Rhyfentown born and bred.'

The sun lowered as they talked, spreading itself like persimmon jam across the sky. The air was warm and alive.

'I might have to train this out when I get home,' Garad confessed. 'You know how it is. You get all revved up in pre-fight time. You sink right into it. You start to disappear and the fight takes over. It needs a release, you know? And when you don't get it . . .'

They trailed off.

It was then that Ghost took her chance. 'I've always wanted to fight you,' she said. 'Well, who hasn't? Shame to waste the chance – unless you're leaving now?'

Garad leaned back against the bench. Ghost could not help but notice how this gesture made the material of their trousers strain and wrinkle against their thighs.

'I won't get picked up for another few hours,' they replied. 'You?'

'I don't travel with an escort. My bike's downstairs. I leave whenever I want.' Ghost grinned. 'There are advantages to being a nobody.'

Garad scoffed. 'You're currently one of Rhyfentown's most famous knights.'

'Neh, well, you're one of the most famous knights in all Seven Kingdoms.'

Garad's expression soured. 'Don't remind me.'

'Oh, what's the matter, all those diamond-encrusted swords weighing you down? Life's so *hard* when life's so easy. Royal escorts and suites at the palace.'

'Coming from you? I've seen you walking the halls of Cair Lleon so often the last few months, the gates must open automatically when you bike up, now.'

Then it was Ghost's turn to sour. 'Not true. I'm only there for those stupid official functions.'

Sensing a hit, Garad grinned. 'Anyone would think you had a lover at the palace. Oh my, is that a blush?'

Ghost stood then, their foreplay having done its work. 'I just imagined knocking you on your back and got all excited. You have fists to back up those words?'

It was a good bout, as she remembers it, even though both were pulled back from hurting each other too much. She thinks now that Garad was favouring her, letting her land hits they could have stopped, especially considering what happened next. A decent round kick of hers left the Silver Angel winded on their back in the grass.

'Nice,' they wheezed.

'Let's stop,' Ghost offered between pants, terrified that they would agree.

'Oh, you're tired?'

'How dare you. Have at me.'

But instead of springing back up to continue, Garad just lay there, magnificently sprawled.

'Come here,' they said.

And then Ghost knew that she was about to get exactly what she wanted.

It had been, she later reflected, a long time in coming.

Garad liked her, that much she knew. Enough to seek her out at functions, introduce her to important people, act like something of a temporary mentor for the evening, the ram shepherding the yearling – though the gap in their ages was less than might be supposed. Garad had won their King the Sword of London at the unbelievable age of nineteen, and Ghost had entered the Caballaria at the relatively old starting age of near thirty. There were only seven years between them, but in fight years they might as well be different generations.

No one *approached* someone like the Silver Angel. They were the kind of knight wholly out of reach, even of other knights, until they descended from their lofty pedestal to pluck their choice from the tree, and Garad was notorious for their absence of plucking. Only now does Ghost contemplate the thought that they simply might be a lot more private about it. No one would be coming up to the rooftop, not until the next bout – which wasn't until next week. Unusually, they were the only fighters currently occupying the monastery. The promise of temporary joy soon to be lost, the heady cloy of jasmine tangled in the breeze and the light drenched in the golden hour with the sun spreading itself like a dropped egg in the sky – all of it gathering to create this time, this opportunity, the awareness that only occurs once every so often of the unique quality of each moment, the only one of its kind in all lives, in all times, this one right here between two people who will never encounter this exact permutation again.

What fucken idiot, reasoned Ghost, would pass up such a moment?

So she dropped to her knees and crawled up the length of Garad's body, hovering over their sweat-streaked face, mouths inches away.

'Neh?' murmured Ghost. 'What is it?'

Garad wasn't smiling any more. 'Our official bout may have been pulled, but there's another way to honour the Saints. A private way.' They swallowed. 'A way I want very much.'

'Be. More. Specific,' Ghost murmured, alive and in heat with the feel of the body underneath her, its hot solidity.

'Specifically? Take off all your clothes, right now,' said Garad.

And so began the most exciting fight of Ghost's life.

They were joyful and mischievous, she remembered, as only those who have temporarily made a world of no responsibilities with a population of just two could be, stripping each other in the purple dusk, fast and hot and wild. Those worlds always collapsed soon enough, and soon enough would come the responsibilities of their outside lives. But one surrender on an evening with nothing else to do was not only forgivable, but practically required.

If only it had stopped there.

If only one evening had been enough.

But it hadn't.

In her defence – if there could ever be such a thing for such an eventual catastrophe – it was Garad who pursued Ghost. Garad who sent her love letters, and messages, and gave her the address to their private home in, of all districts, Alaunitown.

('Why there?' a baffled Ghost had once asked. 'You're Senzatown-born and you work out of Blackheart's palace. Alaunitown doesn't make any sense.'

'No, it doesn't, and that's why it works,' Garad had replied. 'When I say I like privacy, I mean it.')

Worship with Garad was the abandonment and ecstasy of a true believer. A glad and joyful momentary shucking of the self and all its precarious, ephemeral constructions in the face of the endless universe. A way to touch the infinite, and a way to remind each other how very animal, how very human, they both were.

Desire was the gift they gave each other, adding to it each time they met, feeding it until it grew so colossal that by the time Ghost stepped back to try and get its sides into view, it was too late. She'd let it grow bigger than her, so big that it threatened to break her and remake her into something else.

And saints, she wanted to be broken.

In death is life made, and life in death.

'People think you're celibate,' Ghost once teased Garad, as they lay naked together, spent from their latest entanglement. 'If only they knew what I know.'

'I'm not,' Garad had replied. 'It's just that I only ever touch things I love.'

If Ghost had not already fallen before that, it would have sent her hurtling off the cliff.

She was gone. She was in love. Joyously, recklessly, dangerously in love.

There was just one problem standing in the way of giving in to it. She had a secret, one she had guarded since childhood, and this love demanded that she give all of herself to it, even the hidden parts of herself.

Even if it meant the end of her life.

There's not much fanfare in Wardogs. Just grit on the packed dirt floor that scratches under your boots and the rank smell of too many humans penned into too small a space.

Her opponent leers at her as they wheel around the killing circle. He's of average height but slabby, and has far more muscle mass than her. Most everyone does. She's got to be clever to dodge strength. She's got to dredge up those tactics etched into her by another life.

It feels simple. It feels like the thing humans do best and most naturally – watch their own tear each other to pieces; watch and enjoy it.

We like pain, she thinks, *we don't understand a world without it. Suffering is our default, and any time it gets any better than that for us, we get bored and itchy and start to tear it all down again, like a dog that can't stop scratching a mostly healed wound to open it up again, just to feel that sting . . .*

The fist comes for her, lands – would have been square on her face if she hadn't part dodged. And if she hadn't part dodged, muscles twitching with old instincts, she'd already be out of this fight.

'Well, shit,' she says. Hawks up a glob, spits it out on to the grit. 'I just did my face paint, man.'

Her opponent doesn't wait but swings again while she's down.

Another difference from the Caballaria.

That one reverberates through her skull, buzzing its fragile plates so hard it feels like they might get shaken out of their frames, like windows in a quake. Ghost's world contracts to the buzz, all other senses shorted out. She waits patiently, counting out a couple of lifetimes, and then she can see again, and the squeal and hiss and roar of the background trickles back into her ears like soup.

She's on her arse in the dust, her opponent peering warily at her from some distance.

Ghost gives him a wink and stretches her mouth into a smile. It hurts her cheeks like a bitch.

'You sh'd move to Marvoltown, freak,' her opponent snorts over the crowd's animal hooting.

'I was there a few months ago, actually,' she tells him. Her tongue feels numb, turning her words to slurry. 'Day trip. Nice place.'

He snorts. 'Seems like you wouldn't mind going back. Yield.'

'Oh, come on,' Ghost complains, steadying herself against the wall. 'I thought Wardogs went to the death.'

'Only for people who deserve to die.' His scratchy voice rises to be heard over the baying of the crowd.

'What makes you think I don't?'

'Idiot. I'll not give you what you want, you hear?'

'Oh,' Ghost says brightly, 'so you yield?'

'What?' His brow concertinas in quizzical furrows. 'You're down, you were on the damn floor!'

'Right, but you're going to have to put me down proper to win, so if you don't want to do that, you should yield.'

'You're suicidal!'

'And you're in the wrong game,' Ghost says, 'if you don't have the belly to be the bullet in my gun.'

She sees it. The split-second of panicked indecision. The hardening of his face as grim resolve kicks in. He's not making this choice alone. The crowd makes it for him, the witnesses of his life. It's one thing for someone like him to be a coward alone. Much worse to be it where others can see.

Only he's too late. His distaste has cost him. Ghost staggers past his guard to wrap his belly around her fist, pushing it in nice and snug like all she ever wanted was a glove made of flesh to warm her hand with. He loses his breath, he loses everything, collapsing like a broken marionette, and she's on him, a crab-claw razor in her hand, eager to kiss his throat.

He freezes when he feels its caress against his sliceable skin.

'I had you,' he snarls a bewildered snarl, 'I *had* you—'

'And now you don't,' Ghost says, and closes the crab claw shut.

CHAPTER 23

Garad's Apartment, Evrontown
Two Weeks Ago

'You became a Wardogs fighter,' says Garad, with the barely concealed distaste of someone who never had to contemplate sinking that low.

'Neh,' Ghost replies. 'You ought to try it sometime. They call it the "real fight". They say in comparison, Caballaria bouts are nothing more than dancers playing a part.' She pauses. 'Actually, what they say is a lot less polite than that, but you look the type to get easily riled.'

Garad's jaw is tighter than a bow string.

Ghost just about manages to swallow her smile.

The Dugs, Alaunitown
Three Weeks Ago

Long day.

Bad choices lining up like the hangover waiting for Ghost over the horizon. The grim regret of knowing that all she can do is wait it out. Suffer on through, walk the long chasm until she reaches the light once more. A metaphor for life, hangovers.

Sometimes it feels like it's been mostly chasms so far. Is that her choice or fate's? It's hard to tell.

Her latest Wardogs fight was supposed to have been rigged in favour of her opponent – hopped up, so she found out later, on the latest in nervous-system kickers, which explained his constant sweating and the pinpricks of his eyes, an effect of chemicals and not lenses – so now she's won the bout, she's got another couple of enemies to add to the tally, another few people who've taken note of her.

It's almost like you want *to be discovered*, the other tells her sullenly, and then sinks away, too tired to fight against the pull of battered exhaustion.

Such battered exhaustion, in fact, that Ghost fails to notice the tell-tale strangled chirrup of her tampered door lock. She gets all the way inside and halfway across the dark labyrinth space of her apartment floor before she notices a couple of upended candles here and there, which leads her gaze by the nose to the chair in the far corner, the pair of legs currently striping its modest width, the gun held muzzle out atop them, and the cinnamon swirl of hair a little ways above it catching the streetlights outside the window in streaks and glints.

Ghost gives a long, shuddering sigh.

'Oh, you,' she says, as her pulse gamely struggles to respond to the warning adrenalin. 'Is that my gun?'

'Well, I don't own one of these, do I?' speaks the copper-tinged darkness.

The gun point lowers, just a fraction. 'Saints,' says the darkness, 'what happened to you?'

'Got in a fight,' says Ghost.

'With who?'

'Myself,' says Ghost.

'Making as much sense as usual, I see.'

Ghost resists the urge to collapse slowly to the floor.

'I'll trot right past the tired bit about how you got in and go straight to the why,' she says.

'Mostly because where I come from, we don't like it when people we know get murdered.'

'Mostly? What's the rest of it about?'

The gun is held as silent and steady as the one holding it.

'Clearly you're angry about Moth's death,' Ghost tries instead, 'but if it were me, I think I'd feel relief.'

'Relief.'

'That I get to stop dancing to someone else's tune.'

A soft scoff from the copper-tinged darkness above the gun. 'I don't answer to her.'

'And you never will again,' says Ghost.

'You stone-hearted goss,' spits the darkness.

Ghost tuts. 'Such foul language from such a sweet song mouth.'

She takes a step or two forwards, slow enough not to spook out an inadvertent bullet.

'Why'd you kill her?' asks Delilah. 'Because of the test? She wouldn't have told anyone. Not really.'

Ghost shakes her head. 'I didn't kill her.'

'Prove it.'

'All right,' says Ghost, 'I did.'

A pause – disbelief?

'Why?' asks Delilah, the word as hard as the bullet at the end of her arm.

'The test machine. The map. Whatever the fuck it is. She was selling it off to the highest bidder. Sadly, he didn't want to pay.' Ghost takes hold of the pause. 'Neh, I know all about the private sale. Did you?'

Two more steps and she's nearly in grasping reach—

'Stop!' Delilah barks. 'Stop moving! Do you want to die?'

'Maybe,' says Ghost, and reaches her.

The tussle is brief. The singer isn't built for fighting, and she wants this to end. Surrender brings the relief of no choice, or at least the illusion of it. She struggles like a testing cat, *stop start stop start*. Her neck gives so pleasingly under pressure.

Ghost lets go, pushes her off, throws the gun away hard, out of reach of them both, bouncing it off a cabinet and knocking over an unlit candelabrum.

Delilah stares at her, breathing hard.

'If you want to go, go now,' says Ghost. 'Get out.'

'Why, what happens if I don't?'

'You want another turn at trying to kill me, is that it?'

'You don't want me to leave,' says Delilah. 'And you need help to get cleaned up. Where are your supplies?'

Mercifully, nowhere near the gun.

Ghost eases herself on to the end of the bed and directs Delilah from there. A small recess behind the sink yields medicinal fruit. Delilah is all business, moving swiftly and surely, switching on lights, filling up a bowl with clean water, nimble fingers sorting through wound binders and disinfecter strips.

She stands in front of Ghost, looking down at her. 'Take off your shirt,' she says.

Ghost considers protesting, but she can't think of anything clever to say. She wants to be petted, and she's so damn tired. If Delilah decides to take up that scalpel in the medical kit and stab her with it, well, at least that way she'd get some sleep.

Slowly and haltingly, she peels off her shirt. Her body is crusted with dried blood and old sweat, heavy and earthy in front of the sprite hovering above. Air against her skin makes her want to curl protectively into herself. She feels examined, exposed.

Delilah makes unhappy animal noises as her gaze sweeps the damage.

Her cloth-laden hand reaches out. Cold soft shock presses pain buttons. Blood-infused water trickles over the tiny hairs furring out of Ghost's skin, riveting downwards to seep into the waistband of her trousers. Nipples tight from the touch, the air, the water, elemental stimuli. Delilah's hand strokes, sweeps, dabs.

'Why d'you like it?' she asks as she touches.

'What?' replies Ghost. Her voice comes out a little more strangled than she was hoping for. A little less in control.

'Pain.'

Ghost huffs an almost laugh. 'I don't know. Why do we like it?'

'We? I'm not into it.'

'You're not into the safe ones. Cass. Me. Who knows who else from before. Pain of a different kind, but still pain. Ow!'

There's no sorry from Delilah, just a murmured explanation, something to do with crusted blood. Ghost feels those cloth fingers fish into the groove of her spine. It's her shoulders that make her feel the most exposed. The bed sighs around her in rumples as Delilah climbs in, nestling into the space behind Ghost's seat at its end. Ghost can feel the weight at her back, the presence, the flashing ache in her groin that tells her how much she wants the body behind her to press in. The fingers on her back ribs to slip around to the front.

'What makes you think I'm into you?' comes a tickling whisper into her right ear.

'I don't know about you, but I wouldn't clean just anyone,' manages Ghost. 'I'd charge extra for that.'

'Well, you did buy me a couple of drinks,' purrs the sprite.

'Neh, I hadn't forgotten the dumbest choice I ever made.' Ghost arches her spine, pushing into the touch skimming the contours of her chest.

'Let me make it up to you, then.' The body behind her closes in, encircling her from behind, a thigh hugging in on each side of her hip. The touch skirts lower, over the softened pouch of her lower belly, trickles against the triangular crease of her inner thighs.

Ghost leans back, cradling her head on Delilah's shoulder, and willingly opens up her legs. The relief she feels when those fingers stroke and delve their way inside her is gorgeous, comforting, dangerous.

'Cass is dead, isn't she?'

It comes in the drifting part before sleep, when the world has shrunk to a dark, warm cave.

Delilah's head rests on Ghost's shoulder as she asks the question, so the words seem to reverberate through her bones. They are plaited together in a corkscrew of limbs, the bed blankets hot and drowsy-heavy on top.

Ghost says nothing.

Then she says, 'Neh.'

Delilah's sigh is a shudder.

They float along on the bed boat for a while. The air still smells of warm sex.

'I think there's a spy in Moth's group,' comes Delilah's dreamy voice. 'I think they sold Cass out.'

Ghost resists the urge to ask whether the group has a name.

Likely something obvious. The Protectorate. The Defenders. Swords of Justice.

'A traitor to the cause?' she asks. 'Who would they sell Cass out to?'

'To whoever's collecting up godchildren in the area and killing them,' Delilah murmurs.

'Why would they do that?'

'Saints, who knows? But as a start – you can sell them for a lot to the right buyer, can't you?'

Ghost thinks of the sky palace, vials of auctioned blood, high-eyed faces with greed attached to their performing body parts, their weaving, magic hands.

'Why kill what makes trick?' she asks.

'Maybe Cass saw a future they didn't like.'

Another dreamy pause. And then:

'Ghost. I think you're next.'

Ghost stares up into the fuzzy dark.

'Why would you think that?'

'They said the map showed that you're a powerful godchild. Rare. Those are the ones who disappear.' The blankets rustle. 'Joln Chimes says you killed Moth and stole the map to protect yourself.'

'There was someone else. A buyer. He did it. I ran before he could get rid of his only witness.'

'Who is he?'

Ghost smiles grimly into the darkness. 'I don't know, and I've no idea how to find out. I can't defend myself to Chimes – and even if I could, he'd still believe whatever he wanted to. People like him always do.'

Drifting silence.

Ghost sighs. 'So let's review: your friends either want me dead because they think I ended map-maker Moth, or they want to feed me to the neighbourhood kambion-killer.'

'They're not my friends,' Delilah protests.

'No?'

'What if I said I wanted out?'

'Ah, is that my appeal?' Ghost muses. 'I'm your escape?'

Delilah twists like a fish in the sheets. Ghost feels her body being pressed with hands, used to lever weight until Delilah is sat astride her hips, thighs splayed, palms resting on Ghost's belly, the dip that runs down between her ribcage lovely enough that Ghost wants to reach out and stroke it, feel her way into its depression.

'I need you,' says the swaying sprite above her. 'I've never needed anyone in my life before. It scares me.'

You player, you player, you player, thinks Ghost.

But she loves it, loves it, loves it.

'It's all connected,' Delilah whispers. 'Cass' death, Moth and her map. We can help each other work it out, before . . .'

'Before what?'

'Before they take you too.'

'I'm not scared of them.'

But she is.

'Even if I'm wrong about that, the others will open up a dispute against you,' Delilah tries. 'For Moth's death.'

Saintsfuck those idiots. However wrong they might be, she cannot risk anyone from the local guard digging into her past. She was supposed to disappear, transform, discard her old life like a peanut shell. Instead she's been running around drawing attention to herself from every possible quarter.

'And in return?' Ghost asks.

270

'I'm not trying to make a deal,' Delilah insists.

Ghost just smiles. Delilah has the grace to look a little shifty, at least.

'What do you want to happen?'

'I just want to disappear,' Delilah says. 'Start over. Please. I don't have anyone else who can help me. You're my best chance.'

'Then you're really fucked,' Ghost says, but as a formality, an instinctive riposte, because of course she's going to help this wicked little witch. Of course she'll do anything she can. Player or played, it's all the same game.

Besides, she can't deny how much more alive she feels these days, as if her flesh is filling out on her bones, as if she is at last becoming a whole person again. Ghost may soon be a redundant name, one for a past her that needed to hide for a time. If she walks away now, she remains that ghost, with a shadow-her that'll dog her steps wherever she goes.

'I'd never before seen the man who killed Moth,' says Ghost. 'How do I find a total stranger?'

'I can find him,' Delilah replies.

'You know who he is, do you?'

'No, but I know someone who can track him down.'

'You going to tell me how?'

Delilah's eyes are luminous in the room's bistered predawn. 'You have to trust me.'

'Now why,' says Ghost, as she bucks her hips to tumble the hot lap of girl down to the bed and pushes up against her, 'would I do something as stupid as that?'

CHAPTER 24

Lheosne, Rhyfentown
Two Months Ago

Astride his bike, thighs clenched to its flanks and gloved fingers wrapped around its steers, Wyll takes stock of the edifice rearing before him.

An enormous cluster of smoked glass mushrooms sprouts from the richest guts of Rhyfentown. The glass deflects its surroundings with a murky sheen, a machine simulation's idea of a lake's darkest depths. The whole complex is braceleted by a wall, its front clasp a very closed glass screen gate twice his height and as thick as his wrist.

Lheosne. The biggest bio-dome in London, and second only across the Seven Kingdoms to the Queen's own all the way down in Kernow. Unlike the Kernowyen bio-dome, however, which houses everything but humans, Lheosne began life as the ancestral seat of Saint Rhyfen himself, and his descendants continue to live there.

The main house stands as it ever did, a spindly insectoid mansion dating back to pre-Lysander times and the Reckoning of the Saith. In later centuries came the first dome, constructed as an add-on to the main house, and they grew organically over the years across the family land, sprouting like a forest floor. In the following centuries, as Rhyfentown became more and more built-up, Lheosne grew alternately incongruous and harmonious, depending on the architectural flavours of each time – but it never changed.

This is the home of the family of Artorias Dracones, such as it remains – and apparently, according to Moth's map, the hiding place of Art's murderer.

Wyll shifts on the bike seat, paralysed with dismayed indecision. He'd been hoping to think up a plan on the ride over, some reason to explain why he'd come here. He'd told himself it was to confront Art's true killers and have his revenge, but even if he did manage to infiltrate the place and kill any Dracones he came across, there'd be no possibility of escaping the consequences. The repercussions, not only for him, but for London, would be too terrible to bear. But does that mean they should just get away with it?

The only reason Red could be here is if Art's own family are the ones behind his death, but it makes little sense. Art's ascension elevated their own. Before he took the throne, the Dracones were in tatters, friendless and trickless, clinging desperately to the remains of their power, the most diminished of the elite families of London. It seems a strange move, to destroy the source of their reacquired fortunes.

Is he here simply to understand, or does he just want to see Red again? Can anyone really be that pathetic?

Yes, says his father.

Ride away, his mother whispers.

She doesn't come up often in his head. She is the cautious one, the hold-back, the impulse checked. She was always a grey background presence in his life, and his imagined version of her carries on this long-established tradition. He has never been able to work out whether it was fear or apathy that forbade any outward concern for her only son.

Come on, his father urges. *You've come all this way only to ride tail? Get in there and make the people who played you suffer for it. That's the only way you win.*

His mother is silent. He fancies he can feel her quiet disapproval.

His vacillating thoughts are interrupted by a

—*bleep*—

The glass screen gate begins to slide open, its mechanism a sibilant hiss, soft as a breeze through grass.

Wyll has been seen.

Of course. They'd have capturers somewhere discreet, surveying the immediate lands beyond their domain, assessing potential threat. The Dracones have a reputation for being guarded, in lean and fat times alike.

Wyll checks his reflection in the bike's mirror, making sure his Barochi illusion is in place. A bald, pleasant-featured man stares back at him. Given the current negative suppositions surrounding his involvement in Art's death, it would not do to look like the Sorcerer Knight is paying a visit to its potential architects. A man who looks like a vastos in a small department authority debating funds for the local flower fountain astride a knight's machine is, he has to admit, a little incongruous, but if the situation goes to shit town, fast exits are much easier with wheels to hand.

The way is open. Wyll crawls forwards, rolling carefully along the narrow road. Smoked glass doors bar entrance into the spindle house itself, but as he pulls up at the tall set of bike parks at the front – their iron tips are rusting; these things are old – the doors open, revealing a figure wearing a mask. A mask, not an overlay, its surface a hard mould, its features set as a rigid, perfect blank. The eyes bulge in non-human fashion, and the mouth is nowhere to be seen.

Wyll stares at them. The stylised insectoid head stares back. Their body is clad in black clothes of indeterminate form. The effect deliberately obfuscates the shape of their limbs, suggesting a being of ponderous thunderclouds.

'I present my sorries,' Wyll says, 'for not making a prior appointment. I'm here to see Julias Consilias Dracones o'Rhyfentown.'

A fleshy hand, mercifully human, emerges from a sleeve. The fingers open and spread, as if to grasp. Wyll interprets this odd gesture as a motion of invitation. As he approaches, it closes in a flash on his arm. He stops short – his muscles twitch, straining with the sudden, savage need to retaliate – and looks into the insectoid mask.

'Is something wrong?' he asks mildly while his heart beats its panic drum.

Up close, the insectoid mask is not as smooth and blank as it had appeared to be. There are tiny cracks, fissures of long use, and the surface is patchily worn, as if vastos and the mask have been the same creature since birth.

A confusing beat – then the hand withdraws from his arm, and spreads its fingers towards the echoing interior. *Come inside.*

Wyll lays a hand on the thrumming strings of his nerves to quiet them, and then enters the dome. They pass through a bright corridor, its roof transparent to the skies above, the black-robed insectoid vastos a quietly swishing figure ahead.

One or two robed house vastos totter past in distant view. One slows down as they approach – slows down to a standstill, in fact. Its face is little more than a strange circular mouth rimmed with rows of regular points: teeth. Rows of teeth.

It is just a mask. There is someone very ordinary underneath it. Has to be.

The insectoid vastos arrives at a vast glass dome filled with a neatly tamed jungle, wilderness brought to heel. A vast atrium lined with uniform trenches sprouting tree and shrub, clusters of violent-coloured flowers with thick, rubbery petals as big as hand palms. Vines creep and twine over arches and rods, crowding the air far above the head, and further above that, birds chirrup and swoop across the soaring ceiling, landing wherever can hold them with a flutter and a head cock.

In the middle of it all perches an elegant little table laden with a delicately presented spread of food and drink. At the table sits the master of the house himself and a sculpted blonde woman in graceful attire, her hair adorned with tiny seed pearls and her shoulders wrapped in fox fur.

The Lady Orcade is taking tea with the Lord of Rhyfentown. Wyll had no idea they were such friends, but then again, they do each run an entire district as well as an elite family. Presumably they have a lot in common.

Julias looks up as his insectoid vastos enters, and then catches sight of Wyll.

'Who is this, Milio?' he enquires.

'Please excuse my interruption,' Wyll begs in his reedy voice. 'My name is Barochi.'

'Julias,' tuts the Lady Orcade. 'You said nothing about receiving company today.'

Julias cranes his neck in an exaggerated fashion. He looks like an old, wise animal with kindly eyes, tufts of hair, soft as bird down.

'That's because I didn't know I would be,' he says, frowning. 'It's a rare enough occurrence.'

'*I'm* here,' Orcade points out.

'Well, you're the rare occurrence, my dear.'

Orcade gives him a smile, the kind indicating satisfaction with the expected line promptly delivered. Her keen gaze latches on to Wyll.

'Barochi?' she enquires. 'Just the one name?'

'For business purposes, alas,' Wyll says deferentially.

'So mysterious,' murmurs the Lady. 'Well, Julias, if you'll excuse me, I think our visit is over.'

'My apologies—' Wyll begins.

Orcade holds up a half-gloved hand. 'Please, don't feel bad. It was long past time for me to leave. I can be guilty of using dear Julias' delightful company as a way to put off my own business.' She turns to Julias. 'I think you should offer our guest your honeysuckle tea.'

Julias' forehead wrinkles. 'Do you indeed?'

'He grows it himself,' Orcade tells Wyll. 'A special variety. You'll not taste another like it in the dis', I guarantee. The most beautifully delicate flavours.'

'How could I refuse such a unique experience?' murmurs Wyll.

'She's exaggerating,' Julias demurs.

'About the most talented botanist London has ever produced?' scolds Orcade. Their back and forth speaks of comfort and sweet familiarity. They are near enough in age, so it's easy to suppose that they would have been introduced when they were children. There is something pleasant about it, this early bridging of two districts. He remembers the note Julias passed to Orcade in the Consilium meet and wonders if their alliance runs politically as well as intimately.

He listens closely as they say their goodbyes, but they speak mostly of shared gossip. Once Orcade has departed, Julias snaps for a silently masked vastos, who attends to the table, clearing it away with practised gestures.

'The honeysuckle tea, I think,' Julias murmurs to them.

The masked vastos pauses in their clean-up and then bows, disappearing beyond the jungle.

'So,' Julias says. 'Barochi, was it? What is your desire?'

Wyll hesitates. It would be prudent to make sure that Red really is here, but if she appears and sees through his illusion the way she did in prison, he's fucked. What he needs is confirmation of Julias' involvement in Art's assassination – but how to get at it?

'The Artorian era,' he begins, 'has been kind to the Dracones family, itso?'

'Rather more so than his father's reign,' Julias agrees. 'The last twenty years has turned our fortunes around.'

'That is flatteringly candid.'

Julias flaps a hand. 'It's also public knowledge, so I haven't given you much.' His fingernails, Wyll notices, are rimmed with dirt. Soil, presumably.

'And you got on well, despite his illegitimacy?'

'A useful thing about success, it often renders such drawbacks void.' Julias smiles. 'As soon as Art won the Sword – and then kept it, against all odds – no one cared about his origins, least of all me.'

'They did try to take it away from him a couple of times, though, did they not?'

'They did. Mafelon in particular was a terrible event for us all. Just think what might have happened had they succeeded.' Julias gives a little shudder.

'The Welyens would have taken over,' Wyll suggests. 'Perhaps it would have been a good reign too?'

'Ha! Lucky for you, my Lady Orcade is out of earshot. You'd have lost some points with her for suggesting such a thing.' Julias gives Wyll an amused look. 'It took a long time and a lot of work for her to overcome the shadow of prejudice her brother Agravain dimmed her light with. He was the power-mad one, not she. She is far too discreet to go into particulars, but I believe she actually helped them bring Agravain down.'

'And was justifiably rewarded with the Lady of Alaunitown seat,' Wyll agrees.

'Very justifiably. One must recognise loyalty, otherwise where would we all be? At each other's throats all the time, haha.'

'Haha.'

'No,' Julias concludes, 'the Welyens present no danger, except to anyone who threatens London, as it should be. Then, watch them explode! The one who troubles me is the kambion knight.' Julias smiles at the arrival of a masked vastos. 'Ah, here's the tea.'

Under the table, Wyll digs a finger into the palm of the other hand. The pain calms him enough to ride over Julias' casual slur. It felt like a test he needed to pass.

As the tea is poured out for him, he inclines his head at Julias. 'Godchildren are a troublesome species. But which knight do you mean? There's more than one nowadays.'

'Don't remind me,' Julias remarks. 'I mean, of course, the King's own champion, the foolish man. Don't think I haven't tried to counsel him against all that, as well, but Art . . . well. People have their ideas, don't they?'

'He had a thing for protecting them,' agrees Wyll. 'You mistrust the Sorcerer Knight, then?'

'I just think you shouldn't have a tiger on the loose in your house.' Julias indicates the steaming cup in front of Wyll. 'Please do try it, I'm so excited to see what you think.'

The masked vastos chooses at that moment to bump clumsily into their table, upending Wyll's cup and splashing its contents on to the floor.

'Saintsfuck!' Julias screams suddenly. 'You idiot!'

The vastos says nothing, but raises their hands in a gesture of frightened surrender, and begins immediately to clean it up on their hands and knees. Are all the servants here mute? What an odd affectation.

'It's fine,' Wyll says, trying to hide his surprise at Julias' furious reaction. 'Really.'

'No, it's not, *leave* that—' Julias gestures impatiently at the kneeling vastos and points at Wyll. 'Pour out another cup for him. Now. *Slowly. Carefully.*'

The silent vastos does so under the hawk eye of his master, who refuses to look away or speak again until Wyll's cup is filled, at which point he relaxes, sighs and shakes his head, as if to say, 'I try, but what can you do?'

For the benefit of the poor vastos, Wyll takes a sip of the tea.

'The Lady Orcade was right,' he says. 'It tastes extraordinary, as though the honeysuckle blooms right in my mouth.'

Julias smiles, immediately placated.

'So you think the Sorcerer Knight was a threat to the King?' Wyll asks, after a second sip of the glorious tea. It's like swallowing liquid midsummer, hazy and gold on his tongue.

'More like a weapon in need of targets. Point it the right way and it can be an incredibly powerful asset.'

'Like his protégé,' Wyll remarks, while his heart speeds up. 'That Red girl making a name for herself.'

'A pelleren!' Julias enthuses. 'Extraordinary talent.'

'Have you met her?'

'I don't go to the fights much these days.'

It is cannily not a no.

'It's a shame she's not allowed to use that talent,' says Wyll.

'Law's law. And our King might be a touch kambion-struck, but hopefully not that stupid.' Julias smiles. 'Well, Barochi, this is a very pleasant conversation, but perhaps we should approach its business end. Let me hazard a guess on the reason you've come to visit me.'

'Please do,' Wyll says. His tea is half drunk and tingling him pleasantly all over.

'As you're surely aware, I am a botanist,' Julias says, scratching his chin. 'And a decent one, though not nearly as brilliant as the lovely Orcade would insist on. I have, however, managed to turn my modest talents into some lucrative business lines, my own little attempt to keep the family afloat in more difficult times. Necessity is the womb of creativity, as the 'launitowners say. Now, considering your insistence in using a false name and your decision to drop by unannounced, I assume your interest lies primarily in the less, hmmm, official products I offer.'

Well, this just got interesting. An intuition kicks.

'Tidal,' says Wyll. 'You synthesise Tidal.'

'Actually, I also created it,' Julias says with a modest dip of the head.

'Doesn't it intensify magic? I thought you were against its use.'

'Well, no, not entirely, in the right circumstances. All civilisations need good weapons to defend themselves.' Julias cocks a brow. 'But you seem surprised. You didn't know about my hand in Tidal. Interesting. Well, let's follow another path. After all, we have time, don't we?'

Wyll nods. 'I am in no rush.'

'Wonderful!' Julias says. 'Now I have a question for you, if you wouldn't mind playing along. I'm curious as to why you keep talking about the King in the past tense.'

The only sound is the squawk of tropical birds overhead, their presence at odds with the chilled, windswept landscape outside the dome. Inside the dome, all is hazy, and warm, and gold. Just like midsummer in a cup.

'Well, that's because he's dead,' says Wyll.

Somewhere, very faintly in the very back of his mind, an alarm begins to sound.

'How unfortunate,' murmurs Julias, without a shred of surprise. 'Do you know how?'

'Your assassin.'

'*My* assassin?'

Those birds are very loud. His mouth keeps opening before his brain can realise what it's going to say. It's a curious sensation, being disconnected from your own mouth.

'Your Red,' Wyll slurs. 'She's here.'

'Oh, she's not mine,' he hears Julias say. 'No, no. I'm a little chagrined that you think I had anything to do with that.'

He sounds further away. Wyll makes a mental note to look around to see where he's gone, and then forgets to follow it up.

'What's happening?' he hears himself ask.

'It's the tea you've been drinking,' Julias tells him. 'The original plant, when properly treated, begets some curious properties, including a fairly dramatic relaxation of one's guard. Hallucinations as well, I should also warn you. Try to enjoy it. It will be a much nicer ride if you let go.'

Oh no, no, he tries to say. *Please no.*

'Your face is changing,' Julias says, but he is very muffled now. 'Does that happen often?'

Don't see me. Don't look at me.

The cup, the damned cup with the damned poison in it, still rests in Wyll's hand, but now it feels too thick, thicker than a table wedge, thicker than a step, and the sensation is making him want to vomit.

He tastes metal in his mouth.

Glossy deer erupt from his head and gallop, panicked, across the atrium. Illusion or hallucination? It's getting harder to understand what can be touched, or if touch is even a reliable sense of reality any more.

His father appears, his eyes hypnotisingly large, with that expression on his face that used to alert child Wyll to a bad day. He is shaking his head.

You're on your own this time, Wyll.

His mother is standing silently beside Edler, her face lined with sorrowful exhaustion.

Help me, Wyll begs her. *Please help me, Mama.*

But she turns away and fades into the jungle background.

Wyll's hands are itching. He looks down to see thick, fleshy flowers bursting out from the impossible soil of his skin. The one growing out of the back of his left hand, a beautiful mottled orange with furred petals, turns to the one growing out of the back of his right hand, which has delicate silvery leaves as thin as tissue.

Interesting, says the orange flower. *Have you noticed that every single person he conjures is dead?*

Why can't he do alive ones? the silver flower responds, with a genteel, puzzled air.

Maybe it's about guilt, the orange flower considers. *Or maybe it's easier to make people who are no longer around to contradict your version of them.*

Humans are strange.

Strange, yet predictable.

You're cleverer than me, my dear, the silver flower says as it begins to crumble into ash, its feathery remains dusting Wyll's skin.

Well, that's why we make such a great team, the orange flower replies, fading into nothing.

CHAPTER 25

Lheosne, Rhyfentown
Two Months Ago

Wyll wakes wet.

Cold, slithering sheet folds lie heavy against his clammy limbs. He tries to push them off, peel them from his skin. His arms tremble and twitch. Shaking, he levers himself up on to his elbows. He's been stripped of his clothes, clad only in loose trousers, now soaked with his own sweat.

The surroundings swim around him in thick, dark opulence. The room is big, though it appears cosy due to the sheer amount of furniture that perches across its floors and nestles against its walls. Curtains and pillows and rugs sport reds ranging the hues of bright fresh blood to dark clotted wounds, oranges like winter sunsets and tiger stripes, bold yellows of lemon and sandstone. Classic Rhyfentown colours through and through, determinedly old-fashioned.

Wyll rubs his face, trying to clear the clouds in his head. He feels as weak as a day-old foal, his limbs like broken insect legs. The drug-induced nightmares of – yesterday, he supposes – are gratifyingly fuzzy now, only vague impressions of wrong angles and thicknesses too thin and ghosts surrounding him, giving him nothing but their insubstantial backs.

No, wait – the nightmares are not over. There, on the lacquered wall opposite. It's a black hole, and it's growing wider every second, engulfing the exquisitely painted hunting scenes around it. The hole grows large enough for a figure to step through into the room. The sliding door it used to enter closes quietly behind it.

Slim, compact, dressed in a dark, trim robe, the figure's entire face is covered in a mask shaped like a stylised sunburst, radiating its thick rays out from the head like a full circle crown.

It must be another one of Julias' strange servants.

That means he's still at Lheosne. But how long has he been here?

In the few seconds it takes for the figure to approach and halt close to the bed, an array of possibilities flashes through Wyll's mind – while at Lheosne, he grew suddenly ill and passed out and they had to put him to bed/he's under private arrest for performing illegal magic/he's been kidnapped/he's still asleep somewhere else and this is just more nightmare/he's dead and this is one of the seven hells. Presumably Rhyfen's, judging by the décor and the figure's sunburst mask.

The wall opposite the bed flickers with sudden, bright light, which resolves into the head and shoulders of Julias. There must be a projector somewhere above his head.

'Ah, you're awake,' Julias says, sounding pleased. His kindly eyes crinkle. 'How are you feeling?'

Wyll tries to decide on an answer. 'Bad,' he says eventually.

Julias makes a moue of sympathy. 'I'm so sorry. We're still tinkering with doses for that one. Being that you're a large, powerful sort of creature, there was some persuasive argument for doubling the normal amount. Not to worry, there'll be no lasting damage. At least, there hasn't been during the testing phases so far. Life is a gamble, eh?'

Silence descends. Wyll makes desperate grabs for his thoughts. Usually it's a much smoother process to turn them into words.

'Why the fuck did you dose me?' he eventually produces.

'A few reasons. We'll get to the main one in time.'

'But,' a baffled Wyll searches for a way into sense and reason, 'what gives you the right to attack me? We've no dispute.'

'Ah, well. You did enter my house under false pretences.' Julias stops crinkling kindly. 'You were pretending to be some-one else, Si Wyll. Not only very much illegal, but also rather troubling behaviour for such a vaunted knight as yourself. London's Left Hand, the Scourge of the Godless, the Sorcerer Knight, not to mention the royal champion, skulking around the private premises of his King's ancestral home? To what end?'

Answer a question with a question that flatters the questioner. A trick he lifted from Art, who favoured it a great deal when he wanted to give as little away as possible in return for as much as he could get.

'How did you know,' Wyll croaks, 'that I wasn't who I appeared to be?'

'Well, I didn't at first, but I have very talented servants.'

Wyll's gaze cuts to the masked figure in front of him, silent and still with blank threat.

'You can see through illusions?' he asks the figure.

'They can see through yours,' Julias answers. 'But I don't want you to be disheartened. You are, in so many ways, the first of your kind. Or at least the first one to get so famous, which is the only kind that counts for the official stories of our culture.'

'What do you want?'

'I'm more curious to know what *you* want, Si. You're quite a threat. You have been for some time now. Everyone sees you as such, and everyone has their own idea of why.'

'And what's yours?' Wyll asks, while his heart sinks. An old folk song Vivi used to sing to rile him up is playing in his head, the one that goes:

> *haven't you had enough,*
> *enough,*
> *haven't you had enough of being feared?*

'Oh, *I* don't see you as a threat,' Julias assures him. 'I see you as an asset.'

'Which is why you drugged me to incapacity and then stuck some guard dog on me who can tell when I'm trying to fool you?' Wyll croaks out.

'My dear,' Julias says, and then nothing else.

Wyll stares at the projected face before him, puzzled. It has a look of expectant patience on it, but what is he supposed to say or do now? Should he try to fight his way out? Even weakened as he is, he'll still have something in him. He always does. No one digs down as far as he does – they get too scared – but digging down further than you ever thought yourself capable is what makes a champion—

And then it's as though a hand reaches through his chest, wraps its fingers around his heart and clenches tight.

It is the worst feeling he has ever felt in his life. It is beyond any fear he has ever known. It is the fear of having your life slowly squeezed into nothing, and this feeling will go on forever, every moment the one before his last, a constant, horrifying, nameless agony as your heart teeters on the edge of bursting but Never. Quite. Does.

288

Wyll pitches forwards, his mouth slack and formless, his thoughts incoherent swirls of darkening horror.

Then the squeezing stops.

Wyll gasps on the bed like a landed fish.

'How did that feel?' he hears Julias enquire. 'I'm curious. We've only tested it on cats before now, and of course they can't talk.'

To Wyll's utter, devastated humiliation, he can only answer with a great, pained howl.

'Seven saints on earth,' comments Julias. He sounds abstractly pleased. 'Well done, my dear.'

The masked figure steps forwards, their hands in an oddly placating gesture – and then, just as suddenly, they withdraw, as if confused.

'What have you done to me?' Wyll says, or tries to say, each word mangled by his weeping fright.

'Me?' Julias sounds offended. 'I did nothing. That's all her.'

And then Wyll finally understands.

'Take off the mask,' he says to the sunburst.

The masked figure is still.

'Take it off or stay a coward.'

The figure twitches, but holds still. The mask turns back towards Julias, who gives an assenting nod.

A hand reaches up, feels round the back of the skull. The tinny clink of metal on metal, buckles being undone, and then it slides off, and just as in their first meeting, face to face across a fight area with an avid audience in the background, she reveals herself – only this time it's him down in the dirt and she on top, the way he has always wanted it to be.

Red still looks more like sharp angles than the tight curves he remembers – and dreams of – but her recent time out of

289

prison has been kinder. She's obviously been well fed and rested. She stares him down. One hand grips the sunburst mask. The other is loosely curled at her side, as if in readiness to crush his heart again.

He is so afraid of her.

The feeling is exhilarating.

Not a feeling to build anything on to last. A crash-and-burn feeling, a sickening cannibal feeling, all over soon, one way or another – and all the more alluring for its promise of an awful end.

'Fun new skill,' he says to the woman who, from feet away, just reached an invisible hand into his chest and crushed his heart *from the inside.*

'I'm very pleased, Red,' Julias says. 'Now tell me a few dead cats weren't worth it! Ha.'

Wyll presses a hand to his chest as if to reassure himself that it is still intact. It feels like there should be a gaping hole where his heart normally sits. He notices her watch his hand move, linger on its resting place.

'So all this time, you were working for Art's own family,' he says to her. 'Did they hire you to kill him?'

Red's gaze flicks up to his and her lip curls. 'You keep insulting me,' she sneers. 'Did I not hurt you enough?'

'I feel I must defend my honour here,' the Julias protection chips in. 'As I told you before, I've done well under the reign of dear Artorias, and I had no reason to seek his death. However, by all accounts our little heart-crusher did, and I am very willing to support the legality of her claim.'

Wyll bites back a resigned laugh.

Julias already knew that Art was dead. Red had run straight to him and told him all about it, and Julias had no doubt told the entire Consilium. The last few days they must have been secretly mocking his clumsy, pathetic attempts to be someone he is not, condemning his underhand charade.

Lillath, Brune, Lucan, they were fools to think they could fool anyone. Their whole panicked plan had been screwed from the start.

'How does it feel,' Red says softly, 'to be the one drugged and imprisoned?'

'I hate to wilt your stalk,' Wyll bites back, 'but you're not the first person to try and cage me. You'll fail, just as they did.'

It's a decent swipe – her eyes narrow at her missed blow – but Julias cuts in before she can reply.

'As far as I understand your past, Si, you do tend to make a habit of picking up masters. At this point, the pattern rather points towards some orchestration on your part. Perhaps there's something in you that longs for the leash even as you strain against it.'

There is a new curiosity on Red's face. A reassessment. He doesn't like it. He doesn't want to see it.

'I offered you an escape,' he says to her. 'Not a leash.'

Red scoffs.

'It's funny,' Wyll desperately continues, 'how you think this situation is different. That mask is just as much a collar as any collar I've ever worn.'

'More lessons,' Red retorts. 'But I've already learned everything I needed from you. You act like I'm some wayward child and you the patient parent, just waiting for me to stop tantrum-squalling enough to see sense.'

She leans forwards, closer.

Wyll's crushed heart spasms.

'You keep forgetting that I've seen you undone,' she murmurs. 'You'd kill me right now, if you could. Let it out. Go on. Stop *hiding*. Stop *holding back*. I want to see *you*.'

The ghost of a smile haunts her mouth as she throws his words back at him, words said in the heat of their private training sessions mere weeks ago. Private training sessions he agreed to not as a potential mentor, but as a passion-sick idiot. He had wanted her from the first moment they met in that shitty outer dis' arena, the moment he realised he was up against someone who could beat him.

If he let them.

If he wanted it.

And he did.

He springs up from the bed. A fast but clumsy one-two stumble-run to its edge and his arm flashes out and grabs for her throat, crashing her to the floor. A bark of alarm from the wall – Julias, realising too late that his murderous bitch of a distant family member should have known better than to get within arm's reach – but then that savage joy disappears as fast as it came. Strength drains out of him like a pierced battery. He is an upturned beetle, waving its helpless, feeble limbs.

He feels Red disentangle herself from him, leaving him on the floor.

This is the moment, he supposes. The moment she will stop his heart.

He waits.

'Awful, isn't it?' he hears Red say above him. 'The junk they had me on in the clusterloc. Try conjuring something. Go on. Anything.'

'Red,' Julias chides from the wall, 'this sort of mockery is beneath you.' He pauses. 'I'm pleased to see you two getting on so well, though. I expect great things from your pairing.'

Ha.

Well.

This is not an entirely unexpected development from someone like Julias Dracones.

Wyll forces himself to roll on to his back, propping his head up against the foot of the bed as Red turns to the wall.

'What's a pairing?' she asks dubiously.

Julias' large, light-made head glows in the room's semi-dark. 'A controlled mingling of assets.'

Wyll gives a weak laugh. 'That's one way of putting it.'

Red is very still, trying to assess the fast turn of events, he presumes, the sudden shift of power she can now sense but not yet understand.

'Do you really think it'll work?' he asks Julias.

The giant head regards him. 'On what is your scepticism based, may I ask?'

This new direction of the situation is oddly calming. Absurdity often is.

Wyll manages to shift himself into a sitting position. 'My father used to take great pleasure in relating rumours about the Dracones – about all the high families – but I thought he was just being a spiteful gossip. I didn't actually think they were true. It was supposed to be the cause of your family's diminishment over the centuries.'

'The historical precedent was regrettably haphazard,' Julias admits. 'Rather embarrassingly so.'

'Lots of sickly simpletons dying young,' Wyll croaks cheerfully.

'That's all in the past. The experiment has merit; it just needs a more rigorous scientific approach.' Julias sounds mildly annoyed. 'Artorias was a great success, I think you'd agree with me there. Uther bedding an outsider godchild was at my encouragement – and to a lot of opposition, I might add – but it worked out, did it not? Red's mother – that was my idea too. I told them, I said to them, get him with an outsider godchild as well. See if we can't birth a good one out of the match. Of course, *they* just wanted to entrap him off the throne. People can be so short-sighted, it's maddening. But I was proven right, was I not?' He inclines his head towards a baffled Red. 'She's magnificent. A true Dracones godchild, with remarkable talents.'

'What is going on?' demands Red. 'What are you talking about? What is this?'

'Are you going to tell her, or should I?' Wyll asks. His obvious enjoyment is serving only to make her angrier.

Julias gives a little shrug. 'She's not so naïve as to expect my protection to come for free.'

Every inch of Red screams *wary*, but then again, he doesn't suppose she's been able to let her guard down for a very long time. It wouldn't take much to set her off. He should tread carefully.

Or not . . .

'Have you ever heard of the old secret breeding programmes?' he asks her.

He can see by her face that she has.

It was very much the underground fashion for centuries after the Lysander regime. Many remaining godchildren went into hiding, of course, to avoid the rash of hunts and executions that followed, but once things died down a little, there were certain attempts to breed godchild talent back in – not to the general populace, but certain wealthy elites were giving it a surreptitious try. After all, what better way to increase their wealth and power than by having a secret talent in the family for, say, reading people's thoughts, or seeing even the murkiest of futures ahead of time?

The only problem was, it didn't really work. No one, it soon appeared, could be made into a godchild. Talents manifest as randomly as not. Having a godchild parent doesn't guarantee their children will be so – though it does often make it more likely, it's not enough to definitively point at any biological heredity, which, as a science, was experiencing something of a renaissance back then. That meant that families would try to breed it in among themselves, using any family member with even a whisper of talent as a stud – and, anxious about watering down the perceived purity of their own blood, the victims of this unfortunate experimentation were always other family members.

Which inevitably meant that somewhere down the line, small-pool genetics had also played a part, producing generations of elites with alarming health conditions, malformed systems and feeble minds. By the time the theory caught up to the reality, the damage was done.

It was all supposed to have been abandoned as a terrible idea long ago, but rumours persisted that the Dracones family were still insistent on keeping up with some of their old traditions. King-in-the-Ground Uther Dracones, Art's father, had been the warrior-bear exception to a poisoned bloodline. Art had been the same. Wyll can see the twisted logic that has led Julias to want to pursue that bloodline – it's been paying dividends so far.

Red gives a loud, shocked laugh. 'You're obviously joking.'

Julias' brow furrows. 'How so?'

'You really think you're going to . . . *breed* me? With *him*?'

'We've fucked before,' Wyll says. 'I'm sure you can do it again, for the sake of science.'

He tests moving, just a little – but it's not much good. He could probably get to his feet, but after that, what? A weak punch at an undrugged, fully rested heart-squeezing opponent, then stagger safely back down to the floor?

LAURE EVE

'This is a joke,' Red says once more, as if testing the prison walls which have suddenly appeared before her eyes.

'Come, come,' Julias says, 'did you think I'd just need you walking around bursting hearts for me? Your talent as a pelleren offers multiple uses. When you cook a chicken, do you use only the flesh? Certainly not. You cook up the gizzards. You make stock from the bones. You dry the feet and use them for ritual.' He sounds impatient now. Wyll supposes that for him the conversation must be starting to feel like a farmer having to explain to a cow why it should just stand still and damn well get milked.

'I warned you,' Wyll says quietly to Red, 'you're as much of a pet as me.'

'Is it shyness?' Julias enquires. 'It can be as mechanical as you like. A quick daily visit, just until you catch. Then it's all over.'

Wyll can hear her breathing from across the room: the sound of panic. Panic is the fuel that just needs a lit match—

He watches her break and run to the door she came through.

'It's reinforced,' Julias calls over the noise. 'An entry but not an exit. I'm afraid you won't be coming out of the room again until the work is done. If he gives you trouble, you know, just squeeze his heart a little – Red, I really can't talk over all the hammering—'

Red stops.

Then the room explodes.

Wyll curls up, protecting his stomach and wrapping his arms around his head. There's nothing to do but wait it out and wonder if he'll come through alive. Something big and heavy careens into his back, bruising his spine. Probably the bed. Saints alive, but this woman is terrifying. Despite his weakened state, he can feel his groin tugging as he grows stiff and eager.

296

Julias will be pleased, he thinks, and stifles a mad laugh.

Moments later, everything grows quiet.

Wyll checks himself – apart from the ache in his spine and his cock, he appears unscathed – and then risks a look.

Red is standing in the midst of destruction, her chest heaving. She's worn herself out, and much quicker than he'd expected. She looks drained and pale, her legs bowing, and barely aware of the mess around her. The shards of ruined junk poke into the side of her thighs as she sinks to the floor. The Julias image is gone, the projector presumably destroyed. He might still be able to overhear, though. They will have to work quickly.

'Red,' Wyll hisses. 'Listen to me. *Listen*. Do you have to see someone to hurt them?'

She gives him an uncomprehending look.

'Julias – presumably, he's in a nearby room. Do you know where he is? Can you find him from here?' urges Wyll. 'Can you feel his heart, like you did mine?'

He sees the moment she realises.

He can see the war on her face. The decision.

This is a temporary alliance.

She sinks to her knees and her eyes close. Her arm reaches out into the empty space before her. The seconds tick by.

Then her hand squeezes into a tight fist. It shakes with effort. The fingers turn white.

Finally she opens her eyes, and Wyll understands that it is done.

He tips his head back, resisting the urge to fall unconscious.

'Why don't I just kill you too?' he hears Red ask in a low voice.

He gives a tired laugh. 'It must be exhausting to be as angry as you.'

'Like looking in a mirror,' Red retorts.

We are two tricks, he thinks as they stare at each other. *So alike. Maybe that's why it'll never work. We hate ourselves, so we hate each other.*

But he allows himself, just for one moment, a brief fantasy of how it might have gone if they were well met on equal terms. How they could have—

No. Stop. That is all lost to versions of life that never were and never will be. Here and now, they've got what they've got to work with, and it's like oil and fire. It's too late, each of them too far gone.

Never too far, says the quietly hopeful part of him that life has not so far managed to kill, *never too late*—

There is a far-off boom. The walls of their opulent prison room shudder.

A startled Red looks around. 'Was that you?'

Wyll snorts softly. 'I'm not sure I can even stand, let alone throw noises like that.'

'Who—?'

They look at each other.

Neither has the strength to save both the other and themselves.

A loud crunch sounds right outside the room. The impenetrable door to their prison room slides open. Lillath's head pokes through it, looks around the room, then settles on Wyll.

'There you are,' she says, panting a little, framed by far-off shouts and indeterminate bangs. 'Where is she?'

'Who?' Wyll croaks, while his body trembles with the effort he's pouring into it.

'The mythical Robot Lord of Kembri,' Lillath retorts as her gaze combs the room again. 'Red, you fool. Where's Red?'

Right next to Lillath, a saucer-eyed Red stands breathless and still.

Wyll feels the sweat running down the groove of his spine, the clench of every muscle.

He manages to shake his head. 'Don't know. Haven't seen her.'

He refuses to look at Red. If she's too stupid to take the chance that he is risking unconsciousness to give her, then she deserves to be caught.

She's not. He can see a shape inching slowly backwards out of the corner of his eye.

'You sound angry,' he says to Lillath, trying to keep her focused on him.

'Well, that's what happens when people disappoint me.' Lillath sighs. 'Si Wyllt Caballarias Ambrosias o'Gwanharatown, you are under arrest.'

She's almost at the door. Just a little longer . . .

'By whose order? The King's?' Wyll grinds out.

Lillath ignores the goad. Red darts through the doorway just as Lillath turns and strides towards it, missing her illusion-masked quarry by inches.

Lillath disappears through the door behind Red.

Agonising seconds tick past.

Then Lillath returns with two grim-looking guard knights.

'Take him,' she orders, pointing at Wyll.

He cannot even put up a show of a fight.

CHAPTER 26

Garad's Apartment, Evrontown
Two Weeks Ago

Ghost does not give Garad this section of her story either, save for Leon's part in it at the end. Much like us all, in some ways the Silver Angel is very clever, and in other ways extraordinarily stupid.

There's something fun about watching your ex-lover still have absolutely no idea who you are. It's like picking at a near-healed scab, a perverse enjoyment of the sting and the set-back.

That face-changer doc really was worth the trick.

The Dugs, Alaunitown
Three Weeks Ago

An act of servitude or penance.
   An act of adjudication.
   An act of innovation.
   An act of creativity or passion.
   An act of performance or identity change.
   An act of strength or violence.

An act of beginning or ending.

The seven acts a knight performs as the ritual of the Caballaria, your Code-mandated, eons-established preparations in the hours before a fight. Each act is designed to connect you to each holy member of the Saith, as a reminder of why it is you fight, why it is you have chosen pain and sacrifice and glory, and also failure, because even the best knights lose, and lose often enough that if you don't make your peace about such a fact of existence, it'll make you crazy.

Ghost might no longer be a knight but it's hard to shake; it's in the marrow. And she might not be prepping for a fight in a Caballaria arena but it's a justice fight all the same, a fight that may well get bloody in its search for an answer to the questions that have been put to her.

We all need something to hang ourselves on.

For Evron's act of servitude, Ghost waits for a quiet hour and then begins to clean the hallway of her building. It won't exactly transform the place, but at least people'll be able to take a step without landing on an old vomit stain.

'It's over.' Garad's stiff voice. 'You're going to go with him.'

'I don't *want* to go with him,' Ghost had rapped back. It should have come out forceful and sure, but it had sounded like the whine of a sulky child.

'You must,' Garad had insisted. 'It's your duty. We all serve him first, don't you understand?'

Ghost blinks hard and then scrubs harder, banishing the intrusive memory.

For Senza's act of adjudication, she knocks on her neighbour's door, the one who yells at her sister a lot, and spends a dull, irritating couple of hours picking through the causes of their friction. Doubtful it made a difference – both women too set in themselves to bend without breaking – but it serves for her purposes.

When she's done what she can, she climbs the stairs wearily back to her own apartment.

'You're angry,' she had said to Garad. 'That I didn't tell you about him.'

'Of course not,' Garad had snapped, and saints, had they ever been a bad liar. 'We never made any binds. You've always been free to be with whoever else you wanted to be with.'

'But?'

'There's no but.'

'There is,' Ghost had pushed, hungry for the fight, hungry to get all the needling, secret truths they had both been keeping under wraps. 'What you meant to say was, "You've always been free to be with whoever else you wanted to be with, except *him*." Anyone but *him*. Itso?'

One thing pain hates is to be forgotten, relegated to an empty place where it can't cause hurt any more. Pain is all about remembrance.

'He needs you more,' Garad had insisted, and Ghost had wanted to hit them for their silly martyrdom.

'No, he doesn't,' she rapped back. 'I'll ruin his life.'

'Don't be ridiculous. You'll be joy and comfort and safety for him. He needs that. That's what he *needs*.'

'How about what *you* need?'

Garad held themself stiffly. 'I'll be fine.'

Instead of continuing the fight, she did something she'd never done with a lover before.

She told the truth she most wanted to hide.

'I'm sorry,' she had said. 'Garad, I'm really sorry. I like him. But he didn't tell me what he was going to do. He didn't *warn* me. He trapped me and I don't know how to back out.' And then came the next thing she'd never done with a lover before – she cries, hot, thick, fast tears of utter misery. 'It's you I want to be with. You. Always you. I don't want this. There has to be a way we can be together. There just has to be.'

For Gwanhara's act of passion, Ghost sits naked in the corner of her quiet apartment, where the dust has been swept and the candles have been cleared to make enough space for a decent bit of worship. She sits and she roams her own body and mind, fingers and imagination, for a full hour without stopping, her head full of Garad, Garad.

Garad, gathering her into their arms, whispering, 'There is – we'll just explain. We'll just tell him. It's the only way. I don't care what happens if it means I get you. I don't care. Do you understand?'

Ghost had understood very well. Garad's pride, Garad's sense of duty – they would discard it all for her. They would become a new, vulnerable version of themself. They would do that for her.

So she must do that for them.

As she felt Garad's greedy mouth on her neck, as they stripped each other with the trembling urgency of the desperate, the decision was made. She would show Garad the one thing she had never shown anyone in her life.

She would show them what she could do.

With an enormous effort, Ghost banishes the memory, stands unsteadily from her Gwanhara ritual – even as her groin is clenched so tight and the soft parts rubbed so raw they hurt against the thin, light cloth of her underclothes – and for Iochi's act of performance, she recites by heart the infamous speech by Queen Petro in the classical play *Light Fire Snake,* a lyrical, poetical and darkly persuasive justification of the Kembrian genocide the real-life Queen perpetuated in the name of the saints. A controversial choice, she'd chosen it years back in basic knight's training and it has remained one of the very few constants in her ever-shifting identity. Besides, she has no patience to learn a new performance by memory, and memory – memory is a tricksy thing.

The memory of Garad's face changing as she had, midst their hot tangling, given off a great, glad sigh and unfettered herself, for example, might be faulty. She might have blown it all out of proportion, that look of pure, simple horror on the face of the only person for whom she had ever felt such a deep, desperate love. That horror that swam quickly into revulsion.

Maybe it hadn't been revulsion. Garad had just been shocked. After all, Ghost had not warned them of what she was about to show them.

Herself.

Finally.

Once she has finished up Queen Petro's speech, the dull walls of her apartment echoing with the final scream, Ghost moves into her bathroom.

There, laid on the tile, are the tools she will need for Rhyfen's act of violence. A thin, well-sharpened razor blade, swabbing cloth drenched in medicinal-grade alcohol, and neat squares of sticky bandage.

Standing barefoot on the cold tile, Ghost cuts open a small slice just above her hip, a place that won't chafe too much, a shallow cut that'll heal up neat. The blood that comes off the blade she lets fall into the worship space she'd earlier cleared.

The throbbing at her hip recalls an earlier echo, the moment a half-naked Garad had, after seeing what she was, pushed

Ghost so violently from them that she had smacked into the edge of a solid placard, stumbled, and gone down, her side a-scream in blooming pain.

Dazed, she had looked up into a sword point, and Garad at the end of it, trembling, their eyes round as spoonfish and just as wet, the planes of their beautiful lion body tight with visceral hate.

'*What the fuck did you just do?*'

'**What the fuck are you?**'

And Ghost lying there, shock and pain blooming through every nerve and sinew, thinking, *I don't know.*

The final ritual, of course, is Marvol's act of beginning . . . or ending.

It was Ghost who had ended things with Garad.

She had played her hand, and it had been the most spectacularly misjudged play of her life.

Garad didn't like godchildren. Everyone knew that. Ghost knew that. But somehow, *somehow* she'd managed to persuade herself of the transcendent power of love, or some such childish shit. Whatever her reasons, it didn't matter. It was done.

As soon as she saw the revulsion on Garad's face, it was all over.

Her life was over, and the only thing left to do was run.

After Marvol's ritual is done, Ghost draws a bath and takes it long, steaming herself like a dumpling, the air thick and wet and heavy with perfumes, the bath water a faint pink from the dribbles of blood still leaking from her hip cut. Once she is as clean as she can get, she wraps herself up and sits on her bed, leafing carefully through a large book propped open against the pillows.

The book is the only personal possession Ghost took with her when she left her old life. *Too incriminating to leave behind*, she told herself. There is something true in that, but only in part. The rest of it is about reverence. Even if you start out caring nothing for the saints, somewhere along the way, the Caballaria world pulls you all out of shape and moulds you into the newly penitent, one of bendable knees and no hard questions. The book – virgin blank and gifted to you when you pass initial knight's training – is for the documentation of your journey along the river of this strange mess called life. It is your own version of the Code, that ancient-to-present-day collection of writings that forms the philosophical backbone of the Caballaria. Part diary and part personal bible, the book is designed to be filled with your remembrances, musings, pains, pleasures and yearnings. You in handwritten pages – and thus crammed full of insight that Ghost would rather no one else got their eager little peekers on. Besides, one should keep a little mystery in reserve.

Her eyes catch fragments of her past thoughts. It's a stuttering disconnect, like reading a stranger's diary. In between the personal are writings lifted from the Code itself, painstakingly copied out and then annotated in a kind of know-it-all fashion Ghost now finds faintly annoying. Still, it's the original philosophies she's after.

This is how Leon finds her, several hours later – paintless and clean-swept, clad in a simple robe, cross-legged on the bed, deep in words and ideas about how to be alive.

'It's open,' she calls absently when he knocks.

A long pause, long enough to think he hadn't heard, and then he comes in, his tread heavy, his patchless eye roving curiously about.

'I could have been anyone.' He sounds accusatory.

Ghost just shrugs, and returns to her book.

The feel of him watching her is remote. She floats in different waters.

'It's going to hell out there,' Leon says, some time later.

'London's always going to hell.'

'And you're hid up in here meditating like a monk while it does.'

'There's still a ceremony to these things, even down in the dirt.'

'To what things? You en't a knight any more.'

Ghost says nothing. Knights go on being knights outside the arena, she wants to say, but kicks her romanticism under the bed. A lazy, thoughtless phrase. A knight is a construction, an outward facet of the person behind the sword. Not much more than an outfit. Still seems to mean something to her, though.

'What are you up to?' Leon asks suspiciously.

Ghost sighs. She had let him come in. A minimal amount of talk might possibly be expected.

'Got a fight,' she says.

'They do knight's prep for a Wardogs fight, these days?'

'What makes you think I'm in Wardogs?'

He gives her a light scoff. 'Why d'you think they get so many ex-knights signing up? You still have to fight. It's in the bones.'

'Just like you still have to guard people?'

'What's that supposed to mean?'

'Why are you here?' Ghost asks patiently.

He looks around. 'Saints, this is bare.'

Ghost gently closes the book. 'Leon, I have to go soon.'

She rises and crosses the candle floor to her clothes chest. Sheds the robe. Pulls on each piece of the outfit she has chosen for this fight. Tightens up a strap on her thigh until it pinches the skin underneath, aware of his eyes on her movements like a second set of fingers.

'Who's the fight with?' he asks.

'Whoever wants me to take the fall for Moth's death. Not a fan of falls. I like my feet on the ground. I plan to explain this to them with knives.'

A long pause.

'You found out who it is?' Leon asks.

'Maybe,' Ghost admits, 'or it could turn out to be another trap. Either way, considering what's gone down so far, I'm expecting trouble.'

Leon tries again. 'This en't your fight, I told you. If you pursue it, we both get dead.'

'It's like a loose tooth,' Ghost says. 'I just have to keep tonguing 'til it comes out. And with it, blood and pain, I suppose. But then, without those things, how do we know we're alive?'

'Don't give a rat's shit about what happens to me, then, do you?'

Leon's tone has the set of a twice-beat dog. Dashed hopes, expected but still unwelcome.

'Leon, I said I'd let the Grenwald case go, and I have. This isn't about her, is it?'

'Neh? Investigating her cohort's death seems a midge connected to me.'

'You're in a rogitating mood today, I see,' sighs Ghost.

'What's wrong with you?' Leon says curiously. 'You could just . . . hide. You could just do as you're damn well told, and get by, and get on. Instead you keep putting yourself in the bullet path. Why?'

She wants to say: *Because all we have are stories. Stories are the nets we filter reality through. Our own lives, our own memories, the history of our species, are just stories we tell ourselves. If the story I have to tell about myself is one of a coward, well, how am I supposed to live with that? What's the worth in being alive, then?*

She wants to say: *There's not a lot to rest your hat on in this world. Justice — even the crippled, bastard justice we have — it's an idea that means something. Take that away and what's left? Life's got to mean something, or what's the point of waking up in the morning? This is my meaning. This is my choice that isn't a choice, because to choose not to pursue this is to choose a version of myself I don't want to be.*

But Leon's question is a feint — he's moving towards her before she even gets her reply out. It's a good move and he takes her by surprise, but he's tired and old and she's got hours of preparation on her side, and with it a clarity and, for once, a mind and body — only temporarily — fused together to a sharp point. Plus she finds she doesn't mind hurting him. He doesn't deserve pain, but he doesn't deserve clemency either — because no one deserves anything, and we all have to play judge and jury, every day, with everyone we meet, from stranger to dear friend.

In short, Ghost gets him under a knife. He wheezes and kicks, but doesn't do much.

She lets him off, scrambling away. He leans back on one thick palm, the other wrapped round his neck, meat on meat. She is in a crouch, knife out, back to the door. She can walk out any time.

'I suppose this means you decided to try selling me out, after all,' she says.

Leon says nothing.

'Who's on their way? Those palace guard goons?'

Leon says nothing.

Ghost nods. 'It's all right. I wasn't planning on coming back here, anyway.'

There could be a lot to say. She wants to ask him why, in turn, but does it really matter? He could have told them anything to cut a deal – that she's famous missing-presumed-dead Finnavair's sister, that she's an illegal godchild – she wouldn't put it past him to have found out somehow, considering how many other people have worked it out of late. It doesn't matter why, it just matters that she has to run again.

She feels sorry for Leon, someone trying to operate with such limitations, someone desperately scrabbling for a better life but unable to go about it in a way that means being a better human. Everyone's got their burden. It's hard to be alive. It takes work and thought and mistakes and questioning, constant questioning, every step of the way.

She could offer him her own mistakes, make him feel better about his. She could say she's never felt like a whole person, but the shadow that trails behind. The one who got brought out for the violence. The 'bad idea' fuck and the nasty kill. Everyone's got that half, but the trick is in reattaching the bad part of yourself to the good part of yourself again afterwards, to make a whole person who is both, neither, just human.

But she doesn't have time to offer Leon anything. He's made sure of that. He looks tired and small, sat on his arse and looking up at her like a kid who got his ice cream snatched by a bird.

Ghost leaves him in her apartment, surrounded by spilled wax. She remembers the book on her bed too late, but . . . ah, he can help himself to it.

It feels like it was written by someone else, anyway.

CHAPTER 27

Garad's Apartment, Evrontown
Two Weeks Ago

'Did you find your murderer?' asks Garad.

Ghost finds herself enjoying that particular phrasing. 'Neh, I did.'

'At his home, I take it.'

'Oh no.' She smiles. 'He was at a show.'

Theatre of the All-Seeing Eye, Alaunitown
Three Weeks Ago

The building is a half-dismembered corpse.

A metal skeleton rests on fragile legs, latticed gantry ways and girders crisscrossing the sky. Like clean bones, you can see right through to the stone walls of the next building behind it, which itself has a giant hole punched through one wall. A tower spire lies forlornly on its side on the ground beyond, balanced atop mounds of tossed brick and smashed panes of old, thick glass. Whether it's being built up or down is hard to say, but safe and visitable it is not.

So why are there people gathering to enter the skeleton and

311

carefully pick their way through the mess? Why guards at the door checking, presumably, for identification? The street is bizarrely busy for such a disused stretch of the river. Watching a building die dust puff by dust puff must be a spectator sport now, and one that costs a trick or two, judging by the over-wrought finery on the crowd.

Off to the side, Ghost lurks, eyeing the queue. These people are slick as old nags painted up like racehorses and sold at twice their worth. Once they get past the guards, she can see a few of them ascending metal staircases, climbing the building's precar-ious bones to go . . . where? Jumping off the ribs? Is it mass self-end?

'They're the audience,' says Delilah.

Ghost has been loitering here with intent, focusing on keep-ing her mind clear, and even though she's in the sharpest state she can muster, and Delilah's arrival is long-expected, the twisty little tartlet still managed to sneak up on her.

Ghost opens her mouth to be a bitch about Delilah's sudden materialisation – and then sees who she has arrived with.

One step back and two and hand to holster and out comes the gun, its once alien weight fast becoming a comfort in her hand—

'This isn't what it looks like,' pleads Delilah from somewhere behind the brooding bulk of her companion.

Ghost continues to point her gun at Sugar's face.

'Let her go,' she says to him.

Sugar rumbles a disparaging laugh. 'Baseless assumptions,' he says. 'Just like a gun dog.'

'Ghost, he's with us,' urges Delilah. 'We need him. I told you I had a way of finding Moth's killer, didn't I? He's the way.'

'No way I'm going his way,' says Ghost.

'Then fuck you,' Sugar says, and steps away.

'No, wait.' Delilah pulls on his arm. 'We can't find him with-out you.'

'Delilah,' Ghost gives her a pleasant smile, 'what, please?'

'He's a bloodhound,' says Delilah.

Sugar growls at her.

'T'chuss, she has to know.' Delilah turns to Ghost. 'He's the reason the group hasn't tried to skin you alive for Moth's mur-der yet, okay? He could smell the other man at her place. He knew you weren't the only one there that night. So he tracked him down. He's been tracking the guy for the last week. And tonight' – she gestures at the skeletal structure rearing above them – 'he said the man's here.'

'You tracked him all the way here from just a smell?' Ghost says.

'Wanna test me?' Sugar evenly replies. 'I can tell you all the places *you've* been since we first met.'

A moment of tense silence.

Ghost laughs. Sugar looks annoyed.

'Unbelievable,' she says drily. 'With all the people following me these days, it's a wonder I ever feel alone.'

She flicks to Delilah's anxious face. She, at least, seems to believe in this, but with a nose that good, Ghost wonders if Sugar can smell his own ratshit. No one can do what he claims. There's no such thing as a human bloodhound.

There's no such thing as a whatever you are, either, says the voice in her head.

Maybe he's the rat who sold out Cass to a godchild-catcher. Someone that performatively self-righteous is often overcom-pensating for a hidden guilt. She'd had him down as an arsehole from the word go, but didn't quite trust her own instincts, because no one wants to believe that life is often too obvious for

313

a story. Whatever his reasons for inserting himself into this hunt, she needs to have her alarms set to ring. As if she didn't already.

Ghost lowers the gun. For now.

'So what is our man doing here?' she asks, nodding a head to the building. 'And where in seven hells *is* here?'

'It's this new show everyone's talking about,' Delilah says vaguely. 'They're performing in front of some crumbling old Saith church, there at the back. It's being torn down to make a new power station. That's why the building in front is only half finished.'

'They're performing in front of a church?' Sugar frowns in distaste. 'Bit *traditional*, itso? I'd feel like I was at weekly worship with my parents again. Saints only know how many bloody masquerades I had to watch in church when I was a kid. That sort of thing leaves a mark.'

'Nihilists,' Delilah comments. 'Any chance to kick religion.'

'Shut up, both of you,' Ghost says. 'You're really deflating my hunting buzz. Let's go.'

'Where?'

'To this show. Catch him there.'

'We can't just go in there,' says Sugar. 'I suggest we wait out here and follow him when he leaves.'

Ghost raises a brow. 'What, your ability doesn't extend to sniffing one man out in a huge crowd and a building full of a million other smells?'

He glares at her. 'I know what he looks like, okay?'

'So do I,' says Ghost. 'So why are you here again?'

She holsters the gun and strides towards the – for lack of a more obvious word – entranceway. No point waiting around for insults when you can put your back to them.

Delilah catches up to her.

'You're angry with me?' she pants.

'Hmm, let's think.'

'I couldn't tell you how we were going to find him; I knew you might have a problem with it.'

'Astute. Just keep him out of my way while I find the murderous map thief.'

'Wait, Ghost, we can't just go in there right now!'

Ghost halts. 'Why not?'

Delilah looks caught out. 'Because. Because it's a show. We should wait until it finishes and he comes out, then follow him home and catch him there.'

'Or we could talk to him right now, with all these witnesses around so he can't try anything stupid. Sometimes it's better to fight with an audience. Changes the game.'

Delilah's mouth works silently, dredging for more delay tactics perhaps, but nothing comes up, so Ghost walks right into the throng ahead and silently prays she'll lose them both.

The crowd has moved inside, with only a straggler or two passing through. Ghost falls in line at the back and gives the pass checker a big smile. They do not return it.

'Pass, please,' says one, in a bored chime.

'I'm not here for the show.' Ghost touches her fingers briefly to her holster, making sure it draws their attention. 'I'm a God's Gun. You have a registration-dodger in your audience tonight. Just here to bring them in.'

The pass-checkers exchange glances. They work for the show. Theatrical types who look like the only violence they're used to is the fake kind on a stage. They don't have much to do with gun-wearers – few do, and therefore can usually be counted on to defer to the authority of the dark, heavy weapon hanging at her hip. Most people are scared of them, and with good reason.

'You can't interrupt the show,' tries one. 'Can't you wait until afterwards?'

'Promise I'll be subtle,' Ghost says, and walks in without waiting for their nod.

'Hoi,' she hears one call uncertainly, but no one chases after her. She relaxes, climbing on to the metal struts rearing out of the ground, following the example of audience members before her, impressed at the way some of them navigate with the most hilariously inappropriate footwear – either bravery or a lack of forethought, which are often the same thing.

Ghost hears scrambling behind her and turns to find that Sugar and Delilah have caught up. Pity.

Evidently a preshow is under way. Random players pop up behind struts as they climb to deliver varied proclamations.

'PROGRESS,' shouts one, 'BUT AT WHAT COST TO OUR SOULS?'

'Those who dwell in the past,' sing a small chorus standing on a nearby platform, 'drown in entropy.'

Behind the chorus, hanging from girders by thick ropes, is a giant, round, sculptured Eye fashioned out of opaque glass – it's the only way to think of it, with a blazing, capital E – which glares out across the roving audience, judging each of them one by one.

'Subtle as a punch to the face,' snorts Sugar behind her, and Ghost begrudgingly awards him his first few likability points.

She pauses on a large viewing platform and scans the crowd. It might be difficult to find the bald man in this mess. Maybe Sugar will prove useful in the moment after all. As she turns to him, ready to be sceptical about his ability and goad him into proving her wrong, she catches sight of a familiar face.

He is a few feet away, and in profile, but he is unmistakable. Ghost swears.

'What?' Delilah asks in alarm, following her line of sight. When she sees what Ghost sees, she freezes.

'Say, bloodhound,' Ghost casually murmurs, 'recognise that man over there?'

Sugar looks where she's pointing.

'That's the one,' he says with satisfaction.

'That's the man you've been following? The man you could smell at Moth's shop?'

'Neh.' Sugar frowns at her tight tone of voice. 'What's the matter, he's not pretty enough for you?'

Slicked coif of hair. Neat, expensive clothes. Faintly damp sheen to his skin.

'It's the wrong one,' Ghost says. 'It's not him.'

She glances at Delilah, who is staring at Glapissant.

'This is the one I was told to sniff out,' Sugar protests.

'What's that supposed to mean? Told to? By who?'

But Sugar keeps a stubborn silence. Nothing to do but get into his space, let him know threat. '*By who*, soft neck?' she hisses.

'Get the fuck away from me—'

'He's seen us.' Delilah's quiet anxiety cuts them off.

Ghost looks up.

Glapissant is staring right at her like an unpleasant surprise.

That *what in seven hells are you doing here?* look on his face – not only does he remember Ghost, a fleeting encounter at a party several weeks ago, but he's afraid.

317

Ghost gives him a winning smile.

To her everlasting surprise, he turns away from her and begins shouldering through the line of people ahead.

He's on the run.

No thought, no pause and Ghost is bolting after him.

She thinks she hears a bark, some wordless call, from maybe Delilah, but this is no time to stop and do the explain. This bit she'll do alone, fuck Sugar and whatever nefarious plan he had for her – fuck them all, leave them behind where they can't interfere or do her harm. She's the dog and she's got a rabbit to catch.

Her quarry is hard to spot – a slick head and tailored back among the slick heads and tailored backs of the crowd – but as she tracks him she sees that instead of going down to ground, he's climbing, a lone figure tackling the struts that rear all around, scraping the empty sky. Ghost barrels through the line, soft bodies spinning like tops, curses and shouts trailing in her wake, and looks up at the gantry rising dizzyingly over her head. What is it about this echelon and their penchant for being above everyone else? No one takes a metaphor that seriously, do they?

Still, as the chase unfolds, so does her enjoyment, a savage joy at the simple thrill.

The toad flees and Ghost follows, scrabbling across gantry ways, platforms and struts, until he takes a step off an edge, landing on the circular band platform of a tall spire that juts through its hole like a finger through a ring.

Then he disappears, hidden by broken walls.

When Ghost arrives on to the spire's platform, she finds a tight, dizzying spiral of stone steps inside the walls, each spiral leaving her blind to the next and what may be waiting round the corner for her.

Nothing for it.

Gun out, body angled back, Ghost descends.

When she reaches the bottom, her footsteps echoing on stone ground, she realises where she is – the crumbling Saith church Delilah mentioned, the one due for destruction.

The church is the traditional septagon, each room a seven-sided ode to the Saith, each side covered in something of theirs – a symbol, a painted face, a statue icon, an offering. The brief, tantalising scent of jasmine climbs into Ghost's nose as she darts through, Saint Iochi's signature flower, drying bunches of it scattered across his alcove floor. Ritual demands that she stop and offer a kiss and a bare of her throat to each Saith she passes, the gestures so ingrained that her feet get tangled in their unconscious obeisance and she almost trips, righting herself with a curse. No time for niceties, she'll apologise later with a full night of worship – ignoring a treacherous thought about recruiting Delilah to help with the prayer to Gwanhara, saint of passion and the body, as she speeds on—

—and there's her quarry, scrabbling desperately at a sealed entranceway, failing, turning back to see where his enemy is, only to find her on top of him.

Ghost attacks.

It doesn't take long. He is surprisingly weak.

'You are one slippery fish,' she pants as she gets him under her and stops his flailing with a press of the knife to his bare bobbing throat.

'Get that knife off me!' squeals Glapissant.

'Why?'

He gapes at her, surprised, perhaps, at the sheer audacity of the question.

'Cassren Grenwald,' Ghost says. 'Did you kill her?'

'No!' he says quickly.

'No?' queries Ghost.

The toad lashes out, limbs flailing – but when her blade tastes blood, he freezes.

'Careful or you'll cut your own throat,' Ghost says, 'save me a job.'

'Stop,' he begs, 'please – please, I—'

Saints, his glassy eyes are leaking tears. They dribble into his damp hairline, beading along his carefully sculpted ridges of hair. It's been a while since she's been in touching distance of such a tremendous physical coward. This is a man who never has to fight to live. She might be feeling some empathy right about now if she were a better person. Luckily she's not.

She presses down a little, just for the fun of it.

'Wait! Wait!' Glapissant half sobs, his neck stretched comically tight. 'You're a believer! You're a Saith believer, you wear the coin!'

His wide, wet eyes do a dog-like dart to the aforementioned, dangling from its thin chain around her neck, its weight making a pendulum out of it that tocks back and forth above his nose.

'What of it?' Ghost snarls.

'Sanctuary,' he stutters. 'No violence in a sanctuary. No harm comes to anyone in a Saith church.'

'Rhyfen will forgive me,' says Ghost. 'He likes a blood offering.'

'But the others won't! The others won't!'

Fuck him for finding her faultline. She can feel all the saints on her back, whispering, their fingers gripping her arm, staying her hand.

'You'd be damned,' he whimpers, his damp skin glistening in the church's rosy darklight.

Ghost hesitates. Ah well. You sin and then you pay penance for it later. Isn't that how the world works? Lately she's really been racking up the deferred penances and at some point will come the reckoning, but until then, she just has to deal with this sudden weight on her back and the explosion of pain around her throat that stops all else stone-dead—

She can't even gasp, just choke as the leash around her neck pulls her backwards, flailing on the end of it like a reluctant but powerless cat. She lies on her back, blinking up at Saint Marvol's face painted across the ceiling, his pretty slope of a nose threatening to go black on her as her brain gasps for fuel. Her gun's gone too, dropped from her nerveless grip in the attack.

'Where were you? Your godbitch almost killed me!' Glapissant's voice trembles with adrenalin and tears.

And then came Delilah's nervous piping, 'I didn't expect her to run after you like that!'

Typical.

Just typical.

You know what makes the whole thing worse? the other her muses as she watches from inside her head. *This is exactly what you were expecting, and you walked right into it anyway. Did he talk true, that Wardogs fighter, about your death wish? Fine, that's your problem, but it's not my time yet.*

She tries to move. Manages to roll on her side before who-ever's on the end of the leash gives it a pull and chokes her until she stops.

There is a nice long pause, long enough for Ghost to consider all the ways in which she hates herself. Then she feels someone touching her.

A scream swear, and then a 'hold her the fuck still!' from the toad. 'You don't even need to pull that hard, a child could keep her quiet with that leash,' he sneers.

'I *am*, I—'

Ghost's throat constricts to the size of a string – so it certainly feels – and she stills.

The toad appears before her in a crouch, dangling her gun between his thighs. He looks a lot calmer and far less like a squealing toddler who had his cake taken away. Give a weak man a weapon and watch his dick grow.

'You said you'd give me back my sister.' Delilah sounds nervous and shrill. 'Where is she?'

'All in good time,' Glapissant replies, his eyes on Ghost.

'No,' Delilah insists, 'give me her now. That's the bargain: I bring you Ghost, you give me back my sister.'

Ghost can hear that infuriating stubbornness that lies in constant wait behind her teeth, ready for each open of the mouth. *She's got guts, I have to give her that.*

Glapissant doesn't move.

'Did you bring her here?' asks Delilah. 'Did you or didn't you?'

'Bring an incapacitated child to the opera? No, Delilah, I didn't. Your sleepy sister can't even breathe on her own; you think they have the space for that contraption she's hooked up to in a place like that?' Glapissant rolls his eyes at Ghost, a shared moment of frustration. *Women, am I right?*

'Besides,' he says as he stands up, dusting off his trousers, 'you completely fucked this up. You were supposed to get her to come to the Menagerie, where all of this could have been done with the minimum of violence.'

'She didn't want to!' Delilah protests. 'She insisted on meeting us at the show, to get at you with an audience, she said!'

Well, that isn't true. Delilah was the one who told Ghost to meet her at the show. Had Delilah done that on purpose? Tried to create a sliver of opportunity? Had she even let Ghost run off on her and Sugar and ruin the plan, secretly hoping if she did, that Ghost might actually succeed in taking her quarry down?

Glapissant raises Ghost's gun and takes aim. Ghost hears the faintest indrawn breath, a thin hitch of sudden, awful understanding. The gun's bark echoes and ricochets around the church's stone walls, which are purpose-built to glorify any sound made inside, as if drama can make a thing divine.

The leash around Ghost's throat goes slack. There is a loud thump behind her.

Too late to ask now.

'What . . . what?' she hears Sugar rumble.

Idiots find it hard to keep up.

'What, what,' Glapissant mocks. 'She'd served her purpose. Oh, don't look so worried, you're still useful – unless by some unfortunate miracle of genetics, you've suddenly stopped being a godchild?'

A mute silence follows.

'Come on,' says Glapissant with a touch of impatience. 'And bring the gun dog.'

The dog's gun he tosses to the ground. It lands with a heavy skitter and clack. Her gun. The one he just used to shoot Delilah with. Guess that's two murders Ghost can now be blamed for that she had nothing to do with. She's really racking them up.

She is hauled to her feet, forced to move or choke.

It's not my time yet, the other her insists as she is tugged past Delilah's crumpled body.

It's never no one's time, according to themselves, thinks Ghost, *but your time is always your time, your time is when it happens. Now shut up, start thinking, and help get us the fuck out of this.*

The voice is silent.

'You're useless, you are,' mutters Ghost as she is forced out of the church.

CHAPTER 28

Cair Lleon
Three Weeks Ago

'The King is dead! The King's been murdered! He lies in secret state in his palace of black spires while his minions *lie* to us!'

The man screams from a makeshift pulpit, a haphazard stack of metal fish crates, his booted feet searching for precarious purchase on their diamond grilles. Around his neck is a vastos collar of a notable Evrontown shipping family, but it looks old, and the accompanying frayed insignia on his filthy jacket speaks of itself in the past tense. His hair has grown out the tell-tale skull shave on one side, while the other side is long, lank and knotted. He might be free to call the streets his home now, but he's still loud – though just one voice among the line on Oracle Row, the famed soothsayer street of Evrontown.

'Lailoken foretold it all along!' he screamsprays, his lips arrayed in hanging rainbows of spit, 'in his book of prophecies, the book still banned today for all the terrifying truths it contains! But I have a copy! I have *seen* the words, my friends, the words he wrote more than fifty years ago, predicting this very day! The prophecy that runs: "*The forgotten child will come to claim the Sword*",' he pauses significantly, ' "*and London will bleed*"!'

His wet mouth and round eyes disappear from sight, to be replaced by the forgotten child herself, Red Caballarias o'Rhyfentown. She is painted up like she's off to war in a ball-room. They've made her look both glittery and fierce. Outside of a glow screen, she would look ridiculous.

By her side, demure and faded in comparison, stands the Lady Orcade.

'The Dracones family,' she is saying quietly, 'have provided blood proof that Red is a member of their family and the daughter of our late King, and that her right to moldra lagha in the question of her mother's death has been accepted and ratified according to them. They will seek no return vengeance for her part in her father's death. The Welyen family, as well as a number of other prominent families from several districts, are willing to stand behind her claim—'

Brune switches off the projector.

Silence reigns.

'Saintsfuck,' Fortigo says eventually to no one in particular.

Lucan gives a bitter laugh. He has the air of a man who has slept in his clothes, or rather, not slept at all in his clothes. 'Messages are springing up on galdor walls everywhere about it, and in different districts. Rumours are moving through the upwards springs. Half the soothsayers of London are now coming forwards, eager to tell their prophecies of this very moment. The other half are saying that the whole thing is a terrible lie, and that *they* foretold this illegitimate power grab by the other families.'

'Hysteria spreads fast,' comments Lillath.

'Quicker than the sweat-box sicks.' He takes a tired pause. 'It's beyond containment now.'

'What are they asking for?' Brune demands.

'They want to see the King's body, to verify his death

without question, and how and when it occurred. Then they'll force it to an arena dispute between the palace and the Dracones family, with half the elites of London behind them.' Lucan pauses. 'They want Red as Queen.'

Wyll watches the small group echo their cries of disbelief.

'This is ridiculous,' Brune asserts. 'Their proof is flimsy, at best, and even if they do have enough evidence to get it to the arena, no one's going to want a damned *godchild assassin* ruling London. She's not even a qualified *knight*, for saints' sake.'

When Brune gets nervous, she gets personal, Wyll has noticed.

'This can't be their ultimate play,' she continues. 'They know no one will accept Red as Queen. What's the move after this?'

Lucan shakes his head. 'I don't know. What I do know is that we're looking at a very messy, very public arena bout between whoever they pick as Red's champion knight and the palace's champion knight, namely Wyll. Even if we win, I think it might destroy us.'

'I'm not fighting for you headless cocks,' rails Wyll, but it is both foolish and fruitless when they cannot hear him. He sits alone in a clusterloc view room, watching through the one-way flecter glass as Art's Saith discuss his fate without his input or choice. Neither his fury nor his illusions mean much when they can't be seen.

'We have to put the next game into motion,' Brune says as she leans her weight on the table, her gnarled knuckles rising like mountain ranges from its flat surface. 'Here's my proposal. We confirm the rumour of Art's death, but supply all necessary evidence that it was natural. Another heart-stop, just like his father. Runs in the family, say the best medics we can buy. Then we suggest Sirion Dracones as the palace's candidate for King.'

'Sirion Dracones?' Lucan repeats, his tone climbing in disbelief. 'What is he, Art's fourth cousin twice removed?'

'The one who looks like a boiled wart,' Lillath supplies. 'Can he even stand up on his own?'

'He's a little sickly,' Brune concedes, 'a lifetime of ill health, poor boy, but he's long been schooled for at least the *possibility* of the Sword. More importantly, he's entirely amenable. He'll do whatever we require.' She sits back. Her gaze goes towards Wyll, or more accurately, Wyll's shoulder. She can't see him through the glass, but she knows he's there, of course, listening to his future being decided for him. 'And how can he lose when he has the King-in-the-Ground's own champion, perhaps the most famous knight ever to grace the Caballaria, fighting for him?'

They'll rig it. Even if Wyll deliberately throws the fight, somehow, they'll rig it so he still wins. Brune thinks of everything. Brune the fucken strategist.

'This is our best plan?' Lucan raises his hands. 'Saints help us.'

'What about Red?' asks Fortigo.

'What about her?' Lucan replies.

'She has a legitimate claim, by all accounts.'

'Did I hear right? You want to put the King's murderer on the throne?'

'It'd hardly be the first time,' murmurs Fortigo.

'What?' Lucan says irritably. 'What are you talking about?'

'You should brush up on your history.'

'Why the fuck would I do that when it's the now and the future I'm concerned with?' Lucan roars. 'I don't care about how things have been done in the past. We're different. We're *better* than those who've come before. We have to be, or what's the bloody *point*?'

Lillath, quiet as shade, detaches herself from the room.

Moments later Wyll hears the bleep of the door lock behind him, the open-and-shut.

Beyond the flecter-glass window the remnants of the reign of Artorias Dracones continue to argue. Lucan is the apoplectic shade of the hysterically tired, Brune is set to frigidly furious. Fortigo sits silently with his arms crossed, staring into the void. Garad is notably absent. Come to think of it, they haven't been seen around Cair Lleon in some weeks, ever since they aggressively volunteered to verify the body of the late Finnavair.

'The chicken's head's been cut off,' says Wyll, 'but it doesn't know it's dead yet.'

Lillath comes to stand beside him, her gaze lighting on her friends. She says nothing, her expression impressively unreadable.

'Ready for the arena?' she asks.

'I'm not fighting for you,' Wyll flatly replies. 'You won't get me out in that arena for anyone, let alone the sickly boiled wart who constitutes your master plan.'

'No?' asks Lillath. 'Well, if you won't fight for him, do it for London?'

The lightest touch of wryness to her tone suggests her own disbelief in the idea.

'London,' Wyll scoffs, 'the myth you're all so obsessed with preserving. The reality is mess.'

'The reality is always mess,' Lillath replies. 'Our stories make sense of the mess. They process and organise that mess until it feels like truth. They have to, or we'd all go mad. We're not well equipped for staring into the full face of chaos.'

Wyll just sighs. 'Do what you like to me. Throw me in prison, threaten me, torture me. I won't fight for you any more.'

'All right,' Lillath says agreeably. 'Well, what if I told you that it's not you I'm interested in?'

'I know, it's Red – but I think it's time to admit defeat on that one. You handed her to your enemies on a plate.'

The silence that follows is a heavy one. Wyll knows he is dangerously close to an edge, but he no longer cares. Lillath has lost. She just hasn't realised it yet.

He hears her small, disappointed sigh. 'It's not Red I'm interested in. Actually, Wyll, it was never Red. It's someone else, a man I've been watching for quite some time now. He's a fascinating figure. I've been told so many stories about him and the power he commands. People will say all sorts of silly things, of course, because we all need to believe in something greater than the general banality of life. Anyway, this man has been operating quietly across London for years, setting up loose networks of similarly minded people, shall we say. He doesn't look like much, but then, the very powerful often don't.' She takes out a data coin from her pocket, flicks its catch. From its shiny surface pops a grainy image, insubstantial on its bed of air, of a slight, unassuming figure, taken from the back. His head is turned towards the capturer, so that his neat profile and balding head are on display.

'His name is Barochi,' continues Lillath, 'though I'm sure that's not one that can be traced. Not in London, anyway.'

She clicks the coin. The next image is wider, incorporating the man in profile once more, apparently in deep conversation with the figure standing next to him at the side of a kill ring. The figure is unmistakable.

It is Viviane.

The machinery of panic starts up in Wyll's chest. The coin's projection cycles through years of faces, contacts, captures of his comings and goings. Lillath's clever play comes crashing over him like a wave, and he realises he has lost.

All this time, it wasn't Red Lillath has been following.

It was him.

'As I said,' he hears Lillath muse, her scrutiny a palpable weight on him, 'he has some interesting friends, this man. Friends in low places and high. He is patron to a number of curious organisations, the main purpose of which appear to be to protect and defend godchildren. Laudable, some might say. Dangerous, others might say. But to what end? There's the secret Gwanharatown training school he gives money to, for example, the one that houses unregistereds and teaches them how to use their gifts in the most astoundingly unlawful fashion. There's the private group of cross-district adjudicators he employs to rig disputes his way. And I have to wonder, what does a man like this want? What is his ultimate aim? Questions, you can imagine, that keep a Spider up at night. Questions I really need to ask him, and the people he associates with.'

How could you be stupid enough to believe that you roamed without eyes on you everywhere you went? Since the beginning, Wyll. The moment Art took you from the wasteland of your childhood home. The moment he laid eyes on you.

You've never been alone.

'It's not just you that gets affected by your refusal to fight,' Lillath murmurs. 'It's Barochi, and everyone he protects. Because despite what you may have told yourself, this is not a good man. This is a man whose plans make me nervous.'

Seconds tick past as Wyll fights his panic. She can't know everything, even if she makes everyone feel like she does – or can she? It seems that long-held suspicion of his is the only move he has left.

'I'm not the only one with a law-skirting life,' he says desperately.

Lillath looks amused. 'I'm a spy. Law-skirting comes with the job.'

'I'm not talking about that. Hasn't anyone around you ever wondered how you know just what they're thinking? Is everyone really too stupid to question the most mysteriously efficient Spider London has ever seen?'

Lillath affects modesty. 'Stop sticking your tongue between my cheeks. There've been better than me.'

'Prove it,' says Wyll. 'Not even your beloved Art knew, did he? What, were you never tempted by a little confession on the pillow? Neh, he told me you were lovers back in the day.'

'Shut your mouth.' Lillath is all sudden steel.

'When did it first start, your talent for other people's thoughts? What was the kick? Did it start with your bed-players? You got really good at it, right? You gave them just what they wanted? Best lover they've ever had. Hard to turn off such a power over people, right? So . . . the world is unfair, you have an advantage, so it goes. Everyone's got hidden plays. It's fine, it's the natural way of things.' Wyll pauses. 'Only the longer it goes on, the more you can never tell the people closest to you. The decades-long violation of their private selves. How would they react? Could they ever trust you again?'

Lillath gives him a smile of pure fury. 'You have no idea what you're talking about.'

'You're a fucken godchild,' sneers Wyll, 'just like me.'

Lillath leans forwards. 'Prove it,' she says.

Clawing, burning impotence, the rage chasing on its heels, is a rat in the belly gnawing its way through the guts of its prison.

Lillath gives him a small, sympathetic smile. 'Time to go back to the kennel,' she says, and snaps for the guard.

CHAPTER 29

Garad's Apartment, Evrontown
Two Weeks Ago

'Where did they take you after the church?' asks Garad.

Ghost sucks on her sicalo. She needs the calming hit for what comes next.

'Woke up in the Menagerie,' she says finally, through a plume of twilight smoke. 'At least, that's what he called it.'

The Menagerie, Alaunitown
Three Weeks Ago

Steam rises from the bath.

Ghost floats agreeably, noticing neither heat nor wet. All she feels is a vague haze, like being at the point of drunk where time doesn't run all that normal and the brain does lazy hops over the lags and the gaps. Her knees rise from the creamy depths, thighs droplet-streaked.

There's something in the corner of the bathroom. A dark, indistinct shape. A person-shaped shape. In contrast to the brightness around Ghost, the shape in the corner is fuzzy black, as if forming

333

from the shadows of her brain. As if it hasn't yet decided what it wants to be.

The shape flows closer to her, stalking on fuzzy legs.

Ghost asks it who it is.

The figure asks her who she wants it to be.

She doesn't remember saying, but now it's Delilah who stalks towards her, Delilah of the doe eyes and angry, pouted mouth. Little rounded shoulders and little rounded breasts that fit into the grip of a hand, and give so beautifully under pressure.

Ghost watches her approach. She is afraid. She is deathly afraid, and yet she wants more than anything for Delilah to reach the bathtub.

She does. She lowers herself on to a stool next to the bathtub and then leans over the prone Ghost, pushing her thighs further apart.

Then she dips a hand underneath the water.

The water should be Ghost's shield. Her protection from invasion. Underneath it she is naked, soft and pierceable. Invisible fingers find her and press inwards, slowly, sending ecstatically rolling shivers down the length of each limb. Ghost wriggles on the ends of those fingers like a fish on a hook.

She asks Delilah whether she is dead, because she knows, somewhere in the back of her mind, that this is true – somewhere out there this happened, she is sure of it.

Delilah doesn't answer. She leans over the bath, hair dangling, one arm bracing herself on the side, the other arm in the water up to the triceps, her neck stretched across Ghost's field of vision, her expression hidden by the upward angle of her face.

Ghost watches, through her urgent haze, the muscle in Delilah's shoulder bunch as she pumps, each squeeze matching the hot ache she feels between her legs as those fingers push inside, harder—

Ghost tells her to stop, because there's something really important here, something wrong. If only she could remember what it is.

Delilah ignores her, and it would be so easy to give in, saints, she's close. Her hindbrain determinedly ignores her warnings, desperately galloping towards the finish. It's too much, each part of her straining in opposite directions, pulled apart by horses, and in the ecstatic agony it takes to hold herself back, her own hand shoots out from beneath the water and wraps around her torturer's neck, squeezing, just to get her to stop.

Delilah chokes and tries to rear back, flinging arcs of water across the room like arterial sprays from a throat cut, but Ghost has her in her grip and she squeezes – you're dead, she hisses, stop, you're dead – and the body above her flails, scrabbling at the grim purchase on her throat—

Then there is no water, no bath. There is a bare floor and bare walls and hard, cold light.

Ghost comes to her senses to find herself lying prone on a mattress. The mattress lies on the floor of what appears to be a giant tank. Four transparent walls encase her, and beyond them is a larger, indistinct room.

Out of reach of the mattress, sat on a plain chair, a white-haired creature that is not Delilah wrenches and jerks, their pale face a mottled purple. Their hands scrabble at their throat.

Ghost can only watch from her supine position, frozen in total confusion.

The white-haired figure appears to calm. They drag in a shuddering breath.

'Get me out of here,' they squeal. 'Get me out of here, get me out of here, she's trying to kill me.'

The chair they sit on is on ropes. In front of Ghost's bemused gaze, it is lifted up by those ropes, dangling in the air, winched up and out of the tank, the white-haired creature clinging desperately to it. Once it clears the tops of the walls, a giant whirring sound assaults the air. Ghost watches, astonished, as a ceiling is lowered down, sealing off the walls into a large, self-contained box. There are no doors.

The walls of the tank are smooth windows almost twice the height of an average human, made of what looks like thick, transparent glass. Three of the walls are unbroken sheets, but one – the one furthest away – boasts a black coin-shaped hole in its centre. From the coin hole, on the other side of the wall, snakes a giant tube that disappears into the wall behind it. It looks like a worm trying to burrow through the tank.

'What. The. Fuck,' Ghost says. 'What. The. *Fuck.*'

Movement beyond the glass walls catches her eye. The chair with its white-haired cargo has reached the ground on the other side, and its cargo clambers carefully from it, sullenly responding to a tall, slick figure standing with their arms clasped behind their back.

Ghost feels a jolt of hatred flash through her before her brain can catch up with providing its source.

Glapissant.

Ghost levers herself up from the mattress.

The two figures continue to hold some puzzlingly silent discussion, their mouths moving, but with no sound to match it. If Ghost were not feeling so much like a deathly scared rat in a trap, she might have been able to muster a good laugh about how comical they look.

Glapissant's head cocks as he senses movement. Then he holds up a hand to silence the white-haired creature and strides up to the glass wall, meeting Ghost on its other side. His gaze is that of a somewhat disinterested zookeeper examining an animal under his remit.

He presses something on his side of the wall and then speaks.

His voice comes through flat and tinny, but clear. 'You can scream, if you like,' he says, 'but the sound only goes one way, unless I press another button. You can hear me, but I can't hear you. So I'd save your energy and listen.'

She hadn't even realised she'd been shouting. She shuts her mouth.

'I assume you're wondering where you are,' says Glapissant. 'Think of it as an experimental research facility. We call it the Menagerie. Have you heard of it?'

Ghost slowly shakes her head.

'Good,' the tinny voice replies. 'Delilah didn't spill everything to you, then. It was hard to control her at times, even with the threat of her sister's termination hanging over her head.' Glapissant makes an annoyed clicking sound with his tongue. 'Well, Ghost. You're in a tank, as you can see, in your very own room at this facility. Now, the tank is made of . . . oh, some boringly unpronounceable name. It's a very durable, but – up until a few years ago – utterly useless polymer by-product of the factory processes used to make gun moulds. Its most intriguing property was discovered by happy accident – it can both contain and protect against godchild magic.' The tinny voice turns amused. 'That's ironic, eh? A Gun contained by a substance used to make guns?'

Ghost stares at his perfect, clammy skin, his neat, slick hair, his expensive clothes. *This* guy, one of those superstitious lunatics who daubs themselves in deer blood mixed with bat faeces – or whatever the latest fad is these days – to ward off the evil godchildren who could take over their brain? Who'd have thought?

'Now I know what you're thinking,' continues Glapissant. 'You've never heard of this substance. Can't be real. I'm lying. Why don't you try out a little trick on me and see what happens?'

The voice cuts out. Glapissant waits, watching her with a look of absolute assuredness.

He, at least, believes what he's saying.

Ghost keeps still, staring back.

Eventually he presses the button, and into the tank comes his voice. 'No? Feeling shy? Never mind. I must admit, I'm curious to see what your talent is. I'll be so disappointed if it's an obvious one. Delilah assured me it had to be unusual. She had no idea what it was, but she said you came up very strong with her sister. You know, the godchild who tested you. She's a . . . map, of sorts. The most reliable mechanism I've ever come across for determining godchild status and location. Accurate to an astonishing degree.'

The touch on her face down in the cellar.

Too soft and finger-like to be a machine.

The bundle in the bald man's arms as he fled the burning shop. The bundle just large enough to be girl-shaped.

The test machine. The map. It's a human.

It's a sister.

It's Delilah's sister.

And Moth? Their mother, perhaps? Did Delilah know her sister was being sold off? Did she think Glapissant bought her?

Ghost's head throbs. This is getting all kinds of fucked-up.

'You'd be a rare catch,' she hears Glapissant say. 'In which case, I'd be very pleased. Or rather, I might be when I know what it is you can do. Eh?'

He laughs at her.

Laughs.

Helpless fury engorges her, pressing against each organ, swelling in her veins until it feels like she will explode. Only the unbendable iron rod that is her stubborn, contrary, rebellious will keeps it from letting loose. The monstrous toad wants something from her. Denying it to him is the only power she has left.

Glapissant nods, as if this is all so very expected.

'Well,' he sighs, 'I hope you remember that we offered you the nice way first. Poor Wallans here was only trying to give you a gift.'

The sullen, white-haired creature next to him looks away. Throughout the conversation so far, he has been unable to meet her eye, staring off into a corner of the room.

A dremen.

Ghost has never met one before. Dream weavers are supposed to be as rare as an honest thief, yet she just had one in her head, pretending to be Delilah, trying to get her off and provoke a magical kick.

It had felt just like a dream. It had *been* a dream. But the residual ache in her groin and the way the dremen has one hand still wrapped protectively around his throat suggests that the myth is true – with a dremen, what you feel in the dream is so real that it happens to you in the waking world, too. Nightmares in particular must hold more terrors for him than is normal for everyone else.

No doubt Wallans was under duress of some kind to violate her mind like that. The little dremen looks as much a prisoner here as she is. Still, a part of her is sorry she didn't finish the job on his throat.

Glapissant watches her. Now that he feels safe, there is a smug lift to the corners of his mouth and a strut in his walk. She remembers him in the church, cowering underneath her with her knife to his throat, his face crumpled, his voice troughing and peaking in a begging whine.

He looked a lot better like that.

'Of course, there are other ways to provoke a display from you, as I'm sure you know,' he says. 'Near-death does it the best. You see that pipe up there?'

He indicates the black coin-shaped hole embedded in the far wall of her tank with the giant tube snaking out of it. It's big enough for someone to crawl through, if they were small.

'That pipe lets in water,' continues Glapissant. 'The water slowly fills up the tank. Works every time. The tanks were my idea, built to my construction specifications, and they've proved extremely effective, if I may be allowed to comb my own hair, so to speak.'

Cass' dead, waterlogged body. All those dead, waterlogged bodies turning up over the last few months.

He drowns them.

Well, says the other Ghost, *how nice to finally be getting all the answers to the questions that have been driving us mad the last few weeks, itso? Shame it's at the end of the road.*

T'chuss, Ghost snaps back. *This isn't the end of the road, not for you.*

Her captor is smiling with misty-eyed memories. 'The results have often been quite extraordinary. But the combination of the water and the special material' – he pats the wall, and it gives an odd, flat ring – 'contains the results. Never had a tank break yet!' He shrugs. 'Of course it works less well for the mind tricks, but we have other devices for those. For someone like you, though – well. Delilah was insistent that yours isn't mind, and I've been well informed of your capacity for violence. Logical conclusions can be drawn.'

She cannot stop staring at him. Shock, presumably.

Glapissant laughs at her expression. 'Oh, don't look so worried. The water is really a final-stage thing. If you cooperate, you'll be fine. And there are other, less lethal ways we can use. Electrical stimulus, for example. Did you know about that? There was a case a hundred years ago of a pelleren being struck by lightning and inadvertently levelling the buildings around him with the resultant magical shockwave. He died doing it, of course. Even a godchild can't channel that much energy without consequences. But the potential applications are just extraordinary. Imagine being able to destroy buildings, even whole towns, with just one or two human bodies. Little walking bombs – and no one around them would have any idea.'

It must take huge resources to build something like this. Plus, there are two guards on the only door in the room beyond her tank, and presumably more outside the room. She can see capturers embedded into every wall. This can't just be one richly resourced lunatic with a psychotic kink, not for all this. There are others involved.

This is a whole operation.

Ghost starts to feel very sick.

She can hear the toad croaking on about new drug formulations that do interesting things to the physiognomy, still in the experimental stage, some difficult side effects, but oh well, there are always consequences in the name of progress, and she should be examining her tank cage, examining him, every inch of this place, finding weaknesses, formulating an escape, thinking through this calmly and logically and rationally and knowing that she will get out of here, she will see sunlight again, and she will not be trapped in here forever, but instead all she can hear in her head is her own panicked, wordless moans, like a rabbit caught squealing in a snare.

'He left me there a while, to "think things over",' says Ghost.

She takes a suck of the sicalo, but it doesn't calm the tremble in her. 'They turned off all the lights and left me in the dark. I remember thinking we must have been underground, because it was so black inside my room.'

'How long did they leave you in there for?' asks Garad quietly.

'A few days.' Ghost pauses. 'They fed me, but they kept the lights off. It doesn't sound that long, a few days in the dark. But with nothing else to do and nothing else to fix on, you know what happens to a mind like mine? It starts to eat itself.'

Garad is silent.

'When they finally came back in, I felt like I'd lived and died in that tank. I'd have done anything he wanted.' Ghost pauses. 'And he knew it.'

'Ready to show us a little something?' Glapissant asks through the tank's speaker.

Ghost nods. She tries not to look too eager, but she's fairly sure she fails.

'Excellent!' He bursts into a brilliant smile. 'Now what does it take, for you? We have the best and purest-cut Tidal you'll find in London, and any other means that you might need – whether girl, boy or toy.'

And he'll watch, too, of that she has no doubt – but instead of erotic, it'll be anthropological, his interest solely that of a zoo-keeper watching one of his monkeys having a little self-pleasure time. Voyeurism, she'd get. She's even indulged in a little herself on occasion, with the consenting – who hasn't? – but that's not what this is about for him. Somehow, that knowledge disgusts her more.

Ghost holds out a hand, squeezes it into a fist. She is careful not to point her arm at him as she does so, lest he mistake it as the gesture of promised death and take offence. In her head, however, it's his throat in her fingers.

'You need someone to kill?' Glapissant guesses.

Not kill, just fight – but at this point, who cares? This is no longer the real world but a nightmare, and in nightmares you do whatever it takes to survive.

'Any preference on type? A particular visual stimulus?' he asks.

Someone who looks like you would do nicely.

Ghost shakes her head.

He sounds disappointed. Not enough anthropological detail for his liking.

The arrangements are made, and quickly enough – Glapissant is evidently someone to be obeyed. Ghost's preparations are interrupted by the arrival of the selected opponent, a small but sturdy-looking merc guard knight, chosen in obvious deference to her size. Her tank ceiling is lifted off – would that she had impossible springs for feet – and he is lowered in. In one hand he holds a short sword. In the other he holds a gun.

Ha. Guess they want a way to put her down quick, should things not go well.

'Are you allowed to damage the merchandise?' she asks him.

The merc is silent, watching her from under the brim of his

helmet. The allegiance charm sewn into the neck of his clothing is an angular-cut crescent moon, the branding of some private outfit. The one next to it is a fox, symbol of Alaunitown, so at least Ghost now knows she's likely still in the same dis' – and with an apparent abundant water supply to fill up tanks with, it's got to be near the river.

She also notices what looks like thin glass wristbands poking out from his cuffs. Interesting, and useless – at least for him. But now she knows he's afraid of godchildren, she can see past the training that keeps a leash on his panicked hindbrain. Saints, look at him. Eyes bugged wide, every muscle tight with pre-emptive defence. He's already in a losing position, because he's told himself that he has no idea what's coming. No clue what to guard against – mind or body?

It occurs to Ghost – maybe for the first time in her life – how much power she has as a godchild. Up to now, it's been a furtive secret, and every day shaped around the keeping of it. A weakness to be hidden at all costs. But there's a flip to it, and it comes at the point where you just . . . stop hiding it. When you stop collaborating in their control of you, simply by denying them the thing they need to do it.

The power that lies in the discarding of shame. It tastes *delicious*.

A click, and she hears Glapissant's tinny voice.

'Begin.'

She doesn't bother playing it coy. As the guard begins to move in a circling crouch, another Ghost appears directly behind him and taps him on the shoulder.

The guard whirls around.

The look of utter, confused horror on his face is the most hysterical thing she's seen in years. The other Ghost huffs a short laugh, reaches out, takes the gun from his limp, shocked hand and shoots him in the crotch.

He folds, slowly.

The tank begins to fill with agonised screams.

Ghost locks eyes with the other her.

It is always a strange sensation to see herself from the outside, free of distortions from mirrors and the bias of her own gaze. Interesting to note, as well, that the facial modifications she's had done are also on the other her's face. It's been long enough since she's conjured a new version of herself that she wasn't sure how she'd look. The last time was a few months back, in fact, when she died and became Ghost.

The other her nods in agreement, raises the gun, takes aim at Glapissant, and shoots.

The bullets ping off the tank wall. One rebounds and hits the floor inches away from Ghost's feet. She swears. The other her stops shooting, looks at her sympathetically, shrugs.

Glapissant, who had stood frozen, recovers annoyingly fast. Safe behind those impenetrable walls of mysterious material, he walks with quick steps to the speaker.

His eyes darting between them both, he presses the button.

Silence.

Then:

'It's not an illusion.'

Ghost shrugs. Of course not. Illusions can't shoot people in the cock.

'Help me,' groans the guard, still curled like a foetus on the floor. 'Help me, fuck, saints, get me out, fix me.'

The seat is lowered into the tank and the guard grips it like a lifeline, which in a very real sense it is. If they'd left him in the tank, she might have killed him out of sheer fury.

Glapissant's gaze runs greedily over both of her. Only twice before now has Ghost shown someone who she really is. The first time cost her love. The second cost her life. This time, it's all the value she has. A glittering prize she can see reflected in the toad's greedy, shining eyes.

'Extraordinary,' he breathes. 'I've never seen one of you before. Can I talk to the other? Does it understand?'

The other Ghost rolls her eyes and offers Glapissant an obscene gesture. He laughs and claps his hands like a delighted, deranged child.

Does the toad know that not only does his tank keep a godchild's magic contained, but actually amplifies it, like insulation with heat? She's never been able to manifest a double so lightning-quick before. She feels like she's taken four uppers in a row. It makes her want to bare her teeth and hurt someone. It gets her riled.

As soon as he lets her out of here, he's dead. *Everyone* is dead.

The other her grins.

'How does it work?' Glapissant asks. 'Is the copy independent of you, or do you control it? Does it know everything you do? Does it have the same memories? The same capabilities? Do you exist like this all the time?'

She indicates that he'll get all the answers he could want if he lets her out. After all, she needs to talk. And she readies herself. It should be now, while she's buzzing – death for them, escape for her. Once she's out of the tank, it's likely to dissipate fast.

But Glapissant just raises a brow. 'No need. There's another button, my side. When I press it, I can hear you.'

Ghost stares at him.

He presses something on his side. 'Talk to me and you'll see.'

'Fuck you,' says Ghost.

'Ah,' says Glapissant, nodding. 'You wanted out of the tank. Unfortunately, it doesn't work like that. But if you behave well, and you come to trust in our work here, we'll think about taking you out for some exercise, perhaps in a few weeks. Now, please answer these questions and earn your dinner tonight. When did you first notice—?'

It's the 'few weeks' that snaps her, them both, all of it. Without another word, they make the decision together, Ghost and the other Ghost. It's quickly done because there's only one thing left to try. There is a design flaw in the tank – when they came up with this thing, they hadn't ever thought there would be *two* godchildren inside it.

The two Ghosts run to the pipe. It's out of reach, taller than them, not even accessible at a standing jump by an acrobat – but the double leapfrogs on to Ghost's back while she steadies her hands on the wall. She feels the double grip her shoulders, hauling her body weight upwards with barely a wobble, clinging like a beetle while Ghost clenches and braces everything she has, trying to be a tree to climb, and with some effort, her double's got her feet planted on her shoulders, and now they're nearly twice the height. There is a sudden downward push, an awful new weight as the other Ghost bears down, the better to leap up, catch the pipe lip, and then scramble—

The weight is gone. Ghost feels as light as air. She's only faintly aware of muffled shouts in her background as she watches her double's feet disappear, and then her head reappears and her arms extend downwards, reaching.

Ghost bends down.

Springs up with all the strength she's ever had.

Misses her double's grasping hands by what feels like miles.

Fuck.

There's no table in here, nothing she can use to climb closer.

From above her, there comes a deep, throbbing clunk. Then an incomprehensible rushing sound, quiet at first, but then growing louder, louder, like wind through treetops.

Far above her, Ghost's double shouts.

And out from the pipe tumbles a shock of water, hitting Ghost square on the head.

She falls painfully to her knees, ears filled with rushing, body pinned down by the terrible weight of water. It takes everything she has to roll out of its path, enough to get free, stand up, watch in disbelief as it comes flooding endlessly down from the pipe mouth – and starts filling the tank.

Water's already licking at her ankles.

One thing about fight training – whatever else you can say about it, it teaches fast decision-making. Hesitations cost too much.

'You have to go,' Ghost calls up to her double.

'We wait for the water level to get you up to the pipe!' the double shouts over the rush.

Water continues to gush, gush, gush, around her, trying to urge her out of the pipe and back into the tank. Her fingers are white death-grips around the pipe's lip. Any minute now she'll be shunted out of the pipe and back into the tank, and then they're both fucked.

No telling what the water level's like beyond the pipe, or how many guards they're currently ordering to whatever space lies beyond it.

'It'll be minutes we don't have,' Ghost says. 'You have to take this chance – now.'

The double is vehement. 'No fucken way, idiot. I'm not leaving you behind. You're me and I can't.'

'I did it,' Ghost calls. 'I had to. And look at me. I'm a whole person. I fleshed out. You will too.'

The double is shaking her head.

'If you don't go now, we both die,' Ghost says. Cold wet bites and swirls, creeping slowly up her shins. 'If you go, we keep living.'

'No, I can't. I can't let go.'

'I know you're scared,' Ghost says, 'but that's the point. Fear keeps you not just living but alive, itso?'

The double gives a wordless shout as the water torrent nearly shunts her out of the pipe.

She nods and disappears.

Just like that.

I never was one for the long goodbye, Ghost reflects.

The pain in her chest is sudden, sharp and awful. She feels abandoned. Then she remembers that last time *she* was the one who did the abandoning, and suddenly she feels fine. This is how humans live best. We keep shucking off our old shells and expanding into new ones. She's not ready to die, but that's all right. She's lived quite well for someone who's only a few months old.

Outside the tank, Ghost can see Glapissant ordering people around, his face an incandescent shade of red. She smiles to herself. It's a shame she didn't get to watch him die screaming, but maybe her double will. Who knows? There's everything to play for when you've no idea what's coming next.

Her feet are numb stumps. The water is very cold. Its gush fills her ears.

CHAPTER 30

Cair Stour Monastery, Blackheart
Two Weeks Ago

The light in front looks like a comet tail, a blinking ghost that leaves temporary trails across the road's dark.

With his bike purring underneath him, Wyll follows it towards a suffocatingly certain future.

In quieter streets, the bike light dancing ahead of him would be the centre of his attention, but there are no quiet streets in this part of Blackheart, and it must compete with the riot of gyrating street signs above, the glows info projections arcing over the sky, beckoning for his attention. He gives them none. It's easy not to look up if there's nothing you want to buy and there's nothing that you need to know about today's anxious rundown of human misery.

The noise, however, is harder to ignore. Shouts, screams, calls, squeals, rattles, stamps, bleeps and bellows surround his guard phalanx like an outer wall. The crowds they ride past are closer than the sky, and just as unpredictable. There is no perceptible way to tell whether the cacophony is an entertained crowd or a baying mob. Both trick coins and sword charms are rattling on the ground, adding to the confusion of whether the

Sorcerer Knight is in favour or not. The city is on a knife-edge, half for and half against. The best kindling for a war.

Will he be the spark?

A sword charm whips through the gaps between his phalanx's glossy machine hinds, stinging Wyll on the thigh. Barely the length of his little finger, but the bastard was sharpened – it could have cut through his leathers and stuck him in the flesh, damaging him before he even makes it to tomorrow's fight. Some piece of shit out there rooting for that murderous bitch, trying to even the playing field.

The murderous bitch you let go, his father's voice reminds him. *Twice*.

Perhaps it has played out for the best. The arena is where he belongs. The arena is where their world is shaped, their chaos contained. Undermining the Caballaria is undermining the foundations of reason and rule. Without those, human beings amount to no more than pigs rooting in the dirt. If nothing else, he can believe in the fight. It will be one champion against another. Red's vengeance was taken in blood, and the defence of it as moldra lagha will be decided in blood.

And she will lose.

The bike ahead of Wyll slows, a speck against the pointed fortress growing in their sight.

It is the monastery of the legendary Cair Stour arena, a blank monster of lava glass – glossy-smooth impenetrable stone like a black mirror, shaped into a massive seven-pointed throwing star. The only chink in the monastery's armour is the main gate, opening up like an impossible flower as they streak down the main boulevard and slide into the sanctuary beyond. As the gate slides back into place behind the rearguard, the cacophony beyond abruptly dims to near-silence.

Only then does Wyll start to untie some of his belly knots, and then busy himself tying up some new ones. No matter how many times he has fought in the arena, no matter how many times he tells himself it's all pomp and show, the quiet weight in this temple is hard to deny.

In here it is easy to pretend that there are entities larger than he. That the world is in glorious order, and all is as it should be.

He is in the First Blade's prayer room when the monk approaches him.

First Blade is the arm of the star reserved for the King's champion, and though, reportedly, each arm of the monastery is an identical suite of rooms, the rooms situated down the long, lofty corridor of First Blade are just a little more opulent in their simplicity, and it is the only arm decorated in the royal colours of silver and black.

Wyll is half stripped and sweating, light cudgels gripped in both hands swinging forwards and back as his feet beat an aggressive attack step across the black wood floor.

'Praying hard, Si Wyll,' says the monk.

Wyll startles and almost looses a cudgel their way. It drops from his fingers and clatters to the floor. The monk has their loose black rubber hood pulled over their head and close to the cheeks, hiding their face, as is tradition.

Adrenalin from the practice and outrage at their audacity binds Wyll's mouth in shocked silence. Monks do not approach knights, *ever*, unless spoken to first, and they certainly don't enter uninvited, especially not prayer rooms with closed doors.

'It is always nice to see a sweat worked up on the devout,' the monk continues. 'Makes you feel like your life's calling is worthwhile.'

And then they pull their hood down.

The first thing Wyll feels, on seeing who it is, is a surging, gratified relief. Not long before this and he'd have been ashamed of that feeling. Now, seeing someone so familiar breach the walls around him is something like salvation.

'That is the worst disguise I've ever seen,' he says, struggling to swallow a grin.

'We can't all just throw on someone else's skin,' Viviane retorts.

'I meant that no one could possibly mistake you for a monk.'

'I'm a wonderful actor.'

Wyll acknowledges this with a conciliatory nod, and then settles for a pointed, 'How in seven hells did you get in here?'

'Please,' sniffs Viviane. 'Monasteries are like rabbit warrens, there are a hundred ways in. All this nonsense about monks being incorruptible.' They toss a quick look back at the closed prayer room door. 'Still, I don't have long.'

'If you've come for the map,' says Wyll, 'I told you that I have it and I'll get it to you, but I'm a little busy right now.'

Viviane snorts. 'So I hear. Don't worry, I know you have the map safe.'

'It's useless to ask how you might know that, isn't it?'

They give him a tight smile. 'Maybe I'll tell you all my secrets someday.'

There is a tension to them they are not bothering to hide. This is a huge risk, even for someone like Viviane, and despite their flippancy, it would have cost dear, whether by trick, favour, bribe or blackmail. What could they possibly want that couldn't wait?

Wyll eyes them. 'You could have just sent me another message.'

Viviane gives an uncharacteristically sharp laugh. 'This was easier. Truly. Security around Cair Lleon has become rather troublesome these past few weeks.' They look as if they are choosing their next words with care. 'That palace collar around your neck is getting real tight, my love.'

Wyll's turn to laugh. He gestures around him, the place, the situation — *as you see.*

'I'm sorry about what happened with your girl,' Viviane says with soft pity.

Wyll patiently waits for the sudden lancing heart pain to stutter out.

'She was never my girl,' he simply replies.

Viviane takes this in. 'She's a heartless bitch. Fronting for the other side. The whole thing was a play for the Sword. Couldn't wait 'til Daddy swung his last, so swung it for him.'

'There are no sides.'

'Yes, there are.' Viviane regards him steadily. 'And I'm on yours.'

'You're on your own.'

'You keep telling yourself that, if it's easier.'

'Come on, Vivi.'

'No, you come on.' Viviane scoffs. 'Why else would I keep showing up to rescue you — at no small risk to myself, I might add?'

'That's what you came in here for? To rescue me? From a *fight?*' Wyll's confusion grows. 'That I'm going to win?'

'Come on, you really think it's that simple? They've got you fighting some greenback, a total nobody.' They catch his expression. 'Oh, what? Don't try to convince me you're like those depressingly devout knights that refuse to even know who their opponent is pre-fight.'

'Don't be ridiculous,' Wyll says. 'I know exactly who he is.'

It was Lillath who had given him a complete rundown of the champion he faces in the arena tomorrow. The pious Garad would have cut their own head off if the Spymaster had ever tried spilling the beans with *them*, but whatever else her faults, Lillath knows how to play Wyll.

That, of course, is the problem.

Viviane breathes out. 'Thank the saints. Only idiots fight fair, because no one else is.'

'*I* told you that.'

'And I've never forgotten it. Wyll – you're so unevenly matched with this knight that it'd be a clear insult – if it wasn't the biggest bout of the last few decades. What's their play with this?'

He doesn't know, and he can't work it out, and – more worryingly – neither could Lillath. Caradoc Whitetongue, champion for the murderous bastard daughter Pretender to the Sword, is an aesthete from the Lady Orcade's own private stable, known for his beauty rather than his fighting prowess. The kind of fighter who critics use as proof of their words when they say the Caballaria is nothing more than a glittering spectacle for the ever-slavering glows.

'If it were me, I'd have got the Mordred girl to fight as her own champion,' Viviane muses. 'She did almost best you once.'

'Firstly, no, she didn't. Secondly, it was using illegal magic and voided the bout. Thirdly, no one can be their own champion.'

'Prickle. Anyway, you might be interested to know that I got a soothsayer to look at the outcome.' Viviane gives him a serious look. 'I know who wins.'

Wyll scoffs even as his heart skips. 'You and half the city, I presume. Trawling the alleyways for a measly fifty-fifty prediction.'

'I went to someone better. And a lot more expensive.'

'Then I'm sorry you wasted your trick, on both the sooth-sayer and the fat bet you must have laid down after.' Wyll folds his arms. Always a play, with Viviane, and never to do with anyone but themself. 'So that's why you're here? Checking up on your investment?'

'I'm betting for something bigger than a bit of trick, you idiot,' Viviane hotly replies, and then their eyes slide from his as if embarrassed. 'Don't you want to know what they said?'

'I never go to soothsayers,' Wyll replies. 'Things happen how they happen, regardless of whether you can see it coming or not.'

'They said you'd win, Wyll' – no one, no matter what they believe, would feel nothing at that, and his heart rises hopefully – 'but they said the win would cost you too much. That it would break you.'

Viviane is anxious. It's disconcertingly unnatural on them, like a dog dressed in clothes.

'You think I'd let *her* take the Sword?' asks Wyll.

'I think you should,' Viviane replies with passion. 'Who cares? It costs you nothing to lose. But if you win – it costs you all your freedom, and you know it.'

'So you want a damaged killer with poor impulse control as your Queen?'

Viviane looks baffled. 'Same as all the rest. Why break with tradition?'

'Because sometimes it begets change for the better! Art wasn't like that, Art was a *good* person, one in a million in this shitty world, and finally we had someone decent—'

'Yes, a *good, decent* person who had a secret cub with a god-child meretrix and then murdered her mother!'

Prayer rooms tend to be well soundproofed – nothing spoils the divine silence of a monastery quite as much as the torrid shouts, pained grunts and ear-piercing clanging of weaponry that accompany a fighter knight's prayer rituals – but still, voices carry.

The realisation crosses Viviane's face at the same time. They take a deep, audible breath. The sound is oddly vulnerable.

'Everyone makes mistakes,' they say quietly, 'and everyone has to be allowed to. Otherwise you never let them be human, and that's not fair. Then all they are is a saint, and no one is a saint. Not even the damn saints themselves.' They gesture around the painted murals on the walls, those beautiful, stark frozen faces of the Saith. 'It's fine when you're a child, and you've yet to really grasp how inconstant people are. But when you grow up, you have to put that child's game down, or you'll wander through life being perpetually disappointed, feeling like everyone around you is a failure, and yourself most of all.'

Viviane folds themself in tight and looks around the room, as if for hope or inspiration.

'I really am sorry about Red,' they say. 'I'd have helped her, and not just because of our deal. I'd do whatever you asked of me. Why do you think I keep showing up in your life on silly pretexts like maps that probably don't exist and soothsayer predictions that change nothing?'

'The map exists, and it works,' says Wyll, gauging their reaction. 'Still want it?'

Viviane gives a calculated shrug. 'The one who hired me to get it is dead.'

'Who was it for?' he asks, wondering if they'll tell.

'Julias Dracones,' they reply, watching him.

Julias Dracones' official death, as carefully orchestrated by – probably – Lillath, was of a heart attack. Died suddenly and fairly painlessly in his ancestral seat, tending his plants. Presumably the mess Lillath's guard made breaking into the place was well cleaned up by the time less important and more public-facing eyes arrived on the scene.

First Red, and now Viviane. Julias had been quite the dark horse.

'Viviane,' Wyll says slowly, 'what exactly is it that you do these days?'

'I told you. I get people things.' They shift on their feet, side to side, as if using their body to weigh up a decision in their mind. 'I was the go-between between Julias and a business partner he had, someone he used to supply with Tidal. It was her who wanted the map. She runs something called the Menagerie.'

'What's the Menagerie?'

Viviane shakes their head. 'I don't know. And I don't know who she is, I've never met her.'

'I think I have,' Wyll says, thinking about the day he came across Julias Dracones and the Lady Orcade taking tea in a jungle atrium.

First she backs Red's claim, and now this Menagerie thing. Not to mention her ties with the lunatic botanist, Tidal supplier and apparent godchild breeder. She keeps to the background, but once you look, you start seeing her everywhere.

That sly bitch might just be behind it all.

'So,' hazards Wyll, 'what do you think will happen if I keep the map?'

Viviane is watching him closely.

'I never told Julias who I sent to fetch it,' they say. 'As far as he was aware, it burned along with its previous owner.'

At all costs, Orcade must not get that map. No one must have that map but him.

Viviane reaches forwards and takes Wyll's unresisting hand. The touch, any touch, reassures in its simple comfort, its promise of safety.

'You have plans for the map, don't you?' they ask.

Wyll says nothing.

'I can help.'

He shakes his head. 'It's easier alone.'

'But you don't want to be alone,' Viviane pleads. 'You've never wanted to be alone. I *know* you, Wyll. I can't help but know you. And I know myself. All my life, all I've ever been looking for is someone worthy of me. I kept thinking I'd found them. Carr. Titon. But they always disappointed, in the end. They looked strong, but they were weak. But you really are strong. I'm just sorry it took me this long to see it. You seemed so young when we first met, and I didn't trust that. But you're not young now. You're in your prime, and you're only going to get more powerful – with someone like me by your side. I so hope you can forgive me, Wyll. I so hope you can. Because I'm here to serve you, in any way that you need.'

Wyll stares at Viviane. This is different. They've never spoken to him like this before, not with this naked honesty.

'I'll always want to be someone's pet,' Viviane says simply, looking at him direct. 'Now I want to be yours. You think it's the other way around, but it's not my hand on your leash. It's yours on mine. Don't you know what a gift a pet like me is? Nothing else satisfies me like pleasing you. And if I can't find a way to please you, I get angry, and I make the world stop until

I get what I want. I have a fury inside me to please you, Wyll. Point me in the direction you want. I'm the most powerful weapon you've got.'

Vulnerability is a powerful drug. Being offered it by Viviane, of all people, only more so. They stand still, throat bared for his teeth. They stand there begging to be used.

And he could.

Viviane could be an out. Frankly, they're the only one he's got right now. His own dumb pride has prevented him from seeing how rare a gift is talent like theirs, not to mention their tenacity, connections and an all-round genius for landing on their feet. But the sudden loyalty? The profession of love, or the closest someone like Vivi ever gets to it? He doesn't trust it for a moment.

That doesn't mean it can't be useful, though.

Wyll makes a decision. He pulls Viviane into his arms and feels them melt against him with a glad sigh.

'I have plans too,' they promise in his ear. 'Plans to help you. And allies waiting for you in the ring.'

'Just get me through this fight first,' Wyll murmurs back.

He feels their hands skate his hot skin. 'I told you. Throw it. Let her win.'

'I can't,' Wyll says. 'It'll look so ridiculous that it couldn't be anything but staged, and then it'll be disputed, and then' – *Lillath will have my balls, and the balls of anyone associated with me, which means you'd be top of the list, Vivi* – 'I suppose that will drag things out a while, but to what advantage?' He strokes Viviane's hair. 'I've waited things out long enough, and they just keep getting worse. My only way out of prison is to win. For that matter, I don't know that serving Red up to the Sword is exactly going to benefit me either.'

'The other way won't,' Viviane murmurs. 'It'll ruin you.'

'I never took you as one much for prophecy.'

Viviane says nothing while their hands skate lower. They like to use their body as the last tool in their arsenal of persuasion. It works far less well than it used to, but he can let them think whatever they need.

If he loses, Lillath will find a way to lock him up forever on traitor charges and disband Barochi's networks, rendering him friendless and impotent. If he wins, he cements his position as Lillath's favourite new toy.

But maybe, just maybe, there's a third way.

They want a puppet King in the sickly Sirion Dracones? Fine. But not with that fractured, crumbling, headless excuse of a Saith pulling its strings. It isn't only Viviane's hands on Wyll's cock surging him into eager stiffness. It's the excitement that comes with the thought of finally shedding a coward's skin. There is only one way in this world to stop being used.

Time for the pet to become the master.

Good boy, his father says approvingly.

'You'd better get out of here,' he whispers to Viviane. 'They'll be coming to take me to the arena soon.'

'I'll see you afterwards?'

The question in their tone, as if it is now, as never before, up to him when they show up.

'Come and find me,' he says, and Viviane gives a relieved smile.

'Saints' favour,' they say, and take their leave.

Saints' favour indeed.

But which saint favours him, and what do they want?

CHAPTER 31

Cair Stour Arena, Blackheart
Two Weeks Ago

Caradoc Whitetongue is very pretty, very graceful, and very bad with a whip.

Which is unfortunate, given that it's his weapon of choice.

Wyll watches him miss a catch on his opponent and lunge too far, managing to turn the whole fumble into a body roll, from which he pops up with a silly grin and a crack of the whip above his head, narrowly missing his own ear with its barbed tip. And the crowd beast cheers and whistles and claps, as if a lack of talent is something to encourage.

Wyll shuts off the glow screen and lets loose a sigh.

The bowed head in his current field of vision lifts a little, its owner's hand pausing in its brushwork.

'Nervous?' asks the bowed head.

'How dare you,' Wyll responds mock-haughtily. 'The Sorcerer Knight is never nervous.'

Lee DeCyng, famed dresser of the famous, smiles.

'You're right about that,' he says in his thick Iochitown brogue, 'but I was asking Wyll.'

Wyll feels the wet brush tickle carefully along his jawbone

and tries to keep still. Lee's artistry deserves at least that much. He always enjoys this ritual before a fight. It's just him and Lee in the dressing room. All he can hear is the soft rise and fall of Lee's breathing, and all he can feel is the soft strokes of Lee's paintbrushes on his skin. There's something intimately meditative about the combination.

'Wyll is always nervous,' he responds once the brush lifts away. 'Even when he's up against someone who definitely only passed basic knight's training with bribery.'

'I got the impression that she's supposed to be good,' Lee says as he dips the brush tip into a tiny pot. He doesn't follow the fighters of the Caballaria quite as well as their outfits. Fabrics he can remember with astonishing accuracy, but he often has trouble with silly details like names and faces, which is why the pronoun mistake doesn't immediately ring an alarm.

Wyll's desired response goes something like, 'There are so many ways to beat this Whitetongue idiot that the only difficulty will be in making such a prestigious fight last long enough.'

Instead he settles for a more diplomatic, 'Not the best fighter I've ever seen, but people can always surprise you.'

It's not the first time he has been matched against someone far beneath his fighting level. Besides, once you're out in the pit, with the glare of the glow lights blinding you and the roar of the crowd deafening you and your own sweat eager to betray your weapon right out of your grip, anything is possible. Heroes can fall and nobodies can rise. History made in one weak feint, one missed throw, one split-second of well-placed muscle and power.

'It doesn't seem right,' Lee continues. 'I didn't know they could even do that.'

Wyll shrugs. 'It's insulting, but unless Whitetongue has just spent the last few years of his career deliberately making himself look bad in some sort of astonishingly prescient and involved long play to fool everyone, there's not much for me to complain about.'

Lee's forehead wrinkles with a confused frown.

'Si,' he ventures, but then the door to Wyll's dressing room opens so hard that it rebounds against the wall with a dull thud.

The Royal Stable's head trainer stands in the doorframe. Dauntless o' the Dead, they called him back in his fighting days, what with his origins in Marvoltown, the Death Saint's dis'. Daunt is known for a hard face and an impenetrable mien.

'Fight might be delayed,' he announces to Wyll's dressing room.

It's the last thing any fighter needs to hear. It's a lot of hard work getting to this point with calm and control. And now you have to wait, revved up to the gills? Wyll wants to shout. He does not. He forces all reaction down, chokes it 'til it's quiet.

'Why?' he asks Daunt calmly.

'Accident. Whitetongue is out.'

Daunt might be hard to read, but Wyll has been training under him for more than a year, and it's given him some study-time. There is an inflection on that first word that tells a whole lot more of the story.

'What kind of accident?' he asks.

Daunt's mouth twitches. 'Quad ploughed into his bike guard, on his way to the arena. It got announced less than an hour ago.'

'Is he alive?'

'Neh, but in no condition to fight.'

'An *accident*,' Wyll muses.

Daunt grunts.

'That's bad luck,' he says, watching Daunt, who gives another noncommittal grunt – and then his eyes stray briefly to Lee.

One good thing about the laconic, they're used to reading subtle cues and often don't need to be outright told a thing.

Lee nods at Wyll.

'Call for me,' he says. 'I'll stick around.'

He quietly exits the room, shuts the door with a firm click.

Wyll eyes Daunt. 'Faked?'

'I've taken a peek at Whitetongue myself, as is our right. Independent medics have confirmed it. He's done. His right leg's all mangled.' Daunt pauses. 'Might not ever fight again.'

Wyll breathes out. Saints. Game over for a Caballaria knight. Bad player or no, that'll be a hard one to get back up from.

'So they're asking for a delay,' he muses.

Daunt shakes his head. 'No. *I'm* asking for the delay, because *they're* asking to go ahead on the fight with a substitute.'

Wyll sits back with a frown. 'I don't understand. It feels like a play, but why take out your own crappy champion and then throw in a second choice at the last min—'

And then, suddenly, he sees it.

I got the impression that she's supposed to be good.

Wyll's stomach drops all the way to the bowels of the earth itself.

'Who's the substitute?' he asks Daunt.

But, of course, he already knows.

The corridor that leads up to the pit echoes with the noise of the crowd above, reproduced in the arena's bowels as a rumbling roar that vibrates the air, as if he is trapped in an underground tunnel and walks helplessly towards the trag bearing down on him, the fore-echo of a death promise. It smells like old fear in here, the walls impregnated with every fighter who has ever passed through and left behind the tang of their apprehensive sweat.

Fear usually makes him angry, a weapon he has long known how to wield with cool, hard accuracy. Others let their emotions swamp them, thinking that's power. Wyll puts a bridle around his and grips the reins tight. It's the reason he has become such a renowned fighter. He fights with his heart as a clenched fist.

The grip tape on his hands is old – he's been wearing it all day, a trick taught to him by Garad back in greener times – and reassuringly rough against the handle of his sword, the thick, cold metal having been kept gently warm to stop it freezing up his fingers. Another Garad trick. He doesn't exactly miss his first proper trainer – Garad was never good at hiding their dislike of him – but their pride at least ensured that the training he received was likely the best he'd ever get.

That noise. It swells, filling the corridor's narrow space, taking all the air and making it hard to breathe.

'The palace doesn't want to delay,' Daunt had said. 'They're worried about looking weak, and the situation is . . . delicate.'

A lot of meaning packed into one small word, 'delicate'. Cair Lleon is coming into this game on the back foot. The Sorcerer Knight as their champion is the only good play they have, the only way they might win. Even if it's a win tainted with the sullying of Art's legacy, it's still a damned win. No choice, then. He has to fight now. A clean, decisive arena win, showcasing the favour of the saints and quieting the opposition's ability to make good on their clever little sucker-punch.

He should have seen this coming.

Why didn't he see this coming?

Wyll reaches the doors to the pit, flanked by a set of impassive arena guard knights. Beyond them is a raging storm. His heart hammers at his ribcage like a frenzied prisoner.

'Si Wyll,' Daunt says behind him.

Wyll turns his head. Daunt's expression is as unreadable as ever, but the cliff-faced man, in all their time together, has never once called him by his intimate name.

'You are the Sorcerer Knight,' says Daunt. 'The Scourge of the Godless. London's Left Hand. The King's champion.'

My King is dead. She killed him.

The faintest flicker of his misstep registers in Daunt's eyes.

'The King-in-Waiting,' he amends.

Wyll nods. They both know he fights for no third-cousin runt, but a certain self-possessed Spider with one hand already on the Sword. With Wyll's help, she'll have it glued to both palms by the end of the day.

Daunt steps back, and gives a short bow. 'Saints' favour.'

'Saints' favour,' echoes Wyll.

Then he turns to face the rest alone.

An eternal moment later, the doors open. The sound of the crowd slams through like a tidal wave. And as he takes the slope up to hell and emerges, wreathed in the chant of his names, those grand, boastful monikers donned like another piece of his armour, Wyll feels a savage grin paint his face.

At least this one won't be boring, he finds himself thinking, and his heart soars, let loose like a bird to shriek at the sky.

A heft of his sword whips the solid wall of noise into a full assault. This is a bad, wild crowd, flirting with the edge of the cliff and ready to be pushed. A wall of flecter-glass panels eight feet tall and an inch thick ring the pit side to keep out the crowd, as well as any projectiles they might have somehow managed to smuggle in. Despite that, arena guards are already moving busily through the stands, methodically pulling out screaming troublemakers here and there in an attempt to dampen the smoking fires.

Wyll sees the goddess version of his opponent first.

The glow screens fixed above the heads of the crowd, previously filled with Wyll's face and embarrassingly brooding, flexing form – which he always takes care not to look at when he enters the pit, lest he lose faith in the entire circus before the fight has even begun – turn suddenly black.

Then they are filled with her face, which looks impossible, as they all do, smoothed and glorified by the art of the glows. Her slides, her spins, her dancer poise.

Her name.

'THE RED WRAITH,' booms the voice of the nuntias, slamming into every orifice.

The doors at the opposite end of the pit yawn open and out strides a tall, slender figure, swathed in a wall of sound. She moves fast and sure. She looks good. She looks like she belongs.

She plays the game better than him. She had him fooled from the beginning.

That, more than Art's death, is what hurts him most. He'd like to be a better man. He'd like this to be about righteous grief. But it's not. It's about his pride, ripped into tattered shreds by the woman before him. If he is ever to repair it, if he is ever to stand again as a human being of any consequence, he must not only win, but so thoroughly humiliate her that there is no room for doubt. He must appear bored by what little effort it took.

He must not let any part of their history guide his hand.

He must not think of the way she looks when she laughs, rare enough to utterly delight when it comes, her black eyes crinkled into screwed-up half-moons, her head tipped back and her mouth comically wide.

He must not think of her thighs clenched around his sides,

the squeeze and bunch of those powerful muscles locking him in place.

He must not think of seeing her bleeding and broken, how the empty pain in her eyes had made him privately swear to end everything that ever hurt her.

Now *he* must be the one to make her bleed.

Red halts in the centre of the pit, facing Wyll in the start position.

His heart pounds in his ears.

'Good trick,' he shouts to her over the noise.

Fighting as your own champion has historical precedent, back in cruder, dumber days, when a prowess for killing was considered a sign of good leadership. Nowadays it's unthinkable – but the rules still allow for it.

Red stands with one arm weighed down by the cestus, the clawed glove that is her signature weapon, its sharp rapier blades jutting a full foot from her knuckles. She stands stiff and endures the noise of the crowd, the jeers, the calls for her death, the adoration, the lust, the fury.

They stand close, waiting for the signal to move apart and begin the pain.

The nuntias can barely be heard over the lowing of beasts. The paraphernalia of the fight unfolds around them, unheeded. All he can see is her.

'So you wanted to fight me so much that you murdered your own champion,' he shouts.

Moved at last, Red shouts back across the sanded grit, 'It was an accident. Whitetongue isn't dead.'

'He's as good as, and you know it,' Wyll retorts. 'His life will be nothing but agony. Better that you'd killed him.'

Red opens her mouth, but then the lights dip, the bell sounds.

And it begins.

The background roar dims to a low, savage hum. Red moves, and so does Wyll, putting two sword-lengths between them. He can get her on his cutting tip from further away, he has all the advantages, he *has* this—

'Caradoc was nothing to do with me,' Red says, spread into a wary stance.

'That's much worse,' mocks Wyll while he calculates through three different lines of attack. 'You didn't even have the spine to do it yourself' – trying to get her riled, see what mistakes it throws out – 'and here you are, dancing to someone else's music!'

'Look in a mirror, *royal champion*!' Before the whole of 'champion' comes hissing out of her mouth, her arm blurs, cutting a shoulder-shattering blow. Dodging it upends his next move, he jettisons that – *shit, new plan*—

The realisation hits him very hard, sending a rolling sickness through his guts. He doesn't want to fight Red while the world watches. He doesn't want them pitted against each other like helpless puppets, forced into this by sick masters.

He doesn't want to do this.

He doesn't want to do this.

'Stop!' Wyll suddenly shouts. 'Red, stop this! Please!'

And the next, spat like a curse: 'I love you!'

It works. Red rears back, and there's that wound in her eyes, that pain he's seen before, only it doesn't satisfy like he hoped it would, and it's because it's not a play but a truth, and that truth, hidden behind a play, feels small and mean and frittered away on a desperate bid for a meaningless glory that he never wanted.

He just wants to be in bed with her again. That's all he wants. That's it. Just warmth and skin. That contented haze. It's a sad, hopeless realisation, and as he stands there realising it, the wound in her eyes closes over and she lunges forwards and tries to stab him in the heart.

She misses, and the animal part of him begins to crow despite everything, but then a fast spreading numbness below his belly button sounds a warning, and he realises what she did. She feinted. With one hand she feinted at his heart, and with the other she just stabbed him in the guts.

He goes down like a leaking balloon. He's on his knees, breathless with disbelief.

She's trying to kill you. She's really trying to kill you.

'Well, fuck,' he spits.

The crowd beast fades to a dull roar in Wyll's ears as he fights to stay here. Faded ghosts appear and hang in the air around him, flickering desperately. The ghosts of everyone he has ever lost.

It's over.

And then Red is in front of him, her hands naked. Over her shoulder he can see her gloved claw lying discarded, glinting among the dust. She is on her knees in front of him, and he can hear every breath she drags in, every saint invoked in a babbling string, over and over.

'Red,' he says thickly.

'Don't die,' she pleads, 'I'm sorry, don't die, I'm so sorry!'

'Red,' he tries again. She's talking so much, how does she have the energy for so much talk? Even her name is hard for him to conjure. It means he cannot waste any words. It means everything he says has to be exactly what he means. 'Do you love me?'

Red looks around wildly, as if she could escape. 'It's too late for all that.'

'No,' he says patiently, 'it's not. Do you love me?'

'It's too late, I said.'

'Red. Do you love me?'

She looks stricken.

But she doesn't say no.

'Wyll,' her voice is hesitant, tentative on his name. 'I think I . . . I made all the wrong choices. I wish—'

A flat crack rips up the air.

Red stiffens and reels to the side. She wobbles on her knees for an eternal second, arms flailing bonelessly. Then she crumples sideways to the ground.

Wyll stays on his knees and stares at her still form, his mind telescoping from reality. Shouts and shrieks fade into an unimportant background. Red's body seems very far away and ringed in black nothingness, as if he is watching it on a tiny glow screen.

He barely even registers the arrival of an arena white jacket, a figure in a half-remembered dream. The white jacket says nothing, his mouth tightly closed in a thin slash.

Afterwards, Wyll will remember that he was shivering.

He peers silently at Wyll, eyes bulging like a rabbit's, and then shuffles hastily up to the fallen body just ahead. Wyll watches him stop a foot or two away, lift a rigid arm, and then that flat crack sounds again, and Red's body spasms. Wyll feels his own body jump, in sympathy or reaction to the noise, he can't tell which, but he feels it distantly, detached. The white jacket then raises the gun in his hand and positions it into his open mouth.

There is a final crack.

372

CHAPTER 32

Garad's Apartment, Evrontown
Two Weeks Ago

The rest of Ghost's escape from the Menagerie is hazy, dim and half submerged, as are all nightmares of the past.

She sees it remotely like a scene from her long ago, even though it was only a couple of hours back. The pipe's ridges scraping her hands as she crawled, the shock after shock of freezing water trying to push her back from where she came, her fear of what lay behind locking her muscles against the tide so hard that she felt like they could snap, and even now she feels the pull in her arms and legs, like bows strung too tight.

She remembers getting out of the pipe that led down to her tank and finding a tunnel of sorts, the ceiling so low that she could only drag her body along by her elbows in the wet silt, scrabbling desperately with her toes to scoot forwards, every moment a screaming fear that the tiny tunnel would be flooded and she would suffocate and drown inside it, like a dying snail inside a shell.

She remembers one bone-dry tunnel (a difficult moment, when she had lost the water she was following in hope of a route out and was desperately trying to find it again) that had a

373

regular series of ventilation holes cut in its floor, each hole covered with iron latticework, light flashing up from the rooms below and catching her eye as she crawled carefully across each one. She remembers looking down through the latticework. She remembers seeing other tanks, the tops of other prisoner's heads.

She lost count of how many she saw.

She remembers having no idea which way to go, only to choose the pipes the water ran from, crawling along towards its source, please let it be the river, please, please.

She remembers crouching over the entrance to a huge hole in the floor, entirely flooded with water like a small pool. Scared that she was close to exhaustion, scared that she'd be caught soon if she didn't get out, watching tiny wavelets run across the surface of the pool as she hugged her knees, and hoping this meant its water source was close by. Lowering herself into the pool. Taking the deepest breath she could. Wondering if it would be her last. Diving. Swimming.

But Marvol didn't want her, not that day. She kicked frantically through the murk, lungs tight and tighter and tighter, towards some kind of light. When she surfaced, the air was filled with twinkling lights from all the buildings at the river's edge, and the air sliced across her wet face. She was close enough to a bank to half swim, half let the water push her on to the matted reeds at the water's edge. Numb, shaking, every limb a dead weight, she pushed herself on, scared that if she rested now, she'd never move again.

It took a long time to make it to Garad's.

It would have been easy to hate herself for a fool for being back here again, but there was nowhere left to go.

Garad is so still they might have died and she just not noticed.

'How?' they eventually say. 'How—'

'It was either sewage or an old flood-control system,' Ghost explains. 'The pipe led me to tunnels, the tunnels led me to the river. And then I walked to you.'

Hours ago. Hours and lifetimes and no time at all.

Now. Let's see if they've picked up on the most important point of her entire story.

'You can . . . copy yourself,' says Garad.

Oh good. They have.

'It's more like making a temporary double,' she replies. 'The longer they're out of me, the more they start to travel their own path. Up until the time I manifest them, they're just a part of me. A voice in my head.' Ghost shrugs. 'Everyone's got one, as far as I can tell. Mine's just a bit more literal.'

Silence.

'I'm to suppose she had a sister,' Garad tries.

She'd been expecting this, this desperate reach for other plausible explanations. She could let Garad believe that, if she liked. But it's tiring to live like someone she's not. Here she is at the precipice at last, and instead of exhilaration or terror, all she feels is a bone-deep exhaustion. She hugs the blankets tighter around herself and craves a dozen more sicaloes, five shots of neck oil.

'Finnavair o'Rhyfentown never had any sisters,' she says. 'No family at all, not even when she got famous and they could have come forward to claim some of that second-hand glitter for themselves. I've never met or heard of anyone else who can do what I can do. And believe me, I've been looking.'

'I don't understand.' Garad has a sickly expression on their face.

'Neh, you do,' Ghost says.

Garad's mouth opens, and out it finally comes in a half whisper. 'You're Fin.'

Ghost closes her eyes.

She remembers how it is to hear that name in that whisper – but remotely, like it happened to someone else. Because it did. It happened to Fin. The Fin who fucked Garad on the monastery rooftop, the Fin who leaped into a clandestine affair with them, the Fin who fell into the kind of love that feels like hurtling off a cliff, is dead.

A year or so into Fin's courtship with Art, he had said the following to her:

'I don't care who else you're with, as long as it's me you come back to. I just want what's between us. Nothing else exists for me. I don't want to know.'

So Fin hadn't told him. She hadn't told him that she and Garad had begun seeing each other. Garad – fiercely private, protective Garad – wanted it kept secret. As soon as it became public, it became everyone else's. If it was secret, it could remain theirs alone.

But all that had been about to change. The moment that Art gamed Fin, declaring their relationship public, he trapped her. Worse, he did it deliberately, knowing what it would mean for her and doing it anyway. Worse upon worse, she'd understood his reasons. She'd even admired his bravery in being honest about why he'd done it.

He'd known that their public relationship would take a certain amount of freedom from her, but he'd had no idea just how much. His was a peculiar life, and in so many ways an awful one. One she didn't want. One she had *never* wanted. But it took facing down that choice to make her realise it. It took being with Garad to know, finally, that the kind of life she had craved – and dismissed as a fantasy – could exist.

Art had never been very religious. His idea of worship was a quick fumbling between meetings, or a late-night prayer when he was too tired to stand, let alone fuck. Fin forgave him that. He was the damned King of London, after all, and he had his priorities – but she had hers, too. Her role in his life was to ease his burden. But what about his in hers?

She should have told Art about Garad, she knew that. But for two years he'd forbidden her from telling a soul about their elaborately guarded and secretive clandestine meets, and Garad did the same about theirs, and so Fin kept on spinning, unsure, in the middle, acceding to the wishes of both. She'd never envisaged the crisis that would follow because she had no idea how Art really felt – not until he had pulled that public stunt at her bout.

It was a clever move from a master gamer. If only her modest orphan background had been the sole risk the King of London took when he decided to declare his relationship with a street-rat knight to the world.

Later that day, caught in a storm of confusion, she fled to Garad's. And as soon as the door opened and she saw the expression on her lover's face, there was only one thing to say.

'You heard, then.'

Garad just looked at her, and then gestured up into the sky, where the glows were gleefully playing and replaying the moment the King of London had taken off his mask and kissed her in front of a thousand-strong screaming crowd.

'How could I not?' they say.

It was at that moment that a dismayed, shamed Fin understood just how devastated they were. It was in the stiff set of their shoulders. Their careful talk of duty and sacrifice and the King of London's need over everyone else's, but what Fin heard was that she'd snared the heart of the one person Garad would sacrifice their own happiness for – their brother, their King – and therefore for Garad it was all over.

But they didn't understand. There were two reasons she could never, despite his manoeuvrings, be with Art. One was that she was in love with Garad. The other was far worse. Because if he or anyone else ever found out she was a godchild, not only was she fucked, but so was he. He might lose the Sword, and she might lose her life.

There was no choice, not if she wanted to keep Garad.

They had to know.

'Fin?' Garad says again, sounding frightened. 'It can't be.'

Ghost sighs. 'You need more proof? All right. Remember how Fin came to you that night? The night of Art's announcement stunt? You can't have forgotten it. She certainly hasn't. She came to you panicked, and scared, and in pain, and then, in a moment of infinite, naïve stupidity, showed you her last secret. The one thing that gave you the key to unlocking her. And *you*' – Ghost cocks her head mock-thoughtfully – 'told her she was a monster and threw her out.'

'I never called her a monster—' Garad begins.

'Not how I remember it,' Ghost cuts in. 'But never mind the exact words you used, because your actions betrayed your thoughts just fine.'

Garad is supposed to deny, denounce, accuse in turn. It's how pain works. It's how arguments work. Instead, they say nothing.

'Did you ever tell anyone?' asks Ghost.

'Tell anyone what?' Garad murmurs, head turned away.

'That Finnavair o'Rhyfentown, darling of the Caballaria and the King's official lover, was an unregistered godchild. A lifetime liar. A walking scandal-in-waiting.'

The pause stretches on long.

'No,' says Garad at last.

'No?' echoes Ghost, while her heart begins to beat again.

'No,' Garad repeats.

'Why not?'

She waits for a righteous excuse.

'Because I was too in love with her to ruin her life like that.'

Unexpected.

'Even though she'd lied to you,' Ghost counters.

'Yes.'

Ghost scoffs. 'That was stupid.'

Garad ignores this. 'You're saying you're Fin's copy. I mean, her double.'

Ghost shrugs. 'Actually, no. Fin's original double died in the tank. I'm *her* double.'

Don't think about that too hard or you'll go mad, cautions the other her.

'Your face is different,' Garad says. 'Your hair.'

'Had my face recut. Shaved my hair off.'

'Why?'

Ghost just laughs, but now she's been talking so long it comes out more of a croak.

Confused emotions fly across Garad's face like wind-whipped clouds. 'I saw Fin's body,' they say.

'Me too,' Ghost agrees.

'What?'

'I saw my own dead body,' Ghost says patiently. 'Down in the lost station.'

'What' – she watches Garad cast about desperately – 'for the love of the saints, what *happened*?'

'Simple.' She draws in a shaky breath. 'Red.'

By the time Fin got back to her apartment that night from her argument with Garad, she had swum through the agonising shark-infested seas of turmoil and rejection and was now treading water in the calm pond of resignation. Repulsed rejection by the one person she could say she'd ever fallen in love with made things a lot easier, at least. Garad would tell Art that she was a godchild. No point in sticking around and waiting for the moment the palace came for her. She needed an exit, fast.

Two hours later, Red came along and handed her one.

She was at her front door and inside her hall – and just at the point where that bottle of alcohol she had in the back of the cupboard, the one that was so strong it made her eyeballs feel like they were melting, and a long, hot bath (equalling the kind of oblivion that the night she'd just had desperately called for) was beginning to look really inviting – when she heard the sounds.

Rattling. Muttering.

Fin froze.

Someone – some*thing* – was in her apartment.

Her hands were empty of weapons. She had a practice spinner in the bag attached to her bike from an earlier training session, but nothing on her. She hadn't exactly wanted to spook Garad even more by turning up brandishing weapons when she did her big reveal. *Weapons only when you were in control of yourself,* her trainer had taught her. Otherwise, you never touch 'em. Good advice, usually. Then again, she always had a back-up, as it were.

She crept up her hallway. The muttering grew louder. Just behind this door. Pushed it open just a sliver, and—

—breathed a sigh of irritated relief. It was just her old friend Roben. She'd given him a passkey to get in months ago, but he'd never used it before now. He was crouched at the base of the far wall, scribbling and muttering to himself.

'Oh, great,' said Fin. 'I was going to hang up a picture, but this is much better.'

Her previously plain décor had been transformed into a galdor wall. It was covered in words and half-drawn maps and bits of animals and flowers and faces and half-shaped nightmares, all done in smudgy black lines, presumably from the stub of charcoal gripped in his fingers.

Evidently, Roben was on one of his frequent fun-fair rides. Came with the territory, with strong soothsayers. She'd learned to let him just ride it out, rather than trying to do anything about it. Just the way his brain worked. Frightening and strange to behold, but then again, watching someone make a twin of themself must be no day in the sunshine, either. Fin felt a brief flash of sudden, unwelcome sympathy for Garad, chased it with a quick shot of anger, pushed it all away and went to support her crouched friend.

'Roben?' she asked quietly, making sure not to touch him.

'She's a bitch angel of Marvol,' he says, only peripherally aware of her. 'She'll choke London 'til it's on its knees.'

'Who will?' Fin prompted.

He gestured impatiently up at the wall. There, right in the centre, drawn in frantically large letters, was a three-letter name.

Red.

He'd been talking about this for weeks. It was his latest

obsession. He was convinced that the mysterious Red meant something terrible for London, and sometimes his convictions came right in a perfect, undeniable match. Sometimes they didn't, mind you. The hazards of trying to predict something as laughably slippery as the future.

Still, when Roben had a conviction, it was best to at least entertain its possibility, so a curious Fin had gone to great lengths to make friends with the enigmatic young fighter who had bested the Sorcerer Knight himself and caused a sensation across London. All she'd been able to ascertain so far was that Red was closed tighter than a clamshell, guarding a secret core she was too ashamed, frightened or angry to let anyone see into.

She wasn't really sure who Red was or what she wanted – until, as if Roben had summoned her himself, she turned up at Fin's door, frantically high and out of control.

Then things had *really* gone to shit.

'When Fin died,' says Ghost, 'her double was already out. Outside of her, I mean. See, when it's outside of your body, a double is a full double, a flesh-and-blood person. Red killed Fin, but she didn't kill the double. The double woke up next to her own dead body. Now, I suppose no one but me knows what that's like. A unique experience only I can claim. Aren't I lucky? It's pretty fucken strange. And when it happens, the double doesn't understand, at first. You're not . . . fully formed, yet, you know? You're not quite the dead you, and you're not quite a new you, either. You're in this strange in-between, blank as a newborn cow. And there's no one around to tell you what the fuck, or how to think, or what to do. So when the double woke up, there was Red's dead body, and her own. And she bolted. Understandable, you know?' Ghost offers the wall a humourless smile. 'It wasn't until she'd been running blindly through tunnels a while that she calmed down enough to see the gift she'd just been given. Suddenly it all hit her, like three shots in a row drunk fast. Most people don't get to escape whatever sword the saints have hanging over their head – but *she* could. So she left the two dead bodies in the lost station. She went home, packed a bag of clothes and fled London with all the trick she had. Didn't let herself think about it. Just did it. If she'd have thought about it, she'd have fallen apart. She travelled to another Kingdom, found a face man who was supposed to be the best around. That's a story in itself, that one was crazy – but he was as good as they said. Then she had to hide out and heal for a few weeks. Then she came back to London and looked up Leon.' Ghost tips her head back, rests it against the wall, closes her eyes. 'The rest you know.'

Tired. So tired. But her mind feels cleaner, at least, as though by externalising herself, she's swept out the rot, instead of keeping it all inside, leaving it to fester and turn to poison over time.

She waits for Garad to ask why. Why had she come back to London, when she could have stayed away, severed any chance of being outed, really and truly become someone else. She wants Garad to ask, so she can answer that even though she's two Fins from them now, and even though she's ashamed and angry about it, she still finds herself a little bit haunted by Garad. Which is pretty unfair, but life likes a joke, and masochists love a bit of pain, and people often can't let go even when they should.

But instead of an honest conversation, there is only an excruciating silence.

Ghost feels her hope crawl into a corner and get on with the business of quietly dying.

'Listen, do you think I wanted to come here tonight?' she snaps. 'I've got no choice, not now. Leon shopped me. Glapissant's likely hunting me down as we speak. Everyone else is dead. And the King needs to know about this. It's a group, don't you see, some powerful group running the Menagerie, and they're from *different districts*. Elites from Senzatown and Alaunitown working together, at least, and who knows who else.' A shiver of horror runs through her. 'They're making weapons out of us. I know you, Garad – I know you hate us, but I also know you can't let this stand. I *know* you. Anything that threatens Art's rule . . . and this does. Something's going on, something big, and Art trusts you more than anyone else in his life.'

Her eyes have opened while she's been talking, and she's been avoiding looking at Garad, but it happens now, and when it does, she sees big fat tears squeezing out of their eyes and salting their cheeks.

'Oh saints, saints,' Garad is saying. 'Fin, I'm so sorry.'

Ghost feels the bottom of her stomach drop – she feels it go, that old alarm bell of something very wrong. Garad is crying.

Garad does not cry.

'Well,' says Ghost, 'I can't believe I wasn't cynical enough. Me, of all people. That allegiance tattoo on Glapissant's ankle, and on those private guards who warned us off the Cass case. It's a Senzatown tattoo. And guess who's from Senzatown? The original four, those enterprising younglings who came in out of nowhere twenty years ago and swiped the Sword of London. The Tricky King, the Silver Angel, the Mouthpiece and the Spider. So which of you is it? You, Garad? Lucan? Lillath? I know it's not Art, he never had that tattoo anywhere on his body. But I *know* I've seen it before. I know I have.'

Garad just keeps their head bowed, cheeks streaked with salt.

'Garad. You're scaring me. Is it you? Do you run the Menagerie?'

'No!' they spit, managing a wobbling vehemence. 'You really think so ill of me? What you're describing at that place is disgusting to me.'

Ghost sighs out of sheer relief. For a minute there, she'd been very worried that Garad's prejudices had somehow secretly mutated into straight monstrosity – but for good or ill, the Silver Angel still has that stiff moral rod up their backside.

'Look,' she says evenly, 'I'm on a hook, here. You've got me. You know who I am and you can do what you like with me. I'm used to dying, and I'm used to running. I'll tell him everything, if you want. Who I am. What really happened to Fin. Whatever it takes. But you're the only one who can get this to Art, and in secret, apparently, since someone else at Cair Lleon is involved—'

'Fin,' Garad says. 'Art is dead.'

Ghost waits patiently for the joke. 'No, he's not.'

'Fin.'

'I'm not Fin.' Ghost's laugh is of the helpless kind. 'I'm really fucken tired, so you might have to explain the point of this game.'

'Art has been dead for weeks. Red killed him. Wyll's been pretending to be him until we could work out what to do. I couldn't stand everything that was happening, how it was all . . . falling apart like a rotting tree. I walked away. I walked out on the palace. I've been hiding here like a coward ever since.' Garad wipes their tears off with the heel of their hand, their gaze wandering aimlessly. 'Everything's gone wrong. Ever since I . . . did what I did to you. I'm so sorry. It was a sin, the way I treated you, and I've been paying for it ever since. I walked off the path. I lost you, and then I lost Art, the two loves of my life, so fast, one after the other, and it's all gone wrong.'

'No,' Ghost says with utter calm. 'No. There were two dead bodies down in the lost station. They were both lying there. Red and Fin. She was dead. She was *dead*—'

Did you check her pulse?

Did you touch her?

Did you just think *she was dead and bolt like a scared rabbit without checking at all?*

Garad is rising from their seat and Ghost tenses, but they are moving away, moving to a glow pad, flicking its light up to display on the wall opposite Ghost, searching until they find what they're looking for.

It is Red. Standing next to, of all people in the world, the Lady Orcade. There are words blaring above her head.

LEGITIMATE HEIR
MOLDRA LAGHA
CHAMPIONSHIP FOR THE SWORD?

'They announced it a few days ago,' Ghost hears Garad saying. 'How long did they keep you in the Menagerie?'

Days, weeks, lifetimes, no times. An endless bad dream from which she kept trying to wake.

And here is another.

'This isn't real,' Ghost hears herself saying, but it sounds very far away. 'This is a trick.'

Or an alternate world, one that muscled in while she was

underground in a tank. She's surfaced to the wrong reality, that's all. She just needs to go back down into the dark and come back up to the right one, that's all.

'I'm so sorry,' Garad is saying, and their voice, that everstrong, confident shout — bell-like and clear whether they were claiming victory over an opponent in the ring or repelling a lying ex-lover from their doorstep — is gone, replaced by an uncertain sound, watery thin. 'I'm so sorry.'

They have put both glow screen and sword down and they're coming towards her, their hands outstretched, as if to say — what? She's escaped one lunatic, only to walk into the den of another.

'Stop!' she shouts. 'Don't come near me.'

'Fin,' they are saying, 'Fin, I'm really sorry—'

But she's not Fin, Fin is dead, why doesn't anybody understand that Fin is dead and she's never coming back, everyone is dead, everyone and everything dies, and saintsfuck, here comes Garad still, they're going to touch her, embrace her, kiss her — as if everything is all right, as if it could ever be again—

And then Garad finally stops, because it's hard to move when there's a knife at your throat.

Ghost stares at the double of herself who has just appeared pressed up behind Garad, the blade catching the light beautifully, like a line out of a damned poem. She stares at the double of herself who seems to be made out of violence, out of threat, and she wonders if that's all she can be.

Garad is still, wet eyes wide. Their sword is too far away. Stupid cumbersome choice, anyway. They always were too in love with symbolism over practicality.

'Why did you come here?' they ask her.

Ghost doesn't answer.

Garad twitches as if to move forwards – the double twitches and the knife scrapes their throat. Garad stops again.

Ghost notices that the double is trembling as much as she is.

'Fin,' says Garad. 'I need something from you.'

Ghost waits.

'I need your forgiveness.'

Ghost trembles. Waits some more.

'I did something unspeakable to you. Something I have tried to atone for ever since. And then I found out you were dead, and it was like the world ended. I knew I'd have to live with this sin for the rest of my life. This awful weight of what I did to you.'

'What did you do to me?' asks Ghost.

'I shamed you,' says Garad.

The word sticks a knife in her guts.

'I told you that what you are is unlovable. But I love you, Fin. I love you still. I never stopped. So I was wrong. I was completely, utterly wrong. You can't be unlovable, because I love you.'

Ghost is crying too now, a supremely irritating reaction. This is not how it was supposed to go. She doesn't know how it was supposed to go. Some of the more childish fantasies of the past few months have had Garad under a knife and sobbing their eyes out in undone contrition. But this surety is too much. This talk of shame, the thing that has haunted and diminished her all her life, the thing she has tried so hard to discard.

'I'm . . . not . . . Fin,' she forces out between tears.

'Whoever you are,' Garad says with absolute calm, 'I love you. Please, put the knife away. You've been through enough. Let me take care of you. Even if it's just for tonight. Please.'

The double is gone, shit. Couldn't sustain her any more, not with all this saintsdamned crying she's doing. Hard to be violent when all she feels is a beautiful, overwhelming relief.

She feels Garad's arms around her, Garad's strong ropy arms, Garad's hands, those hands she fell for, those hands she had all over her, back in another life. She feels herself gathered up, transported to another room. Laid on the cold tiles. The sound of water, this hot and steaming and laced with pungent soap.

'Trying to knock me out?' she croaks.

'You really stink,' says Garad. 'Stop fighting and get in the bath.'

Ghost manages a shaky laugh. She is gently stripped of her foetid river-soaked clothes, and then helped in, sinking into hot comfort.

Afterwards, Garad carries her to their enormous bed, and lays her down among its soft hillocks of blanket and pillow.

'Don't go,' says Ghost. She was supposed to think it. The bath has opened her all up.

'You're safe,' Garad replies, swathed in sweet, dark, bedroom gloom. 'I promise.'

'Don't go,' she repeats, unable to say more.

Garad is still.

For a moment she thinks she's gone too far. That it was all a lie.

Then she feels Garad sliding into the bed next to her.

'Ask for it.'

'What?' murmurs Ghost.

'Whatever you want,' Garad murmurs back. 'If I can give it to you, I will.'

Ghost draws in a steadying breath.

Courage, now. Don't fall at the final post.

'I want you to comfort me,' she says to Garad.

She lives and dies inside the silence that follows.

'Fin used to mean something specific by that,' she hears Garad say.

'I know,' whispers Ghost.

And when she feels warm, long fingers begin to explore her, she finally, finally feels safe enough to let go.

Garad only ever touches things they love.

PART III

Let Gwanhara gift you life to spend,
Then take your rest at Marvol's end.

— Saith proverb

CHAPTER 33

The Menagerie, Alaunitown
One Week Ago

'Welcome!' the man trills, the greased ridges of his hair glistening under the bright, flat light. 'Welcome to the Menagerie!'

They callian him Glapissant, and the slippery name becomes him. He has a trim frame draped in expensively demure clothes and a little too much perfume. He walks them through the building's main entranceway, prattling on in a practised, charming fashion.

'I'm flattered to give a personage as illustrious as you a tour of this facility,' he calls over his shoulder.

'I'm flattered to be granted the opportunity to see it,' Wyll courteously replies.

'And I'm so happy our wonderful intermediary here could set this up.'

Viviane, walking beside Wyll, gives Glapissant a brilliant smile. 'Well, dear Julias always spoke so highly of this place. He said it was the most important project in all of London.'

'Dear Julias,' Glapissant mechanically repeats, as if he learned the art of expressing affection out of a book on mathematics. 'It's hard to believe he's gone.'

'So hard,' Viviane agrees, and then, with a little laugh, 'especially since that means I'm now out of work.'

'On the contrary,' Glapissant replies, 'we need a steady supply of Tidal for our operation here, and the Menagerie's agreement with him transfers automatically to the inheritors of his biodome estate on the event of his death. The Menagerie's owner made sure of it in the contract. Julias was, though wonderfully vital for his age, rather chronologically advanced. And you just never know when Marvol might take it upon himself to pay you a visit, itso?' He pauses, and then gives Viviane a brilliant, encouraging smile, as pure and cold as cut diamond. 'And we'll let it be known that the Menagerie would prefer to continue dealing with you rather than with the estate directly.'

Viviane inclines their head with a grateful expression. 'Then I am very grateful to you.'

'Be grateful to the owner of the Menagerie,' Glapissant replies. 'We are lucky to have a mistress both canny and generous.'

'I'd like to pay her a quick visit,' Wyll says, 'after the tour.'

Glapissant hesitates. 'I'm not sure she's here today. She's a very busy woman.'

'I've heard that she is.'

Glapissant gapes at him, and then utters a tittering little laugh. 'Well, of course, of course, you would know, would you not?'

Wyll just smiles.

They enter the facility proper, Glapissant waving his arms towards various areas and explaining them in grandly expansive tones. They walk along a wide, elevated gantry that runs halfway up the towering walls of an enormous warehouse, affording them a bird's eye view of the spread below. There are separate sections divided by walls, rows and rows of rooms without ceilings, and a heavy mix of people busy in each one. Medics pour over glow screens together, or operate various delicate-looking instruments and machinery. Vastos track like ants between rooms, delivering and transporting goods and information. Guards line each room and the corridors in between.

Then there are the rooms with the tanks. There are a lot of tanks, and none of them are empty.

Wyll tries to place the feeling of familiarity the whole place is giving him, and then he has it – it's like a cattle market.

He becomes aware of a lull in proceedings. Glapissant is looking at him expectantly.

'It's extraordinary,' Wyll offers.

Glapissant looks pleased. 'Thank you so much. Yes, we're very proud of what is being achieved here. Hundreds of years of stifled progress will soon be swept aside. The strides we're making are unprecedented. We are wiping away the cobwebs of misinformation and fatuous superstition. Medicine, tech, weapons – the applications are dizzyingly endless. If I can contribute anything to our species, it's knowledge. I've always hated that feeling of things being kept from me, ever since I was a little boy. Curiosity saves. Without it, we are little more than animals killing each other for coin, don't you think?'

'Absolutely,' agrees Wyll. He wonders if he knows any of the cattle.

Focus, he tells himself. *You are not here for them. Not today.*

He turns to Glapissant. 'Well, this has been illuminating, and I thank you. Now I'd like to speak to the mistress of this facility.'

Glapissant hesitates, clearly torn between his duty to said mistress and the desire to obey the 'illustrious personage' he has before him. 'I'll send word. She can have someone come and meet—'

'Oh, there's no need for that,' Viviane says smoothly. 'Why don't you just take us to her now? We'd love to surprise her. We're all good friends.' They tip their head and give Glapissant a sweet smile.

Wyll watches him curiously. He has never really seen the direct effect of Viviane's talent on someone else, as he has historically been the subject of it. It's fascinating to watch. First Glapissant frowns, as if his brain knows there is something wrong but cannot put a finger on what it is. Then he goes blank as Viviane's mind gently wraps around his own and strokes. Then he curls into the stroke like a happy dog.

'Absolutely,' he agrees. 'The Lady Orcade does enjoy a surprise.'

Viviane laughs, Glapissant laughs, and then he takes them to an ascender, a smooth affair of smoked glass that transports the trio to a decidedly more private part of the building.

The hallway up here is plushed and hushed, the lighting and décor more that of a tasteful house. Glapissant stops at a door and raises his hand to press the arrival bell, but Viviane stays it.

'That would spoil the surprise,' they coo. 'Let's just open it and go in.'

Glapissant hesitates – a small struggle of assertion – and then laughs assent. He produces a key coin from his pocket and flicks open the catch. A small projection of a stylised W blooms from the coin. The door quickly responds, sliding noiselessly open.

Wyll steels himself for the best performance of his life, then walks through.

The room beyond is an elegant receiving room fit for any upper echelon of guest, but it's the open door on its far side, and the noises coming through it, that catch his immediate attention.

'Ah,' he hears Glapissant say, a note of sudden anxiety in his voice, 'I think she's busy with a guest—'

Wyll glances at Viviane. Now there's a third person to deal with. They had been counting on getting Orcade alone.

'Forgive me,' Glapissant hisses at them both, 'but this appears to be a personal meeting and we should not intrude. Can I take you back downstairs to wait?'

Very personal, judging by the strained animal moans coming through the doorway on the far side of the room.

Wyll hesitates, frozen with indecision, maybe even decorum, but Viviane has none – either that, or they're attracted to the scene like a dog to a rabbit's tail – because they move forwards before anyone can stop them. Cursing silently, Wyll abandons the dithering Glapissant and follows. Anyway, there's no need for panic. At the moment he and Viviane are just rude, it's just a breach of etiquette, and the situation is possible to ride without any alarm bells ringing, considering who he looks like right now—

But when he reaches the room beyond and sees who awaits him there, all their plans crumble into dust.

Viviane stands frozen in a small, bright bathroom in front of a panting Orcade, whose clothes are in disarray and whose blonde knot at the back of her head sprouts hair as if it has been savagely pulled.

Standing next to Orcade, her hands gripped full of the woman's flesh and her own disarray showing, is the one who has clearly been doing the hair-pulling. Lillath, her cheeks painted rose from her exertions, Lillath, fully dressed but never so naked, Lillath of the watchful gaze and air of benevolent omniscience – benevolent until you try to live in a way that displeases her – Lillath the illustrious personage Wyll has been pretending to be in order to gain access to the Menagerie,

Lillath the key that opens every lock, because who would ever refuse the Spider of London access to anything?

It had been a generic gamble, choosing Lillath as a disguise. How unfortunately specific it had just become.

The two Lillaths stare at each other.

They are lovers.

Lillath and Orcade are lovers. The Spider is in bed with the architect of her own Saith's downfall. They are in on it together and saints be fucked, it all begins to make an awful kind of sense, they are *lovers—*

Viviane is the one who saves them both. Abandoning their hold on Glapissant, they throw everything they have at the real Lillath. Defences down, mind utterly focused elsewhere, caught unawares. The best and only chance anyone has ever had to beat her.

Lillath's mouth opens. She twitches. Viviane takes a step forwards.

A heavy silence settles over the room.

Orcade, in a remarkable display of self-possession, pulls herself out of Lillath's now slack grip and smooths the loose hair back from her face.

'Who are you?' she politely asks Wyll. 'You're not Lillath, so who are you?'

He lets it go. Might as well. In a contest of who can prove they're the real Lillath, he'll lose fast.

'Ah,' says Orcade, as Wyll is revealed. 'I see.'

She looks a little pensive, but apart from that, her shock is so impressively well-hidden that he almost wants to applaud. She gives the air of someone running a hundred different permutations of the situational outcome to land on the one that will net her the most gains.

'Lillath?' she prompts, gazing at her curiously. 'What's happening?'

Lillath's eyes are locked on Viviane's. Viviane's are locked on hers. Neither moves.

'It's a fight,' Wyll tells her. 'A godchild fight.'

Orcade glances sharply at him, and then at Lillath, whose body gives a minute tremble. She takes a step back, away from her lover, and by the look on her face, Wyll realises something very important, a piece of leverage that could make all the difference: *she didn't know.*

Orcade had absolutely no idea that Lillath was a godchild.

And now she is beginning to doubt everything, every little interaction they have ever had, doubt her own desires and search her memories for evidence of the presence of another mind in control. Wyll knows this, because this is what happens when you discover that your feelings might not have been entirely your own.

She is beginning to doubt *Lillath.*

'Vivi?' Wyll gently calls.

Viviane gives a tight grunt, but otherwise makes no sound.

This means it is a hard fight. There's a chance they might not win.

All right. Now it's Wyll's turn to be decisive.

Without another glance at Orcade — it's a small bathroom, there's only one exit and he's currently blocking it — he moves swiftly towards Glapissant, who is peering anxiously through the doorway.

'I do hope you haven't killed him,' he hears Orcade say after a moment.

Wyll straightens. The man had crumpled like a paper doll.

'Just incapacitated,' he says, leaving Glapissant's body in the doorway where it fell. He isn't completely sure, actually – it can be hard to tell – but he's done his best.

'Good, thank you,' murmurs Orcade. 'He is quite useful.'

Wyll glances down at the still man with distaste. 'In what way?'

'He has a superbly strong stomach.'

Orcade is now several feet from Lillath, pressed against a wall, her arms folded close to her body, calm but tight, her gaze owlish as it flicks constantly between the three threats in the room. There are no guards within screaming distance, no alarms to raise, the body of her slippery vastos is blocking the only exit, her best weapon is currently otherwise engaged, and she cannot beat Wyll in a fight.

So he turns his attention to Lillath.

He stalks carefully closer, watching her body for any flicker, any tremble that might suggest a muscle tense, a movement, a decision, a choice. He moves so close to her that he can smell her hair.

Still she does not move.

His gaze flickers over Lillath's shoulder to Viviane.

Let's even the odds even more.

Weapons are not permissible in the Menagerie, but strength is a weapon no one can relieve him of. For a vastos, Lillath keeps herself in good shape, but she is no match for Wyll's muscular weight. He locks one arm around her chest to pin her arms, the other around her neck, and squeezes tight. Her body reacts. She kicks, flails—

'Vivi, put her to sleep!' he pants.

The body in his arms wriggles and slides like a maddened fish.

'Vivi!'

Viviane's jaw is clenched, teeth bared. They cry out like a

knight putting all their body into the swing. Wyll tries to keep Orcade in his line of sight, he tries to hold everything together—

Viviane sinks to their knees, now on all fours like a dog. The body in Wyll's arms limpens, lolls, sags, drags him down with its sudden weight.

He sets the unconscious Lillath carefully on the floor and straightens.

'The rope you have tied around the toilet, there,' he says politely to Orcade. 'May I borrow it?'

Two bodies lie in the bathroom, one tied to the toilet. Viviane watches them both through the open doorway from their hunkered position on a chair in the receiving room beyond, their elbows on their knees. They look tired, but well enough to keep guard.

Wyll and Orcade sit in the receiving room together on a facing pair of pretty divans. Orcade has fixed her hair and straightened her clothes. Her hands are folded neatly in her lap.

'Shall I ring for tea?' she asks Wyll.

Wyll smiles. 'Of course not.'

'How uncivilised,' tuts Orcade. 'There's a jug in the corner that still has a little water in it. Can I get some? I'd at least like to wet my throat before the interrogation begins.'

She nods to a small table, set with a tall, transparent glass container and a cup.

'I'll get it for you,' Wyll says.

Orcade laughs. 'I'm not that old.' She rises to her feet and crosses the room. Viviane tenses, watching Orcade turn her back on both of them as she takes up the jug and pours out a glass.

As her back is turned, Viviane gives Wyll a rueful look. Just water.

After a moment of fiddling, Orcade crosses back to the divan with the water in her hand. She takes her time arranging herself comfortably – a little insolently, thinks Wyll, a tiny rebellion, the only kind she can manage right now – and takes a long gulp of the cloudy water.

'All right,' says Orcade, swathed in calm. 'What is it you want to know?'

'Did you arrange Art's assassination?' asks Wyll.

'No. That was all your fearsome lover Red.' Her small smile suggests the mild satisfaction she feels at revealing her own knowledge in turn. 'I simply took advantage of Fortune's wheel-spin. We are all creatures subject to a chaotic universe. That's why soothsayers are so pointless. Predicting a possible future out of the hundreds that could occur is hardly a useful skill. It is annoying when they can see the secrets of the present, though. There was one – extraordinary girl. She might have been a valuable asset.'

'What happened?'

'Glapissant occasionally gets a little too excited with his play-toys.' Another flicker of amusement crosses her face, presumably at the flash of disgust she just saw on his. 'You should let him keep running this place for you. The benefits outweigh the costs, with him.'

'What in seven hells makes you think I'd keep this place running instead of burning it to the ground?' Wyll asks.

'I'm no soothsayer, but I have good instincts about people. That's served me well' – a conciliatory shrug – 'up until now. You always were a bit of a wild card, Si Wyll. Just like your Red. I really didn't think she would go through with killing Art. I have a lot of admiration for unpredictable people, even though they're generally not very smart. They're also a lot harder to control, which means, unfortunately, that they do need to be put down at some point.'

Wyll stares at the self-possessed woman before him. He sees Red's body crumple in front of him, falling sideways, eyes blank, shot dead by a sweating, desperate white-jacketed man who then turned the gun on himself.

For a moment he struggles to suppress the killing urge her words arouse. He fancies that Orcade sees it on him. She looks faintly amused, as though he's doing something silly and pitiable.

'But you wanted Red on the throne,' he says.

Orcade shrugs. 'Neither of us did. She was simply a node on the path. A swing in the fight.'

'Neither you nor Lillath.'

Orcade just tips her head.

Saints knew how they met, or how it came about. A mutual, dangerous attraction, or perhaps they were each playing their own game – or perhaps it was both at the same time. It usually is.

'Lillath wants to keep control of the throne and you want to run the Menagerie operation uncontested,' Wyll says. 'Maybe even financed and distributed by the palace, eventually. Red was the best play you had to get what you wanted – Cair Lleon bending to your terms. But now that's done with, neither side wants an unpredictable bastard daughter in charge; they want someone they can control. So Lillath strikes a deal. She'll make sure someone malleable gets the Sword – a soft runt like Sirion Dracones, let's say – and she'll run things from behind. And you'll have her ear on all issues, meaning she gets to do the hard work of keeping London from falling apart, and you get to concentrate on launching your new godchild-weapons tech empire.

Which, in the long run, may make you more powerful than Cair Lleon. And Lillath surely knows that, but you can bet she has plans in place to check you further down the line. A perfect partnership, as long as you don't eat each other first.'

Orcade gives him a genuine smile. 'That's some of it,' she agrees. 'You know, I always thought it would be your ambition and not your magic that would lead to Art's downfall.'

'Well, you were wrong.'

'Was I?'

'I had nothing to do with his death.'

'Did you not?'

Orcade takes another delicate sip of her water, her eyes on him.

'Thwimoren,' she says. 'Such an *intriguing* personality.'

'The one talent you don't appear to have represented in your little farm downstairs,' Wyll replies.

'Not for lack of looking,' Orcade admits. 'Have you ever found another one like you?'

'No,' Wyll admits in turn. 'Not for lack of looking.'

'You must be relieved. You get to be powerful in a way no one else is. Look at what happens when you have a common talent, like soothsayers. People don't take you seriously. They look down on you, not up.' She sighs. 'Do you know why I never tried to collect you?'

'Because people might have noticed the disappearance of the Sorcerer Knight?'

Orcade looks impatient. 'Don't be ridiculous, anyone can be disappeared without too much in the way of consequence. You just have to work out what story to tell about it to everyone else. People are generally quite averse to conflict; they'll avoid it any way they can. The ones who aren't, well. They tend to run things. Sometimes not for long.' She muses. 'No, it's because soon you'll be pointless, Si Wyll. Projection tech is set to look as real as real. We're developing a wearable device that will throw up an illusion, like a full-body overlay. At that point, your power becomes obsolete.'

'And yet, look where I am because of it,' he serves back, nettled.

Orcade's smile is faint, and all the more chilling for its vagueness. 'Not for long.'

She finishes her water in a long draught, looks forlornly at the empty cup like she's thinking of asking for more, then decides against it and sets the glass carefully on the floor.

'I have a question for you, if you don't mind,' she says.

Wyll just waits.

'Do you think you're a good person, Wyll?'

No.

'I don't even know what it means to be a good person,' he replies.

'I tend to find that good people usually have a clear idea of it,' remarks Orcade. 'And even if they mostly feel uncertain as to whether they measure up, they at least try to. Whereas you've given up trying, haven't you?'

'I don't understand what you mean.'

'What a shame.' She looks drained, pressing into the divan as if its solid weight is the only thing holding her upright. 'So, what happens now? Did you come here planning to kill me?'

'No,' says Wyll.

'That's a little naïve of you. But have your plans changed? Do you want to kill me now?'

'No,' Wyll sharply repeats, knowing he means yes, knowing she can hear it. 'I want you exposed. I want everyone to know the game you played. I want London to turn its back on you.

I want you friendless and alone, and I want your whole saintsforsaken family to crumble into dust.'

Orcade manages a stiff nod. 'I regret that I must disappoint you.'

She seems to be struggling to breathe well.

An ominous foreboding blooms, spidering across Wyll's chest.

'Good luck,' Orcade whispers. 'There are so many more players than you know.'

Then her mouth opens wide and she vomits on to her lap.

Wyll leaps up and backs away, horrified, disgusted, enraged. Viviane springs from their chair and runs over – *to do what?* thinks Wyll, *it's too late* – and Orcade keeps vomiting, her body hurling over itself, bucking and spasming, eyes bulging from their sockets, small hands clenched white.

It is over quickly.

When Orcade goes still, Viviane bends down, picking up the glass with its clouded water dregs and taking a cautious sniff. Their nose wrinkles in disgust and the glass is launched from their hand into the corner of the room in one jerky, adrenalin-shuddered throw.

'Poison?' Wyll asks.

Viviane nods. 'Cat's milk. Stinks.'

'Why in seven hells would you have a jug of it just standing there in the room . . .' Realisation hits. 'Maybe it was meant for someone else.' He thinks of Lillath. Such a dangerous partnership would always have a short life. 'Though it's hardly a discreet way to end someone.'

'Maybe the point was pain.' Viviane gulps in a breath. They look odd.

'Are you all right?' asks Wyll, suddenly afraid. Is he about to lose his newly acquired and extremely useful weapon?

Viviane takes a moment to reply, the way someone might when struggling with something that has suddenly gone badly wrong.

'I felt,' they say, and then they stop, breathing hard, 'some of that. Her dying.'

Wyll darts forwards almost before their legs begin to buckle.

Their escape from the building is easy.

So what if the Menagerie's premiere Tidal supplier walks a little unsteadily, and looks a little pale? When they are accompanying the Spider, no questions are asked. And no one sees Lillath's unconscious body slung over Wyll's shoulder, because he doesn't want them to.

Glapissant, upon being awakened from his enforced slumber to see Lillath's sleeping form and Orcade's dead one, was made to understand the situation quickly enough. In a move that surprised neither Wyll nor Viviane, he was entirely agreeable to their proposed plan. Glapissant is a businessman and knows a good deal when he sees one. He will make the transition as smooth as possible.

Orcade's body will be found, and there will be many questions – but the answers from any witnesses will indicate that they saw the Spider of London visiting the Menagerie, going upstairs to visit the Lady Orcade – who subsequently drank poison – and then the Spider taking her leave.

Any way you look at it, Lillath is pretty fucked.

The pet has become the master at last.

CHAPTER 34

Garad's Apartment, Evrontown
One Week Ago

When Ghost wakes, for one moment she is convinced she sees glass walls all around her, and beyond them, a roomful of toads, croaking and hopping and staring through the glass with wet, blank eyes, staring at her with a token curiosity.

Then, mercifully, the conviction fades. She is in an elegant bedroom with tall windows that let in the gauzy springtime light that is sprinkling the rumpled sheets around her naked form. In this moment, she is safe, warm and content. It's hard to remember the last time she felt like this, but then again, she still feels uncertain and new. Not quite Fin and not quite Ghost, not any more – but Ghost will do for now, the ghost of a Ghost.

From outside the peaceful stillness comes a clatter, sounds of movement.

Ghost makes a token nod to being clothed and follows the noise outside the bedroom, down the hallway to the kitchen, where Garad hovers in front of a laden stove brandishing a stirrer.

Ghost clears her throat.

Garad turns, throwing the stirrer in her direction. It misses, clattering against the wall and spraying an indeterminate sauce across the floor.

'Shit,' Garad says dismally.

'Sorry,' Ghost replies, amused.

'It's fine, I'm just not used to someone else being here yet.'

There is a fascinatingly distracted and ungainly air to them as they dance around.

'What are you doing?' enquires Ghost.

'Cooking breakfast.'

'Are you sure?'

'You're scrawny,' declares Garad, pointing the reclaimed stirrer at her. 'We need to get you fattened up.'

'Sexy. Sort of thing a farmer says to a pig before they roast it.'

'Sit down.'

Ghost sits, enjoying herself.

'How'd you sleep?' asks Garad.

'Like the dead.'

Garad sighs. Ghost chides herself. A better person would give them time to get used to all this before they brought out the bad-taste jokes.

'So since when did you start cooking?' she asks. 'You used to eat out four times a day.'

'Neh,' Garad says as they poke and flip and stir, 'but I haven't been out much recently. I've just needed to stay away from everything, for a little while. So it was either learn to make food or have raw oysters for every meal.'

Ghost isn't the only one who got too lean, but more than their doubtless rather variable cooking, she realises Garad's weight loss might be connected to the heaviness that has settled in their eyes and nestled on to their shoulders like a dumpy cat.

It's grief, of course.

Art was always the rudder they steered their course by. Now he is gone, they must feel adrift.

'I'm so sorry,' says Ghost.

'About what?'

'Art.'

Garad's back is turned to her, so she cannot see their face, but the sudden stillness in their body speaks loud enough.

'You couldn't have prevented it,' they say. 'You died trying. That's more than enough.'

'I know. I'm just sorry.'

Garad sighs. It is a long, trembling sound, but fluid rather than brittle. 'As am I.'

'He was a good man,' says Ghost quietly, 'but it sounds like she had a claim to his life.'

Best to get this out there now. See where things stand.

After a long, dangerous silence, Garad nods. 'Sounds like she did.'

No one is exempt from consequences, not even Kings. Though the consequence of Red's actions has been to bring a city to its knees. How about that for an example of everything wrong with moldra lagha?

'I owed her for Roben, though.' Ghost pauses. 'And me, I suppose, though she could hardly be blamed for contesting that. It's annoying that you can't claim from the dead.'

A few days ago, through the privacy and safety of Garad's personal glow screen, they had watched Red win the bout against the Sorcerer Knight that would hand her the Sword of London, only to lose her life moments later at the hands of an assassin.

It was almost a shame, despite everything she had done. Ghost had to admit that she had been a beautiful fighter. In

410

another version of her life, she'd have made it all the way to the top of the Caballaria. In another life, perhaps she and Fin might even have been friends, pitted against each other as professional rivals, winning all their bouts, laughing with each other at all tomorrow's parties, rolling in trick and fame and the sure knowledge of never again having to fight to live.

Sounds dull, comments the other her.

Garad turns with a pot in their hand. Ghost watches them carefully shovel a mound of fluffed, glutinous rice into a bowl on the table in front of her, and then set down an accompanying plate of charcoaled meat strips that she decides she will be very polite about enjoying.

'Which is your favourite of the currently circulating theories about who had Red killed?' she muses as Garad seats themself opposite.

They huff a bitter laugh. 'The white jacket was no doubt blackmailed into it, and the self-end that followed, with promises made to take care of his family afterwards. Could have been the palace. What remains of Art's family. Orcade. Wyll.'

'Not Wyll.' Ghost frowns. 'He looked devastated.'

'He's a good actor,' Garad mutters.

Ghost shrugs, tucking into the rice. To her, he had looked utterly undone. The weakest, in fact, that he had ever appeared in his public life. Rare is the person so fractured that they can be *that* good an actor, but everything, it must be acknowledged, is possible.

Garad bites into a charcoaled meat strip. 'Oh, these are getting better. I think they might become my signature dish.'

Ghost chews absently, her mind whirring. 'Well, I hope he's more than just a good actor,' she reflects, 'because he's the one we need to talk to.'

411

'About what?'

'The Menagerie, Garad. The conspiracy.'

Garad pauses. Lays down their fork.

'To do what?' they ask, watching Ghost.

'Shut it down, of course. He's the only one left with enough power to do it. And you said yourself, he has no love for Cair Lleon. If someone at the palace is involved in the Menagerie, he won't hesitate. He has the means – and the anger.' She finds herself getting excited by the prospect. 'Saints, I wouldn't like to be in the room when he finds out what they've been doing to his own. He'll tear them limb from limb.'

The halting silence coming from across the table is really damping her fire.

'What's wrong?' she asks.

Garad is silent.

'You don't want to put him on to whoever's doing this, do you? Because they're your friend.'

'Were,' Garad says. 'It's been many years since I could claim closeness with Lillath. She took her own path. We all did.'

Ghost's heart skips a beat. The wheel with roses flourishing from each spoke. It's the De Havilland family symbol. That's where she's seen it before.

On the skin of the Spider of London.

So the Spider is all tangled up in the web of the Menagerie. Is that why Garad quit the palace? How deep does it run? Who else is involved?

'Let's just go,' Garad says suddenly. 'Let's just leave.'

Ghost stares at them, struggling to catch up. 'Leave? What do you mean, *leave*?'

'You did it once before. Let's do it again.'

'Garad, I . . . I don't understand.'

'Then let me be clear, Fin: my life here is over. In the past few months, I've watched everything I've built over the last twenty years go up in flames. My King is dead. My career is done. My Saith is broken. My oldest friends are no longer people I recognise. I have nothing. Nothing.'

There is no vitriol, nor self-pity, about them. They are calm, collected and quiet, holding Ghost's gaze.

'I want to leave London. The only home I've ever known. I want to go before it's too late and I succumb to the same disease that killed Art and corrupted Lillath, Lucan, everyone who steps foot into Cair Lleon.'

'What disease?' asks Ghost.

'Blind righteousness.'

A long silence follows.

Ghost searches for the right words. 'Garad, I'm so sorry for your suffering. I am. But I just can't let this be. I was there. I *felt* it. You talk about disease, about rot? The Menagerie is a symptom of that – a bleeding, infectious sore.'

'We don't have to go to Wyll,' Garad counters. 'I've got plenty of contacts in the glows. We can just make sure it gets out there that way.'

'You're joking,' Ghost hotly replies. 'Give the decision over to public debate? Oh good, well, you know how well *that* always turns out. There'll be a lot of hand-wringing, and arguing over whether it's justifiable or not, in the name of progress, fa la, oh me oh my, but *someone* has to understand how these, these *creatures* work, just in case they try to take over the world or something, and in the meantime, people get tortured and then drowned when they're not useful any more, and their corpses flushed out into the river like sewage! And no one *cares*!' Ghost strains forwards in her seat. 'This is not a fucken

413

moral debate. Someone just needs to go in there and destroy it, now. And *he* would. He wouldn't give a shit about politics. You know he protects us. You know how much power he has. He'd just tear it down. And that's what needs to happen. That's what I *want*.'

'Because you're frightened of it,' Garad says quietly.

'Yes! Aren't *you*?'

Garad's mouth opens, but nothing comes out.

Ghost sits back. 'Fuck the saints,' she says with a bitter laugh. 'You really *don't* like godchildren, do you?'

'It's not that,' Garad sharply retorts. 'Don't you dare.'

'But you'd rather leave than help me destroy something that almost destroyed me. And you know, Garad, the only reason I'm alive right now is due entirely to the thing about me that you hate. So where does that leave me, in your eyes? What am I? Are you afraid of *me*?'

Garad just waits, patiently, until Ghost subsides.

'Yes, sometimes I'm afraid of you,' they say, and Ghost's head rears. 'What were you expecting me to say? I think anyone is capable of anything. I've seen the evidence of that with my own eyes, from both commons *and* godchildren. But you're power-ful. Of course I'm afraid of that. I'm also intensely excited by it. That's the magic of you.' Garad takes her hand across the table. 'Look, I understand your reasons, I really do. But vengeance never sates.'

'This is not about vengeance—'

'I think it is,' says Garad patiently, 'otherwise you'd be con-tent with exposing the place instead of destroying it. Fin, I don't think you're going to get what you want out of this. It's not going to feel good.'

This patience, this calm, is a new facet to her old lover that

Ghost is not really sure she cares for. She takes her hand out of Garad's.

'You seem to know a whole lot about me for someone who isn't me,' she snaps.

'Well, if we were all hermits, then it wouldn't matter how I saw you, Fin, but since who we are is made up of how others see us, as well as how we see ourselves, I think I get a say.'

Ghost chooses to let the constant use of her dead name slide, as well as the rest of it. Negotiations about all that can come later on, if she's lucky enough to get a later on.

She wants to call Garad a coward, but she can't, not quite. It doesn't ring like that. It's something else, but she's not sure what.

She leans forwards. 'Garad, I need to do this,' she says simply. 'I am going to go to the one person with the power to kill this thing, and I'm going to point him at it, and I'm going to smile when it's done. And you can either help me, or get out of my way. But please, don't try to stop me.' Under the table, Ghost laces her hands together and prays. 'So which is it going to be?'

Garad puts down the remaining stump of the charcoaled meat strip in their hand and gives a gusty sigh.

'I'll help,' they say quietly. 'But we do it my way.'

CHAPTER 35

Cair Lleon, Blackheart
Yesterday

This place is so ugly.

Can a ruler's energy change an environment to reflect it? The way they carry themselves and the way they treat everyone around them is an infection, passed along and along, like ripples out from a thrown stone.

If that's the case, whoever it is in charge in Cair Lleon now likes fear, because this place, if fear had a smell, would stink of it. It is in its dampened silence. Its rustling of quick, quiet movement. Even though the hallways are as full as ever of walking, talking bodies, there is no hum. No . . . no *life*.

And to think, Fin might have been Queen of all this, thinks Ghost.

Queen of? No. Queen in, but not of. No Queen has ever ruled this nest of spiders, and in the end, just like spiders, she'd have been eaten alive.

It feels like a lucky escape. Fin might not have been able to set guilt aside and feel relief at all the choices she has made that led her away from this place, but Ghost can – even if it took her dying to finally cut those ties. Her world these days might be more uncertain and a hell of a lot less opulent, but the one she left within these walls feels somehow more insidiously danger-ous. Out there, people may want to kill you, but at least they usually don't bother to hide it. In here, it feels like death hap-pens in secret, and as a rather unwelcome surprise.

The size of Ghost's escort guard is doing wonders for her ego, but a lot less for her sense of safety. These knights are positively bristling with weaponry. It's like walking in a phalanx of human hedgehogs. They bring her to an imposing door. Beyond is a small, comfortable-looking antechamber with the discon-certing addition of mirrored walls.

Her escort lead turns to her, indicating the antechamber.

'You wait in here until the other door opens,' he says.

'You're not coming in with me?' Ghost glances at the mir-rored walls. 'Takes a lot out of you, being alone with yourself.'

'You're never alone in the palace,' the knight grimly replies, and any more jokes she had lined up dry up in her mouth.

The door is closed.

Ghost stares at the mirrors. She tends to avoid looking at her-self too deeply these days – it can get confusing to try and remember which face to expect to see – but having little other choice over, say, cricking her neck by staring up at the ceiling, or examining the floor between her boots like a naughty child, she might as well give the woman in the mirror a thorough going-over.

Not bad. A bit thin, maybe. Some of her strength has gone, and she'll have to work hard to get it back. It's all the stress of recent times. Plus perhaps all the sex of even more recent times. Ghost grins. That's better. Think of Garad and those strong, deliberate hands of theirs.

There is a soft click. The door to her left swings open.

'Enter,' calls a deep, familiar voice.

Ghost runs a hand over her shaved scalp, comforted by the bristles against her palm, and walks in. The room beyond is dimly lit and hot, too hot. Its furniture is bare bones; Cair Lleon's opulence, so ubiquitous everywhere else, noticeable for its absence. But the heat and the stripped appearance are soon forgotten in view of its occupants.

The familiar figure of Si Wyllt Caballarias Ambrosias o'Gwanharatown – the Sorcerer Knight, the Scourge of the Godless, London's Left Hand – sits in general contemplation on a plain chair near a dead fireplace. He also stands a little distance away with his arms folded and a penetrative stare on his face. Two more of him are arranged near a window. Three ring a weapons rack over by the far wall. All in all, Ghost estimates there are at least a dozen Si Wylls in various attitudes around the room, who all, when she enters, stop whatever they were doing and turn to look at her.

She swallows.

'Fuck me,' she says in awe.

'He won't, but I might.'

That's a different voice, lighter and liltier, coming from behind. Ghost spins around. Flanking the door she just came through are two more Wylls, silent and watchful. Next to one, leaning casually against the wall, is a lithe stranger with soft, tumbling hair, alluringly dark eyes and a boldly appreciative smile.

Ghost's head feels soupy and thick, as though filled with honey instead of brain fluid. Maybe it's the heat in here – they must have the wall generators cranked up to the limit – or maybe it's the disconcerting number of Sorcerer Knights currently prowling the room around her, but she doesn't even have the wherewithal for a ready quip.

'T'chuss, Vivi,' says Wyll – every single Wyll, it sounds like, a dozen of the same voice speaking at almost the same time.

The lithe figure shrugs in response.

Ghost tries to decide which Wyll to look at, but every one of them looks just like him. She finds herself flitting from Wyll to Wyll like a fly that can't decide which shit pile to land on. It's not helping her soupy head. It would be nice if she could stop feeling overwhelmed enough to appreciate the sheer marvel arrayed in front of her. Has there ever been a more powerful thwimoren to walk the streets of London?

'So you wanted to speak with me,' say the Wylls. It takes a microsecond more than normal for the sentence to finish coming out of every mouth, and the effect is jarring.

'Neh, Si, but I was expecting just one of you,' Ghost says. 'This is like trying to talk to a bee swarm.'

'Security measures,' the chorus replies. 'You may have come vouched for by Si Garad themself, but that's the only reason I'd grant you an audience. How could I refuse my former mentor, after all? I'm a little disappointed that they didn't come with you, however.'

Disappointed means suspicious.

'Seems like they had a falling-out with some people here, and are no longer as welcome as they'd like,' Ghost says.

'So you came alone,' muses the chorus of Wylls. 'Brave choice.'

'No,' she counters. 'Garad is waiting for me outside the gates. They were anxious to support me.'

And ready to raise hell should Ghost fail to reappear after her meeting is due to end. Garad was extremely clear on this point. Ghost had mocked them for being overly cautious, but now she is not so sure.

'They needn't have been,' the Wylls murmur. 'The people they clashed with are no longer such a threat.'

What an intriguing statement. If it came from anyone other than perhaps the most powerful magician knight London has ever seen, it would sound like nothing more than a laughably outrageous boast.

'I was surprised you asked to meet here, in the palace,' Ghost ventures. 'I'd have thought you'd prefer somewhere else. Less . . . showy.'

'I don't leave Cair Lleon much these days.'

So he's either a prisoner or a paranoid. But which? Does he have any power at all any more, or is this a fool's errand?

'Show me your talent,' says the chorus of Wylls, breaking Ghost's ruminations.

'That's forward, for a first date,' Ghost says. 'I came to talk with you, Si, not play show and tell.'

'When you first approached me through Si Garad,' the deep voices mingle, 'I made it clear that I only grant audiences to other godchildren, and I was assured that you are. I want to see your talent. Then you can talk.'

The dead Finnavair Caballarias o'Rhyfentown was extremely careful never to be outed as a godchild, and she only knew Wyll well enough for polite pleasantries at public Caballaria functions. He doesn't know who Ghost used to be. She came here under the guise of being a student of Garad's, come to solicit advice from the former. She came here as Ghost, not Fin, and her new face seems to be holding up under his scrutiny.

'There's no need to be worried about breaking the laws against magic here,' says the chorus of Wylls, misinterpreting her hesitation. One of them spreads their hands to indicate what currently fills the room, and the others laugh. The sound is horribly loud.

'I'm not,' says Ghost. 'Just shy.'

'Someone with as much power as you hardly needs be.'

'How do you know how powerful I am? You've not seen anything yet.'

'You've already been assessed,' the Wyll chorus assures her. 'It couldn't tell me exactly what you can do, but it could tell me how strong and unusual your talent is.'

Hoo, whistles the other her. *That's a familiar description, itso?*

It might just be a coincidence, Ghost ponders.

'You have something that can do that?' she asks. 'Like a test?'

The Wylls do not reply. Just watch her.

Well. Clearly she has to impress him to get anywhere in this meet. Might as well take a little risk.

'It didn't used to belong to someone calling herself Moth, by any chance, did it?' asks Ghost.

It's a good leap. Several of the Wylls flinch. Mouths fall open in surprise.

She definitely has his attention now.

Fuck the saints – the neat little bald man who went looking to buy the map off Moth that night. It was the Sorcerer Knight. He'd thought it was a machine, then he went down into the cellar and realised it was a girl, a godchild. Realised Moth was selling her own daughter to the highest bidder. Evidently he'd been displeased with this discovery. He took Moth's daughter, killed Moth – and maybe he would have killed Ghost too, if she hadn't run.

Well, look at that, she's finally found Moth's killer. Shame there's no one left to acquit herself with. Delilah is dead, Sugar apparently prefers the wrong side of this fight, and the rest of that activist group – if there was ever a 'rest' to speak of – have gone to ground. Understandable, considering their decimated ranks. She doubts she'll have any more trouble from whoever remains, whatever happens next.

The Wylls open their mouths. 'I recognise you now,' they muse. 'The girl skulking around the shop that night. Well, well. Didn't you just get much . . . more . . . interesting.'

A freezing cold shiver runs down Ghost's back.

Stupid reckless idiot. Why give him a reason to shut you up?

'Vivi,' comes the choral hiss.

The lithe figure lounging behind Ghost begins to speak. She'd all but forgotten they were there.

'She's got information she thinks you should have,' Vivi says in an assured voice. 'Something that makes her angry. And frightened. Something she thinks will do the same to you.'

That soupy feeling in her head. Vivi is *inside* her.

For the first time, Ghost notices how much she has begun to sweat. Maybe it's a good thing she had no idea what she was walking into here, or she'd never have come.

'And her talent?' the chorus asks.

'I'm not sure,' says the damned mind reader. 'It's like . . . an argument. A constant debate between two voices. Like she can—'

It happens fast and instant, as always.

As her double appears and locks a savage arm around Vivi's throat from behind, choking them quiet, Ghost speaks.

'Where I come from that's called head rape, and I *really* wish people would stop doing it to me.'

Vivi kicks and scuffles. Ghost's double, to their credit, is having a hard time holding them still.

'Enough,' calls the chorus. 'Vivi, stand down. *Stand down.*'

The command is so forceful that even Ghost finds herself twitching to obey. It works on Vivi – they quiet at once. Ghost's double does not relax her arm. Vivi gives Ghost a venomous glare, but keeps still.

'So I'm not the only one who can make copies of himself,' the Wylls comment. The choral effect masks the overall sentiment, rendering his reaction chillingly hard to figure out.

'My trick's better,' says Ghost.

'Neh, it is. No wonder you shone so bright for our little tester.'

'Not the first time we've met, she and I,' Ghost says. 'She probably got all excited at the familiar face.'

'You just can't stop goading people who are a threat to you, can you?' her double says tartly.

'Shut up,' Ghost retorts. Saints, she has such a thick Rhyfentown accent. Does she really sound like that? How embarrassing.

She can see the Wylls closest to her double prowling gently, shifting closer.

'Talent such as yours, I feel like we should have come across each other before now,' they say.

Not much time until her upper hand vanishes as swiftly as it arrived.

'All I want to do,' says Ghost, 'is tell you what I came to tell you. That's all I want. Then we can all go back to our happy, separate lives in entirely different locations. 'Cord?'

'Accord,' the Wylls whisper, and she has to forcibly clamp down on another shiver jerking its way down her spine. 'Let Vivi go. Then talk.'

Ghost lets her double disappear. It takes too much out of her to keep her out for long, and there might be a need for her again later, if this continues going downhill.

Vivi stumbles, almost falls at the sudden loss of weight against them. It's petty, but there's a little satisfaction to be had at seeing that. She suspects that Vivi is not often graceless.

Ghost gathers herself. 'Is there anyone listening in?'

'I can't guarantee not.'

This is exactly why she didn't want to meet in the damned lion's den, but he'd given her no choice.

'There's an experiment going on,' says Ghost.

'An experiment on what?'

'Us.'

Silence.

Fuck it. There's no point being coded or coy, not now, and if there really are palace people listening in, well, then she was screwed the moment she stepped into the room. She opens her mouth to vomit it all up, every nasty detail, every damned evil thing she has seen in the last two months, when the Wylls interrupt her.

'Of course,' they say. 'The one who makes a twin who escaped. Glapissant has been looking for you.'

You know, reflects Ghost to herself, after a few missed heartbeats, *no one could accuse you of not being cynical enough, and yet somehow reality keeps beating you at it.*

'You already know about the experiments, then,' she says.

'I've seen the Menagerie,' the chorus agrees.

Silence.

She feels carefully watched for her response.

'Funny,' she says after a pause.

'Funny?'

'Funny. Funny because I came here thinking that as soon as you heard about it, you'd want to raise all seven hells to shut it down.'

'Why would I want to shut it down?' ask the Wylls.

Ghost feels a nice lick of anger warming her up. Better than cold fear.

'What I saw there,' she says, 'gave me nightmares. It was people as *things*. To be prodded and starved and drugged and electrocuted, just to see what happens.'

'Not any more,' says Wyll. 'Better people have taken over.'

'Better people,' scoffs Ghost. 'Like who?'

'Like me.' Vivi gives her an insolent bow.

She wants to run. Her mind conjures images of Glapissant waiting outside the door for her, dragging her back to that tank . . .

'So you're a sadist as well as a mind raper?' she says to Vivi, and loudly claps her hands. 'Good choice!'

The claps echo around the dark room like gunshots. The Wylls shift tensely on their feet, half rise out of chairs.

'And you're a hysterical toddler,' says Vivi to Ghost. 'Who would you rather have in control of our power, us or them? How do you think wars get won? By whoever has the best weapons.'

'And an arms dealer too, now?' Ghost gestures at the nearest Wyll. 'Quite a catch you have here, Si, congratulations.'

Vivi turns to Wyll. 'Please let me hurt her,' they plead.

'You're pathetic,' spits Ghost with furious terror. 'What do you get out of this, puppy? Is it in your nature to fawn at someone's feet? Is that how you feel alive?'

Vivi just cants their head. Far from being angry, they seem amused.

'Yes,' they say. 'When the someone is worthy of my fawning. How do *you* feel alive?'

With an effort, Ghost focuses back on the Wyll nearest her. The rest be damned.

'I've heard about you before, you know,' she says. 'And I don't mean the Sorcerer Knight. The other you. There's the official one who pours money into hostels, pays for disputes where a godchild can't afford it. All that stuff makes you look good to some people and bad to others, but at least charity, any kind of charity, earns a grudging kind of respect. Of course, your enemies say that the hostels are illegal training grounds for talent and the disputes are corrupted, bought off in favour of the godchild before they ever get to the arena floor. Do you really think so much of us? Because I've met some godchildren I'd cheerfully stab in the guts. It's a surprisingly long list.'

And now you're on it.

The Wyll nearest to her pushes off the wall he's been leaning against.

'People are stupid, petty, vindictive, small and dangerous,' he says, and just the one voice, after that buzzing chorus, is like a drink of cool water on a bowel-achingly hot summer day. 'That includes godchildren as much as any. Sometimes, perhaps even more so. Hard lives make monsters as often as martyrs. But in our society, a power imbalance has existed for too long. We've been fed lies about our own culture, our own natures, to keep us controlled. We've been told we are rare aberrations, mutant pets to be used when useful and kept down when not.' The Wyll closest to her leans forwards. Ghost resists the urge to lean back. 'But the map is perhaps the greatest and most precious resource of the last hundred years. It's going to change everything, I can promise you that. *Everything*. So my suggestion to you is this: choose the side that's going to win.'

Every Wyll's face is filled with savage excitement.

'How will Moth's daughter change everything?' Ghost asks.

'You'll find out.' His head cocks. 'If you stay.'

'Stay?' She looks around. 'Here?'

'I like your anger,' he says. 'I could help you direct it.'

'Train me like you did Red, you mean?'

Finally, a blow that lands. The atmosphere gets a nice little edge to whet her blade on.

'Were you behind it?' she pushes.

'Behind what?'

'Red's grand plan to kill her own pere.'

Were you the one I should have had down in that tunnel?

'No, I wasn't behind it,' Wyll says. 'Everyone who was behind it is dead now.'

'Who?'

'The former owners of the Menagerie, for one. They had an impressive change of heart when I showed up. One's dead and the other's in the Menagerie, and likely to remain there indefinitely. Still upset with me for taking over the place?'

'Maybe you weren't behind it,' Ghost says, 'but I need to know. Did you know what Red was going to do? Did you help her?'

Silence. The longest silence. She's just about decided that he'll never answer when it comes.

'Maybe.'

And then:

'I'm not sure, any more.'

He's lost his mind, whispers the other Ghost.

'She's frightened,' Vivi murmurs. 'I can taste it.'

'Stay with us,' Wyll urges Ghost. 'Help us get our power back.'

Run, run, run.

'I'm not sure your puppy would like that,' Ghost tries.

'I can share.' Vivi is prowling.

'There's already two of me to go around, thanks.'

'Mm,' Wyll says, 'and I can make a hundred of me.'

'Right, but only one of you is real.'

'Which one? Can you tell?'

'I stay,' says Ghost, 'and you put me in a tank to see how I work.'

'No, no. I told you, all that barbarism is over. All that's required now is that we take blood and genetic samples, painlessly. Everyone does it. Even Vivi. Even me. And we'll all enter training programmes specifically designed to improve our talents.' The Wyll nearest her is practically twitching with excitement. 'Think of what we have access to, now – drugboosters, scientific exploration, medical enhancements. Think of being free to understand yourself for the first time in your life. Think of being *free*.'

'I am free,' says Ghost, 'and I understand myself just fine.'

Wyll dismisses her words. 'You have no idea what you're capable of. You've been living in the dark your entire life.'

Sometimes it's better to see only so far.

'What would I do?' Ghost stalls out loud while the rest of her works frantically on escape routes. 'If I came and worked for you?'

'Whatever you like most. Something involving violence, at a guess.'

'Great deal. Would I have to live here at Cair Lleon, though?'

'Oh dear,' says Vivi, dripping with acid, 'what's wrong with the largest, richest and most beautiful house in the entire world?'

'Well, I'd want a playmate. And I can't bring Garad. I heard they got banned from the palace when they did their angry walk-out.'

'Oh no,' muses the Wyll chorus, 'bans no longer stand when the person who made them is no longer in charge.'

'Hard to run things from a tank, I suppose.'

'She's not in a tank. And she's there voluntarily.'

Something about the way he says it suggests otherwise.

'Good for her,' babbles Ghost. 'She always struck me as a team player. Well, I'm very flattered and I'll definitely think about your offer, but right now I have an appointment I need to make, so I'm going to go.'

'So soon?' murmurs Wyll. 'Stay for dinner, at least.'

There are so many Wylls, and they keep damn moving.

'Garad's expecting me. They're waiting right outside the gates, remember? They're a nervous sort, these days. Can't even be five minutes late without them raising alarms.'

He seems to understand the warning. Seven of the Wylls give Ghost a smile. She turns, takes confident steps towards the door, expecting with every step to feel hands on her. Maybe even a syringe stuck into her arm.

'We'll invite you both back,' the Wyll next to the door says. 'You and Garad. Very soon.'

And Ghost understands exactly what he means.

'Garad will be thrilled.' She grasps the door handle. 'They've really missed the place.'

The walk back through the palace is limitless agony.

When she gets outside, makes it all the way across the grounds and then spots Garad's tall figure astride their bike, she wants to cry with relief.

Garad salutes the guard knight who has been with them while they wait, and the knight respectfully salutes back, moving away.

'Well?' Garad says softly.

'We need to go,' Ghost replies just as softly, and then gives them a sweet smile. 'Right fucken now.'

Their face drops. They turn on the bike and upkick the engine. Ghost slides behind them and grips their waist with all the strength she has.

She'd been too blind with recent trauma to see it, but Garad was right. Cair Lleon is riddled with disease. Everyone who steps foot in that place succumbs.

Will telling the world of the Menagerie change anything? Will it be the match that lights the powder keg? There are so many matches these days, it's hard to tell.

Maybe it's too late. Maybe the rot has spread too far.

Maybe it's just too damned late.

CHAPTER 36

Private Viewing Room, Cair Lleon
Now

The last of the projection fades, its luminous cloud-glow lingering even as the machine shuts down. Oddly beautiful, oddly alive.

Its small audience is silent, unreadable in the necessary dim.

Glapissant turns to them, his hands held behind his back and his chest puffed. He waits, his air of respectful patience in deference to the luminaries before him. His posture is one of surety, both feet firmly planted on the comforting pillar of provable facts.

One member of his audience stirs.

'How many godchildren has this ... map ... seen in the immediate area you just outlined?'

'We're still counting,' Glapissant replies, 'but we're up to fourteen thousand, three hundred and fifty-two. Extrapolating for various population densities in each area of Blackheart – and before we're at the full total – that puts the figure at nearly a million.' He pauses. 'And that's just Blackheart, obviously by far the smallest district. If we widen—'

'How many total in all of London?' interrupts the audience member.

'Through our calculations, we project that the total figure will come out somewhere around thirteen million.'

Guttural noises of outrage and disbelief fill the room. Wyll watches the audience carefully. They are all focused on Glapissant, lost inside their own minds as they process, or too caught up in performing to each other. Only one has their gaze going in his direction – Brune, the questioner.

She can't see Wyll properly – he stands far behind Glapissant, and what little light there is doesn't reach his face. Nonetheless, she looks.

'You're positing that more than half of the total population of London is a godchild,' she says, her authoritative voice cutting across the spluttering around her.

'Posit? No,' Glapissant says. 'Calculate, yes.'

Another audience member cuts in, 'It's ridiculous, impossible. It's an outrageous lie.'

'Medical data,' Glapissant replies. 'You've all seen the reports. You've spoken with her doctors. Watched the recordings of her brain patterns. Seen as she's picked out, with perfect, unbroken accuracy, godchild from common in test after test with our registered volunteers. What more evidence do you need? We are not discussing saints' miracles here, Lords, Laerds and Ladies. We are discussing hard, verifiable science.' He cants his head. 'We are discussing a new world order.'

After that, it takes a while for things to regain any sense of calm. Glapissant and his sense of theatrics.

Still, monsters are useful, too.

'Well,' Lucan says with a laugh, 'you always put on an extraordinary show, Wyll, I'll give you that.'

Wyll inclines his head. Around them the small crowd of Cair

Lleon's most influential pick at the tiny expensive pastries that the palace has laid on for the post-meet mingle. They are down in the Green Room, in the bowels of Cair Lleon. A private, discreet place, perfect for the private, discreet nature of this gathering.

Lucan has his most charming, affable face on.

'Your . . . consultant there, Glapissant,' he says. 'He's a common?'

'Yes,' Wyll replies. 'Verified by the map.'

Lucan considers this. Never before has there been a definitive way to pick out a godchild. He has doubts, but he understands the implications. The potential.

'Interesting for a common to be so invested in exploding that bomb,' he says.

'Not really. He has a scientific mind. Resolutely apolitical.'

'Mmm,' Lucan muses. 'In my opinion, no one is apolitical. They'd have to live underground to be so, no?' He gives a little laugh.

'He essentially does,' Wyll replies. 'What were your thoughts on our presentation?'

'If it's true, the consequences are, of course, astounding. I'm curious to know what you plan to do with the information.' Lucan gives another, more annoying little laugh. 'Start a civil war?'

Tread carefully. You've spooked the horse, don't make it bolt.

'That's the last thing I want,' Wyll insists with firm sincerity. 'London needs strength right now, not more division. I'm asking for your help.'

Lucan looks caught out. '*My* help?'

'You are Cair Lleon's Mouthpiece. I'd have thought it would be obvious. Why else would I come to you? Everyone in this room is here because I believe it is in London's best interests to work together with those in the best and most useful positions of power. As you say, the implications of this information could be devastating.' Wyll pauses meaningfully. 'Or they could be the beginning of a journey towards reconciliation and equality.'

Lucan's portly belly swells gently over his belt. Old captures of him show a slender man with bright eyes and an infectious grin. Time and wealth have not been favourable to Lucan, Wyll reflects. His hand comes up and claps Wyll jarringly on the back.

'I always knew Art's trust in you was well placed,' he says. 'And now here you are, making brave moves to continue his legacy. Congratulations on an extraordinarily well-played game.'

'What game?' Wyll enquires.

'You'll be taking the Sword, of course. And why not you? Any palpable competition has been taken care of, for now. And with this information, well. London is going to need a ruler who represents the interests of more than half its population, wouldn't you say?' Lucan grins at Wyll's careful silence. 'There's no need for obfuscation on the matter, not behind these walls. I'm for you, Wyll. It's time. You've shown us that. If you'll have me, I'd like to be part of your Saith, just as I was for my best friend in the world, and your mentor. Oh, don't answer now. Think about it, of course. I have a number of ideas about how best to approach it. Let's talk tomorrow, if you have time?'

Wyll inclines his head. 'By all means.'

'Excellent!' Lucan booms. He gives Wyll a deferential head nod. 'From Si to Sire in less than four years. Extraordinary work. Just extraordinary. One would think you've been planning for this all your life.'

It's done.

It's done. And now to see what the cost of it will be.

What a horrifying way to live, never to know ahead of time how a thing might play out. Fortunately, he now has working for him two of the brightest soothsayers to be found – literally; they glowed so much for the map that she gave a great squeal and burst into noisy tears when she felt them. It took a whole afternoon and a slew of drugs to get her back in working order.

The audience are all gone, every last one of them constrained to secrecy by the usual palace contracts. He is all alone in his private rooms. Now, finally, he can allow himself to climb down from the dizzying wall-tops of risk.

Well. He is not quite alone. Never quite alone, nowadays.

A quiet presence has materialised beside his chair.

Wyll turns his head. Standing before him, shaking her long dark hair back with a toss of the head, is the infamous Red Wraith herself. Mordred Dracones, Red to those privileged enough to have been let so close. Black eyes gleam in the lamp-light as she catches his gaze.

For a moment, he is struck dumb by the visceral gut-punch the sight of her face and her body still delivers to him. Then he recovers.

'Well?' he asks her.

Red shrugs. 'Lucan hates you,' she says. 'He kept thinking about Lillath while you were talking. He's convinced you've had her killed.'

'I'll have to arrange for him to pay her a visit at the Menagerie,' muses Wyll.

'You think she'll behave in front of him?'

'I think she will with the right incentives. He doesn't know about her *partnership* with Orcade. I doubt she wants him to find out she was bedfellowing a Welyen and secretly destroying all

435

their schemes for her own ends.' Wyll reflects. 'Perhaps it's time Lucan learned some truths about his oldest remaining friend.'

'First chance he gets, he'll strike at you,' Red warns.

Wyll nods. 'Nevertheless, we have to keep him close. For now. What about Brune?'

'She's more guarded,' Red says. 'She's biding her time, waiting to see where you're going with this. Keeping a tally of warning signs.'

'Warning signs?' Wyll scoffs. 'Like maniacal laughter? Mood swings?'

'You'll be her third King,' Red quietly points out. 'She has . . . experience.'

Wyll leans back in his chair. 'She's a long-gamer. A life diplomat. That means prudence. I don't think I need to worry about her until I start, say, openly slaughtering the serving vastos whenever I get bored.' He reflects. 'And she might even tolerate that, as long as she approves of my policies.'

He hears the swish of bare feet on rug. Feels warm, firm hands on the back of his neck, stroking the vulnerable skin there.

'You're tired,' observes Red from behind him.

He hesitates. With her, and only with her, he can be honest. Soft and open, just the way he always wanted. It is his secret indulgence. His release.

'Am I doing the right thing?' he asks the room.

There. His worst fear. Once given voice, it hangs anxiously, waiting for judgement.

'How can you doubt?'

The fear fades at such surety, relieved to be dismissed.

'Who else was there?' continues Red behind him, as her

fingers press and roll against his flesh. 'You prevented London being taken over by greedy technocrats and their disastrous puppet rulers. People who would have reduced us to drugs and guns. Enough is enough. All your life you've been used, Wyll. We all have. Time to use back.'

'Yes,' he says, nodding, but he is never sated, always eager for more affirmation. 'Yes. But maybe there was a kinder way. A less . . .' He falters.

'You're scared of being disliked.'

'No.'

'Yes,' comes Red's amused voice. 'You love the fear and awe but you hate it too, because it isolates you. But you're not alone any more, Wyll. You have me. And we're going to fill Cair Lleon with godchildren, just like we talked about. Imagine it. People openly being able to express themselves. No more illegal magic. It'll be done on the streets, casually, just because we *feel* like it. Saints. It'll be glorious. It'll be freedom.'

'You still,' says Art, 'need rules. Rules negate chaos.'

The dead King is standing feet away, one elbow on the mantelpiece in an attitude of casual repose.

'Chaos is necessary,' Red scoffs at him. 'Chaos creates movement. Without it, we stop. We wither and die. You might as well put us all in one of Glapissant's tanks.'

'It's a balance,' Art gently rebuffs. 'It has to be a balance. Indulge too much in the ecstasy and the passion of freedom and you're just another addict. It's a drug, and it reduces us to animals, and we have to be better than that. We have to be.'

Red's hands leave Wyll's neck. She circles him, puts her back to Art and drops down to her knees in front of Wyll with her face tilted up to his.

'Fairness has never been won by playing fair,' she tells him earnestly as she undoes his belt. 'You told me that yourself, a long time ago.'

'I know,' Wyll murmurs, helpless in the face of his own need. 'I know.'

'For the greater good,' Art reminds him from the mantelpiece.

'Yes. For the greater good.'

'He can watch,' says Red, as her hands pull gently on Wyll's trousers, freeing him to the air. 'I don't mind.'

But Wyll dismisses Art with a blink. If it isn't private, the intimacy he craves from it gets lost.

He feels a mouth engulf him, wet, dark, hot. He feels her weight on his knees, her body nestled in between his thighs. The sheer glad comfort of it. A sensation to lose yourself in. A sensation that stops thought and self.

'I love you,' he tells Red. 'I love you.'

She moans into his cock, burying him in her throat up to the hilt. This close and the illusion slips a little – he can see Viviane's messy light hair showing through underneath Red's dark gloss. It gets harder to hold on to it, harder to concentrate when they fuck. It's a delicate balancing act between keeping control and letting go.

She pulls back for a moment, her head tilting to catch his eye with her throat full. Viviane's softer planes are there, hovering ghost-like behind Red's foxy, pointed cheeks. Or perhaps it's that Red is the ghost and Viviane is real.

Either way, it's good enough.

It's good enough.

CHAPTER 37

Hemstede Burial Mound, Rhyfentown
Now

Ghost stands braced astride her bike, her gaze on a familiar sky-line from one of the tallest natural hills in all of London.

She roves over its raw jags, its cultivated spires and brooding flat tops, its glassy gleams and dark, muted grandeur. It is a kind of grief that she feels. An ache for an anchor point she once had and is now untethering herself from.

London. Her mother and her father.

We could try and kill them, if you like, whispers the other her.

Who? she silently asks herself.

Every person we think shouldn't be allowed to exist and influence the order of the world, the other her replies. *We could spend our life doing that. We like to kill. We could become revenge's wolfhound. It might be a short life, but we get more of it than everyone else. Think about it. Isn't that a worthy way to spend the precious time we have on this earth?*

Ghost thinks about Red, revenge's last wolfhound.

No, she says, *not really.*

'Ready, my heart?' asks Garad.

They are standing next to her, astride their own bike, the wind whipping at the silver strands of their hair. Their face is

439

lined, marked, shown up for its age in the sharp spring sunlight, and it has never looked more tantalisingly vulnerable, more human and more alive.

'London will keep turning without you,' they said to her recently, and it is a painful truth, and a happy one.

Ghost wants love, and she wants adventure. To get them, she has to leave her old self behind once again. But it's not such a sacrifice when you remember that the only thing in every universe that stays the same is the inevitability of change.

Saints, she thinks wryly as tears fill her eyes, *it's not* that *good a view*.

But it is familiar, and much of its beauty comes from that.

Ghost wipes her face, bares her teeth at the skyline, and then smiles in pleasure at its comfort, the vision and feel of it that is hers, that she gets to keep for as long as she likes.

As they kick the bikes and ride off together, she offers up a prayer of gratitude to Saint Marvol for the lesson, and turns gladly towards the unknown.

It's the only way she knows how to live.

ACKNOWLEDGEMENTS

This book would not exist without the music of:
Alice In Chains
Boy Harsher
Burial
Cold Cave
Makeup and Vanity Set
Public Memory

A heartfelt thanks to musicians. Your stuff makes my stuff go.

Huge thanks to Jo Fletcher and everyone at JFB and Quercus, without whom *Ghosts* would remain a hideously malformed first draft of a Word doc that no-one would ever read.

Finally, thanks to London. I lived in you for twelve years and you only got more interesting as time went on.